A PERFECT STORY

ELÍSABET BENAVENT

sourcebooks
casablanca

Published by Sourcebooks Casablanca, an imprint of Sourcebooks
P.O. Box 4410, Naperville, Illinois 60567-4410
(630) 961-3900
sourcebooks.com

Originally published as *Un cuento perfecto* in 2020 in Spain by Suma de
Letras, an imprint of Penguin Random House Grupo Editorial. This edition
issued based on the paperback edition published in 2020 in Spain by Suma
de Letras, an imprint of Penguin Random House Grupo Editorial.

Cataloging-in-Publication data is on file with the Library of Congress.

Manufactured in the UK by Clays and distributed by
Dorling Kindersley Limited, London
001-343425-July/24
10 9 8 7 6 5 4 3 2 1

my heart. Nothing is that serious, and your life isn't going to end. Just…new possibilities will open up.

Look, let me tell you a perfect story, okay? One that will seem perfect too, in the beginning. Once upon a time, there was a modern princess. She didn't have a castle or sit sighing on a balcony where she could look out over her entire kingdom. She didn't comb her ridiculously long locks with a brush made from enamel, gold, and horsehair. She wasn't waiting for Prince Charming to save her from the wicked witch.

Although…I'm pretty sure my mother counts as a witch.

What I mean is, somehow, those princess stories still clutter up the corners of our minds. Sometimes they're microscopic, and other times they loom large. There are no more princes on horseback or little birds helping us get dressed for a date that will lead to love and happiness (I mean, really…sometimes it's hard to believe they made us think some nerd was capable of sweeping us off our feet), but we still believe in stories. In fairy tales. And they've convinced us we want to be princesses.

Take a look at Instagram. You don't have it? Well, don't download it just to see if this is true. But…I'm sure you'll know what I'm talking about. Perfect lives. Lives of luxury. Photos where you can almost touch that hazy fantasy of a dream existence. Shiny, glittering, every hair in place. Yes, most of the time, social media is trying to sell us unrealistic perfection that pushes us to find something that doesn't actually exist. Now little girls want to be version 3.0 of the princess in the story, with a designer bag, clutching a mysteriously pink coffee on the edge of an infinity pool in Tahiti. It doesn't sound bad, it's true. I want it too…but the difference is knowing that there's no perfect life behind that photo. Just…a life.

1

ONCE UPON A TIME...

MARGOT

So your boyfriend dumped you. You might even hate your job. You probably spend your days yearning for things you'll never be able to afford. Have those extra summer pounds teamed up with the ones from Christmas? Don't worry. And don't worry if you don't fill out your bra. Or if the chairs at restaurants squeeze your thighs. If your mother never approves of anything you do...and anything you don't do, of course. If you gave your heart to that idiot. If you feel like you're married to your mortgage. If your boss is a fucking psychopath. If you suspect you've been cheated on, that you're going to get fired, that you've put your foot in it.

It doesn't matter! Seriously. I promise you, it doesn't matter. And one more thing: if you get frustrated or even bitter watching TV or looking at magazines or social media and seeing how wonderful and easy other people's lives are, I'll tell you a secret: they're not. The thing is, everything is always more complicated when you see it up close. For example, I had everything, and I lost it all just by putting on sneakers and going for a run... I didn't have everything, and I didn't lose it. Pay attention. I'm telling you this from the bottom of

I say that from personal experience. No, I'm not an influencer or a YouTuber or a model, but, in a way, I've been observed, examined, judged. How? Well, I lived (was trapped, more like) in a fairy tale, the old-fashioned kind that isn't always as shiny as it looks. I was born into an upper-class family. I was born with a string of aristocratic names and a hotel empire attached to them. When I was born, members of the royal family even went to my baptism. I was born condemned to be a princess in a story I didn't believe, but nobody ever thought to ask what I, Margot, believed in.

I know I had a million privileges at my fingertips that other people don't have, but…just let me tell this story my way.

Once upon a time, there was a woman who had everything and a boy who had nothing.

Once upon a time, there was a love story trapped somewhere between success and hesitation.

Once upon a time, there was a perfect story.

And only you can decide how it ends.

2

SUCCESS. APPROPRIATE AND ANODYNE.

"Where are you vacationing?"

That was Mama's favorite question. She asked it at Christmas, when the family was all gathered around a table creaking under the weight of glasses, cutlery, and silver crap as useless as it is old. She asked it during Holy Week too, when we're obligated to go to her house to eat *torrijas* made by a rotating cast of cooks, each one inevitably fired.

On the anniversary of Papa's death, when we traveled to our grandparents' country house to lay down flowers and hear mass, she would ask us too.

"Where are you going on vacation, girls?"

And the reason she always asked exactly the same thing was mostly because she's an old-fashioned snob who worried too much about what would happen if high society didn't see her daughters skiing in Switzerland, lazing on a boat in the Mediterranean, or sunbathing in French Polynesia. That and being skinny enough to see your hip bones through your clothes were the only things that mattered to her. Oh, and "marrying well," of course. Marrying successfully.

No shit, Sherlock.

The first time I heard her talk about success, I was too little to understand or question the characteristics she valued. The idea calcified in my mind, like the word *caterpillar*, which I always pronounced "capertillar" until one day I finally understood what it meant, but not quite like that. Success for my family was the baby in a baptism, the bride in a wedding, and the corpse in a grave. The only respectable aspiration, the very purpose of human existence. A pain in the ass. And this concept felt like a school bully: either you were with him or you were a victim of his whims. And that's where that same tired question came from too.

"Where are you going on vacation, Patricia?"

My sisters and I shot each other looks and smiled stealthily, our eyes glued to our bowls of vichyssoise light, which was more like dirty leek water that smelled like a pond. It was the first sentence my mother had uttered to us since we started the dinner to celebrate my sister Candela coming back to Spain for my wedding.

Yes. My wedding. Welcome to this story that starts where others end happily ever after.

"I'm not asking you. I already know you're going on your dream honeymoon." My mother lifted her gaze to mine, seized her glass, and smiled at me.

"Your dream," I heard Candela whisper, forcing an imitation of my mother's old-fashioned, aristocratic accent.

"Alberto wants us to spend the first two weeks of August traveling, but with the children…" Patricia, the oldest, shot a warning glance at Candela, trying to stifle a smile.

"I want to go to Greece," my brother-in-law explained as he glanced at my terrorist nephews, who had already eaten and were playing suspiciously quietly in the drawing room next to the dining room.

"Traveling with them is exhausting," my sister insisted. "I think we'll rent a house in Formentera for the month."

"Formentera?" Mama looked worriedly at Lord Mushroom, as we called her second husband, and then at Patricia and Alberto. "Isn't that full of—"

"People?" I tried to cut her off before she said something offensive.

"Well, people, yes, but…I'm referring to…people…you know…"

She waved her hand vaguely. This often happened to her, not being able to find the words. She would often…leave things unsaid. Mama is…well, she's lazy in a way someone can only be when they've never understood that "work gives dignity." She's the closest anyone in this century has been to those ladies Kate Winslet hung out with in *Titanic*. Ladies whose only job was regular cosmetic surgeries resulting in majestic, stretched cat faces. As always, she'd just gotten some little "nip," so she was pumped full of her customary pills, ones that take away her pain and, if she swallowed them with alcohol (which she usually did), even eliminated that pesky sensation of human existence.

"Why not Saint-Tropez?" she asked after a sip of wine.

"Because…" Patricia looked to us for support. "Isn't Saint-Tropez pretty passé?"

"Ah, you're right." She nodded. "But Menorca sounds better than Formentera, don't you think, darling?"

Her husband, Lord Mushroom, nodded. He had a noble title, but the truth was, he was like a fungus, very regal but with zero pulse. Sometimes we weren't sure that he had even a hint of life in him, but other people insisted he could form complete sentences. We also suspected he'd been getting lip fillers lately. Every once in a while he had the weirdest pout.

"And you, Candela? Where are you vacationing? You'll have to find somewhere warm to make up for your life in Iceland—"

"I live in Stockholm, Mother, which is the capital of Sweden, and…I had to take off quite a few days to come here." She made a face. "So I'm going on vacation in your guest room."

"Working all day," my mother sniffed disdainfully. "People will think you don't have a penny to your name."

"Well, if I took a few selfies in the room you put me in, I could convince some of my friends I've been to Versailles. Rococo is also pretty passé, Mother. So eighteenth century."

Patricia and I dabbed our mouths with our napkins so they wouldn't see our smiles. The staff cleared our plates and were serving the second course in less than a minute. A steaming filet mignon was placed in front of each dinner guest…in front of me, a cup of kale.

I looked at my sisters. I looked at my brother-in-law. I looked at my mother.

"Oh, darling." She smiled at me. "Sautéed kale. Really good. Really healthy. Very low calorie."

"But…" Candela started to say.

"Just wait until you see how great you look in your dress."

I took a deep breath, plastered on a fake smile, and cut off my sister.

"Thank you, Mother. Cande, don't worry about it."

"With all the beautiful names you all have, I don't know why you insist on calling each other these ridiculous nicknames. Like you. *Margot*. Margot? What kind of name is that? Margarita. Ana Margarita Ortega Ortiz de Zarate."

Present.

Sounds fancy, right? Sounds like a girl who sweats perfume and shits popcorn. An aristocratic grandmother. A mother with a cat face. A mushroom with a noble title for a stepfather. Ana Margarita Ortega Ortiz de Zarate was, in this case, a character, only presented to the other members on the board of the family business, the people interested in society news, and the name that appeared on official documents. For everyone else, that person didn't exist. And thank God for that because she was a bore.

Me, the real me, was Margot. Along with the diminutives when my sisters wanted something, the affectionate nicknames from the men who loved me, the monikers I had been baptized with behind my back in the office, which were an open secret: the marquess, the automaton, or, my favorite, Madame Overtime.

And believe me, Margot didn't feel any sympathy for Margarita, the image that she somehow projected outward. The way everyone else judged me was not how I really felt, not even close. People usually constructed an image of me starting with my origins, but… does that really say anything about me? It says more about my potential investment portfolio really. But we are not what we have, for better or worse.

By force of habit, I'd already learned how to fake a polite smile and sneak out of the society parties I couldn't avoid. Candela, my middle sister, was always allergic to anything my mother might like. Patricia was better behaved…probably because everyone adored her. She's one of those beautiful women who makes other people feel sympathetic.

There wasn't much conversation. In front of our mother, we always found ourselves with nothing to say to each other. Speaking trapped inside these characters we performed for Mama was so awkward that we preferred to stay silent at dinners and be ourselves when we got away from her. That's why we soon retired from that overwrought room where even the oxygen seemed like it was enrobed in velvet.

"Don't leave me alone here, you assholes," Candela groaned as she walked us to the door. "That woman scares me."

"That woman is your mother." I laughed.

"Take me with you. I'll share a bed with any of your children. Even the one who pisses himself at night. I don't care," she whimpered to Patricia.

"I still don't know why you wanted to stay here instead of at my house," I insisted.

"Because you're getting married!" she said as if it were obvious. "And I'm terrible with all that veil stuff."

"Go to a hotel," Patricia proposed, rummaging through her bag. "There's no room at my house."

"You live in a mansion. What do you mean there's no room?"

"Ugh, look, you're a pig, and in two days my sofa will be buried under a mountain of dirty underwear. Ugly, dirty underwear."

"Don't be stupid," I offered again. "Come to my house. He won't mind."

"By the way, why didn't he come today?"

"He had work to finish up before the honeymoon."

"Liar," Patricia added, beckoning to her husband and finally extracting her phone from her Céline bag.

"Bye, Alberto!" Margot said.

"Why do you think that's a lie?" Candela asked, waving a hand at our brother-in-law.

"He didn't come because he can't stand Mama. And look, I get it."

The three of us smiled conspiratorially and hugged each other.

"Good night."

"Lock your door. She turns into Catwoman at night," Patricia joked, pointing up the stairs.

"She wishes. She's more like…like if she swallowed the wardrobe of the entire cast of *Cats*, only skinny."

"See you tomorrow."

"I'll come get you at work," Candela threatened.

"Don't even think about it. I still want them to respect me."

"And what does that have to do with me?"

"You dress like Indiana Jones."

"Indiana Jones? No way. She dresses like a communion photographer."

Patricia and I burst into laughter, and Candela gave us the middle finger.

"You two are disgusting snobs."

"Good night, María Candelaria Ortega Ortiz de Zarate."

~~~~~

As much as they insisted, my sister's car could not fit her, my brother-in-law, their three children, and me. Plus, I lived about fifteen minutes from my mother's house, and it was a warm, lovely evening in early June. The streets, the Madrid that I grew up in, were livelier than ever, even at that hour. I adored the city for that, even though the north, my family's land, was the love of my life.

As I walked, I was thinking of Candela. I wondered if she still harbored some hope that one day Mama would see the light and realize she had three amazing daughters who were more than just work. For a long time now, I had assumed that she would never embrace us or worry about our dreams or apologize for all the things she imposed on us and that we weren't and would never be. Candela was probably the one it mattered least to: she had lived in Stockholm for years practicing as a doctor, and she had a full life designed purely around her desires. She never let the family yardstick make her doubt herself. She was my hero. I felt for Patricia, but I felt adoration for our middle sister.

For me, not letting the family judgment affect me was more complicated: I had always felt somehow obligated to participate in the family traditions, the business, the social events...even though I felt out of place. In a world where the only important things seemed to be shiny (success, beauty, money), a girl like me, even with all my last names, was nothing more than an impostor.

Run-of-the-mill. Neither pretty enough, like my sister Patricia, nor conveniently intelligent, like Candela. I grew up knowing that I was the bland youngest daughter in a family that always aspired to excellence. My mother believed success was embedded in our DNA...imagine her disappointment when she found out her little progeny didn't excel at anything. They signed me up for violin classes, but I only managed to produce a lament that sounded like a cat in heat. They made me attend equestrian classes: the horses hated me and had a predilection for chewing my hair and kicking me. That wasn't going to be the girl's talent, but they kept trying: not an Olympic yachtswoman nor an "it girl" nor a celebrity shaman. Look, I say this with a lot of respect and a little bit of envy because I'm still terribly mediocre. Invisible.

According to Mama: neither tall nor short, neither fat nor skinny enough, neither pretty nor ugly enough, neither clever nor stupid, neither literary nor scientific. I was in the loop with every group but didn't belong to any of them. And according to Lady Meow, as Candela called her, it's better to be criticized than not talked about at all. What was I going to achieve if I didn't stand out in any way?

Do this. Do that. In the end, the only thing I seemed to excel at was not being contrary. Because I didn't have a clear vocation, I ended up following family advice to take a position in the business. THE BUSINESS. The family empire: someone had to do it since Patricia and Candela didn't show even the slightest interest.

I know my mother lamented giving birth to me instead of a little gentleman because she always told us the business world was for brave men with a lot of talent.

It took me five years to figure out that my true vocation was rejuvenating the brand and making it competitive and modern in the digital age. Not everyone has to have it all worked out in preschool. Ever since then, I've always been seen as the "daughter of" because in our world, it seems like women are invisible unless they have that prefix or "wife of," but that was something I had come to terms with. Of course, "the brave men with a lot of talent" weren't going to be pleased that a thirty-two-year-old woman was on the board and had a voice in serious decisions. Important lesson: never make an effort to eliminate prejudice from someone's eyes because they probably see what they want to see. It took me a long time to figure that out, and…someone had to come along and show me.

When I got home, silence loomed inside the cavernous flat. The lights of Madrid twinkled through the floor-to-ceiling windows in the living room and followed me as I crossed it barefoot, my shoes in hand, to the bedroom, which I found empty.

Puzzled, I took out my phone. I had a missed call and a message.

I'm going to grab a drink with my friends.
I won't be back late.

I texted back:

I love you, just got home.

I took off my clothes. I put on a nightgown. I wiped off my makeup. I slathered on my face creams. I sat on the bed and looked out the window.

Two days to go until my wedding. I was going to marry the perfect man. I had a huge apartment in the center of Madrid and a closet full of clothes. I had a giant engagement ring, and I knew that the following night at our rehearsal dinner, my in-laws were going to give me an emerald necklace that had belonged to the family for generations. I had a job and a chauffeur. I had stocks. I had a social life and a bottle of champagne in the fridge.

And even with all that…what mattered most was the overwhelming sensation that I had nothing at all.

3

~~~

FROM BAD TO WORSE

DAVID

She was talking, but I couldn't hear her. Well, to be honest, I could hear her, but I was only able to catch a few words here and there. What she wanted to say had become clear in the first few sentences, so as I often did, I lost the nuances of the discussion, spellbound by her features. Jesus Christ…she was so beautiful. She was incredibly beautiful. She had a special magnetism, the aura of a femme fatale who could cause emotional suicide. She had it all. To me she was the most incredible girl in the world.

I had always liked the pointy shape of her mouth because it seemed to kind of match her character. Suddenly, a word would get snagged on a corner and reject calm in favor of the storm. She was a storm. With her platinum-blond hair and her asymmetrical shoulder-length haircut, somewhere between French black-and-white films and hipsters at music festivals. She was a girl with an explosive body. I'd be lying if I said the first thing I noticed was her eyes or her style. Crazy curves. The day I met her, excuse me, but I fell in love with those two perfect nipples showing through her shirt.

This babe always knew what to wear to drive anyone crazy. Her outfit was never the most logical option… She'd wear something totally outlandish to have a beer in the most tucked-away place in Lavapiés and then wear baggy jeans full of holes to her business meetings. She was like that with everything… Nobody understood her, and it's lame, but that's what I fell in love with (besides the nipple thing, which Freud would probably say points to some childhood trauma).

How many tangos have been written about women like her? How many dudes like me have fallen at her feet?

"David, are you listening to me?"

I bit my bottom lip and felt annoyed. I was much happier in my daydream than answering her.

"Of course I'm listening to you, Idoia, but there's been nothing for me to respond to for a while."

Her red-painted lips froze in a smile, but…it wasn't a smile that put you at ease…more like one that had a bite. There are few things that bother me more than condescension, and coming from her, it was even less tolerable hearing all the "you're so young, David" or "you'll learn that in the years to come." She had thirteen months on me. Call me crazy, but I don't trust the wisdom accumulated in that year and thirty days of difference.

"We agree then, don't we?" she said finally.

At this point in the film, I had very few options. One was to be honest and confess to her that, even though I hadn't been paying attention to her little speech, no, I didn't agree. That would involve debating each point with her, one by one, that she had been putting on the table and…we were standing on a corner, in the middle of the street. I didn't feel like airing my dirty laundry there; it wasn't the time or the place. It would be really embarrassing. I never liked to grovel, but I suspected that I'd been doing that a lot ever since we started our thing. Plus, after everything she'd said to me, I didn't want to give her ears the gift of hearing that it was a unilateral decision that hadn't taken me into account, as an equal.

"Totally agree," I declared.

I went to take a step back to leave before I gave myself the chance to beg. My mind flashed to an image of me on my knees, whimpering and licking her legs and…it disturbed me. I had my pride, but I was very hooked on Idoia, and it could probably happen. Maybe licking her in the middle of the street was a product of my imagination being overly prone to drama, but let's be honest: we (her, me, the kebab guy on the corner, her yoga teacher…) all knew that I was capable of begging for her. I wanted to leave with what little dignity I had left after that talk so I could still imagine cool music playing as I walked away, the rest of the passersby watching me in slow motion, not even blinking while everything exploded spectacularly behind me. But the screening of that particular mental film would have to be canceled for now because Idoia clutched my wrist and pulled me to her. I looked at her mouth and her breasts, bulging out of her black shirt, pressed against my torso. I closed my eyes for a nanosecond; she wasn't wearing a bra. Not that she needed one. Those glorious tits stood up perfectly on their own… Her surgeon made sure of that. *DearGodPleaseDon'tLetMeGetABoner*.

"What are you doing?" I let myself ask with a smile but a furrowed brow.

"Giving you a kiss goodbye."

I should have refused, I know, but I told myself she was the one who proposed it. I couldn't deny myself. It was too soon to accept the truth: that for her, to keep her by my side for five seconds longer,

I would have thrown myself on the ground and let her walk on me like a carpet. Dudes are proud idiots, but at the moment of truth, we would bow down to the first evil villain who scorches our hearts.

And we kissed. We kissed how everyone should kiss. Like a goodbye at the train station. Like in songs that people dedicate on jukeboxes. Like the protagonists of an award-winning drama who fell in love off-screen after the film premiered.

Fucking Idoia. Nine months together and she waited for that moment to give me the best kiss, incredible but short, like all the good moments with her. That's probably what got me hooked on that relationship: the ups and downs, the intensity, the feeling of free fall.

I didn't feel her pulling away from me, but when I opened my eyes a few seconds later, she was already touching up her lipstick, looking into a little mirror she had taken from her bag.

"I'm going."

"Bye," I responded, my voice cracking like a nerd's.

"I'll call you so you can pick up the stuff you left at my house."

"You can keep it."

She didn't say anything.

"Good luck, Idoia," I persevered.

"Same to you."

She smiled, tucked away her lipstick and mirror, and, with a flip of her hair, turned to go, nothing else to say.

"You know where to find me if you ever need anything," I heard myself call out, just to see her turn around.

Come on, come on. Come back. Come back and I'll crawl if you want me to crawl. And I'll buy a dog collar so I can follow you around at your feet. Come back, look at me.

"If she comes back, she's yours, dude."

But she didn't.

Her platinum hair vanished into the crowd bustling around Hortaleza Street. At this time on a Friday in June, there were thousands of people. Even so, I waited like a dope for a few more minutes, forcing myself to pick out her figure from the throng, hoping she would come running back, throw herself on me, wrap her legs around my hips, and stick her tongue in my mouth again. No one's as big a dumbass as me. Or a romantic. Or a pig.

In the movies, the guy is always shielded from the harsh reality by a glass of some very strong liquor, which he drinks without wincing while a middle-aged bartender, armed with great advice, listens to his sorrows.

But in real life there was no glass for me… I was the bartender, and, I swear, the last thing I wanted was some drunk telling me his whole life story.

I sighed and checked the time on my old cracked phone. I was late for inventory, and Ivan would already be at the bar.

~~~~~

"Dude!" Ivan greeted me from behind the bar as I ducked in under the half-open shutter of the club where we both worked on the weekends. "A sight for sore eyes!"

"Sorry I'm late. I was with Idoia. We had to talk."

"Blessed Idoia. She's like human evolution: she turns monkeys into men."

Normally, I would have laughed at that, but this time I emptied my pockets next to the cash register and grabbed a notepad without saying a word. I had spent the short twenty-minute walk to the bar reviewing the shreds of the conversation that I could recreate in my memory…a pretty difficult task because I had disconnected mentally during the first cascade of reproaches.

Immature. Head in the clouds. An out-of-touch romantic. No vision of the future. Unhealthily shortsighted. Needy for constant affirmation. Emotionally dependent. A penchant for using "freedom" as an excuse to justify my mediocrity. Unadventurous and resigned to being an underachiever with my three part-time jobs. My scruffiness. "Sharing an apartment" (crashing on their couch more like) with my best friend, his girlfriend, and their seven-month-old baby. Never having a dollar in my pocket to make plans or go on trips. Burping after the first sip of beer.

That bitch had really done a number on me. She never seemed to complain when I was eating her out every single day, the stupid whore.

Okay. I was pissed off. What phase of grief was that?

Whom was I trying to fool? I was sad. Very sad.

"Are you listening to me?" Ivan asked.

I snapped out of it and stared at him blankly. He was leaning against the bar with a rag over his shoulder, wearing his favorite checkered shirt, and smiling in a way that looked dopey to some but I knew was simply honest. He snapped his fingers, and it infuriated me. Like a little boy getting told off in class and feeling humiliated by his classmates' laughter.

"David, you're spaced out."

"No, Ivan, I'm not spaced out," I snapped back as I turned around, pretending to count the sodas we had in one of the fridges behind the bar.

"I was telling you, for the hundredth time, that you should bring her home whenever you want. Dominique wants to meet her, and…I do too. Seeing her photo is fine and all that, but…I don't know. We're going to end up thinking you're hiding us because you're ashamed of us."

"Don't be a dumbass."

She was the one who didn't want to meet them. She was never "really into" mixing with my people, she would say. Not with Ivan and Dominique or with my crew from the village.

"You already told me she's elegant and sophisticated," Ivan continued, "and she has that super modern job, but…we're still good people in the hood."

"Uh-huh. Listen, is it better if I start in the storeroom?"

Ivan came closer and studied my expression with a furrowed brow. His hair was even more disheveled than usual. I normally joked with him, inventing stories about a surfer soul who grew up in Madrid and surfed on the M-30, but that day the fact that Ivan had abandoned his dream of living by the sea seemed much sadder than normal.

"What's going on?" he asked me seriously.

"Nothing."

"Is it because of the night the little one had? I'm sorry, dude. Her teeth are coming in, and…you know they say if we had to deal with that pain as adults, it would drive us crazy?"

"It's not that, Ivan. I live in your house, and you don't even charge me rent. I'm not going to complain about your baby crying at night." I leaned against the bar and felt a current of grumpiness, sadness, and frustration zip down my spine.

"So?"

"Nothing. It's…" I sighed. I didn't want to talk about it. "It's… this job. I can't handle any more brats screaming for their drinks."

"Ah, well…" He shrugged. "It is what it is. We're bartenders."

"Bartenders, messengers, florists, dog walkers…"

"After all that studying, my mother says."

"As if that guaranteed anything," I muttered as I headed back to the storeroom.

"Hey!" Ivan snapped. "Seriously, what's your deal? You're fucking up the feng shui in here with all your negativity."

I snorted and slumped against the wall. Ivan wasn't going to stop until he wheedled it out of me. It was better to confess now.

"She broke up with me."

"What?"

"Idoia broke up with me."

"But…why?"

I grabbed the notepad again and kept walking toward the storeroom as I said over my shoulder, "She doesn't have time for me because she has to focus on her job. If I were more mature, more reliable, had anything to offer…she would make an effort, but me being me, it's better to leave it here because we don't have any future. Well, to be honest, I'm the one who doesn't have a future, apparently."

"You don't have a future? Why not?"

"Don't make me repeat it all over again. Bad vibes."

"But…what a bitch! Who does she think she is? What is she talking about? She doesn't deserve you, dude… She doesn't deserve you… You know what I mean? What's going on here is…"

Ivan's voice drifted away into nothing as I submerged myself in the chaos of the storeroom, which, as always, smelled damp and stale. Like floors sticky with beer, sugary liqueurs fermenting in the corners. The dark side of the moon, the dirty side of a club where hundreds of boys and girls go to make out on the weekends.

I guess Ivan's words would've comforted me if I had stopped to listen to them, but I didn't give him the chance. Whatever he said, he wouldn't be able to talk louder than the voice in my head confirming everything Idoia had said to me. It was true. Apart from a bunch of pipe dreams, I had little to offer, even to myself.

I was a twenty-seven-year-old guy with no cash in my pocket. I was a dude with no guarantees for the future. I was a kid who had not even the slightest idea where he would be in a few years. No higher education. No masters of the universe. No connections. No long-lost rich uncle. I, David, was the living example of what a poor kid shouldn't aspire to; freedom, the real kind, costs too much money.

I perched on a box of Coke bottles and scrunched my hair in my hands. My life was a disaster. I envied people who had time to lick their wounds. I envied the guy in the movie with his glass of whiskey and a bartender who looked nothing like me. I envied everyone who wasn't me because I was a real mess and nothing ever turned out how I wanted.

I took a deep breath, looked at the ceiling, and wondered why the fuck I still felt so full in spite of everything. I was overflowing with desires.

Shit, I was going to end up choking on my own hunger to be loved.

4

VERTIGO AND PRINCE CHARMING

MARGOT

Patricia smoothed the pleated skirt on my navy-blue taffeta Dior dress and whispered in my ear that I looked beautiful while simultaneously hurrying me toward the hotel entrance.

The terrace and garden of the Hotel Relais and Chateaux Orfila Madrid were crammed with guests dressed in couture, toting designer handbags and dripping with eye-wateringly expensive earrings and necklaces. They were all there to celebrate my imminent matrimony. Almost eighty percent of the guests were work or family obligations. The only real friends there, the kind of friends who hold your hair back when you're puking after hitting the sangria too hard, were my sisters. I had friends, of course, but I never felt like I could be Margot with them. Who are you inviting to your parties and your boat trips, Margot or Margarita? Sometimes I pined for a huge group of friends so much it drove me nuts, friends to go out with, to have fun with and tell secrets to… I never felt comfortable with the girls I used to go out with, same with my friends from college.

When I arrived, I got a pretty insipid smattering of applause and hundreds of eyes looking me up and down. I was prepared, but, after the afternoon my mother had given me, this was the cherry on top to throw me into full panic. I smiled as I tried to shove down the already familiar sensation of drowning, as if the air was getting to my lungs through a filter that only let half through, the same way I felt whenever I had to go to a board meeting or face "society" gatherings.

I still hadn't recovered from my mother being such a pain in the ass at her house while they were designing my personalized cocktail for the wedding. And now I had to pretend to be delighted to make small talk with all these strangers.

I tugged on Candela's wrist and leaned discreetly toward her.

"Find Filippo, please. And do you know who Sonia is?"

"Yes." She nodded. "Slim, shoulder-length hair, big eyes like an abandoned puppy."

"Exactly. If you see her, let me know," I requested.

"You invited your secretary?" my mother asked.

"She's my personal assistant, and, yes, I invited her."

"Why on earth would you do that?"

I rolled my eyes and waved her off to go get another drink. My mother glared at me, as if trying to send threatening brain waves about how I could ruin my own life if I didn't stop being so stubborn and act normal, but I pretended not to see her. Patricia pulled her phone out of her bag and started to type while Lady Meow stalked off.

"You never switch off. How are sales? And the blog?" I asked her.

"The website," she corrected. "Blogs are so 2008."

"Please spare my life."

Patricia designed jewelry. Of course she couldn't dedicate her life to anything less glamorous. Okay, fine, I was being shitty and jealous. The truth is she was really talented, and after Mama made her study law, I was really happy she had been so successful.

"The website is going great," she clarified. "You should see it. Take a look and I'll send a messenger with whatever you like. That way you can take it on your honeymoon."

She glanced up from her phone, winked, and sighed longingly.

"I'm going to find Alberto and the kids. Enjoy your night."

"Don't leave me alone," I pleaded through gritted teeth.

"I'm not leaving you alone. I'm leaving you with your prince."

Patricia drew an arc in the air with her hand, elegantly gesturing toward him as he made his way over. Him. Candela winked and gave me a thumbs-up, and I returned the gesture. As soon as my eyes met Filippo's, my stomach shrunk until it would have fit in my right fist, and everything was calm again. Him. My prince. I still couldn't believe I was about to marry him.

~~~~~

Filippo was tall, really tall, and had hair so blond it would blind the sun. He was handsome; no, not handsome, hot. Everything about him was right, from his height to his demeanor to his tailored clothes. He had broad, toned shoulders and a cheeky smile that showed off his perfect teeth and eyes that were an incredibly deep blue. He was physically perfect, the man of your dreams for any woman who had ever dreamed of a man, and not just because of his incredible physique. It might sound cliché, but the thing I fell in love with was his smile. Well…his sensibility too, the way he was a perfectionist and how he'd always treated me like the only woman who mattered on the face of the earth since the moment we met. Not ordinary or dull. With him, I was special.

Who would've thought…? When we met at a soporific party at the Spanish embassy in Rome (where I had been forced to go for a work commitment because we were building one of our boutique hotels in the Italian capital), I thought he was Norwegian. Or Icelandic. Maybe Swiss. I never would have guessed he had been born there, in that city, and that he spent part of his childhood summers running around getting tan on the grounds of one his parents' many houses in Tuscany.

He spoke to me in English. I answered him in Italian (which I don't speak fluently, but I can get by in) when I noticed his thick accent, and he launched into a rapid, brutal monologue that I didn't understand a word of. When he finished, he smiled. I did too.

"Let me get you a drink," he finished off in Spanish.

Back then, I was "hanging out" with a guy I'd met years before in grad school. I wasn't really convinced I liked him, to tell the truth, but sometimes human beings do these things: they make themselves believe that what they feel is chemistry when it's actually just anxiety. Right before the summer, my mother had sat me down for a "polite" conversation to tell me I couldn't be too picky about men if I didn't want to end up alone.

But it wasn't like that with Filippo. He was like Cupid's arrow to me, like in the stories that inspire fairy tales. He was incredible, candid, magic, and a little nuts. I have to admit that, at first…I didn't even believe he was hitting on me. It was too much. I figured such a good-looking guy would just be looking for someone to chat with during a boring event. When it started to become more than obvious that he had other intentions, my mind created a convoluted and twisted conspiracy that this was all a plot by other members of the board, that they had paid Filippo to flirt with me and then, in a maneuver I hadn't quite figured out (maybe stealing confidential information from my laptop using technology only MI6 knows), used him to prove I wasn't prepared for my role in the Ortega Group.

After he chivalrously walked me back to my hotel and asked for my phone number, I sent a message to my sister Candela telling her my suspicions, and her answer, composed entirely of curse words, snapped me out of it. All I had to worry about was the normal stuff: not getting too excited and/or him hurting me. At the end of the day, I'm not 007, I'm just an idiot with an important name.

The next day, after a work meeting, he took me to Florence to have lunch. He sent me a message saying a car would collect me outside the hotel at eleven, and…it made me really grumpy; it seemed like he was trying to impress me with a display of wealth. And I had already been through all that with a few posh Borjamaris and Pocholos who had courted me on Lady Meow's insistence. But it wasn't like that. He showed up in a pretty ramshackle taxi that smelled like peanuts, which took us to the train station, where we headed off to Florence. We had lunch in a teeny little place that only had about four tables and an improvised bar screwed to the wall that was no more than twenty centimeters wide. I asked him to recommend a local specialty, and…he went nuts. He made me try everything: wine, cheese, charcuterie, a bite of truffled mortadella, an incredible soup, and some crostini. Afterward, we bought gelato, even though it was February and freezing, and strolled toward the Duomo. I was stuffed. Me. A woman used to always being hungry. I didn't think I'd ever go back to killing myself with crazy diets after meeting him. He liked to see me enjoy things.

The sun set on us standing on the Vecchio bridge, kissing.

I was so sure it was a fling, romantic but brief, that I didn't worry about playing games or whether it would be appropriate for me to sleep with him the first night. I, the girl who ruminated on everything for days, who made pro-and-con lists and researched for months sometimes, asked him if he wanted to come up. And he said yes.

Our goodbye was incredible. They brought us breakfast in bed. We repeated, with a lot more rhythm and coordination, what we had done the night before, and we showered together, clinging to each other and kissing like only two strangers who will never see each other again can kiss. I was barely even sad to leave; I figured I was leaving the story at its climax. And it was better this way, so nothing would tarnish the memory when, decades later, I told my niece about it over mugs of warm anise.

But, surprise, Filippo called me that Monday.

"*Dolcezza*...what are you doing tonight?"

Never, ever underestimate an Italian. They always have an ace up their sleeve, like revealing that, actually, they live in the same city as you.

He worked for the Italian embassy in Madrid. He was thirty-three years old. He had four more or less serious relationships behind him, including his most recent ex, with whom he had discussed marriage. They had never set a date. Now she was married to a pilot, a childhood friend, with whom she had a little girl...and Filippo was her godfather. He was even perfect that way: he maintained beautiful friendships with all the women who had passed through his life. He liked good music; he was a great dancer; his laughter was booming, deep and sexy; he got really tan on vacations; he loved drinking a glass of red wine after dinner; he had the softest hands I had ever touched in my life; and...he fell in love with me. Besides his pride, I became his greatest weakness.

I don't know how it happened, but it happened. He got down on one knee in Nara, Japan, in the fall, after a courtship of a little over two years. And finally, we were about to get married.

~~~~~

"*Dolcezza*." Filippo leaned down to kiss me on the lips, making a chorus of guests wolf-whistle and applaud, although we both ignored it. "You look beautiful."

"Me? Have you looked in the mirror?"

"It's just a suit," he beamed.

"All this is mine?" I threw him a lascivious but discreet look as I stroked his chest.

"I'll show you everything tomorrow."

"Tomorrow?"

"Your mother told me"—and I loved the accent that all these years in Spain hadn't managed to erase completely—"you won't be sleeping at home today."

I raised an eyebrow. "I don't like that plan."

"Your sisters are supervising everything. Everything will be fine. Plus, I'm sure that once you're a married woman, your mother will stop meddling."

"Patricia's been married for seven years, and our mother still criticizes the way Patricia tells the girl to iron the crease into her kids' uniforms."

"But our kids aren't going to wear uniforms." He smiled cheekily. "They're going to be normal, running around covered in dirt half the time, and they'll hate their grandmother."

"Guess they'll take after their mother then." We smiled. "But enough about my mother; she'll be entertained by the open bar pretty soon. Come on…I'm going to say hi to your family and start greeting the guests. We must comply with social protocol."

He kissed my hand where my rock of an engagement ring sparkled, and we started to stroll around, our fingers interlaced. I squeezed his hand a little when I realized that this was the first of many parties where I'd have to pretend I wanted to be there.

5

BRIEF PREAMBLE TO PARANOIA

My mother shook me awake at dawn. The weak morning light filtered in through the huge windows of my ground-floor hotel room. She didn't seem to care at all that we had finished the rehearsal dinner late and then it had taken me another hour to get to bed because of her. Apparently, sleeping in my house with my future husband the night before the wedding was a terrible idea. Much better to sleep in one of the rooms in the hotel where the union was going to be celebrated...eighty kilometers from Madrid. The hotel was a parador with beautiful gardens, famous for the food that would be served at dinner, with an incredible sunset...but it had shitty beds. So on top of sleeping little and badly, my back was stiff and I felt like I was moving as elegantly as a headless rotisserie chicken slowly rotating with a stick shoved up my butt.

Lady Meow brought me breakfast in bed. She materialized with her hair pulled back in a turban, a robe, and furry slippers lined with matching silk, glowing and beaming, and whispered to me: "Welcome to the happiest day of your life." She must have been terribly happy to take the weight of my spinsterhood off her shoulders, but I don't think she thought it through; the only reason I didn't die of shock was because the universe seemed to want me alive. First, being woken up by a lady in this getup, sitting next to my bed, whispering; second, accepting that the woman who gave birth to me, who is little more than a stranger, is bringing me breakfast in bed for the first time in my life; third, realizing that said breakfast is plain green tea. It was all too much for someone who had just woken up and was showing symptoms of latent neurosis.

Still, despite how frugal the breakfast was, the tea stayed untouched on my bedside table. I tried, but I couldn't swallow a thing. The anxiety from the night before had taken up residence inside me; it was like having a brick lodged in my guts. It felt like it was even pressing on my lungs.

When Candela showed up in my room, relief flooded me because I thought I was saved. She could fix it all; she always calmed me down, like the day before when my mother told the makeup artist that the eye shadow she was putting on me made me look like a whore, and my sister threw her out of the room and threatened to shave off one of her eyebrows. Candela was a Marvel superhero disguised as a babe who doesn't know how to put an outfit together. Her hair was pulled up in a messy topknot that revealed her shaved undercut, and she was carrying a bun she had managed to pilfer from the free buffet.

"I don't want it." I shook my head.

"What are you talking about? It's made with real butter, you snob!" she retorted, offended.

"I was just going to call you. I don't feel good."

She shoved me violently onto the mattress and pulled my shirt up over my head.

"Do you have to be so rough? Nothing even hurts there!"

She didn't even bother answering; she put on her "I know what I'm doing" face and started digging into my belly.

"I'm telling you, there's nothing wrong with my stomach."

"You don't have diarrhea because of the nerves?"

"I hate that word," I complained through clenched teeth.

"What word? *Diarrhea?* Come on. It sounds so nice. Think about it. It's almost like an explosion of liquid poop."

I pushed her off me, slapping her hands away.

"Tell me what's bothering you," she demanded.

"I mean, I don't know. It's like a pressure between the top of my stomach and my chest."

"Your chest? Pain or pressure?"

"I mean, I don't know. Pressure, I think. What do you think it is?"

"It could be asthma, an anxiety attack, stiffness, or a heart attack."

Patricia came in then, just as the words *heart attack* were still hanging in the air, and she stared at us, surprised.

"Wait, what's going on here?" She leaned over me, like I was on my deathbed and she had to say goodbye. She was wearing yoga pants and a Balenciaga hoodie that could have fit four of her inside. "It's your wedding day; you can't be sick."

"How much did that hoodie cost?" I asked her, my brow furrowed.

"Nine hundred euros."

"Shut up!" I yelped. "You're insane!"

"But it makes me look super young."

"And stupid. I have one just like that from H&M," Candela declared. "Can you let me work?"

"Nothing's wrong with her. It's just nerves, whatever's bothering her." Patricia flopped down on my bed and shook me. "Your wedding is today! Relax and have fun. If all goes well, and it seems like all's going well, you'll only get married once in your life. Filippo is crazy about you, the wedding planner you found is a psychopath control freak, the weather is supposed to be perfect, not a cloud in the sky, and if there are any hiccups…like Lord Mushroom getting wasted too early…I'll take care of it. I've always wanted to punch that guy."

She dragged a smile out of me, which made me feel a little better, but it didn't seem to have the same effect on our sister.

"I'm going to get my stethoscope."

"You packed it in your suitcase?"

"I never take it out of my backpack." She shrugged. "Medicine runs in my veins."

Ten minutes later, I was sitting on the sofa with Candela probing me.

"Hurry up," I whined. "I have a lot to do."

"You shouldn't have that much, Lady Important. For the fortune you paid, they should be wiping your royal ass," Patricia grumbled, rolling her eyes.

"Shh! Shut up, you birdbrains. Take a deep breath one more time."

Patricia and I exchanged sheepish glances, trying to telepathically send the message that Candela could be really annoying.

"Enough?" I asked when she took the piece of metal off my chest.

"No. I'm going to take your blood pressure."

"Oh my god…"

"You're the one who feels like shit."

"I don't feel like shit! I just have…I dunno, anxiety or something. Can't you just give me a pill and move on?"

"I have to know what to give you, don't I? What do you think?

That we just have a first aid kit full of magical pills shit out by unicorns in Lollipop Land for times like these?"

"Jeez, look at you. Such a charmer." I was intimidated.

She slapped on the cuff to check my pressure and threatened me to keep quiet. After a few minutes of silence, Candela pulled off the stethoscope and looked at me seriously.

"Your blood pressure is very high."

"Define *very high*."

"Very high for a woman of your age who is completely healthy and isn't being chased by a lion. And I have to say this, Margui…" And her voice broke a little on the end of my nickname. "You don't have to go through with this if it's not what you want."

"What are you talking about, you nutjob?" I clutched my chest. "You're making me nervous, for fuck's sake."

"This girlie is not well." Candela shook her head. "This little girl does not want to get married."

Suddenly Candela was acting like she was seventy-seven years old.

Patricia pulled away and smiled like a movie star on a red carpet.

"It's just nerves, Margot. You've always been a perfectionist." Patricia stroked my back with her iPhone in her hand. It felt like she was scanning me.

"What if I am having a heart attack? It could be a heart attack and you're here, trying to peer pressure me into thinking I don't want to get married."

"She's the one saying it." She pointed at our middle sister disdainfully. "All she wants is chaos. She's like the Joker."

"Margot." Candela made me look at her and fixed me with the scariest stare I had ever seen. I couldn't express my fear that it could actually be a tropical disease that someone had brought to the office as a souvenir from spring break. "If you love Filippo, if you're sure about what you're doing, then I'm asking you—no, I'm begging you as a sister—to let it go. It's here! Everything is fine! Stop looking for problems where there aren't any. Stop believing something bad has to happen. This is your fairy tale, and despite whatever Mama made you believe, you deserve it."

It was like a slap. But only because it was true and, at the same time, an open secret: ever since I had gotten engaged, I had been waiting for something bad to happen. It couldn't all go so perfectly. Not for me.

And...yeah, I know, I know. It's very predictable what was going to happen next, but if I don't tell you, you might not understand.

6

PARANOIA

The dress was digging into me atrociously, but not because it wasn't well tailored or because I had gained weight. It was supposed to be that way. If it didn't fit to the exact millimeter, pretty much painted on, it would be baggy on the curve where the back ended, and it would slip down my shoulders.

I had taken forever to find my dress. At first everyone, including the wedding planner and the personal shopper, insisted that I should choose a haute couture dress from a famous designer. I tried on…I don't know how many. Valentino. Chanel. Even a few cocktail dresses by Saint Laurent that could be altered and transformed into wedding dresses. Nothing. There was nothing I liked; I felt like I was wearing a costume.

So I had no other option but to trust someone to convert the mental image I had of my perfect dress into something real. And here it was, materialized. A dress that a bespoke designer, From Lista with Love, had sewn according to my exact wishes, my dreams, my personality…and the real one, not Ana Margarita Ortega Ortiz de Zarate. A boat neckline, half sleeves, backless down to the waist, a small sash topped by two lined buttons, and a drop-waisted skirt. Simple. Without the eccentricities or the modern things some brides who are hoping to appear in the glossy pages of fashion magazines want. A low bun, a silk bow around it in the same white as the dress, and dusty-rose shoes that were mostly hidden under the skirt. My grandmother's earrings. My engagement ring. Everything in its place.

I looked in the mirror, took a deep breath, and felt the seams of the dress groaning as they pinched my skin.

"You don't like it?" the hairdresser asked, pulling a few strands loose from the updo so it would look natural.

"What? Huh? Yes, yes. I like it a lot."

The dress was perfect. Incredible. The most beautiful thing I had ever seen in my life. The hairstyle was comfortable and elegant, natural…just like the makeup, nothing overdone. Everything, down to the manicure, was perfect, but the only thing I could see when I looked in the mirror was how fast the vein in my neck was pulsing.

"It would have been more elegant if you could see your hip bones, but there's not much we can do now," my mother said, and she sighed.

"You look incredible." Patricia held her breath next to me, and I knew she was trying not to cry. "Tell your auntie how beautiful she is."

My nephews, decked out in shorts and button-up shirts with suspenders and bow ties, and my niece in a frilly dress, all shouted at the same time that I was very pretty, not because they thought so but to get their mother off their backs. The next second, they launched into chasing each other around me until, as we all feared, they ended up in a tangled brawl of kicking and biting.

Everything was too bright and spinning. Them, the room, my

dress, the mirror, everyone else. It was like I was seeing everything through a kaleidoscope. And I was breathing hard. All I could hear was my own panting.

It was hot. I was hot. But my hands were cold.

"Bah," I eked out.

"Take this." Candela came over with a glass of water and the half pill I hadn't taken earlier, after I had drunk two sips of gazpacho for lunch. It was a mild benzo. "I guess you needed the whole thing after all."

"I'm fine," I lied.

"Don't even think about drinking anything for a few hours," she whispered. "Or you'll end up like Mama."

For a second I felt like I was alone with her, but when I turned my back to the mirror, I found a room full to the gills with women staring at me. What the hell were all these people doing here? People infecting the air with their motivations and emotions, like the spit that flew everywhere after a sneeze. There was jealousy, derision, admiration, affection, happiness, disbelief. Everything.

I grabbed Candela's wrist. I wanted to be left alone with my sisters, but I couldn't get the words out.

"Young lady!" One of my mother's friends ran over. "Are you dizzy?"

I shook my head. Another one brought over a chair. My mother-in-law kept palming my forehead to check if I had a fever. I hadn't even seen her come in. Whispers. The word *pregnant* floated through the air, though I don't know whose mouth it came out of. The lumps in my throat, my chest, and my stomach all contracted. I didn't know if I wanted to scream, faint, or burp. Maybe fart. Voices kept spinning around me, like spirals of smoke leaving me blind and deaf and making my throat dry and burning. What if I was dying? My heart thudded sickeningly against the seams.

A familiar voice asked, very politely, for everyone to get out except Candela and Patricia.

"These are emotional moments. Let's go and let them enjoy some privacy."

Sonia. Blessed Sonia. She was an angel without wings.

Patricia fanned me as I heard the door opening and my mother inviting everyone to go to the chapel and find their seats.

"All the seats are assigned, dears. You'll find your name there."

I waited for her to go to the chapel with the rest of the guests, but she came back. I noticed this even through my closed eyes and the sound of the fan. It felt like her presence made the air thicker again.

There were still twenty minutes to go before the ceremony.

"Might you deign to tell us what's going on with you?" she scolded me in a low voice. "What is all this? A cry for attention? For God's sake! You're the bride! You're not getting enough attention? You need to behave like such a brat in front of all my friends?"

Nobody answered. I tried to wave her out of the room, but nobody paid me any attention.

"Okay, what do you want?"

"Air," I managed to squeak.

Patricia ran to open the windows. The smell of fresh-cut grass wafted into the room, just a few feet from the garden, on the back end of the farm the hotel was on.

"Margot, this is a classic panic attack to a T," Candela whispered.

"No. No. No way," I whimpered.

I swallowed. I felt like my dress was cutting off my circulation. I felt pressure even in my throat.

"Can you unbutton my dress?"

"There's less than half an hour before the ceremony," my mother announced.

"The dress. Please."

"If you had listened to me and followed the diet. A minute on the lips and a lifetime on the hips."

"Mother, could you shut up please?" Candela groaned. "Can't you see she's white as a sheet and she can't breathe?"

"Well, then do something. That medical degree can finally come in handy."

"Yeah, because it's always been so useless."

"I'm not allowed to speak?"

"Patri…" I tugged on her hand. "Tell Filippo to come here please."

"Ay, Margot…that's bad luck."

"Please. Tell Filippo to come here."

Patricia looked at me, hesitating, before she stood up and made for the door. Candela and my mother had launched into a full-blown passive-aggressive argument in muted but cutting tones. Accusations were hissing around me like poison arrows.

"Stop now. Please," I begged.

Candela shut up and started to unbutton my dress.

"It doesn't matter if you're a little late." My mother's mouth, inflated by punctual injections of hyaluronic acid, pasted on a hyena's smile. "Elegant brides always play hard to get. You don't want them to think you're in a hurry or desperate."

Candela held her breath and swallowed; then she rubbed my back tenderly.

"Better?"

"When I see Filippo, then I'll be better."

"That's bad luck."

"Bad luck doesn't exist, Mother," she snapped back tensely. "Life happens. Sometimes it's good, sometimes it's bad."

The door opened, and Patricia appeared with a smile.

"Close your eyes. He's too handsome to spoil the surprise."

"He's always handsome," I answered.

Filippo filled the room with a special light. Everyone, including my mother, smiled with a kind of relief. He always provoked that reaction.

"*Dolcezza*." He smiled as he sat next to me. "What's going on?"

"I don't know." My voice came out strangled.

"Could you leave us on our own?" he asked my sisters and my mother.

"There's no need," I cut in.

"Is there something you want to tell me?"

"No. No. I just wanted to see you. I'm… I need air."

"*Amore*," he whispered into my neck. "You're nervous. But we've already been living together for a year, and…everything is going great. This is just a formality. With a big audience, but still a formality."

"I can't," I heard myself say.

"What do you mean you can't?"

"There are too many people."

"So what?" He smiled. "Come on, Margot… You gave a conference in Los Angeles in front of a thousand people in another language. Compared to that, this'll be a cakewalk."

"What if I can't do it?"

"Of course you can."

"But what if I can't?"

His brow furrowed.

"Margot…"

I closed my eyes and panted. It felt like the air was dissolving when it arrived in my chest and my lungs always needed a little more.

"Filippo…" I moaned, on the edge of bursting into tears. "It feels like I'm drowning."

"You're not drowning. And this is nothing."

"It's a lot."

"Well, we should have thought about that earlier. Right now there's nothing we can do. We'll just get it over with, and then it'll be done."

"There are hundreds of them." I closed my eyes.

"So what's the problem?"

Hundreds. Thousands. Eyes watching. Slithering. They were like slugs, they left behind a shiny, slimy trail of prejudice, of criticism, of judgment on my skin. Disgust in my stomach. An unpleasant tingling on the back of my neck. Like millions of insect feet scampering over my body.

I was driving myself crazy. I gulped air. I pushed on my temples and curled into a fetal position.

"Filippo," I heard Candela say. "Maybe you should consider the possibility of delaying a little."

"What?"

He sounded very severe. Him. The titan. The dark part of a great man.

"She's obviously having a panic attack, and…I mean, I get it. There are five hundred people crammed into a chapel, the grounds are packed—"

"It's not like we weren't expecting all that," he insisted.

"Anxiety can't be controlled. If reason could intervene, anxiety wouldn't exist."

"Margot." Filippo was next to me again. "Take a deep breath. Calm down. I'm here with you, okay?"

I didn't move despite feeling his hot breath on me. It was like when someone says to the other person who feels awful the classic phrase "Come on, you're fine." *Ah, well, thanks so much, now I'm totally happy; thanks for your help.*

"I can't," I groaned.

"You're going to have to, *amore*."

I lifted my head to get air. My lap was cutting off my oxygen.

"There are two hundred people from the embassy and from the... how do you say it...the Italian government. There are...civil servants. Important people who respect me. I can't allow myself to be—"

"Filippo, you're not helping," Candela jumped in to defend me.

"It's not helping, I know. But this is life. Life is like this. We were lucky to find each other in a world where there are millions of people, and this whole thing is ridiculous."

"Why don't we give her a few seconds alone?" Patricia proposed, leaning grimly against the wardrobe with her arms crossed. "Let's give her a few minutes, stop crowding her with our opinions and let her see the light."

Filippo gently took my face between his big hands and made me look at him.

"*Dolcezza*, I need you to look at me. It's me. I'm the love of your life. All you have to do is come out of here and do exactly what we did in the rehearsal. Say yes, yes, yes and sign a paper. You'll have your back turned to all those people; you'll only see me."

The breath of five hundred people dampening the back of my neck. Gross. I shuddered.

"This is ridiculous." He was starting to get agitated. "Ridiculous, Margot."

"It's a lot of people."

"They're just people. I don't get it. I don't get how suddenly you—"

"It's a lot of people," I repeated.

"Don't do this to me, Margot!" he replied firmly. "It will bring shame on my family."

"Okay. Okay. Let's go calm down." Patricia took Filippo by the arm and dragged him away. "Let's all get out of here. Let's give the bride a moment to breathe. And if we have to delay the ceremony by half an hour, then we delay it. More was lost in Cuba, and they came back singing."

"That's enough, Lady Proverbs," Candela teased her as she showed my mother to the door.

"There's one for every occasion." She smiled. "Margot, babe, we're going to leave you alone, okay? When you're ready, call us. We'll be in the hallway waiting. You calm your tits. Sit, relax, smoke a joint…"

"She doesn't smoke," Candela said.

"Well, maybe now's a good time to start. Come on, my love. You take deep breaths and forget all this. Everyone in the chapel shits too. Remember that. Okay, chop-chop, everyone out."

Filippo stood in front of me and took a deep breath, looking very serious.

"I'll be waiting for you outside, Margot."

~~~~~

The door swung shut, and the room was left in relative silence. The echo of faraway conversations drifted in through the open window, a gentle noise like water trickling over a riverbed of tongues and teeth. Birds were singing. Leaves were rustling in the soft June breeze. The footsteps of my sisters, my mother, and Filippo were moving farther away, muffled by the carpet, and when I couldn't hear anything except the old house breathing, I felt like I could breathe too.

I don't know how many minutes went by before I stood up from the sofa. All I know is that suddenly everything felt different. Like when you went back to school after summer vacation, you changed classrooms with a new class, and even though it was the same school with the same students, it felt different. I looked around the room like I had never seen it before. The heavy Castilian-style furniture. The dusty imitation-Persian rug. The curtains fraying at the edges. The fake, dust-laden luxury. This room was like me. A false projection.

Hit me, truck, I'm like a mothballed velvet curtain, nibbled to shreds for who knows how many years.

Panic was flooding my veins at top speed. The truth is I can't explain where the anxiety and the visceral need to run away were coming from.

I heard my teeth grinding together. Gasping. The room. The stone walls. My suitcase open on the perfectly made bed. The bathroom with the light on. The carpet. The shadow of the horrible imitation antique lamp on the opposite wall, painted beige. All of it. All spinning around me, like I was at a funfair. And me in the middle of it all. Me. Me. Me. Me.

Blackout.

You know the noise a high voltage tower makes when the energy cuts off? Imagine the sudden relief when a sound you didn't even know you were hearing disappears. Suddenly everything calmed down. Yes, I know. What kind of fucking explanation is that? I don't know. But everything calmed down. Everything.

But it wasn't me.

The person who pulled on sneakers under her wedding dress. That wasn't me.

The one who opened the window and jumped out. Definitely not me.

The one who sprinted across the perfectly manicured lawn to the road. No fucking way. That wasn't me.

The one who everyone watched from the door of the chapel, running in some random direction... Nah, nah. It wasn't me.

The one being chased by Candela, Patricia, my niece and nephews howling with laughter, Lord Mushroom, Filippo, and a few guests. What are you talking about? That wasn't me.

It was me, and it wasn't me. But... that person who wasn't me has gotten herself into a pretty big mess, huh?

7

DEPRESSION

DAVID

Dominique had lived in Spain for twenty of her twenty-two years, but some people still considered her a foreigner. More like a citizen of the world, smarter than most and prettier than anyone. When Ivan introduced me to her, I was stunned. As stunned as he must have been the night he first laid eyes on her in a metro station and she smiled at him. They fell in love at first sight, just like in the love stories that don't happen to guys like me. They were both good and healthy, and in each other, they had found someone who they could share beautiful things with. That was my mistake. I always ended up falling in love with people who brought out the worst in me, who made me feel insecure, like a big kid, who made things not just difficult but impossible. I fell in love with the antiheroine because I couldn't be bothered with Superwoman. I always liked the villains, even in the comics I read as a teenager.

I was delirious. My head had been trapped in a delirious state ever since Idoia left me. I would think these things over and over, sometimes feeling sorry for myself and judging myself because no girl had ever made me feel even close to what I had felt for her. And in that moment, seeing my best friend's beautiful girlfriend rocking her baby, I was more sure than ever that I had made a lot of mistakes in my life.

"When did I start fucking it all up?" I asked out loud.

"Whoa, the lump on the sofa is talking. Look, my love, the walking dead." She propped her daughter, Ada, up so she could see me, and she gave a gummy smile, her face still red from the tears that had woken her from her nap.

"Seriously, Domi, when did my life go to shit?" I ran my fingers through my hair, overwhelmed.

She sat down next to me, balanced her baby on her knees, and smiled.

"Oh, God, no," I moaned. "Don't smile at me like that with your beautiful face before you rake me over the coals."

"What are you talking about?" She laughed at me like I was crazy.

"Your boyfriend does the same thing. You're both so sweet. You smile first to stupefy people, and then you give the death blow. Go on then, shoot."

"David…you've been glued to that sofa for a week."

"That's not true. I went to work."

"In the same shirt."

"But I showered."

"I'm not so sure about that."

I leaned back and groaned.

"I know you liked Idoia a lot," she acknowledged gently.

"I loved her."

"You really liked Idoia a lot, okay."

I sucked my teeth; I was never going to convince her that this thing with Idoia was true love.

"I know you believe you loved her, but love, my boy, is something else," she assured me.

"It's not feeling alive, having heart palpitations, feeling like you have your hands full?"

She put her hand on my forearm, halting my speech.

"Love isn't waiting for her to respond to a message or measuring your own self-worth based on how much attention she gives you one day, knowing the wind will blow in another direction and she'll change her mind the next."

"That's the thrill of it—"

"No. That's a misunderstanding of love. If it's torture, it's not love. Love is fun. Super fun, actually." A smile broke across her beautiful, clear, trustworthy face. "You feel so comfortable and so yourself with the other person that you could be doing almost anything. You feel capable. And you laugh with your mouth full, fighting, cooking, and even in bed. David, really…love is much lighter than anything you've felt. It makes you fly; it doesn't pin you to the sofa hugging… what even is this?" She pointed at a piece of clothing I was clenching, which I snuggled whenever I was on the sofa.

"One of her shirts."

Domi picked it up gingerly between two fingers, as if it was a test tube full of a lethal virus, and held it up in the air.

"One: this couldn't be any tackier. Two: it smells like death. Three: you're being ridiculous."

She put Ada in my lap and carried the shirt over to the trash, where she tossed it without a second thought. As soon as she came back over, I went to retrieve it. A little wash and it would be mine forever.

"Your mother is a cruel vixen," I murmured to the little girl.

"I'm not a vixen. Do me a favor."

"Whatever you want. I live on your couch," I murmured. "Because I'm a mediocre dude with no aspirations and blah, blah, blah."

"David, we're not making ends meet and you do the grocery shopping, you help around the house, and you take care of Ada. It's a win-win—"

"Yeah, right, fine."

She snapped her fingers at me gravely while her daughter gummed my beard.

"Take a shower. A nice long one. Sit and listen to 'All by Myself' while you cry and complain because the love of your life abandoned you, but then stop wallowing. It's Friday and I know you have work, but you're a bartender in a shitty club, you're young, you're cute, and you're free. If you don't sleep at home tonight, we won't call the police."

"I need to find my own place," I muttered, feeling miserable.

"Go take a shower and get laid for fun, fucking hell!"

She took the baby and pointed at the tiny bathroom we all shared.

I dragged my feet and heard her mutter that I could thank her later. I felt the urge to spout some drivel at her. I was angry, and I felt like I had the right to feel like a piece of shit, a kind of cocoon of grief and anxiety. Who cared if I looked like shit at work? From Monday to Thursday I juggled jobs as a florist and a dog walker, so I didn't think either the flowers in the storeroom or a pack of dogs would care about my scruffiness. But Domi was right. It was Friday, and I had to go back to the bar, and smelling like dick with greasy hair might be a problem there.

I had no choice. I needed the money.

~~~~~

The club was jumping. It's one of the things I've never understood about Madrid. It was a beautiful night. What drove people into a skeezy club where they just got elbowed all night? And where it's hot, because 120 souls in a club, dancing, drunk, and—ninety percent of the time—horny, create lot of heat. I guess the answer to the question is that there are always people in Madrid. Everywhere. On the terraces; in the alleys snaking through neighborhoods like Malasaña, Lavapiés, or La Latina; in the "old man" bars where the walls are covered in photos of dishes already faded by the decades, where you can still smell a whiff of tobacco; on the rooftops of hotels with clubs and fake speakeasies. That's what happens in the capital; there is life everywhere even when you want to be alone.

But Dominique's speech got under my skin. I couldn't get it out of my head, the kind of love she had been talking about. It was floating around me constantly, like a puff of smoke that wouldn't take form.

At first, I fell into a mistake more cliché than putting a beret on a French character: looking for someone to help me get over the pain.

I know, I know. Super dirty, but we all do it. We're human, and we all grew up hearing that the best way to get over someone is to get under someone else, so getting laid for fun by a girl who was probably in the same situation as me was my first plan. I scanned the horizon looking for someone (preferably with short blond hair, a cold look, and pouty lips) with whom I could try to make a date for closing time, but…I didn't find anyone. No. Actually it was exactly the opposite. I saw tons of people, but none of them were Idoia.

I watched couples making out passionately in the corners, and I found myself wondering if they loved each other in a fun way.

Fucking idiot, of course most of them had just met that night. Why would they be thinking about love?

It seemed stupid to me. I was obsessed with the stupidity. Having fun with love? Fine, maybe in the honeymoon stage. But, like everything else, the one who has the upper hand would always be having more fun, and let's be honest, love has always been a power struggle.

"What are you thinking about?" Ivan asked me as he restocked the fridge and I filled some highball glasses with ice.

About Idoia. How I'm dying to send her a message. How I'd love to see her appear in the doorway. How nobody is like her. How I want to kiss her again and listen to our songs while I trace hearts on her back, and now, I want to drink myself to death.

"How much I hate this job." I grinned at him like a lunatic.

Despite the deafening volume of the music, the girls I was serving heard me and burst out laughing. I pasted on a friendly face and turned to them, raising my voice above the song of the moment.

"Nothing personal, girls. Did you know the bartenders have to clean the toilets too?"

"Noooo!" all three screamed in horror.

"Don't listen to him." Ivan laughed. "We've only had to do that a few times. There's a cleaning crew."

I made a face, implying that my colleague was lying, and pulled a bottle off the shelf behind me.

"It's not such a bad place to work, is it? You probably meet a lot of people," one of them said. She was a brunette with full lips, enormous eyes.

I don't want to meet a lot of people. I want to climb into bed with Idoia and wake her up with my tongue.

"Okay, fine. It's not so bad."

"Where are you from?" she wanted to know. "You don't have a Madrid accent."

"Nobody in Madrid is from Madrid." I plastered a half-smile on my face and put the bottle back in its place.

"That doesn't answer the question," she said teasingly.

I pushed their drinks over and opened the sodas with a bottle opener and a flick of my wrist.

"Tanqueray gin and tonic, vodka with orange juice, and Barceló with Coke Zero. That'll be thirty-six, ladies."

The one whose round it was waved her card and tapped it against the card reader to pay.

"Goodbye, Mr. Bartender who's trying to be mysterious," the brunette called out.

"I'm sure that won't be your last drink. So I'll probably see you again."

I smiled, but as soon as they disappeared into the crowd, my smile vanished. This was my least favorite thing about being a bartender: having to pretend I had no personal problems.

"You were flirting." Ivan elbowed me.

"What're you still doing here?" I laughed.

"Enjoy it, David. You're single." He winked.

"I guess so." And I flashed him the fakest smile in my repertoire.

"You feeling better?"

"Yes," I lied.

He slapped me on the back and headed over to a group of guys who were waving at us, desperate for another drink or a round of shots.

Enjoy it… you're single.

Two rounds of Jäger shots demanded by screams. One "Do you

have chocolate tequila?" from the mouths of two little girls who didn't look like they were legal. Three winks. One "What time do you get off?" Two "What a rip-off" and one phone number scrawled on a napkin.

Immature. Head in the clouds. An out-of-touch romantic. No vision of the future.

Fuck it. Maybe Idoia didn't turn around when I stood there waiting like a jerk for her to look at me again, but could I let her go believing I was all of those things? How could I let that happen? My fucking chest was full of feelings and things I wanted to share with her. I wanted to marry her, have kids with her, adopt a dog, a sheep, fifteen cats. Whatever! No. I was sure I could still do something about our relationship.

I didn't want to get laid for fun. I already had the person who could take away my pain. And I knew whom I was going to focus my attention on. I was very clear about who deserved my efforts.

I wasn't going to be down in the dumps. Of course not. The breakup wasn't going to discourage me. Quite the opposite. It would have a purpose. It would make me better. Turn me into a man.

If you're thinking that I realized I was the person who could get me out of my own pain, whom I should focus my attention on, and who deserved the effort…you obviously think I'm smarter than I am. No. Really, even though I suddenly felt like my life jacket was inflating and I was floating back up to the surface, I was actually filling my pockets with stones, like Virginia Woolf. Because suddenly all my brain chemistry had decided that…I was going to get my ex back.

And I guess that decision is what led me to her…and I'm not talking about Idoia anymore.

8

~~~

CONSEQUENCES

MARGOT

My mother's wails and her subsequent fainting à la Victorian lady (resulting in her falling face-first into a golden footrest, which, come on, even I found funny) didn't get to me. But it did get to my eye twitch. My eye twitch was seriously affected and decided making my eyelid samba was a good idea.

My sisters' funereal silence did more than get to me; it freaked me out. I was scared they were judging me the way I knew everyone else was and also that, when all this passed and waters calmed a little, Candela would open her big mouth and say the forbidden words: *told you so.*

But on the list of two hundred problems my running off down the path of an empty lawn had caused, the only one that really mattered to me was in front of me right then: Filippo.

His forearms were resting on his knees, and his head was hanging down, avoiding even looking at me. I wished he would, but I wasn't in the position to ask for anything. I ran out on our wedding and left him at the altar and let him down when it came time to give explanations in front of five hundred guests. I wriggled out of his arms and sprinted across the lawn outside the hotel and squeezed through a hole in a fence. It's best not to even mention the state of my wedding dress.

"Say something," I pleaded in a small voice.

Ever since he had come into my mother's house, where I was imprisoned "for my own good" after they "hunted me down" in a gas station restaurant a kilometer and a half from the wedding venue, he hadn't opened his mouth. All he had done was sit opposite me on the footrest my mother had crashed into when she fainted, frozen in the same position he was still in now.

When he heard me, he lifted his head, but for two eternal minutes, he still didn't utter a single word.

"Please," I begged.

He lifted his chin and looked at me. I had changed my mind, but I didn't want him to. I didn't like what I was seeing at all. None of it seemed familiar to me; this was some stranger version of Filippo who didn't even want to be near me. But I mean, every action has a consequence. That's one of the first things we learn in childhood, and I guess our existence is supposed to be simplified by learning this, if we possess the skill of thinking before you act, which I don't.

"You ran. Away. From our wedding."

The pauses between the words were heavy, as if he had to drag up every tiny syllable weighed down by shackles from the depths of his disappointment. I swallowed, and this time, it was my head that drooped.

"With no explanation, without even talking to me, without saying anything to me," he insisted.

"I did talk to you."

"You told me there were too many people and you couldn't do it. You couldn't do what? That's as good as saying nothing."

"I was filled with… I don't know. Panic."

"About marrying me?"

"No!" I looked up at him. "Of course not. I want to marry you."

"You wanted to marry me. Don't use the present tense."

"I *want* to marry you, Filippo."

"Don't insult my intelligence. Don't hurt me even more, Margarita."

"I'm not trying to hurt you and…don't…don't…don't call me Margarita. I'm Margot to you. Just Margot."

"To me, you're the woman who escaped down the highway on our wedding day. You're the woman I loved who broke my heart, Margarita. Let me call you whatever I want."

I sniffed and looked at the ceiling. Bobby pins were digging into my scalp.

"I don't understand what happened to me. I think I need help," I said.

"You need a lot. You made me believe this was all real."

"That's enough, Filippo," I said, dripping with hostility. "You've made it very clear you think I was tricking you because I'm the worst person on earth, but you're wrong."

"So then what?"

"So then I don't even know what I did or how I did it. I don't even know how I got to the fucking gas station, for fuck's sake."

I covered my eyes. I had spent my whole life avoiding being whispered about in society, but…now I was doing it in grand style: Heir to the Ortega empire flees her wedding down the highway and is found in a Galp gas station drinking a Coke. It was going to cost me a fortune to stop that news leaking to the press.

By the way…how had I planned on paying for the soda, now that I think about it?

"What do you want me to believe? That you have mental health problems? I live with you, Margot." I was flooded with relief when I heard my real name. "I know you don't. You're completely sane."

"I've been feeling really weird lately, Filippo. Really, really weird. I'm not sleeping, I've been distracted, anxious. Sometimes I find my socks in the fridge and I throw yogurt into the laundry basket."

"Oh, for God's sake."

Filippo stood up and started pacing around the living room. He had taken off his suit, just like I had taken off my beautiful, trashed white dress. His legs, in tight dark pants, roamed around the room that was decorated to the hilt. Minimalism and my mother didn't get along.

"You're not crazy, Margot."

"Well, I ran out of my wedding to the man I love. How else would you explain that?"

"Simple." He looked at me again. "You don't love me as much as you say. Or you don't love me as much as you think."

"Filippo, please."

"Margot, you jilted me at the altar. You jil-ted-me-at-the-al-tar."

"Shit." I curled into a ball in Lord Mushroom's wing chair.

"No. You can't run away from this too. You jilted me at the altar in front of my whole family, my mother, father, sister, nonna… My nonna is a hundred years old, Margot."

"Don't make me feel even worse."

"Besides my nonna," he continued, "my boss was there. And my boss's boss. The guests included eight work colleagues. A minister from my country and…wait, there was also my uncle, who's a bishop."

"Fine, I've caused problems with the Italian state, the Spanish embassy and the Vatican. Anything else?"

I watched as he leaned against the ornamental fireplace and crossed his ankles. His elbow on the mantelpiece, his fingers in his thick blond hair. His eyes cold. Like ice.

"What did I do wrong?" he asked, still not looking at me. "I always treated you with respect, like an equal. I respected your professional ambition, your beliefs, your schedule."

"Filippo, that's what a normal couple does."

He shot me a furious look.

"I loved you more than anyone has ever loved!"

God. Not the opera, please. I squeezed the bridge of my nose and braced myself for the next hit.

"I was crazy in love. I left my apartment to move into yours! I put my plans on the back burner. I always prioritized our relationship like it was the only thing that mattered. I put up with your mother, for the love of God! That has to be worth something."

I had to give him that one, but all I could do was nod.

"You know what, Margot? You're right. You need help. And I'm sorry if I'm being harsh, but the fact that you made me a laughingstock in front of five hundred people took away the love filter. Do you know what you seem like? Like you're thirty-two years old and you don't even know who you are or what you want. You always do things because you think they're expected of you, right? Yes, you do need help, but not mental help. You need help to learn how to live and be free, dammit."

I hung my head and tucked my knees into my chest.

"Your inertia drags everything around you down. Even me. Because you don't care about all the things you are, Margot, you're obsessed with what you are *not*, and that is exactly what happened to you today. Your fucking obsession was more important than our love." His voice broke, and I buried my head between my chest and my knees, cocooning myself. "Fear that people would say…what? That you weren't elegant, that you hadn't chosen a good dress, that the food was cold? You broke everything because of the opinions of people you don't care about!"

I looked at him and shook my head while two round tears made tracks down my already washed face.

"Now what?"

"I'll fix it," I promised.

"It can't be fixed."

"Of course it can." I sobbed. "Filippo, this is our fairy tale."

"I don't believe in fairy tales, Margot, and you shouldn't either. Live your life through your own eyes, not everyone else's. That would be a good start."

I ran my hand under my nose and then swiped away a few tears. As he headed toward the door, Filippo said, with a determination that I never could have imitated. "I'm going to leave Spain for a while. My bosses told me I should enjoy the month and a half I had taken off even though I didn't…didn't get married. And I'm going to do just that. I'm going to go sailing with some friends and maybe read on a beach. And during this time, until I get back, I don't want you to call or text me because I need to figure out if I can forgive you for what you've done, if our love carries more weight."

"You're leaving me? I mean, you're going to live"—I wiped away my tears—"like a free man the whole summer and then you'll decide? Because I don't like that, Filippo." I sobbed. "I don't want this to turn into a summer of you getting revenge on me by fucking other women."

"No, I'm not leaving you, though you have no right to demand fidelity from me right now. All I'm trying to do is see whether I miss you after a few weeks, if I can forgive this humiliation. Then we'll talk."

"When?" I cried.

"Don't call me or text me. We'll talk in September."

"It's June!" I whimpered. "That's more than two months."

"That's how long I estimate I'll need to make my mind up. If you're upset about that, we may as well throw in the towel now and say goodbye forever." When I didn't say anything, he nodded, taking my silence to mean I accepted his conditions. "Goodbye, Margot. Have a good summer."

I heard the door click shut from where I was cowering in the wing chair. My mother's voice moved away with Filippo's footsteps toward the exit of the humongous flat in the Marqués de Salamanca Plaza. I was sure she had been trying to eavesdrop on our conversation, worried that her daughter was throwing away her opportunity to redeem not being special through a good marriage. The door to the building closed too, and I swear I could hear my ex-fiancé's footsteps going down the stairs outside. I let my nails root through my hair as much as my hairstyle would allow and then rested my cheek on my knee.

My mother poked her head into the room and then came in. Her heels tapped along the floor with a sound muffled by expensive carpets.

"Margarita, it would be better if you take a vacation. Nobody in Madrid should see you right now. We don't want this turning into an even bigger incident, do we? You…just behave. Show him that you regret what you did and he'll forgive you." She patted me on the arm. "And get your feet off that chair. It's a Louis XVI, and it cost two thousand euros."

9

HOW LONG CAN GOSSIP LAST?

"Before you decide anything, you should go out and get wasted."

Candela looked at Patricia in shock, as if she couldn't believe she agreed with her suggestion.

"Amen, sister."

"Yeah, right?" Patricia put the phone face down on the table and smoothed her hair. "All three of us could go get dinner and drinks. Spill the tea while we get sauced. Dance a little to forget it all."

"You have tea to spill?" Candela teased.

"Ah, darling. When you don't have problems, you look for them. And if you can't find them…you imagine them."

They both looked at me, and I blinked, like it was the only way I could communicate with them after what had informally become known as the INCIDENT.

"You have to move. You've been in the same position since yesterday."

"Same position and zero verbal communication."

"My mother threw me out of her house yesterday because she didn't 'want gossip.'" I pointed out. "So that's inaccurate. I did a lot of things yesterday: I ran through a field to flee my wedding, I drank a Coke in a gas station, I broke my engagement, I put my feet on a horrible chair that could have been a prop from *Beauty and the Beast*, I ordered a Cabify, I came home, I sent you two a message, I ate two lorazepams for dinner, and, because even the pharmaceutical industry hates me and it didn't have the desired effect, namely sleeping for at least eighteen hours, I got up to take another one at nine in the morning, but you wouldn't let me. So, no, I haven't been in the same position since yesterday."

"Do you remember her being so grouchy?" Candela looked at Patricia.

"Yes." Patricia nodded.

"Ah, well, I guess I must have idealized you both with the distance because I'm suddenly realizing you're not that pretty either."

Patricia rolled her eyes. There was no point telling her she wasn't that pretty; she has mirrors in her house.

Candela went over to my wardrobe and rifled through my clothes, taking the initiative to get the plan rolling immediately. Patricia sat next to me and murmured softly.

"Have you heard anything from Filippo?"

"Do I look like I've heard anything from Filippo?"

"Come on, Margot. It's not that deep. How long can gossip last? We're living in the information age. These things are a trending topic for a few hours and then they disappear. So what if there are photos of you on the internet squeezing through a hole in a fence to escape your wedding? Anyway…you're a badass! I never would have thought you had it in you to cause a scene like that."

"Hey, come on," Candela hustled over to me. "I put together an outfit for you. Now all you have to do is shower and get dressed. I'll book us a table at… Is Perra Chica still cool?"

She held up two hangers with clothes so badly mismatched I didn't even recognize them.

"That blouse goes with the black pants hanging next to it, and that skirt goes with the pale-pink shirt in the top drawer," I said.

"Well, clothes can mingle with other garments, you know? It's not considered adultery."

"Candela, serious question." Patricia elegantly lifted her ring finger. "Are you color-blind?"

I flopped down and sighed.

"You're doing this all wrong. Candela is the one who should be giving me a pep talk about how the INCIDENT doesn't really matter, and, Patricia, you should be choosing the clothes for going out tonight."

They both whooped.

"So we're going out then?"

"Yeah, of course." I turned my back to them. "Close the door behind you when you leave."

After twenty minutes of jiggling hangers at me and trying on my shoes they realized I wasn't going to go out on a bender with them under any circumstances. I know they had good intentions. They're my sisters; I don't think anyone loves me as much as they do. But they weren't thinking it through. If they had, they would have realized that being seen the day after my failed wedding drinking in some trendy bar would be super tacky. And that wasn't all: it just didn't make sense.

I wanted to get Filippo back, not forget him. I wanted to get back our Sunday mornings, reading on the high stools in a home I hated without him while we listened to Italian music that I didn't know. I wanted to get back nights cuddling in bed, telling each other how our days had been. I wanted our Thursdays when we ate Vietnamese food, for fuck's sake. And I was hungry.

"I want Vietnamese food."

~~~~~

So that's how I ended up spending Saturday in one of Filippo's old shirts, wrapped in our duvet (even though it wasn't exactly cold) eating Vietnamese spring rolls like the world was ending. My sisters were there, but I couldn't tell you what they were doing. I didn't even answer the consoling messages from my godfather, a member of the board. The whole world could go to hell.

~~~~~

Now I know that the only thing I wanted was to stay quiet and let the days pass without needing to make a decision. Everything was so bleak that I felt like making any decision would mean I was unable to go back and settle the chaos. I was so scared…any decision seemed like a huge potential fuckup.

The normal course of action, I guess, would have been to listen to myself. *You didn't just hightail it from a wedding for no reason. Panic always has an invisible little friend who whispers shit in your ear.* If I had known what mine was, maybe I would have understood something. But, besides that, on a much more superficial level, I didn't even know if I wanted to hole up at home or do the opposite, run away to find the meaning of life. For the love of God, I couldn't even decide whether I wanted my tea hot or iced in the mornings…

But, on Sunday, while Candela jabbered with her mouth full of ultra-processed candy that Khloe was her favorite Kardashian, I decided I didn't want anything that they assumed would comfort me in that moment. I didn't want nights slathering on face masks, pretending to watch TV while I stuffed myself with sweets and then feeling bad because I was going to get fat and then thinking it's fine because once in our lives we should all indulge ourselves and wallow in our own misery and…then back down the rabbit hole to start the cycle again. What I wanted was to forget that I'd had some kind of breakdown that had destroyed my life. I missed the feeling of control over myself, and I only had one place on earth where I felt like a boss bitch: my job. Ironically, there were no objectives that felt impossible to reach there; everything was a question of time and effort. Between the four walls of my office, the world was manageable…as long as I didn't have to see anyone or go to a board meeting.

I figured the best way to slowly get my life back was…returning to normality. I guess acceptance goes through phases and I was still in the first phase.

~~~~

I always felt more comfortable in my office than in my house. In my palatial and jaw-dropping apartment on Paseo de la Castellana, I always felt like I was living in the set of an ad or a hotel lobby. Manufactured coziness, too flawless; I always felt like sitting on the couch would mess everything up. But my office was…warm. It didn't matter if there were papers scattered everywhere, if the last meeting had left a trail of dirty coffee cups, or if the trash was overflowing. Hard work calls for disorder.

Plus, my office was a beautiful place. Pleasant. Nothing garish. It had a beautiful brown carpet that reminded me of the Swiss chocolates my sisters and I bought at the airport on the way home for the holidays, with modern and elegant furniture and a beautiful painting I had bought for my apartment but ended up hanging there because it was where I really felt at home.

As soon as I got into the building and breathed in its familiar smell, I felt much calmer. There in my crystal palace, everything was calm, and Patricia was right…how long would it take, in the height of the information age, for everyone to forget what had happened? Life goes on. Everything would get back to normal sooner or later.

I got onto the elevator. I greeted the regular mail room guy with a smile. I took a sip of my latte. I breathed in deep. *Fine. Calm. Serenity. Real life…*

The elevator doors opened opposite the reception desk, where Sonia should be sitting, but…nobody was there. Nobody except noise. Actually, more than noise. I would call it a hubbub. Like in the villages when the open-air dancing ends but people still want to party. Bursts of laughter, scattered whoops, even a few snatches of music filtering through the voices. And that definitely wasn't normal.

A speaker was playing so loudly it was making the glass vibrate, and I started to walk toward the room where my team was gathered, passing by reception, the photocopier corner, the kitchen, and the coffee machines. I poked my head into the hallway and saw Sonia trying to call them to order; I could hear how nervous she was, tutting in all directions, saying they were jerks, that this wasn't right. When I heard, "Don't bite the hand that feeds you," and a loud and blunt "Ingrates," I knew the score.

The laughter continued when I appeared in front of them, where they were crowded around a computer screen.

"What's going on?" I asked, serious, contained, cold.

The iciest silence you can imagine settled, crushing us all. Inside

I was losing my shit, so humiliated that I could feel each and every fiber of my jacket rubbing against my skin.

My whole team stared at me in shock and terror. And Sonia let out a horrified yelp.

"Argh!" she squealed, and her hand flew to her chest. "Marg... Margarita." Her eyes darted around frantically but didn't find what she seemed to be looking for and finally landed back on me with a horrified expression. "Go to your office. Don't worry, I'll take care of this mess."

I gestured to the owner of the screen they were all looking at to turn it around, but he didn't move. I twirled my index finger, praying and crying inside that they couldn't tell how I felt. A boss, even one who aspires to be a good boss, can't show how crushed they are by feelings, or their team will feel like there's no one at the helm.

"Margarita," he begged. It was one of my managers, by the way. Someone I trusted.

"Turn the screen around," I managed to get out. "And don't even think about minimizing what you're looking at because I'll call IT and get all the skeletons out of your computer. And that'll be way worse."

He sighed and turned it so slowly I thought I would scream.

Two memes. That's what was causing so much hilarity, two memes. Of me, of course. In one of them, a photo where I was sprinting in my wedding dress and they could see the shoes I was wearing were Nike. Underneath someone had added their very famous slogan: "Just do it." Fine. The worst part was, it was clear that someone who had been invited to the wedding had leaked the photo. But, if that weren't bad enough, the next one was a replica of the poster for *Runaway Bride*, where they had replaced Julia Roberts's face with mine and Richard Gere with Luigi's, Mario's brother, the video-game character.

I had to remind myself to breathe.

I didn't scream. I didn't send them to HR. I didn't even give them a "you're all fired, you dicks" look. I just nodded, turned around, and walked to my office without looking back.

I hadn't even had time to turn my computer on when my phone started ringing and the CEO's name appeared on the screen. He was obviously the poor sap the board had saddled with this task.

"Yes?" I answered after swallowing the lump in my throat.

"Margarita…how are you?"

"Fabulous." *Keep your cards close, Margot, you're in hostile territory.*

"Right, um…could you clear your calendar for a last-minute meeting?"

"My calendar is clear. I was supposed to be on vacation, as you might recall."

"Yes, right. I didn't want to bring it up."

"Well, I brought it up, so let's stop ignoring the elephant in the room."

"Okay. Come to the meeting room in half an hour, please. The board would like to speak with you."

Sonia had to put three lime blossom tea bags in my cup and rub my back for five minutes. I thought I was having a heart attack.

Have you seen the movie *300*? Yes? Well, no spoilers just in case, but there's this moment when the protagonist, Leonidas, is forced to visit the Oracle of Delphi, where he asks the Ephoros something I won't reveal. The Ephoros are a gang of hooded beings who have very bad vibes and make your skin crawl to the max. It's not just that they look like they've suffered from some archaic disease…

The thing is they look like the disease personified, with eyes. Half pus-filled blisters, half zombies. If you've seen it, you remember them, and if not, well, you get the idea. That's exactly how I saw the members of the board, even down to the hooded capes. Mostly made up of men who gave you goose bumps. As soon as I joined the heart of the power at the company, I had to make it very clear I didn't find the jokes about breasts, hookers, rape, and brothels, and the comments about my clothes funny at all. But I mean, really, not at all. Still, they scared me. They were like those Ephoros, but in suits, ties, tacky cuff links, and hideous but expensive shoes.

You can imagine how much I wanted to see them that day of all days. Shit. They had all been at the wedding. Couldn't they cut me some slack?

"How's it going?" I asked, steeling myself as I walked in and found them all sitting in their chairs, around the enormous table where we held meetings.

"Fine. Sit down, Margarita, we'd like to talk to you."

Instead of the strong tea, I should have taken a pill. Or a shot of whiskey. Something to help me stomach the paternalistic undertones.

"We're speaking as equals, right?" I asked as I sat down.

"Of course, Margarita. We're colleagues."

"Of course. I do hold thirty-seven percent of the shares of this group."

They all nodded.

"I say that because I'd like to point out that I didn't have the luck of meeting my father in this lifetime. They say he was a good man. I don't need anyone to come in and try to be a father figure... Am I making myself clear?"

"Perfectly." The president took the lead.

Fucking shit. I never should have approved this guy being appointed. He was like Krampus. Only without the goat legs.

"You see, Margarita…what happened on Friday was…"

"Intense," I filled in the blank for him.

"It must have been very difficult for you. A traumatic experience. We understand you're looking for a little comfort here at work."

Comfort, that son of a bitch said. What a douche.

"But?"

I hate *buts*.

"But we think it still might be a good idea for you to take your vacation. All your vacation days. The business owes you seventy-six days off."

"Well, these have been hard years," I pointed out to guilt-trip them for their monthlong vacations every summer, plus a week off every winter to go skiing.

"Yes, and we think it might have taken its toll. That's why—"

"I appreciate your intentions, but I would feel better coming in to work, to be honest. I want to keep my mind busy."

"Margot…" My godfather, one of the men my father trusted, turned to me. He was the only member of the board I would save from a burning building. And he didn't look like the Ephoros. "You know I would never support anything I thought was bad or unfair to you, but…you have to take these vacation days. You're thirty-two, and you have to do some self-care and put yourself first."

"I don't need a vacation," I lied.

"Well, we think you do."

"You had an incident with your staff today, right?" another one pointed out.

"So let me get this straight…I have to take my vacation days because I need to rest and think about myself or to get the stink a little further away from the business's premises?"

"Margot, please…take the vacation," my godfather pleaded once more.

"Do I have a choice?"

"No."

I put my elbows on the table and buried my face in my hands.

"Don't do this to me."

"The business will put any of our hotels at your disposal so you can rest, relax, get away from all this—"

"I don't want to get away."

"Well, you should."

I scoffed and stood up.

"Sweetheart…" my godfather called out before I hurried out of the room. "Enjoy a few days. A month if you want. Come back whenever you want, but…really, you need to stop and think about what's important, and right now that's not work."

When I got to my office, I only had the strength to wordlessly beckon Sonia over. I don't think I had ever been so sparing with my words to her as I was that day. She called one of the company cars to take me home. And when I got there, I peeled off my suit, climbed into bed, and ignored Candela until she finally gave up.

10

HEADSTRONG

How long does gossip last? Well, in theory, not very long...unless there are memes. If they make memes about it, then it lasts a little longer. A few weeks, my sisters told me. It was a matter of a few weeks. I just had to be patient. And I was patient, that's for sure... because with the amount of dignity I had lost, I had extra room in my soul to cultivate it.

According to my calculations, Candela should have gone back to her job. She always said that if you asked for more than a week off in a row at her hospital, they gave you dirty looks. But this time, when I asked when she was going back, she told me that she had a ton of vacation days saved up. She could go back when I got out of this mess. I had to deal with my whole life collapsing. Too much tragedy for me to be worrying about her.

Nobody can beat my stubbornness, so I tried to do it my way: I had to have a normal life. If I continued with my life as normal, it was only a matter of time before Filippo understood that what had happened was nothing more than a breakdown. Some kind of chemical imbalance in my brain had probably caused the whole episode. I told Candela about my hypothesis and took her silence as approval, ignoring the baffled face she made at me. *Common sense must prevail,* I told myself. I needed to feel like I was in control of myself and my destiny.

So I thought it would be great to burn off a little energy at the gym. No use dragging myself home to a house devoid of life but full of Filippo everywhere: his clothes in the wardrobe, his cologne in the bathroom, my condoms (mine because I bought them) in the bedside table.

"Have you heard from Filippo?" Patricia asked when I said I wanted to go to the gym.

"What does that have to do with anything?"

"I dunno, but…have you heard anything from him?"

"No," I groaned.

"Fine." She sighed. "Going to the gym doesn't seem like a good idea to me. Just watch out for the guys at the desk," Patricia warned me. "I stopped going because getting into the locker room is like passing a polygraph."

"I need some endorphins," I replied, convincing myself more than anyone.

And I really did think it was a good idea. The first day I did the machines, said hello to a few acquaintances, bought an isotonic drink with no added sugar, and strolled back home. The second day I went to a boxing class and really gave it to the punching bag using more force than technique. But…the third day, what had seemed to be limited to just a few glances showed its true face when my personal trainer asked me (at top volume), while cheering me on to keep bouncing the rope, if it was true I had left Filippo because he had a tiny one or if I was really a lesbian.

Experiment over. Conclusions: exercise doesn't solve your problems, and it's actually just medieval torture disguised as healthy habits. Oh, and people are stupid.

So I gave up and flopped into bed, like a dog in the sun, scrolling through photos of Filippo and me when we were happy and I wasn't running away from anything.

"Why don't you spend time doing all the stuff you normally don't have time for?" Candela suggested, when she came home and found me with a bowl of spaghetti, tomato sauce smeared around my mouth. "Treat yourself a little, Margot, babe. It's not the end of the world, just…an impasse."

Fine. That seemed like a good idea. I would throw myself into making my house cozier. I would start there, with something I complained about a lot but never made an effort to solve. I would change the curtains in the bedroom and the cushions on the couch. Maybe now was the time to fill the freezer with food that would make me feel good and give me energy. Everything went terribly, of course.

I went to a decor store that was near my house, an employee showed me a bunch of samples, and I started crying because the shade of blue she pointed to reminded me of the color of Filippo's eyes.

I guess going to the fruit store was the chronicle of a death foretold. I asked the lady to recommend some sweet fruit that would cheer me up a little, and she asked if I was more into bananas or figs. I was so deep into my spiral of self-pity, so defensive, that I told her to go to hell and left without paying for the two flaccid avocados I had in my hand in a paper bag. They were like two blackened cushions inside a recycled scrotum.

"Let's go to the cluurrb," Patricia said when I asked her to bring me some mandarins and explained why I couldn't go back to the fruit store downstairs. "Seriously. Do the normal shit we all do after a breakup. Eat chocolate, cry, drink wine, and bust a move in a tiny miniskirt."

"This isn't a rom-com," I moaned.

"Come on, we'd all like to go out. We always have a good time in the end." When she saw my pout, she sighed. "Why don't the three of us make a plan? We need to make the most of Candela being here a few more days. I don't think it'll be long before she goes back to Chiquitistan."

"That's not even a country."

"Geography was never my thing."

"Obvs."

They had been taking shifts with me. Candela seemed delighted to spend more time with me, and it's not like Patricia was sick of it, but...besides all the work she had looming over her and the shared responsibility of organizing a family with three young kids, she was even more stressed than usual, and it was easy to see.

We decided we'd perpetrate the crime on Friday. At least, we planned it like it was a crime. Even in *Money Heist*, I don't think they ever organized a raid as carefully as we did that night out. Because it was a postbreakup girls' night out, of course, but it was a lot more complicated than that. It couldn't be in any of those fancy clubs where my former classmates went on the weekends. Or one of the cool and super hip dive bars that Filippo's little sister had recommended to me (and I had never once set foot in). Nowhere I could run into anyone I knew and especially anyone who worked under the Ortega Group umbrella. Somewhere as unknown as possible, where they played music you could dance to, where there was a lot of alcohol and darkness, and where there was no way I'd bump into the poor fruit seller who I had told to go to hell.

And no. I didn't run into her there, but I did bump into the most beautiful complication of my entire life.

11

MARGOT'S DESPAIR

Candela trawled the internet to find an adequate dive bar for our night out. Because I had ditched my fiancé at the altar and he had run off with orders not to contact him until September, it was like two breakups at once for the same person. At that point I didn't care about anything. After listening to "Miss You Like Crazy" by The Moffatts more than six times, the world lost its nuance and started to blur at the edges.

But Candela found the perfect club because that's how she is. She doesn't know how to put together two articles of clothing, but she knows how to find things. So the only thing we had left to do was reserve a table at some restaurant nearby where they served pitchers of sangria to hordes of tourists.

Patricia left her children with Alberto; they had planned a movie night with popcorn and candy, and they were ecstatic because they were going to watch something with superheroes. She was worried they'd have nightmares after, but the truth is Captain America would have nightmares if he met my niece and nephews, not the other way around.

She came over to get ready at my house, where Candela was already waiting because, actually, she had basically turned my apartment into her lair. She was pretending to be staying at our mother's house, but there were a camping backpack in my spare bedroom and colorful clothes scattered everywhere that told a different story.

"Jesus. It looks like a Desigual exploded in here," Patricia said when she stuck her head in.

"What should I wear?" Candela asked.

"Nothing lurking behind this door. Let's go to Margot's closet. She has cool stuff."

Candela chose the only thing from my wardrobe that she seemed to like: a short camel-colored romper with a brown belt. *I bought that for our honeymoon*, I thought when I saw her try it on to make sure it wasn't too big on her. *Actually, you didn't even buy it*, I corrected myself, *your fucking personal shopper, who's pretty and blond and charges through the nose, bought it. And it doesn't even matter anymore.*

"He still hasn't texted me," I muttered, rummaging through my shoe rack in search of plain sandals.

"That was the deal, right?"

"Do you think he's flirting with other girls?"

"No," they chorused.

There's a saying about how adding poetry to truth is like a spoonful of sugar. Well, the same thing is true for lies. Sometimes it makes them more digestible.

~~~~

I systematically said no to all the outfits Candela picked out. Now that she had seen herself looking pretty in the mirror, she seemed to believe she was suddenly a gifted stylist. I rejected everything Patricia picked out as well, but that was because all the clothes in my wardrobe had an order and a system that they didn't seem to understand. So I took two neighboring hangers and got dressed in what was on them. They were in the "informal cocktail" section of the wardrobe, which my personal shopper usually indicated to me through black hangers, so there was no danger of making a mistake: a black polka-dotted shirt with short sleeves and a cross-over neckline, worn with matching jeans, cropped at the ankle.

"Something's going on with Patricia," Candela murmured while we were waiting for a cab in my lobby.

"What?"

"You heard me. Something is going on with Patricia. She's acting really weird."

"She's not being weird; she's stressed. She's thirty-six, has three kids and a successful business. How would you be?"

"Dead. But that's not what I'm talking about. Seriously, look at her."

We both turned discreetly toward her, where she was tossing her head to fix her hair, her gaze glued to her phone.

"She's doing it again." Candela nudged me.

"Doing what? Being pretty?"

"No, idiot. She's on her phone again."

I rolled my eyes.

"Cande, that's normal. You're the one who's not. And I'm not saying you're better than us, but I get that you're not used to it because you still have a phone with an antenna. You can do a lot on phones these days: read the news, manage your calendar…"

"I know that! But she's doing something else."

"What?" I asked, intrigued.

"She spends all her time chatting."

"It's called 'WhatsApping' now," I corrected her.

"Whatever it's called. She's talking to someone all the time."

"Cande, she and Alberto have three kids. Do you know the mental load that entails for two working parents?"

"Well, no, but given that my work often involves saving lives…I get the idea that her life isn't that easy."

"Don't do that," I pleaded with her. "Don't twist what I said."

"I'm telling you something's going on."

"And what exactly do you think is going on?"

"What if she's thinking about getting divorced?"

I looked at her, shocked. "You're insane."

"Or maybe they want to move to another country. They both have international range and…" And the more she fleshed out the theory, the more convinced she seemed by it.

"Or maybe she wants to kill us and get our inheritance."

"I already donated all of mine, so good luck."

I laughed.

"Stop making predictions. Nothing's going on with her. This is just…how she is."

Candela didn't seem to agree, and I shrugged, not really caring. I don't know whether I didn't want to worry myself more or if it was because I didn't want to share space in my drama.

But, like I've said many times, Candela is the brainy sister. I shouldn't have brushed her off, if only to save myself from her smug look when, after our first glass of sangria, Patricia started spilling piping-hot tea.

"I have to tell you something."

Candela's slightly bulging eyes gleamed smugly. "I knew it," she muttered. "Something's going on with you."

"Or not?" I said in a last-ditch attempt to win my bet. "Isn't it just stress from work and your kids and—?"

"No." She lifted her glass, scratched from so much use, and took a sip of the concoction this bar dared to call "sangria."

"There's something that…"

I looked at them suspiciously. "Oh…I get it. You've been plotting. You wanted to make me feel better by inventing weird gimmicks like 'My life isn't as happy as it seems.'"

"No one's life is as happy as it seems."

"Yours is," I accused her. "Don't try to cut in."

"Can you let her talk?" Candela chewed me out.

"Yeah, yeah. Now she'll invent something like, 'For months my pubic hair has been growing at a superhuman speed, and I look like I'm always wearing bike shorts.'"

"That's pretty good."

"Can you both shut up?" Patricia snapped, filling her glass. "I'm trying to tell you something. And God knows this is hard for me."

"She and I"—Candela tilted her head toward Patricia with the kind of disdain you can only have for a sister you love wholeheartedly—"haven't been plotting anything. I never agree with her, not even about… Well, I can't think of any examples. Nothing. We don't agree on anything."

"Will you let me talk?" the former insisted.

"I just want you both to know, I think what you're doing is really heartless. Can't you just be normal and get me drunk to try to make me forget him for just one night? No, you have to plan a—"

"We haven't planned anything!" Candela yelled at me.

"You trailer trash!"

"I don't know about any trailers, but you're really frigging getting on my nerves."

"I think Alberto is cheating on me."

Candela and I dropped the pieces of bread we had been poking each other with and stared at Patricia in surprise.

"What are you talking about?"

Patricia took a deep breath and nodded. She looked like she was holding back tears, just like the afternoon of my wedding. Ex-wedding. Supposed-to-be wedding. The wedding I bailed on.

"I think he's cheating on me, for fuck's sake."

"That's impossible," Candela attested. "That dude has been crazy about you since freshman year. His whole world revolves around you, Patricia, for God's sake!"

"I'm as sure as I am that Mama named me Patricia after the Roman patricians."

"And she named me Candelaria after Papa's aunt whom she couldn't stand! Mama's an idiot, but you're not. Alberto's not cheating on you. He's totally pussy-whipped."

"'Pussy-whipped,' says the trailer trash," I needled her.

"I know how to stop your heart and keep it from showing up on the autopsy," she said to me with a smile.

"He comes home really late, and when he's home, there's always something to do, calls, emails…not to mention all those trips to conferences and plans at the club."

"You both go to the club," I pointed out. "Actually, all five of you go."

"Of course. The best lies are half-truths. He takes his wife and kids to his fucking love nest. That way there's no suspicion…"

"You're really tying yourself up in knots, girl," I assured her. "You're paranoid."

She filled her smudged glass again and downed it practically in one gulp, which she had already done while Candela and I were threatening each other.

"But…" I leaned toward her, trying to create a little more of a conspiratorial ambiance in the greasy bar where in two out of every three groups someone could be heard shouting, "Olé!" in an accent from somewhere north of Roncesvalles. "Patricia, how could he cheat on you? You! You're smart, interesting, your days have more hours than the rest of us mortals, you have a thriving business, your kids wear matching clothes…with each other! And on top of all that, you're awesome…"

"Mama always told me." She grabbed her forehead in that gesture that was so her. "It doesn't matter how much you take care of yourself, there will always be something to improve and some woman who doesn't suffer from it."

"What language is she speaking?" Candela asked me.

"I let myself go and…"

We looked at her, our eyes wide.

"Is she serious?" Candela turned to consult me again.

"Stop asking me!" I complained. "I'm in the same boat as you."

"Come on, Patricia. Are you an idiot?"

"No." She sobbed as she groped blindly around the table looking for the almost empty pitcher of sangria.

"Come on, then."

"Stop. I know he's cheating on me."

"Are you serious?"

"You cunt! Yes!"

"Oh, okay." Candela simmered down for a few minutes while I stroked Patricia's arm like she was a puppy. "Well, then you have to decide what to do."

I looked at her with a furrowed brow as the waiter deposited a plate of anemic-looking croquettes on the table.

"Can you bring us another pitcher of sangria?" Patricia asked before turning back to Candela.

The three of us dissolved into silly giggles, almost in tears. It had been an intense few days.

"I miss having a mother," Patricia complained.

"We have a mother," I reminded her.

"Well, then I miss having a mother who doesn't meow."

This time I couldn't hold in my cackle, and it echoed loudly across the table where a fresh pitcher of sangria had just landed.

The bill wasn't as cheap as it should have been given the quality of the food. If the night wasn't marred by severe food poisoning, it would be a miracle. Although judging by the giggles emitting from Patricia, it was looking more and more likely that it would all go to hell with us having to drag her home draped over us and hold her hair while she vomited up the two pitchers of sangria she had chugged. And the worst part of it was…Candela seemed to be finding everything hilarious too. Wasn't I supposed to be the one forgetting everything for one night? Apparently, I was the only one who had suddenly developed a tolerance for alcohol. It wasn't fair.

The doors of the club looked sketchy. They made me wonder why they needed a bouncer so big he looked like he'd been trained at Guantanamo.

"How did you find this place again?" I asked Candela as we waited for the two girls in front of us to find some ID.

"On Google, duh. It had good reviews. Friendly atmosphere, popular music, and the drinks aren't bad. And apparently one of the bartenders won a beauty contest not that long ago."

"Interesting." Patricia nodded. "Excuse me, could I bum a cigarette?"

One of the guys waiting behind us offered up a cigarette and a lighter in a fraction of a second, very helpful.

"Since when do you smoke?"

"She quit the first time she got pregnant," I confessed to Candela. "She smoked since she was sixteen, but she never let me tell you."

Patricia took a deep drag with her eyes closed.

"This is such a good sisters' night out." She nodded to herself.

"Yeah," I replied, slightly ironically. "Now, not only am I worried about my life, I'm worried about yours too. Praise be."

"Relax! What's the worst that could happen? It's not the end of the world! We're going to dance with two hunks who'll take away all our pain."

"Hunks? Patricia, they asked the girls in front of us for ID. What exactly do you think we're going to find in there?"

"I dance very well, and I'm legal." The head of the guy who had given her the cigarette suddenly popped up between us.

I shot Candela a dismayed look, hoping she would throw me a rope, but she was still finding everything hilarious.

The club was very dark. Music was blaring; I could feel the rhythm thumping in my chest. The packed crowd was heaving rhythmically and almost sexually. A couple was making out against the cigarette machine. Two girls were dancing sensually. In the back, two guys and a brunette were involved in a threesome that seemed exciting even to me, and I was depressed.

"Let's hit it!"

My sisters took me by the arm, and I slung my bag across my chest. This environment was completely hostile to me. I felt like I was heading into a jungle without even a rusty machete to grab if things got ugly.

We elbowed through the crowd to get to the bar. A couple of pretty and efficient girls were slaving away, slinging drinks with both hands. There was a perimeter of people clamoring for their attention.

"This bar is slammed," Candela yelled. "Let's go to the one in the back?"

"We might need spelunking equipment to get there," I shouted back, trying to make myself heard over the din.

But Patricia was already cutting a path through the people.

"Excuse me!" she shouted when she touched down at the other bar.

A blond boy looked at her and raised his eyebrows to invite her to speak.

"Can we get some shots and some drinks?"

"Gimme a sec, please. My buddy just went to get more ice, and I'm all alone."

"Don't worry, love, I'll wait for you."

"Patri, please," I pleaded. "Don't drool."

"Did you see him?" She turned back to us with her eyes wide open. "Mama mia!"

"I think he's the same age as your son."

"Hey, we're interesting thirty-somethings, and he's not a kid. Let me flirt. My husband is cheating on me!"

When she turned around, a boy who had appeared out of

nowhere looked at her with a half-smile as he loaded bags of ice onto the bottom shelf of a freezer. He ripped one open with one fluid motion and filled an ice bucket with it. He had a mop of dark hair, dark eyes, an upturned nose, the face of a boy…a naughty little boy, the kind you fall in love with at the school gates, who steals your first kiss and breaks your heart. Except with a patchy beard.

"What do you think? My husband is cheating on me!" Patricia screamed again.

This one seemed to like her too.

"He must be a scumbag!" the bartender played along. "So you should leave him. Pack your bags."

"Really?"

"Three gin and tonics." I leaned over the bar, wedging myself between them to cut off the conversation. I looked at Patricia. "Stop telling him your whole life story, for God's sake."

"Ask him for three shots and his phone number."

"Shut up!" I shot back nervously. "Your teeth are glowing in this light, and it's scaring the shit out of everyone."

"Let's see…let's see." The boy leaned over, trying to get my attention. "You seem like the leader. Talk to me. Shots of what?"

Had he heard the part about the phone number?

"Um…lollipop shots?"

"How 'bout I give you girls rainbow shots?"

Someone else might have been offended. To tell the truth, any other moment in my life, I might have been offended. But…it made me laugh. I ducked my head so he wouldn't see me smile.

"Tequila! Three shots of tequila!" my sisters both shouted at the same time.

"Dear God…" I groaned.

"Margot, turn up a little, come on!"

I sighed and turned back to the bartender with an embarrassed look.

"So…three gin and tonics with…um…whatever kind of gin you want and three shots of tequila."

The boy kept looking at me with a smile that had a certain whiff of superiority.

"What?" I asked, embarrassed.

"You don't go out much, huh?"

I shook my head.

"Don't worry! Have a little fun."

"I am having fun!"

But he didn't hear me. He had shot like lightning over to grab a bottle of gin from the top shelf.

"He's a hottie!" Patricia yelled.

"No way!" Candela and I answered at the same time.

I agreed the guy was cute, but I didn't want to egg on potential revenge cheating.

"Ay! Rosalía!" Candela yelped when the next song started.

"Ooh, you're so with it."

"Always cool, never uncool sis."

Three highball glasses full of ice appeared in front of me on the bar, and a look of horror made my lips part.

"In highball glasses?" slipped out before I could stop it.

"For someone who doesn't go out much, you have a good pout, hey?" the bartender responded.

I took a second to analyze whether Patricia was right and he was more than just a cute guy. Brunette hair that urgently needed a cut (disheveled, very disheveled, like skater boys from the 2000s), deep-brown eyes, full lips. Twenties…early twenties? Or late twenties. He was one of those ageless boys who could have been about to graduate from high school or college. He was wearing a black shirt with the name of the bar printed in white across his chest, and the truth is, it was flattering, but…it wasn't like that…nothing crazy. I don't know how to explain myself.

My fiancé (ex-fiancé? Ex? Future husband? Boyfriend?) was one of those men who caused a stir wherever he went. If we went out to dinner, our table always ended up being the center of a swarm of furtive glances and drew whispering from gaggles of girls. "Look at that dreamy dude." "Whoa, what a hottie." "Some people have all the luck." All Filippo was missing was a fanfare of trumpets to announce his arrival. He was the prince of the story and the measure I used to rate other men's beauty, so…in my opinion, as much as Patricia was drooling over him, this guy didn't seem like all that to me.

What was Filippo doing right then? Was he out partying with his friends? Was he leaning against the bar in some club? Probably, but a more glamorous one, an elegant place full of pretty girls, the kind who pop stars and athletes fall in love with and who…

"You wanted tequila shots, right?" the bartender asked, breaking my train of thought.

"Whatever you want, babe!" I heard my older sister shout.

"Tequila," I hurried to say.

He smiled at me and slid three shot glasses and a plate of lime wedges across the bar. He grabbed a bottle from the well and filled all three glasses with a single fluid motion.

"Forty-eight," he said to me.

"What's that?"

"That'll be forty-eight euros," he repeated, almost shouting.

"Um…can I pay with a card?"

He held the card reader out to me so fast it caught me off guard. I gave a little jump and started rummaging anxiously through my bag. I glanced up at him, and he was watching me, amused, unknowingly bobbing his shoulders along to the song. My fingers finally brushed my phone in my bag, and I held it out to him, confirming my payment with a tap.

"Do you want a receipt?" he asked.

"Not necessary."

He tousled his hair, pulled his head to one side to crack his neck, and looked back at me. Brown eyes, common but…sad.

"If I'd known I would've charged you double," he teased.

I furrowed my brow, and he paused for a second.

"It was a joke."

"Right." I smiled. "Thanks."

I turned around to hand out the shots and the limes to my sisters.

"Hey," I heard behind me.

The boy was still there when I turned around. We held eye contact for a few strange seconds before he raised a shot that matched ours between his fingers.

"To you girls," he toasted.

Patricia let out a little shriek of joy after downing the tequila in one gulp; Candela cracked up, and I…I stood there holding my shot, convinced that this boy had recognized me in the crowd. Not for being the rich girl who had fled her wedding but as the other two saddest eyes in the dive bar.

12

SAD EYES

DAVID

You learn a lot about psychology as a bartender. But like, really a lot. I guess movies always portraying us in the role of confidants isn't completely unwarranted. We hear a lot of stories; more than we'd like, to be honest. Sometimes you're not in the mood for first-world problems, and other times, you're not ready for the drama some people lug around with them. We all carry our pain on our shoulders, and it's not always what we think it is.

That was the vibe I got from that girl. She was lost even in her own body, like a foal still figuring out how to work her limbs. Clumsy. Frightened. Lonely.

Judging by her manicure, the state of her hair, and the gloss of her clothes, this girl didn't have the same problems as me. She had plenty of money left at the end of the month; she had a beautiful home and a good job. She was fashionable—discreet, but fashionable; her wardrobe was full of clothes to flaunt on occasions I couldn't even imagine. And yet…she was alone. Lonely, really lonely. Lonely in a way you can only be when you don't even have yourself. Like me. We both must have given off some kind of sonar signal that makes you feel comfortable with someone you've just met. The DJ continued to remix one hot song with another, and although reggaeton dominated all of them with its relentless beat, "Sola con la Luna" by Anni B Sweet was playing in my head. Idoia told me once that she liked it, and I was hooked as soon as I heard it; one afternoon, lying in bed, naked, she asked me to change the music.

"I'm sick of this broken record."

"I thought you liked it."

"I did."

That's how she was. Whatever was good today would be the butt of her jokes tomorrow. Is that what I was becoming right now? Maybe she was in bed with some other guy, one with a good job, a car, an apartment, and plans for the future, who she was telling that her ex was a poor devil who served drinks in some hole-in-the-wall club in Huertas.

Ivan and I switched ends of the bar at two thirty. We always did this so we could see different people and not keep serving the same faces the whole night. We took turns restocking too because the one closer to the storeroom was always in charge of this. As I served two Jäger bombs (that shit is going to kill someone one of these days) from my new lookout post, I saw them. The two blonds were dancing more or less in rhythm, clearly drunk, while the girl with the sad eyes was moving timidly, looking all around her, as if she was really worried that someone might think she wasn't dancing the right way and give her a citation. It reminded me, somehow, of the way I loved Idoia. I took payment, grabbed my phone from my bag, and glanced at it: no notifications.

I bit my cheek. If I wanted to get Idoia back, I had to do something. It was clear waiting for her to regret her decision wasn't going to have any effect.

"What's up?" Ivan asked me.

"Nothing. Why?"

"You're making a weird face."

"We don't have enough fifty-cent pieces or euros."

"Want me to go see if the girls have any?"

"Sure."

I would've told him we didn't have any glasses if that would get rid of him. I love Ivan, but sometimes he doesn't understand the way I see the world. I've never been good with words. I never really known how to express how I feel or what I want, mostly because I never really have it very clear myself. Like when I left school in my final year and I just told my parents, "It's not my thing." There was much more behind it, like the panic about being swallowed by routine and not finding a job in the field I was studying.

I saw the three girls go to refill their drinks a bunch of times, but always at the other bar. I kind of felt like the girl with the sad eyes was avoiding me, but finally the other girls nagged her into coming back. The truth is, my end of the bar always had the shortest line at this time of night because it was way in the back.

"What can I get you?" I smiled.

"Three gin and tonics and three tequila shots."

The sad girl turned around like a shot. Her hair was shoulder-length, straight and shiny, brunette, and flew around her face. "No, eh? I can't handle any more."

"One more, please!" the prettiest one begged.

I ducked down and looked for something behind the counter. When I popped up, the sad girl was leaning over with a furrowed brow, like she was looking for me.

"Ah, there you are," she said.

"Of course. Where'd you think I went?"

"I don't know. Narnia? My sister's a pain. She thought maybe you had escaped through a trapdoor."

"Your sister?" I asked, grabbing a bottle of gin from behind me.

"My sisters." She pointed at the two blond girls, who were waving at me enthusiastically. "I know we don't look alike. They must have found me in a cabbage patch."

"That's a nice story. The girl who came out of a cabbage."

"I don't like how that sounds. Listen…" She tucked her hair behind her ear. "Don't give me tequila."

"Why not? You still sound pretty sober."

"It's not getting me drunk today, but it is making me nauseous."

"Give us three, hey!" her sister insisted, as if she could hear her.

"Here, this one's on me." I tried to help her out. "And I'll drink hers for her. Okay? Your sister doesn't look like she can handle her tequila very well, and we don't want puke on the bar. It kills the vibe."

The other two started to cackle, and I glanced sideways at her for her thanks. The girl with the sad eyes pressed her lips together and smiled with her mouth twisted like a knot.

"Listen…what time do you get off? You should come party with us!" proposed the one who I thought was the oldest.

"Me? No way! I'm beat. When I get out of here, all I want is a hot shower and to fall into my bed."

My couch, I corrected myself silently.

"Ignore her, please."

The girl with the sad eyes, besides being humiliated, seemed to be miles away from the music playing. On the one hand, her voice reached me more clearly than the others, and on the other, it was as if only ten percent of her was there.

"You wanted a gin and tonic, right?" I asked her.

"Yeah, but…"

I pushed three rocks glasses over to her and raised my eyebrows so she'd notice the change in glassware.

"You didn't like the highball glasses, so, look, I went and found other ones. They're not wineglasses, but it's better than nothing."

She threw me a look of disbelief that was funny and tender; I liked it.

"Let's see…" I took out three tonics and poured a little of each into its corresponding glass. "That'll be thirty-six."

"I'm paying," she offered.

"No, no. Get out of here."

"I'm paying!" the older one yelled.

"Quit it."

"Don't take your wallet out, you'll lose something," the one with the sad eyes insisted.

"You want to leave me?"

"Jesus, you're a nut… You're sleeping at my house, right?"

"No, no. I'm going to *my* house."

"Great, your kids are gonna love hearing you vomit in the garden."

"You're obsessed with vomit," added the other blond, the one with the clever eyes.

"You sure you don't want a bottle of water instead?"

"I want to find my fucking phone to pay!"

There was the typical scuffle between siblings that's pretty fun to watch. I remembered my brother, my sister, and me fighting over a can of condensed milk last Christmas. And the time my friends from the village walloped each other over a kebab.

I smiled. I missed them. Maybe Cris, one of my lifelong friends, would give me the perfect excuse on his birthday to get a night off from the bar and go home to catch my breath.

The commotion of the sisters fighting next to the bar brought me crashing back to the club, which must have disappeared completely for them because thanks to being so full of drinks, they were tussling and yanking each other's purses. Unsurprisingly, the fight ended with the older one's purse flying over the bar, smashing into the liquor shelf and spilling everything inside it all over the floor.

"Ah, fuck your meowing mother!"

I bent down to gather up her stuff and also so they wouldn't see me laughing. They were characters.

"Little one..."

"Don't call me *little one*! That's so cringe. Hey, sorry, okay?"

"No worries." I leaned against the bar and handed over a designer purse, a wallet, a lipstick, and a few tampons. "Did you have anything else in there?"

"The keys to your house?"

I let out a chuckle. One of the sisters started to laugh while the youngest one laid into her.

"You're both so corny! I swear I'd almost prefer the kombucha."

I took out a little flashlight from the back pocket of my jeans I used whenever something like this happened and looked around my feet. I found a few crumpled bills, a business card, and the keys I assumed were for her house. I slid them across the bar, but they were already on their way out.

"I swear I knew it. I knew it! 'Let's go out partying, Margot, that's what you need!' And it's total bullshit! Piano-sized bullshit," the sad girl was ranting.

"Hey!" I yelled. They kept getting farther away. I couldn't hear what they were saying anymore, but it looked like they were still sniping at each other. "Hey!"

I came out from behind the bar and skirted around a few couples grinding on each other to get to them.

"Girls." I showed them what I had in my hands.

The older one opened her bag so I could drop it all in and came over to give me a kiss on the cheek. The other blond couldn't stop laughing, and the youngest looked like smoke was about to come out of her ears.

She put a cold hand on my arm, and I looked at her. She seemed smaller than she was. She was medium height, normal build. But... she seemed so helpless. She leaned over so I could hear her without having to yell.

"Hey, sorry for making a scene, okay? I'm really sorry."

I shook my head, stepping back. She smiled and grabbed her sister's arm, the one who was dragging them outside, glass in hand, with the excuse of getting some air. Excuse because...they never came back in.

No. The girl with the sad eyes didn't stay stuck in my head because of a crush. Nothing to do with that. It was just...a glimmer. Of what? I don't know. Maybe of the promise that trying to steer life in one direction meant it was going to drive you crazy by going the opposite way.

At six in the morning, when the lights came on and the few customers left headed toward the exit, Ivan slid a phone with a small crack in the screen across the bar.

"Is this yours?"

"No."

"I'll put it in lost and found, okay?"

"No, no. Give it to me. I know whose it is."

Twirl, twirl, sad girl. Twirl faster.

13

RESPECTABLE DAUGHTERS

MARGOT

The first thing I thought about when I woke up was my mother. Not like: *Oh, maternal being, come take care of me.* Mama had children because it was her duty, not because she had much of a protective instinct. Mostly I thought of her because of the guilt of a convoluted thought, something like *If one little rager does this, imagine the old lady's hangovers!* She finished off cava, anise, grappa, and grape liqueur and mixed it all with pills…How did she survive?

A ray of light beamed through the window straight into my eyes, but I didn't have the strength to push the button next to the bedside table that would activate the blinds. It was 11:40, and I had spent two hours dozing and waking up every half hour. The worst part? When I was asleep, I always forgot that I had single-handedly turned my life into hell, and waking up, it all came crashing back.

Next to me, a face down lump groaned.

"Why is it so bright in here? It's worse than the Sahara, girl," she moaned.

Candela was still wearing my romper.

I climbed out of bed and was grateful I had drunk two glasses of water and taken an ibuprofen before I went to bed; otherwise I probably would have died from the hangover. I remembered the inelegant phrase ,"Those who aren't used to underwear get chafed by the seams." If you're not used to going out, four drinks trigger an apocalypse.

"Should I order breakfast?" I asked my sister.

"Close the blinds and let me sleep."

She had taken over my guest room and my bedroom, and now she was ordering me around in my own home. Unbelievable.

I took a shower, pulled on some jeans and a blouse, and went outside. I had woken up craving a raspberry croissant from Mama Framboise, and a walk would do me good.

I thought about calling Patricia to find out what state she had gotten home in last night, but I was scared she'd still be sleeping and her husband would answer the phone. But speak of the devil, just when I was about to take the first bite, sitting at a table in the back of my local café, my phone started to ring, and my brother-in-law's name appeared on the screen.

"Shit." I threw down the croissant, shook my hands, and took a deep breath before answering. "Hello, Alberto. What's up? Everything okay?"

"It's not Alberto; it's me," my sister whispered.

"What are you doing, crazy girl?"

"What am I doing? My life has been hell since I woke up…at eight in the morning. Santiago sat on my chest, and I swear I thought I was dying of sleep apnea."

"That kid of yours…"

"Except he didn't just sit. He took a running start. Basically. I'm going to have to talk to the school counselor and see if they've noticed any psychopathic traits in school. I'm scared he's going to kill me in my sleep."

"Don't be an idiot." I laughed.

"Where's Candela?"

"Still sleeping. I came down to get breakfast because she's taken over my house and now it's her way or the highway."

"Fine. Even better. The fewer people who know, the better. Margot…I dropped my phone in the bar last night."

"What? What are you talking about?"

"It must have fallen out of my purse. Seriously, Margot, we're so stupid."

"Why didn't you call me from your landline? You scared the shit out of me, you bitch. I thought Alberto was calling to demand explanations."

"Why would he want explanations? I hosed down the puke in the garden."

"Why are you calling from Alberto's phone, you pain in the ass?" I whined, ignoring the fact that my thirty-six-year-old sister had vomited on her doorstep at dawn.

"I'm calling from Alberto's phone because my kids hid the landline, first of all. And second…because the bartender has my phone."

I furrowed my brow and looked up. Dappled light played across the ceiling, chasing itself every time a car went by on the street.

"The bartender? The one you were hitting on last night?"

"I'm sure it wasn't that big a deal. The way I remember it, it was a mutual flirtation."

"You're the worst. That boy was not flirting with you. He just wanted us to leave."

"Well, now he has my phone."

"How do you know?"

"Ah, girl, for God's sake. Because I called it to try my luck. He told me that he plugged it in to wait for someone to call and claim it."

"Sweet of him."

"Yes, very sweet, but I can't go get it."

I raised my eyebrows. "And you want me to go."

"Yes."

"No fucking way! I never want to see him again for the rest of my life! I mean, come on, I'm way too embarrassed."

"Margot, that boy will have seen people vomit and piss themselves at the same time; an angry woman saying nice things to him is not that deep."

"God, you sound so gross. If you were a guy, I'd hang up on you."

"But I'm not a guy, I'm your sister, and I need you to go get my phone."

"You go! You can escape for half an hour."

"I live in the sticks, and I went out partying last night, and I came back home looking like hot garbage. Now I have too many points on my bad mom card to reoffend." When I didn't answer, she softened her tone and changed tack. "Margot, I want to stay with my kids today. Weekends are meant to be spent with family."

I sucked my teeth and then snorted.

"What if Santiago ends up developing a narcissistic and unstable personality because his mother didn't give him enough attention?" she added.

"Because you didn't spend one Saturday morning with him? Let him live, for God's sake! All that kid wants to do is eat colorful cereal and watch cartoons."

"Just what I need. Then they'll accuse me of feeding my kids ultra-processed foods. I have to make carob brownies today; I promised them."

"Please tell me you're joking." I rubbed my forehead.

"Sugar is the new cocaine, Margot!"

"Jesus Christ. You're the worst."

"My phone, please," she whimpered. "Being a businesswoman, a mother, a cheated-on wife, and a brushed-aside sister is too much for me."

"Not to mention favorite daughter."

"So much pressure..."

"Okay. When do you want me to go?"

"Today. I don't want Alberto to notice and have to explain it to him."

"You didn't tell him you lost your phone?"

"No, and he doesn't know I called you from his either, okay? So keep your mouth shut."

"You do the weirdest shit, babe." I covered my eyes, even though she couldn't see me.

"The boy gets in to work at ten," she insisted.

"Can't I just send a messenger from Glovo?"

"Do whatever you want, just get my phone back, please. It's super urgent. And necessary. And...a national emergency. I. Need. My. Phone."

What my sister really needed was a phone detox.

I was going to send a Glovo, but the truth is it seemed kind of rude after how kind the bartender had been to us. I think it was a combination of being taught to be a people pleaser plus the aversion I felt to ever being seen as a hag like my mother.

Anyway, I needed to get some fresh air, instead of flopping on the couch, miserable, pretending to watch some American reality show with my sister while I replayed, over and over, everything I had ruined with Filippo. It's like when you're trying to fall asleep and your brain suddenly connects to the mental image of the most embarrassing day of your life or you start to analyze why you didn't get along with your math teacher and all the things you could have done to fix it. No. Nothing would be fixed at home, and a stroll would work wonders on me, like it had that morning, and while I was at it, I would burn off the million and half calories I had ingested over the last three days. Deep down, Mama would never disappear from my head.

Patricia had made it pretty clear that the fewer people who found out, the better. I knew asking Candela to come with me wasn't an option, so I had to come up with a plan so she wouldn't want to join me. The only thing that occurred to me was the obvious one:

"Mama called me. She wants me to go over for dinner. Are you coming?"

She didn't even need to answer because I already knew my plan had worked.

~~~~~

I remembered the street the club was on but not the name, so I wandered around the area until I recognized the doors. It was very early, and I was surprised to see that the bars were already open at this hour. It was Saturday, but…who wanted to go into one of these dumps at 10:00 p.m. on a Saturday in June?

I started to head determinedly toward the door, but the bouncer casually threw the butt he had been smoking to the ground and stopped me.

"Where are you going, Little Red Riding Hood?"

"I'm meeting someone inside."

"Well, either you're early for your date or you got the wrong place. We're not open to the public until eleven thirty."

"No, I'm meeting one of the bartenders."

"Which one?"

"Um. The brunette one." I ran my hand over the top of my head, trying to emulate what the boy must do to comb his hair every day, judging by the results.

"The brunette has a name. It seems pretty suspicious to me that you're meeting him and you don't even know his name."

"My sister left her phone here yesterday." I sighed. "We spoke to him, and he told us to come collect it."

"Ah! The tall blonds."

"Yup, those ones." I nodded, bored. People always remembered my sisters. The small one who wasn't blond, no one noticed.

He waved me in, and I went through the door. God, this place was even worse with the lights on.

I spotted him immediately. He was propped against the bar, talking to his colleague. He was telling him something about a message he had sent right before he went to bed and saying he was sure it would do the trick. Who and what the trick was were left hanging in the air when they both turned toward me with a smile.

"They sent you?" he teased.

"They sent me. That's what happens when you're the youngest."

"That and getting all the uniform hand-me-downs."

I smiled politely but reluctantly, and he hopped behind the bar.

"Here you go. I have it right here."

"Thanks so much. That was very thoughtful of you."

"That's how David is," his colleague pointed out with a half-smile.

"Yeah, that's how I am. By the way, nice to meet you. I'm David."

I don't know why my first instinct was to stick my hand out for him to shake because that's not exactly the norm here. But it didn't seem to matter to him because he took it in his, still smiling. Someone should have told him all his effort not to seem sad didn't work, even though he had a beautiful smile, guileless and calm.

"I'm Margot. Charmed."

"You're not from around here, are you?"

"Um…well, yes. I mean, my family is from Galicia, but I was born here."

"What's with that name? It doesn't sound very Galician."

"No. The thing is…it's more of a nickname. My real name is Margarita." Why the hell was I telling him that?

"Margarita. A classic name. *Daisy* in English."

"Yes. Daisy." I shifted uncomfortably. "Like Donald Duck's girlfriend."

"Can I get you a drink?" his colleague offered.

"No, no, thank you."

"Come on, Margot. A beer? It's too early for a cocktail," the blond one insisted. "And the wine we have here…honestly, I don't recommend it."

"No, we don't recommend it. It'll give you kidney stones for sure," David teased.

"No really, I have to get back."

"Not even a Coke?" He raised his eyebrows.

"Well…okay."

I asked for a Coke Zero, and the other guy served it following all the rules, with ice and lemon in a highball glass. David tried not to laugh when he saw me approaching the glass reluctantly. I took a sip. I felt stupid. They were both watching me with scientific interest. I didn't know what to say. They didn't either.

I began to weigh possible conversation topics. "It's a nice night." "Such a nice temperature for the middle of June, right?" "Do you like your job?" "Do you know I'm on a forced vacation because I ran away from my wedding?"

"David…" the bouncer yelled, saving me from the silence. "Visitor. Should I let her in?"

Anyone else would have missed the tension that flitted across David from head to toe, but part of my job was being on the lookout for signals. He stood up straighter, inhaled sharply, glanced at his friend, and smoothed the shirt of his uniform.

"I'm not expecting anyone else."

"She says her name is Idoia and you sent her a message last night telling her to come."

The smack he gave his friend was as quick as it was well aimed. Then he started doing a silent jig before he obviously tried to chill out, grabbing his chest through his shirt.

"Ah, yes," he said in a slightly deeper voice. "Tell her to come in."

The blond guy and David looked at each other and high fived discreetly before the latter disappeared through a door that said, "Private."

She came in. And everything changed.

Sometimes, even today, I start thinking about what my life would have been like if that girl hadn't appeared in the club while I was there. If I had said no to the Coke or if I had sent a Glovo to get my sister's phone. Actually…what would have become of me, of my life, of my dreams, if my sister Patricia hadn't lost her phone? Life is random. There's no destiny, there are just moments.

Have you ever thought about what you would be like if you had been able to design yourself? I have. I thought about it a lot when I was a teenager. Being dull suited me well because I went unnoticed, but what I actually dreamed of was the opposite. I guess that happens to all of us. If you're blond, you want to be brunette; if you have curly hair, you wish it was straight; if you're skinny, you want curves. I guess if that weren't the case, a lot of companies dedicated to feeding our insecurities so they can sell us things to magically solve them would go bankrupt. But look, I wanted to be explosive. With platinum-blond hair, shamelessly lightened at the salon, long legs, big boobs, high and round, waist and hips with the exact measurements society demands for standard beauty. Marlene Dietrich's look and Ava Gardner's mouth. The charm of black-and-white movies mixed with the obscenity of the filthiest porn. Sexy, mysterious, beautiful, attractive, angelic. Not so much to ask, right?

Well…if I had been able to design myself, it would have been in the image and likeness of the girl who had just come in, wearing a tight plaid skirt clinging to her hips. I looked at myself, with my Levi's and my white blouse with the sleeves rolled up, and I felt invisible. She stared at me, and instead of feeling more real, I just felt smaller.

"Hello," she said slowly and slightly condescendingly.

"Hi," I responded.

She clunked her bag onto the bar; despite the stuff spilling out of it, including men's underwear and a box of condoms, all I could look at were her red lips.

"Hello, Ivan," she said lazily. "Because you must be Ivan."

"Ivan. That's me." He pointed to his chest, dazed.

She winked, sure of herself and aware of the effect she had on men.

"David's not here?"

Ivan looked toward the door he had disappeared through, but he didn't add anything. The silence was killing me.

"He'll be right out," I heard myself say.

She looked at me like a stool had learned to talk.

"Sorry, and you are?"

"Margot."

"Margot?" she said mockingly.

"Yes. What about you?"

"Idoia."

"Charmed. David'll be right out," I parroted.

For the love of God, this felt like a scene in a Tarantino movie. Basically…someone should have been brandishing a machete.

David came out with a garment in hand and, without kisses or even a greeting, handed it to her with a cold smile.

"Your shirt."

"I wasn't in a rush to get it back," she said.

"Right. Sorry about the rush, but…I did want my stuff back."

She looked scathingly at the bag, as if it were the most pathetic excuse in the world to see an ex. Because that was clearly what was happening here. David had texted Idoia with the excuse of getting back the junk he had left at her house before the breakup just to see her. It was the most transparent plan in the world. I almost felt sorry for him. So young. So in love. So…devoured by a girl who had used him as a snack.

"Thanks a lot. Ah…" And here David was fast on his feet. "Idoia, have you met Margot?"

"Yes, we just introduced ourselves."

"Should I go?" I asked like a dummy.

"Of course not." He smiled at me when he caught his ex's gaze on me. "Sorry, Idoia, it's nice to see you, but we made a plan to grab some dinner before people start showing up."

When he pointed to me, I looked around to see if he meant someone else, but there was no one but us.

"I'm in a hurry too," she announced.

"Great. We won't take up any more of your time then. Do you want to walk out with us?"

She nodded, looking me up and down, analyzing each and every one of the loose ends this story was leaving in its wake. I didn't know how to do anything but smile and stand up.

"See you later, Ivan," I said in a small voice as David slung his arm around my shoulder.

"Pizza?" David asked me, completely naturally.

"Uh…okay."

Next to us, Idoia was walking slowly and her heels rang out, crunching the little dignity I had when I left the house, which was now floating in the half-drunk soda. I understood everything and didn't quite understand anything. But I couldn't help but find it strangely exciting, almost fun.

"Listen, David…" Idoia said when the neon sign of the club was shining on our backs.

"What's up?"

The blond glared at me, and either through that glare or telepathically, I got the impression that she wanted to talk to him alone. In a flash, I weighed my options: if I stayed, it would make things difficult. If I left, it would probably make things easier for him. It was clear he wanted to get her back, even if his plan did have quite a few loose ends to tie up.

"I'll leave you guys alone for a second," I muttered as I walked off.

He grabbed my wrist, pretending it wasn't necessary, but I smiled at him and took a few steps away.

What was I doing? Should I stay there a little ways off but watching them? Answer emails leaning against the wall? Leave?

I watched them talk. She was obviously annoyed. I don't think she was jealous and possibly smelled that this was all a theatrical performance, but…there was still a glimmer of doubt, and I don't know why, but I wanted that doubt to blossom into something enormous until she couldn't think about anything else. I didn't know him at all, but…I felt for him. You get it. Two completely different situations, two pairs of equally sad eyes.

He seemed sure of himself, but his gestures gave him away. His hands buried in his jean pockets, his bottom lip between his teeth, his gaze darting around, going from her to the street and from the street to me. I didn't even think about it.

"Hey, David, don't make me wolf my food down like always. You know it hurts my stomach."

He raised his eyebrows for a second, surprised, but then played along.

"No, no. Come on." He reached for my hand, and when I got closer, he grabbed it. "Let's go."

Damn. He was a good actor.

"I don't get it." She crossed her arms, making her perky, suggestive breasts rise even higher, and kept talking like I wasn't there. "We broke up two weeks ago, and suddenly you text me asking me to return your stuff as soon as possible, in some big hurry…"

"Idoia, I left a couple of T-shirts at your house and my iPod and I need them for a trip. That's all."

"A trip?"

"Yes, a trip."

"With who?"

"With Margot." David pressed me against his side.

OMG. This was crazy.

"And where are you going?"

"Where was it again?" he asked me.

"Santorini." I threw out the first thing that popped into my head. "You're gonna love Greece."

"But you're always broke," she retorted.

"I dunno." He shrugged. "I guess it's a priority thing."

"Okay, fine. Well, then…great. I'm happy for you." She faked a smile and pushed a lock of hair out of her face.

"I'm happy to see you too, Idoia. Take care."

Without waiting for a response, David let go of my hand and wrapped his arm around my back, and we took off in the other direction. The street was full of people, almost all of them tourists. There was a pleasant breeze, noise and laughter were wafting out of the bars, and a man who I barely knew anything about had his arm around my shoulders and was leading me in an unknown direction.

"Damn, girl, you're good at that," he cracked up as we crossed the street.

And what do you think I said? Did I ask him if he was crazy? Did I ask for an explanation for why he got me involved in this mess? Did I demand he stop touching me? Did I threaten legal action? No.

"Are you seriously still using an iPod?"

14

~~~

NINE DIGITS

"I'm really sorry." David was still cracking up.

"You're nuts."

"No, no. Did you see her face? If we'd rehearsed it, she would've died from disgust. Fucking A, it went so well…it was like magic!"

"The capital's next up-and-coming comedic duo. That's us." I smiled and looked over my shoulder. "She's still there, dude, watching us."

"Holy shit." He laughed. "She's the type who turns away immediately. Do you think she's jealous?"

"I think your 'bring back my stuff' was the weakest excuse I've ever heard in my life, so I don't know why, but there's an ember of a doubt now."

"You think so?" he asked me again eagerly.

"Yeah, yeah. It worked for you, don't ask me why."

"Because of you!" He smiled at me. "Margot, girl, I don't know you, but you're the best!"

And suddenly his eyes were shining. It made me jealous.

"I hope karma doesn't come back to bite me."

"I don't know about karma, but I have ten euros in my pocket, and there's a sick pizza place right over there. Have you eaten?"

"No."

"Great. Lemme treat you."

I didn't have any expectations. Maybe that's why, when he brought me to one of those holes-in-the-wall that sell pizza by the slice all night, it seemed like a fantasy to me. Fuck. It smelled forbidden, and I was hungry. Had I eaten anything for lunch? Ah, no. The last thing was the croissant from Mama Framboise.

I picked ham and mushroom. He got carbonara. We bit into them as we walked, no airs and graces involved, and when I realized I blushed.

"What the fuck am I doing?" I said out loud, peppering my words with a nervous laugh.

"Eating dinner," he replied simply.

"But I don't even know you."

"Calm down," he teased, "it's just pizza, no strings attached."

"That's not it. The thing is…I'm shy."

"And a very good actress." He grinned.

"Yeah?"

"I don't know what you do for a living, but I'd say this is your hidden calling."

"My hidden calling is trying out beds."

David spun toward me with a smile.

"To sleep in or to…?"

"Hey, stop!"

"I was going to say to jump on."

"Yeah, right, of course." I laughed and held up my pizza in a kind of toast. "Listen, thanks for the pizza."

"Two fifty. Can you believe it? It's the best in Madrid."

"No way! The best pizza in Madrid is from Ornella. There's one that comes with truffles the size of my fist."

"And what do you drink with it, Moët?"

"You know Moët isn't the best champagne in the world, right?"

"I don't know. They like it a lot on Instagram."

"I didn't take you for an Instagram user."

"Well, I don't know if I'm a user. I don't even know how I managed to download it on my phone."

"What do you have, a calculator that makes phone calls?"

"Yeah, basically." He took his phone out of his pocket and showed it to me.

I snatched it with no sign of what my mother would assume had been our exquisite education. It was the most rudimentary device I'd ever seen in my life. Almost, almost, almost…as bad as my sister Candela's. Seriously…it looked like one of those Nokias that were cool in the early 2000s. I was speechless…and not because I was a snob, but because these days even the little old grannies looked up the bus schedule on their smartphones.

"Are you kidding?" I cracked up. "How long have you had this relic?"

"Hey! Gimme a break! All I use it for is making phone calls and sending WhatsApps. It works fine for what I need it for. The whole looking-at-Instagram part is just a bonus."

"That's great." I smiled and gave it back to him.

"I'm sure you have one that can make you dinner."

"Dinner no, but I'm lost without it." I stopped in the street and looked at him. "Wait…where's my sister's phone?"

"I don't know. I gave it to you inside." He pointed back toward his work.

"Fuck, I left it on the bar." I sighed.

"Don't worry, Ivan will keep an eye on it."

In my hand, I was still holding the half-eaten piece of pizza in a paper bag dripping with grease. He was standing in front of me, and I had known him for, what, fifteen minutes? The night before didn't count. And I was the kind of person who found conversations with strangers outside of a business environment to be hard work. Yet here I was, chatting with him, eating pizza, and laughing. What was happening to me? Ever since the Saturday before, I kept finding myself doing weird shit, being someone who wasn't Margot or Margarita, and who I wasn't sure I trusted.

"I…I have to go," I told him.

"Um." He took another bite of his slice and pointed down the street where we'd have to keep walking to get back. "Come on, let's go."

We didn't say anything for the rest of the walk. I mean, we didn't say anything out loud, but I never really stopped talking in my head. It was all so weird…and the weirdest part of all was that, underneath it all, I didn't feel awkward. I had spent all day thinking about a thousand fuckups…a whole week thinking about all the fuckups, really, and this little sliver of time had been…I don't know, calm. Pleasant.

I looked at David. He was chewing as he walked, waving left and right at people who were wandering in and out or lingering in the doorways of the clubs. He was comfortable too, but he gave off the air of just being like that: an adaptable person, who was happy with me and would be happy anywhere.

"Listen," I heard myself say, "you know in the long run it's not going to work out for you, right?"

"What?"

"That girl...you planted a seed of doubt in her mind, but she won't take long to figure out you made a pretty big effort for her."

"That's not true. What were we just saying? We made her crazy jealous. I know her. She thinks I had a date with you and I'm getting my life back together and—"

"No," I disagreed sharply. "I did what I could, but there wasn't much to save. Believe me. When a couple breaks up, the best thing to do is at least let some time pass."

"Are you saying that from experience?" He shot me a cheeky look.

"The last thing I would do is put on a show to make him jealous."

"So you are saying it from experience." He smiled at me, greeted the bouncer at the club where he worked with an affectionate pinch, and held the door open for me. "But I'll tell you when you leave someone, trying to make them jealous wouldn't make much sense."

"You're assuming I broke up with him?" I asked.

"It's always you girls." He rolled his eyes.

"Your love life almost makes mine seem like a movie." I smiled.

"What do you know, smart-ass?"

I pointed at his eyes with a warm smile.

"Wear sunglasses if you don't want us to see it, stud muffin, because those eyes are screaming."

His brow was furrowed, but he was still smiling, though that didn't calm me down much. What the fuck was I blabbering about? I took a deep breath and went over to the bar where his friend was still standing, trying to put space between my sudden role as a love adviser to strangers and the real me.

"I left my phone," I explained to Ivan before David caught up with me and ducked behind the bar, licking his fingers.

"Do you want your Coke? I saved it for you in case you came back. Sensational acting, by the way."

"Yeah, yeah." I looked down and grabbed the phone he was holding out to me. "But I'm leaving now."

He smiled, and I offered what was left of my pizza to David, who took it, not even skeeved out that I had already bitten into it.

"Good luck," I said. "And thanks for saving Patricia's phone."

"And thank you for your…what did you call it?" he asked his friend. "Ah, yes, your sensational acting."

I laughed and took a couple of steps back.

"What if she asks me about you, what do I say?"

"That you dumped me because you couldn't stop thinking about her," I threw out without thinking.

"That's even less sexy than the message about getting my stuff back."

I walked toward the door.

"You know your floor is super sticky?" I called without turning around.

"Everything here is sticky, Margot. You can't expect any less in hell."

He almost got a cackle out of me.

"You're both weirdos."

I said goodbye with a sweet smile. It was, without a doubt, the filthiest hole-in-the-wall I had ever wilded out in in Madrid, but I had to admit the owner had an eye for hiring staff.

I had already reached the street when someone grabbed my arm.

"Wait!"

David stopped in front of me, visibly hesitant, holding my greasy leftover pizza in his hand.

"I don't want any more pizza," I said.

He rubbed his forehead and then crinkled his nose.

"This is going to be weird," he murmured, taking a pen out of his back pocket and grabbing my hand.

I looked on dumbfounded as he wrote a string of numbers on it.

"What are you doing?" I grumbled.

"This is my number. I don't really like talking on the phone, but text me if you ever want to tell me about your eyes, you know? Sad people need someone even sadder to understand them."

He stepped to one side, and I stepped back. I didn't know what to say. I hadn't thought my eyes gave anything away. I wanted to flee, but at least this time I wasn't wearing a wedding dress.

I took out my AirPods and shoved them in my ears. People were walking by happily, laughing, stumbling, but their smiles never faltered. Is everyone lucky in Madrid? Everyone except me. Even that poor devil, who thought making his ex jealous with someone he had just met was a brilliant idea.

While I was walking, I kept skipping songs: *I'm sick of this one, this one is annoying, we listened to this one the night we…Filippo loves this one, this one was going to play at our wedding…* I couldn't help but notice none of the playlists I usually listened to would work. All the songs were a minefield of phrases or memories. It's amazing how a melody can transport you to another place and another time. It was too tempting. I knew that if I took refuge in my memories, I would never get out of there.

I opened Spotify and randomly clicked on a playlist. "Someone You Loved" by Lewis Capaldi started to play. I picked up the pace and shoved my phone in my jean pockets.

How hard was it for Filippo to send me a message? One. One tiny message. One that said: Margot, I'm in Italy and I'm fine. I'll find a way to forgive you.. A little dash of hope, something to hold on to, an ember of peace, or a sign that the road didn't end there. Although, at this point, I felt like I'd be relieved even to hear the opposite; at least I would know where I stood…

I skirted another group of fashionably dressed girls. I could see them talking animatedly, but all I could hear was the sad song that told the story of someone who had become so accustomed to being loved. Why is fate such a dog? I mean, you could also surmise that I had just kept skipping songs until I found the one that would hurt me the most.

I fumbled for the phone in my pocket again.

I stopped dead, and a couple slammed into my back; I said sorry, probably shouted it because the music was blasting in my ears. I turned off the music—I couldn't handle one more song, no matter what it said, and when I saw an empty taxi, I hailed it, recited my address, and opened WhatsApp. I typed. I deleted. I typed. Deleted. Typed. I read it six times, and then I pressed send.

I just need to know you're okay.

I couldn't help curling into a fetal position, pressing my chest to my thighs in the back of the taxi. The images of fleeing playing in an endless loop. My mother screaming. Filippo sprinting across the lawn. My niece and nephews giggling. Patricia with her hand on her chest, incredulous. Candela begging everyone to calm down. My shoes. The Nikes I had packed in case I felt like running a little on the treadmill before we started getting ready, but I couldn't use because the hotel didn't have a gym. The Nikes that were now grass stained, like the hem of my dress.

My phone vibrated, and I hurried to read the message, praying it wasn't Candela asking me to pick something up for her on the way home from dinner at Mama's house.

September, Margot. I can't say anything else.

I pressed my cheek against the window and sighed.

"Do you want me to turn the AC up?" the taxi driver asked me.

"No," I mumbled. "I just want September to get here."

"Be patient. We still have two very hot months to go."

I wiped away a tear before it became obvious I was crying, and as I let my hand fall into my lap, I noticed what was scrawled on it.

Sad people need even sadder people to understand them.

15

~~~

A PLAN

Candela was still skipping out on her job in Stockholm. When I asked her about it, she gave me even vaguer explanations than before. This led me to the hypothesis that she had called to take more days off, using up all her vacation days, trying not to leave so many dumpster fires behind her when she finally went home. She had a lot more fires to put out than my imminent descent into hell. Patricia was losing her mind, and not because she missed her phone, which I sent over with a messenger from the business on Sunday morning.

On Monday, at the crack of dawn, she showed up at my apartment, perfectly dressed and glam, holding a box from the bakery, which she wasn't even going to smell (because she didn't eat sugar, which is the new cocaine), to tell us with a smile that she had gone on a fishing expedition in her husband's wallet, calendar, laptop, and car, and she had proof of his infidelity.

She laid it out on the living room table, setting aside the vase of fresh flowers someone refilled every Monday.

We were still in bed when she arrived, but she ordered the "staff" to wake us up. I feel the need to clarify that my house was not a hive of butlers, housekeepers, interns, and cleaners, but every day Isabel, a very affable middle-aged lady, took care of chores and some cooking. It was 7:20 in the morning when Isabel came into my room.

"Your sister is here," she whispered, as she flipped the switch that opened the curtains. "She insists you get up. She says you have to make a plan."

I looked at the ceiling and fantasized, happily, about the chandelier falling on me. I didn't want a dramatic death, just a few weeks in the hospital.

"I'll be right there."

She let me take a shower first at least. And while I was putting on pants and a shirt from the corner of the wardrobe labeled "around the house" (first and second drawer right next to the en suite bathroom), a sentence got stuck in my head like an earworm. It was like when you wake up humming a few verses of a song that you don't remember listening to recently, but it plays on a loop in your head all day: *You have to get out of here.*

"Okay, what's going on?"

Patricia was sitting on a stool at the breakfast bar in the kitchen with her legs crossed and a cup of coffee in hand. Isabel was making breakfast, but I went over and kindly asked her to leave it for now.

"I'll make myself a coffee."

"Nothing else? A bowl of fruit?"

"A ten-diazepam omelet, please," I grumbled. She smiled. She knew Patricia and the face she put on when she wanted everyone to think everything was fine. "Please call Sonia and ask her to come over after lunch, whatever time works best for her."

I needed my right hand here. I needed to keep myself busy, and she might be able to bring me some reports so I could stay up-to-date on how things were going at work.

Patricia pointed at the table, at the statue of Christopher Columbus, with an almost blank look in her eyes. There was the proof of the "crime"…a handful of receipts.

"What is all this? And why didn't you wake Candela up?"

"Because she told me to go to hell in seven languages and one wasn't even verbal, that's why. What you have in front of you is—"

"An art exhibition that exposes how our lives are controlled by consumerism?"

"No. They're receipts."

"For what? Diamonds and motels?"

"Restaurants and parking lots."

"Oh my god."

I turned on the coffee maker and stood there, glued to it, like it was my best friend. Every drop of coffee dripping into the cup gave me the will to live.

Patricia had also brought a paper copy of her husband's calendar. She had copied appointments and reminders from his Google Calendar while Alberto was taking a shower, and now, on top of cross-referencing the receipts with the calendar, we also had to learn how to decipher Egyptian hieroglyphs.

"For the love of Manolito," I said, with one of the small but filling croissants in hand, "do you even know how to write?"

"You try copying a month of appointments while your husband is in the shower. He's bald! He doesn't need to wash his hair or put on mascara, Margot. Do you have any idea how fast he can be?"

Candela deigned to show up when the will to live the coffee had gifted me was already draining away, and as proof of the whims of genes and how different sisters can be from each other, she seemed pretty hyped about all of this.

"OMG! This is like playing Clue!"

"Yeah, except with my husband. If he's cheating on me, I swear I'm getting new tits."

Logic and my family have had a complicated relationship for years; this was nothing new.

"Do you think I ran away from my wedding because of some recessive gene that's active in you guys?" I suddenly blurted out.

"No. It was because of your lack of emotional awareness, but nothing that wouldn't go away with a few vacations in one of your hotels."

"Our hotels," I corrected.

"Your hotels. I'll remind you that I sold my stock and donated the money. The only thing that belongs to me from the business is the last name," Candela said proudly, seconds before immersing herself in the facts we had gleaned from the chaotic stack of papers.

I looked at Patricia who, wearing the coolest and most flattering plastic glasses, smiled at me before she said, "But they are a little bit mine."

It didn't take long to figure out there was nothing noteworthy. Receipts for lunches with clients that corresponded to the millisecond with what Alberto had scheduled in his calendar. When they started declaring that he could be using code names to hide his affairs, I decided to leave. And I climbed back into bed. Face down. With any luck, I'd suffocate.

~~~~~

Sonia, as always, warned of her arrival far enough in advance that I could get dressed and spruce myself up.

I led her into my home office (not nearly as warm as my office at work) with a Diet Coke (she hates Coke Zero) and a burning desire to ask her to kill me.

"Hey, boss." She smiled tenderly. "You look good."

"I better. I'm wearing seven layers of Double Wear by Estée Lauder."

"Then you're going to have to take it off with gasoline."

"Yeah, like the Kardashians."

We gave each other a hug just with a look. Some people you only need to look at to feel their arms around you.

"I thought you wouldn't want to see me." She sat down across from me and whipped out her ever-present iPad, where she had the entire universe organized. *Damn she's good, the bitch.* "I thought you were going to rest and all that."

"My sisters won't let me. They're playing IRL Clue."

Sonia raised an eyebrow. "Did they kill someone?"

"Let's drop it. The less you know, the better," I joked. "Give me an update?"

She wrinkled her nose.

"What?" I asked, alarmed.

"I don't want you to think I haven't been doing my job."

"I never think you haven't done your job because you do yours, your colleagues', and sometimes even mine. What's going on?"

"I don't want to get into something that's not my place," she said, avoiding eye contact.

"I called you."

"Let's see…" She sighed and ruffled her hair a little, kind of scratching her scalp in the slightly annoying way she always did when she was stressed. "I brought a bunch of updated material, but I don't think I should give it to you."

"And why not?"

She raised her right hand. "I solemnly swear that what I'm about to say is not a judgment or even a criticism."

"Spit it out, you troublemaker."

She bit her lip. "The board is right: you need a vacation."

"Like everyone in Spain right now."

"I don't know if everyone else in Spain has an eye twitch, drinks seven Coke Zeros a day, and ends up cursing and trembling like a crumpled leaf."

"Are you telling me I need a psychiatrist?"

"No. You need to rest. And to talk to someone."

I put my forehead on the desk. "You're telling me to get an urgent appointment with my psychiatrist, right?"

"No. Margarita—"

"Call me Margot, please."

"Margot…I cleared your calendar until the end of August; the business owes you seventy-seven vacation days." Her faltering hand crept closer to mine until it finally landed on top of it. "You've been under too much pressure, and you're going to end up getting sick or—"

"Going crazy."

"I don't know, but…I really think you need to get out of here. Stop seeing all of us and…find yourself."

"Well, when I find myself, let's see what I tell myself."

Sonia smiled.

"I'm sorry to ask, but…have you spoken to Filippo?"

My breath caught. "We texted, but…it's not looking good."

Her fingers squeezed mine.

"I'm going to be really honest, okay? You pay me to be, and you pay me well, so I'm going there: rumor has it that the rest of the board is pressuring your godfather. They say the fact that you fled the day of your wedding indicates that your mental state is not suited for a position with so much responsibility and that you're buckling under the pressure. Someone mentioned that your mother has made comments about your delicate state."

"She's a cat who drinks too much; nobody will listen to her."

"But it bodes very well for them to believe her. They want it to be true. You know better than anyone that they don't—"

"They don't want me there, got it. Any other information about how disastrous my future is looking?"

"It's not disastrous. You just have to do what they want you to do. It's simple: make the most of the opportunity and leave for you, not for them. Leave for all the things you don't even know you want because you never have time to do them. Leave for the part of you that's sad and for the part that's going to be happy. Leave for me too because I can't. Leave, Margot. Leave and lounge around on some beach, for the love of God. You're the heiress of a hotel empire, and you're using a shade of foundation from Siberia. You don't need to constantly prove you deserve it, okay?"

Sonia tugged on my fingers and raised her eyebrows.

"You're fucking Ana Margarita Ortega Ortiz de Zarate. Get out of here. And don't come back until you've forgotten your computer password."

We stared at each other, and a tiny smile pulled at the corner of her mouth.

"Nobody…listen to me carefully because I'll never talk to you this way again…*nobody* runs out on their wedding when they're happy. And you deserve to be happy. Like me. Like your sisters. Like the boy who brings us our lunch orders. Leave and figure out what's missing."

16

~~

THERE'S A GUY...

Sonia smiled and shook her head.

"Where would I even go?" I asked, side-eyeing her.

"You have hotels all over the world. Pick a destination out of a hat."

She grabbed her iPad, her fingers flying across it and, when she found what she was looking for, turned it toward me. There was a world map on the screen.

"Close your eyes and point."

"What are you talking about?"

"Come on!" she smiled. "I'll take care of all the planning."

"That's not your job."

"But you can't live without me."

"That's true."

"Come on!"

I closed my eyes and dangled my finger over the iPad. Then I let it drop. A giggle burbled up from Sonia's throat.

"What, what? Tell me I didn't pick North Korea."

"Greece. Greece is amazing."

"Have you been?"

"Yes. In one of the business's hotels, taking advantage of the employee discount." She winked. "You're gonna love it."

"Traveling alone? Seems like you don't know me very well. I'm going to be babbling to myself within the first half hour."

"Well, then take one of your sisters."

"What do you want? For me to open the plane door and depressurize the cabin? They have their own mess, and Greece is not part of their plans. You come."

"I can't." And, embarrassed, she put the iPad down on the table.

"Why not?"

"Well, because I'm your assistant, and…it would be really weird for you to take me on vacation with you—"

"You're my right hand." I smiled.

"No, no way, Margot. It's better if we don't. You go alone and enjoy it. I'm sure you'll meet people and—"

"I'm not going on a singles cruise."

"If you keep going like this, I might sign you up for one," she threatened. "Why don't you ask one of your friends?"

I thought about the last girls' trip I had gone on. We went to Ibiza. They were all obsessed with taking bikini photos on some yacht, and when we went out to dinner, they spent the whole time taking photos of the food, the drinks, and us dolled up and posing like we were finalists in a beauty pageant. I was bored just thinking about it.

"Maybe I don't have any real friends," I said finally.

"You work too much."

"That's not why. It's because by the time I realized how shitty my friendships were, I was already too in love with Filippo, and I had no desire to go out and find new adventure buddies."

"Life is much more than love. Or, to put it another way, you can love much more than a man."

"I know. I'm pathetic."

"No." She shrugged playfully. "Because nobody pathetic has the ovaries to run out on a wedding with five hundred guests. Plus, you're about to set off on one of those trips everybody dreams about. You, your quest, and a luxury destination."

"Maybe you're right."

"As always." She smiled. "You have it all, Margot, but you've been looking outward to find it."

"The board is only approving my absence so that—"

"The board can go fuck themselves."

I side-eyed her again and let out a cackle.

Me alone. With my suitcase, my book, and juggling between finding myself, getting my life back, and making sure no one in the company has any reason to fire me because of my mental health. Come on. If I had been a man, would there have been such an uproar at work?

"Okay…fine. But…I don't want them to have any reason to rip me to shreds, so book good hotels but nothing crazy. Nothing the Kardashians would choose."

"Done."

Greece. Imagine that. Almost like it had always been there, waiting. Wasn't that the destination I pulled out of thin air for the trip with the bartender? I laughed. What if…?

"What's so funny?"

"Me?" I looked up at Sonia, who was studying my expression. "Well…I don't know. The other day I met a guy and…"

She sat up straighter. "What do you mean you met a guy?"

"No, no, look, I went out with my sisters in Huertas to some sleazy club, and Patricia lost her phone. One of the bartenders kept it safe, and I was the one who had to go get it the next day. I don't know how it happened, but suddenly, I was helping him make his ex jealous, playing the role of my life, pretending to be his new 'friend,' and telling her we were going to Greece soon and that he was going to love Santorini. It made me laugh when I realized I just picked Greece again."

Sonia raised her eyebrows.

"Are you serious?"

"Totally." I laughed. "I can't believe I ended up in that situation either. The club was ratchet, by the way. The worst."

"What was it called?"

"The truth is I don't even remember. The bartender was named David. He gave me his number and everything."

"So you could keep pretending to be his girlfriend and making his ex jealous?"

"No. Um…" I started to wonder whether continuing this story was a good idea because it was getting a little too intimate. But… how could something with a stranger be too intimate? "He told me he could read something sad in my eyes and that he was sad too. He mentioned something about how sad people need each other to be understood."

"That's the worst excuse I've ever heard to hit on someone."

"That wasn't what he was doing." I looked at her and smiled. "He was…young, one of those wild guys. A kind of…I don't know how to explain it, a prom king mixed with a lost little boy. He's crazy about his ex, and to tell the truth, I'm not surprised. When I saw her, I thought about how cruel genetics are. That girl and I aren't even from the same species."

"Well, well, well," she muttered.

She looked at me, and her expression softened before she breathed in, straightened up, and smiled with her teeth. "We're just in a bit of a slump. Then…"

I nodded. She never lost perspective. That's why I liked Sonia so much.

"Would you text him?"

"I would." She laughed. "But I'm not trying to get back together with anyone, and…underneath it all I don't think much about the consequences of my actions. But you're Margot."

I looked at her, confused. "What does that mean?"

"It means you don't do anything without thinking through every possible scenario. This story has more possible endings than, I don't know, bubbles in this glass."

She held up the soda and thrust it into the air in a kind of ceremonial toast and took a sip. I should have said something in response, but the truth is I was still entranced by the bubbles flitting up and down, dancing in the sweet dark liquid. They seemed…free.

If only that hadn't seemed so tempting. If only I hadn't taken it as a challenge.

The door of my office slammed open, and my two sisters burst in, excited, elbowing and shoving each other, fighting over who got to be the first to tell me the results of their investigations.

"We've got it!"

"What do you have? You found something?"

"Bah, this is just a bunch of useless paper," Candela complained.

"But we have it!"

"A thread to follow or the emergency number for the Lopez Ibor psychiatric institution?"

I could tell Sonia was struggling to hold back her laughter.

"The detective! We have the detective!"

"He accepted my case!" Patricia barreled over, thrilled. "And wanna know the best part?"

"He's going to swindle you?"

"No! He's really good!"

Her cracked screen showed the photo of a guy in his forties, very handsome, grinning from his website. The slogan of his business: "Your trust, his secret: my job."

It seemed so horrible to me that I couldn't say anything more than:

"Fuck."

17

~~~~

SAD PEOPLE

I was lying in bed clutching my phone. My sisters had gone to pick up my niece and nephews from school, and Sonia had gone back to the office to finalize the details of my upcoming trip. I had already drafted an official email for the rest of the members of the board where I informed them that in the end I had decided to get away from it all and enjoy a vacation. A long one. That's the benefit of having an obscene amount of stock in the company.

I had also written and sent an email to my department to share with them, in a very formal manner, my profound disappointment in their behavior the previous week.

I still had a window of peace before Candela came back home. An album was playing that reminded me of my time in the United States, when I went there to do my master's. I tried to make friends, but everyone was too competitive. Maybe that was my problem: I didn't like competing the same way I didn't like taking risks.

I had always walked in the shadows. I had always been responsible. I had always considered the possibilities, the results they could lead to.

I had never thrown myself down one path without looking back. Until I ran out of my own wedding.

What if what Sonia said was true? What if there really was something that wasn't working? Well, I bailed on our wedding; there had to be some explanation. Maybe…maybe a part of me was scared to really throw myself in headfirst before I experienced more. I had never done anything crazy. I had never made a mistake or had my heart broken; everything before Filippo had just been a rehearsal.

But…what would be the point of all this time lying fallow if I didn't change? A little. I'm not talking about a trendy haircut or a new red sports car. What if…I just opened myself up to the world?

It wasn't easy, and I regretted it two hundred times before he answered, but I felt proud of myself for the first question I drafted in a newly started conversation with an almost unknown contact that…was about to change my life.

MARGOT

So what about you, what are you sad about?

DAVID

What are you talking about? Who is this?

MARGOT

The weird girl your ex thinks you've involved with.

DAVID

Ah! Margot.

MARGOT

Which isn't a Galician name.

DAVID

WhatsApp suits you.

You're nicer.

MARGOT

I am nice.

DAVID

You're right. There's an abyss between the two terms.

MARGOT

Are you going to answer me? Why are you sad?

DAVID

The love of my life left me. Don't you think that's enough?

MARGOT

Yes.

DAVID

Did you see her? She's perfect.

MARGOT

A goddess.

DAVID

If you're going to be sarcastic, I'll block you.

MARGOT

Sarcastic? Your ex is a goddess. She almost made me reconsider my heterosexuality.

DAVID

I would convert to Mormonism for her.

MARGOT

Dude, with the phone you have, you're only one step from churning your own butter.

DAVID

You're thinking of the Amish, not Mormons.

MARGOT

Can you explain to me why a complete stranger is giving me religion lessons?

DAVID

More like general culture, but if what you're really asking is why you finally decided to text me, I'll tell you it's because it's easier to talk to someone you don't know who has no reason to judge you.

MARGOT

Everybody judges. It's inevitable.

DAVID

Is that why you're sad? And don't try to tell me you're not.

Did someone make the wrong conclusion about you?

MARGOT

No. I lost the love of my life too.

DAVID

According to your criteria, that's not a good enough reason to be so sad, so there must be something else.

MARGOT

Typing...
Typing...
Online...
Typing...
Online...
No.

DAVID

You know what really doesn't make sense? Texting to a stranger who you can vent to and who isn't going to judge you, even if you tell him your father is an otter, and then still lying to him.

MARGOT

Clear something up for me, what does "otter" mean in your slang?

DAVID

I'm just getting home from work and my only aspiration is to have a passionate love affair with a ham sandwich and a shower, and you're lying to me and talking to me about otters.
Margot, smh, what am I going to do with you? I don't deserve this.

MARGOT

I didn't mean to bother you.

DAVID

Margot!! Please! I'm fucking around. Come on, let's do something. I promised to talk to you on WhatsApp, but it's actually more complicated than talking in person. What are you doing tomorrow from 9 to 10?

MARGOT

In the morning or night?

DAVID

That's why I like you, pretending you have other plans.

MARGOT

I'm just deciding if you're an idiot or...

DAVID

The other one. I choose the other option, whatever it is.

Tomorrow at 9. In the morning.

I'll send you the address now.

I'll wait five minutes. If you stand me up, I'll bounce and block you, but with no hard feelings. Okay?

MARGOT

Okay.

18

~~~~

THE CRAZY DOG WALKER

DAVID

When I saw her show up, I couldn't hide my smile. I could pick her out from the crowd among the people hurrying along the street on their way to work because she exuded that probably unconscious vibe that made her seem lost wherever she went. As always, she was wearing a pretty discreet look: jeans, a thin blouse, and flats. But all the clothes and accessories she wore, everything, had a shine of luxury that I can't explain. Her plainness was elegant, I guess. And she was beautiful.

I don't know how these thoughts connected, but I wondered what Idoia would have worn for the meetup. She probably would've shown up in an evening gown and combat boots or a red latex miniskirt with a white men's shirt and white sneakers.

Margot jumped over a couple of dog poops and planted herself in front of me, not quite knowing how to greet me or where to look. I held out my hand to her, stifling a laugh; deep down I liked seeing her so lost. It was the opposite with Idoia, and lately I had been starting to think the only women I would ever feel comfortable and like I could be myself with them would be Dominique, the girls from my village crew, my mother, and my sister. I don't count my grandmother because she always made me feel tiny. None of this looked good for my social life. Or my sex life.

"Good morning," I said to her.

"Good morning."

I gave her a short but firm handshake, possibly accompanied by a roguish smile.

"You're making fun of the way I greeted you the other day, aren't you?"

"No." I smiled. "I was trying to make you feel comfortable. I guess that's how people greet each other on your planet?"

"I'm starting to regret coming. By the way, can I ask what you're doing with all these dogs? Are they all yours?"

I looked at my feet, where a German shepherd, a French bulldog, and a dalmatian were all sitting, waiting politely and panting.

"They're my clients."

"Your clients?"

"Yes."

"But don't you work in that club?" she asked, her forehead wrinkled with a kind of disdain.

"Yes. But I have other jobs."

"Jobs? Plural?"

"Every morning, from Monday to Friday, I collect these gentlemen and that lady," I pointed at them, "and then after a walk and a little play, I bring them home. Tuesday, Wednesday, and Thursday afternoons I help out at a florist."

She raised an eyebrow.

"You have three jobs."

"I'm a babysitter too, but I charge for that in a different way."

"In sex?"

I burst out laughing and decided to take a step forward. My kids followed politely behind me, just like I taught them.

"No, buddy." I glanced at her. "Ivan, my colleague from the club, has a seven-month-old baby. I live with them. Well, with Ivan, his girlfriend, and the baby. We share costs, and I take care of Ada sometimes when her parents' work schedules overlap."

"Does Ivan have another job too?"

"He's a waiter at a café from Monday to Friday." I shrugged. "You don't make much in the hospitality industry."

I wasn't surprised to see a spark of stress in her eyes.

"And where do you work?"

Hesitation. She looked at me hesitantly. She didn't want to talk. She was like those girls I had met up with from Tinder before Idoia, the ones who didn't want you to know any more about them than their names so things didn't get complicated.

"Actually"—I took a shortcut, not looking at her as we kept walking—"let's make a deal. We'll only talk about our problems and our deepest, darkest traumas, but we won't tell each other about any day-to-day stuff. Does that work for you?"

"I don't even really know why I came."

"Because I'm a charmer." I grinned at her.

"I pay a guy with an office full of prestigious degrees the trivial sum of a hundred euros an hour to talk about traumas and secrets."

"Yeah?" I asked, tugging gently on Walter, the German shepherd, who was straggling behind sniffing a tree. "And does that work for you?"

"No. Honestly, not really, judging by the circumstances."

"Give me a headline."

"I'm not going to give you a headline. I don't even know you."

"Do you know what bartenders, dog walkers, and florists all have in common?"

"The type of contribution to Social Security?"

"Yes, we're all self-employed, but that's not what I'm talking about. Listening. I know how to listen."

"Explain something to me." She swung her bag around to the side, not looking at me. "Why did we meet up?"

"Because you did me a solid with my girlfriend."

"Your ex."

"My ex, you grammar Nazi," I teased her.

Margot shot me an indignant look, but I cut through her airs with a cackle.

"That's why you wanted to meet up today?"

"No. It was the eye thing, buddy."

"Don't call me buddy, God," she said and sighed.

"Two pairs of sad eyes recognize each other. Remember? We're both sad, and we both know how to give good advice. We might not know how to get our own lives back on track, but maybe we can help each other."

"But why?"

"Well, because we crossed paths. That has to mean something, right?"

"That we both live in Madrid and my sisters have very bad taste in choosing nightclubs."

"Maybe. Or maybe not. I don't know about you, but I'm not really the kind to meet up just to figure something out."

I squeezed through the gap between two hedges, and the animals followed me. Margot didn't hesitate either. As soon as they recognized the place where they ran and played every day, the dogs got jumpy, at least until I unhooked their leashes and they could run with each other, brothers and sisters after so many walks together. I could easily watch them from here, and the park's only exit was behind me. They were safe, so I turned to Margot. Her gaze was lost on the dogs racing around, drawing concentric circles on the grass, and she had a pretty indecipherable expression. It was instantly clear to me that she was not one of those girls who, like me, often told herself she had nothing to lose.

"What's the problem?" I asked. "Apart from losing the love of your life and all that... He's not dead, is he?"

"No!" she groaned. "He's alive and kicking, enjoying his summer on a yacht on the Amalfi coast."

"Fuck, that's flossy! So he's rolling in it, huh?"

She looked at me like I was a real weirdo, and I rubbed my thumb and forefinger together in the universal gesture for money in case she hadn't understood me. She didn't answer.

"Okay, let's do it the other way around: Idoia is the woman I've loved most in my life. I had never felt even half what I felt when I was with her. She was...she was a savage, a witch, a magician, a lady, a goddess...all rolled into one, all at once and all the time. She made me feel alive. And free."

"Free? Did you have an open relationship?"

"I'm not talking about that kind of freedom." I leaned on a tree trunk and whistled for the dogs, who were getting a little rowdy. "I'm talking about...I didn't feel like being with her stopped me from being free. Being tied down didn't bother me."

"Being tied down? Your concept of relationships is..."

"When you're with someone, you're tied to them in one way or another, right?"

"I guess, but it's your own choice, not because you're 'tied.'" She repeated the word intentionally.

"Now you're getting it."

"So what happened? I mean, why did she dump you?"

"Because I'm not enough for her."

She raised an eyebrow. "Are we talking about your economic situation?"

"Economic, social, and, to finish me off, even religious. It seems that I'm a poor boy accustomed to being mediocre, and I built a nest there, in the shit, where it's warm but it stinks."

"I mean…" She rubbed her temples.

"I sleep on my best friend's couch; I'm aware that…"

"No matter how little you earn from your three jobs, it should be enough to get you minimum wage, which…should be enough for you to rent an apartment. Even in Malasaña. An apartment with two other guys, on some cool, trendy street."

"That would tie me down to a house and…what if I want to pick up and fly the coop tomorrow?"

"Do you want to fly the coop tomorrow?"

"It's rhetorical. A hypothetical."

She looked at me like I was crazy, and something in her eyes made even me start to consider the possibility.

"That's a personal choice," she declared. "You live in your best friend's house…I'm going out on a limb here, okay? I'm guessing it's because they took you in because they thought it would just be for a few days, but now the situation is dragging on. Then they became parents, and you realized that having someone helping out around the house worked for them. And being there worked for you too because you trust them, you feel comfortable, they give you affection…"

"Are you psychoanalyzing me?" I looked at her like she was being a bummer.

"Okay. I hit the nail on the head."

"Not exactly, but…I'm fine where I am."

"And you wouldn't move in with Idoia?"

"You'd have to ask her. I think the mere mention of the possibility would make her break out in hives."

"What did you guys do as a couple?"

I glanced at her, but I played dumb.

"I don't know. The usual. We hung out in her apartment; we went out every once in a while for dinner or to go to a concert. We drank wine in bed. We fucked."

Her look went through my skull like a shot. "Fascinating. Did you make plans for the future?"

"I already told you we didn't."

"So tell me something… How were you planning to get her to stay with you if you didn't give her anything in exchange?"

"I gave her love," I scoffed, offended.

"What about what she gave you?"

"Love," I answered, not very convinced.

"Right. Yeah. And with a lot of love, she told you, 'Fly, fly, little birdy.'"

I groaned, and she smiled.

"If I'd known we were coming to a park, I would have at least brought a thermos of coffee." She sighed. "If you want to get her back, you can't just make her jealous. That girl knows she's the only one for you in the whole world. She has you wearing blinders and, listen, I get it. But you have to show her your life doesn't revolve around her, that you're making plans and you know where you're heading."

"And where am I heading?" I asked her.

She shrugged coyly and smiled. Of course, it was good advice, and even I knew it. It wasn't easy, and it didn't sound at all like what I wanted to hear, but I guess those are two hallmarks of good advice.

"Now your turn. While I reconsider where my life is going."

"How old are you, by the way?" she asked.

"Twenty-seven."

"You're still young."

"You talk like you're double my age."

"No, but I have five years on you."

"Ooooh," I teased. "Age is just a number."

"For you guys, maybe. We dry up."

The blow hit me in the middle of the forehead, and I turned back to her, surprised.

"You're a witch!"

She laughed. And she did it wholeheartedly.

"Come on. Your turn."

She glanced at the dogs and bit her bottom lip. "I...ran out on our wedding."

"What?" I blinked.

"I ran out on our wedding."

"That sounds like a euphemism for *jilted him at the altar*."

"You said it, not me."

"You jilted him at the altar?"

"Hey!" she complained. "I didn't ask any stupid questions!"

"Okay, okay. Keep going."

"Well...since I left him at the altar, let's just say he doesn't think too highly of me right now."

"He hates you?"

"No, but he told me he needed a few months to think about us."

"But do you want him back? If you dipped out on your wedding... By the way, were you wearing your wedding dress?"

"And a pair of Nikes, yes."

I let out a snort of laughter, and she covered her face.

"That's pretty badass. Hey, I bow down to you." I gave her a pat on the back.

"I don't know why I did it." She sighed. "I love him. I want to live with him, travel with him, tell him how my day went every evening while he opens a bottle of wine and we listen to music."

"What are you, living in a Hollywood movie?"

She raised her eyebrows, like I didn't get it.

"The truth is," she went on, "I had a panic attack, and I bolted without thinking twice about it. I humiliated him in front of a lot of people... Maybe I should accept that something wasn't working."

"Something big wasn't working. Was he good in bed?" I asked.

"Shouldn't you wait to...I don't know, not be a fucking stranger before you ask me a question like that?"

"I already told you, I can't handle being left hanging. Good or not? You can just move your head."

She nodded, and I smiled.

"Do you hate his family?"

"No. I hate half of mine. His...are pretty amazing."

"Did he treat you well?"

"Like a princess."

"Then I don't get it."

"Me either," she claimed.

"What were you thinking about when you ran off in Nikes and a wedding dress?"

"Don't have too much fun, hey?" she warned me. "I wasn't thinking, David. I was just…running."

"Like Forrest Gump?"

"Something like that. Like it was all too much for me, like I couldn't live up to it."

"Then maybe you're the problem in the relationship. You feel like you're not enough…"

Judging by the look she gave me, I'd say that was good advice too.

"What if you spend this summer doing things for you? Travel, enjoy, YOLO, go a little crazy. Take it like a…what does that Izal song say? A wild loop."

"What song?"

"I think it's called 'Bill Murray.' It goes: 'I know I don't have much more time on this wild loop.' I always thought it meant like a kind of vital limbo where you don't think too much about the consequences of your actions."

"Then I have to get into a wild loop, and you need you get out of one."

"Something like that."

"Well, I know where I need to start. What about you?"

I looked at the dogs and started to walk toward them, rummaging through my pockets for some treats that would convince them getting back on their leashes was a good idea. What was Margot suggesting? That I should look for something shiny to distract me from my fears while I got the reins of my life back?

Walter, Milagros, and Aquiles paused their scampering around as they scarfed their treats; Margot watched us, absorbed, as if her brain was made up of a million tiny teeth and she was chewing the words into a liquid she could inject directly into her nervous system.

I went over to her, threw her a smile, and moved past, leaving her behind. Ten meters later, she was by my side.

"So where are you going to start?" I asked her.

"By leaving."

"That doesn't count. Running away isn't the answer."

"It's not running away. It's almost obligatory. Let's just say… everything in my life points to me needing to get away for a few weeks. I'm lucky enough to be able to swing it with my…work life."

"So where are you going to go?"

"To Greece."

I stopped dead, and the dogs' leashes yanked them back. I turned back to her, and she gave me a cheeky smile that spread to me. I stared at her, and she stared back.

"Greece?"

She nodded.

"Athens, Santorini, and Mykonos. I can already see myself there, in a hotel with sea views and an infinity pool with the best sunsets in the whole Greek Cyclades."

"Dear Margot…that's our trip."

"Too bad you can't come with me."

I'd be lying if I said I thought about it because it didn't even cross my mind. No. I left it there, just one more funny story, like our handshake greeting. But after I dropped the dogs off at their houses, when I found her on the corner holding two lukewarm coffees, I knew, like you can only know things that haven't happened yet, that she wouldn't be. No. Margot wasn't a funny story; she was one more step in my stupid obsession with never wondering what if.

19

~~~

INSPIRATION

MARGOT

I wasn't even home yet when I got the first of many messages.

What are you doing this week?

Under other circumstances, I would have run a mile, but I knew David didn't want anything like that from me. We both wanted to get our partners back, and we felt like we could help each other. In my case, David was an inspiration. It reminded me of when I was in boarding school and I was assigned a seat next to a student who was flunking out. His grades improved, and I learned to let my hair down a little within the regal and rigid atmosphere that reigned over the school. My grades in music and art improved, and it was thanks to him that…well, I can neither confirm nor deny that he was my first kiss.

But it was different this time. I wasn't going there. It was…in a way, it was exciting. Or more like exhilarating. David was a strange but interesting person. He aroused my curiosity, which had been lying dormant for some time.

When I texted back that I didn't have any plans until I left for Greece, he asked if I wanted to grab a drink the next evening. I suddenly understood why I was opening up to a complete stranger, because suddenly I could talk about what had happened to me and I was finding it easy to express myself: he was paying attention to me. To me. To my feelings, to what had happened, to the why behind what I had done or what I said. What I had to say seemed important to David, and we weren't even work colleagues. That made me feel good.

We made a plan for me to scoop him from the florist and go get a drink somewhere quiet, where we could talk: David wanted me to give him advice on how he should go about getting his life together. I didn't put too much thought into it. I had nothing better to do, and he got me out from under the duvet, out of the spiral of crying and scrolling through old photos.

I spotted him in the back as soon as I got there. He was wearing a shirt that had been white at some point in its existence and jeans hidden under a black apron covered in stains. His hair was messy and tangled, and his eyes were fixed on the flowers he was arranging.

"Can we help you?" two ladies asked me.

"I'm here for David." I smiled at them.

They looked at me. They looked at him. They looked at each other. They were in their seventies, and you couldn't miss the fact that they were sisters. Judging by their expressions, they were surprised that anyone, or at least anyone who looked like me, would date him.

"What about the blond girl?" I heard one say to the other.

"Shut up, shut up. It's for the best."

"David! Someone's here to collect you!"

"I'm just finishing the everlasting flower bouquet for the restaurant. I'll be out in five minutes."

"No," one of them said firmly. "Come out now. You don't leave young ladies waiting."

"I didn't know there were any young ladies in this florist," he retorted mockingly.

He stuck his head out, saw me, and smiled. "Gimme one sec?"

"Of course."

When he finished, the two sisters had already told me how the shop was a family business with more than seventy years of history, and they had given me a little posy to put in my bedroom, but when David came out, he decided it wasn't good enough.

"Not those ones!" he had the nerve to complain. "Amparito! You gave her funeral flowers, for God's sake."

"Gladiolas aren't funeral flowers, you animal!"

"Get them outta here. They give me bad vibes." David ripped the flowers out of my hands, threw them on the counter, and grabbed stems from a few buckets overflowing with different blooms.

In the blink of an eye, he wrapped what he had picked in brown paper and tied a string around it. He put it in my hands and turned back to the two ladies to argue, like a goalie, about which flowers were best for graves, and I…I didn't know whether to freak out, run away, or burst out laughing. In my hands, I was holding a small, tight, and almost trivial bouquet, a mixture of dark green, white, red, and purple. I never would have chosen a bouquet with those colors, but…it had turned out so beautifully! It seemed like something living, eccentric but exciting, like an impressionist painting, like a sunset, like…David?

"Oh forget it. I give up on you two," he said with his eternal lopsided smile, and he came back to me with the air of a teacher. "Young lady, these are eucalyptus leaves, this white one here is called *statice*, and the ones that look like strawberries are *gomphrenas*, not to be confused with *gonorrheas*."

"You were doing so well," I said warningly.

"Bah…this lilac-colored one is salvia. When we get it in red, it's sick. Plus, they all dry phenomenally. You have to cut the stems two fingers' width from the end, diagonally, like this."

"David," I cut him off.

"Pure magic, queen, this bouquet is pure magic." He waggled his fingers at me, sweeping them through the air, making it clear that he felt he held great power in his hands.

~~~~~

I had reserved a table at a restaurant I loved, but I didn't tell him. First of all, because I was embarrassed, and second, because…with the way David looked I couldn't let myself be seen there with him. He hadn't even changed his shirt.

"Do you always walk around like this?" I asked him.

"Do you always walk around like your shit doesn't stink?"

I turned back to look at him and gave him a pretend haughty look. I couldn't help smiling.

"I mean, when you met up with Idoia, did you always look like such a slob?"

"I just got out of a florist. What do you want me to wear? A suit? I get covered in dirt, water, pollen!"

"You could bring a button-up and change into it when you leave."

"A button-up shirt? Like for weddings?"

I stopped on the street. "Did you just say *for weddings*?"

"Listen, lady, who wears a button-up on a regular day just because?"

"Billions of dudes? Plus…that shirt has a hole in it."

"They all have holes." He shrugged. "The tags bug me, and I rip them out. It's only a matter of time before they get a hole."

I couldn't believe it. I opened my mouth to speak, but he cut me off.

"Anyway, I don't need to walk around like I'm going to a job interview all the time."

"I bet my left hand you go to job interviews like this too."

"I'm cute. I don't need much."

I let out a giggle, and he started laughing too.

"No, seriously. I have no clue about fashion. No fucking clue. Idoia is very trendy. She works in the industry. She's always…avant-garde, you know?"

My lip curled.

"Define *avant-garde*."

"Full of personality."

"Like she was in an editorial for a fashion magazine?"

"It's all Greek to me," he teased. "I mean she wears stuff I never would've thought could go together, but somehow it works on her. She's a trendsetter."

"Ah, like my sister."

"What?"

"Nothing. So…you didn't think you should've cleaned up your act a little for that? I know it's superficial, but if she likes fashion so much, I would say one of the reasons she left you is your holey shirts."

"Help me then."

"I wouldn't be much good for that."

"I don't know about that. I don't want you to tell me how you would dress me because I already know I'm not going to wear a button-up, but I'm sure you have more of a clue than me."

"No way. Filippo is the one who has style. Someone chooses my clothes for me."

"What do you mean someone chooses your clothes?"

"Exactly what I said. I pay a girl to buy me clothes for whatever I have coming up. Then she organizes my closet into sections: work, free time, vacations, around the house…"

"I can't believe it. You're worse than me." He started to laugh. "Come on, let's go, I'm hungry."

~~~~~

We headed into Malasaña. Colorful hair, vintage bags, beautiful shoes on broken cobblestones already sticky with spilled beer, even at this hour. David walked calmly, like someone very secure in his skin. He was rambling about a place that served delicious hot dogs, but I wasn't paying attention. I was thinking about shopping. How could something so natural seem so complicated to both of us? It just flummoxed me. I got overwhelmed. I never knew what to wear or not wear and what looked good on me. Sometimes, in the lunch-room at the office, I still found myself accidentally staring at a clique of girls who looked elegant, sexy, and filled with personality with just a couple pieces of clothing. On the other hand, even though I spent a pretty interesting budget to dress like I should, I always seemed… bland. Well, not bland; elegant, but in a plain way, like a model from a photo in a clothing catalog who doesn't move, who doesn't feel comfortable, who would never go out dancing in those pants and won't feel the pain from the heels on those shoes.

"Do you like spicy food?"

I looked at David, jutting my chin out to meet his mocking gaze. Whoa. He was taller than I remembered. I had gotten lost in my thoughts, and I didn't realize we had gotten to the place he had been talking about: El Perro Salvaje.

"I mean...yes. I guess so."

"What do you mean you guess? Come on. Can I get two Boxers and two IPAs, please?"

He took a twenty out of his pocket and gave it to the girl, who gave him back a few coins. We'd have to be miracle workers to stretch that bill in the restaurant where I had reserved a table. I took my phone out and surreptitiously sent Sonia a message:

Cancel the reservation, please. All the details are in my Google Calendar.

"What are you thinking about?"

I turned back to him and stowed my phone in my bag. He was leaning against the counter, drumming his fingers on it. Every once in a while, the girl behind the counter was peeking over at him. I couldn't tell if it was because the noise was bugging her or because she thought he was cute.

"About why we find shopping so tricky."

"I don't think it's tricky. It's just not something I do a lot."

"Well, that shirt gives me the ick."

"You should see what I wear to sleep."

I laughed.

"It must be because you have pretty-people complex." I sighed. "My sister Patricia went through it at your age. You never make the most of it. In fact, you usually fight the hot."

"What are you talking about, you nutjob? I'm a stunner."

"That's why your girlfriend dumped you," I muttered.

The girl at the bar turned around like a shot. Wow. I guess she was interested after all.

"That one's looking at you," I whispered.

"Idoia," he enunciated slowly, raising his eyebrows. "Idoia is the only one we're interested in here."

We ate the hot dogs sitting on a bench, in a plaza a little farther along. It was teeming with people. Every bar patio was hopping. The whole plaza was buzzing with conversation and laughter.

"So how am I going to figure out where my life is heading?" David asked, the corners of his mouth speckled with chili.

"I mean, I don't know."

"How did you know where yours was heading? Things seem to be going pretty well for you."

"I had it easy. I went into the family business."

"Wow. I'm jealous."

"Jealous? Don't be. Honestly, I never figured out what I wanted to do either. I just let myself be carried along. Except with Filippo, he was always a force of nature…"

"All right, lemme see a photo of this Filippo guy, come on. He can't be that hot."

"I mean what we had was…the clichéd love at first sight, but I'm not gonna lie; he's really hot. Like a prince."

"I'm gonna puke," he teased.

"First, wipe your mouth. You missed some."

I took my phone out of my bag and opened Instagram. Neither of us had very many followers because our profiles were set to private; thank my lucky stars, he hadn't blocked me yet. I scrolled through his profile, but before I could pick a photo to show David, I froze.

There was a new post. One where he looked really good, holding two beers, laughing, in a black T-shirt. Two beers. Was the other one for a pretty, striking girl, like David's ex-girlfriend, something I would never be? I struggled to swallow, but I made myself take a sip of my IPA.

"What's up?" David elbowed me gently.

"It's him. He just posted a photo."

"Fuck." He wiped his mouth with a napkin and whistled. "Holy shit. Okay, you're right. He's a hot enough dude to freak out over. Next to him, I'm more dog than human."

I didn't answer. I was reading his caption, in Italian.

"What does it say?" David asked.

"'A beer in Positano is the best life can do for me right now.' Do you think he misses me?"

"No."

I turned toward him, my eyes as wide as dinner plates.

"Thanks for your help," I bellowed.

"He's pissed off right now, Margot. You get that, right? You ran off on the day of your wedding. How would you feel?"

"Like shit."

"Have you thought about what you would do if the situation were reversed?"

"I would be begging him to come back."

David gave me an astonished look. "Seriously?"

"Of course. He's the love of my life."

"And you would grovel in front of a guy who left you at the altar?" His raised eyebrows made it very clear that the correct answer was no, but my mouth wanted to form a yes. David realized this and tried to stop it, like someone who thinks you're not ready for the truth. "Look, Margot, this hunk of a human specimen doesn't miss you…yet."

"I guess you men are simpler than us when it comes to facing your feelings, right?"

"Yeah, we are. Give it time."

"Do you think the other beer is for a girl?"

"He wants you to think that, I bet, but it's probably for the buddy who's taking the photo. That dude seems like he'd have a pretty flashy phone. He's not going to let the first girl he meets take photos of him while he goes to get beers."

I looked at him, perplexed. "You're even weirder than me, and I never thought I'd say that to anyone."

"You gonna finish that?"

I handed over my hot dog with a sigh.

"Hey," he said with his mouth full. "Just because there's a chance that he went to grab a bite with some girl one night doesn't mean you can't fix it with him."

"What if he falls in love with 'some girl'?"

"Then that means he didn't love you very much."

I looked at him, and he smiled. He had a piece of onion stuck in his teeth. I smiled back.

20

EASY

Candela started hounding me about where I had been as soon as I got home. Suddenly, reliving our boarding school days by living together didn't feel like such a great idea because I didn't have any desire to have to explain myself about this…or about anything. A few days before I had started experiencing a kind of fatigue that went way beyond physical. It was like I was tired of everything: TV, food, the conversations I heard on the street, radio, music, books, shows, all the shady messes my sisters were getting into, and even my own train of thought. Everything that was familiar to me, but especially anything that smelled vaguely of an interrogation.

Where was I coming from? From eating a hot dog and drinking two beers with the bartender from the dive bar they dragged me to when they were trying to help me get over my breakup.

"I just grabbed a bite with some friends," I lied easily.

She wouldn't understand it. I didn't even really understand it myself.

David messaged me the next day to ask me if I wanted to make plans, but I dragged my feet. I felt like it would be weird to suddenly be attached at the hip overnight. I had just met him, and even though it was true that he was one of the few people I felt comfortable with… it didn't seem normal to me. Deep down, really deep, our nascent friendship seemed weird to me. It had nothing to do with the fact that I was part of the board of a large multinational and I held a significant amount of its shares and he had three low-paid jobs. Or even with the fact that he was wearing black sweatpants when I met him in a park to pick up dog poop. It was just…he was the first and only person outside my normal life (work, social events, family) whom I had struck up a relationship with, and I didn't want to impose or obsess or entrust my whole heart to someone whom I still didn't really know, no matter how good his intentions might seem.

That evening, when I was already desperate at home, not knowing what to do, he texted me with the strangest proposition I had ever received in my life:

Wanna watch a movie and then talk about it?

He had told me he lived in Vallecas, and I lived on Paseo de la Castellana, but that night we watched *12 Angry Men* together despite the kilometers of distance. They were showing it on one of those oldies DTT channels, and we messaged about it the whole time it played.

~~~~~

Patricia suggested we meet up on Thursday morning. She needed to check how her jewelry brand display in a department store downtown was doing, and then she had been summoned to a meeting that wasn't going to leave her time to meet for lunch. So she thought a late breakfast was a good excuse for the three of us to catch up. And the plan seemed perfect. To them. I wanted to sit at home eating Doritos and watching *My 600-Lb. Life*, but, as usual, no one asked me what I felt like doing.

"I ran into Mama on the street," an ashen-faced Patricia said as soon as she sat down at the table where Candela and I were already settled and served. "She was drinking a mimosa on the patio of Hotel Wellington. Do you think we should be worried?"

"Look, look! Look how worried I am," Candela tossed out while she stuffed a huge bite of *tortilla de patatas* in her mouth.

"How's the store going?" I asked.

"Fine, fine. Listen, tomorrow I have to go see the detective. You're both coming with me, right?"

Candela nodded vehemently. The truth is she was living for this whole hiring-a-detective-to-trail-our-brother-in-law thing. She thought it was the best thing ever. I, however, pretended not be interested, looking at my phone.

"Hey, are you not coming?"

"I can't," I dropped without looking at her. "I have things to do."

"Aren't you on vacation?"

"Yes, but…I'm going on a trip," I informed them. "And I have things to finalize."

"What do you mean you're going on a trip?"

"Well…I was talking to Sonia, and she thinks I need to get out of here and find things I like to do. Rest. Sunbathe."

"Ah, well, if Sonia thinks so…" Candela threw down a piece of bread from her sandwich and cleaned her hands on a napkin. "Who's Sonia again? The one from work? The one with the eyes like an anime character, right?"

"My personal assistant."

"Your secretary," Patricia corrected disdainfully. "The one who was in your office the other day."

"You know you've inherited your mother's idiocy?"

"Well, I've noticed you inherited her flat ass," she retorted.

"Hey, hey, hey," Candela waved at us to calm down. "You, stop being such a snob! And I'll inform you," she pointed at me, "that I'm with Sonia. But I'm crashing at your house until you come back."

I rolled my eyes. "For fuck's sake, Candela. Fine, but you can't stay anywhere except the guest room. It's a pigsty in there, and I can't handle the chaos."

"Fiiiiiine," she muttered, chewing. "I'll stay 'til Patricia figures out this thing with Alberto. How long are you going for?"

"Two weeks. Or more. I don't know yet. I'll see."

"Sounds good."

"Hey! We're talking about my appointment with the detective!" Patricia protested.

Guess we're not going to dedicate more than two minutes to my terrible emotional state.

"So what do you have to do tomorrow?" Candela interrogated me with one eyebrow raised.

"Errands," I lied, stirring my café con leche. "Buying things."

"And you can't go some other day?"

I considered it. Maybe it was an obligation of being a good sister to go with them on any pointless mission, even if I didn't agree with it and thought it seemed like hot garbage. But…a feeling of utter apathy settled in the pit of my stomach. I didn't want to go.

"I can't," I heard myself say. "I already made plans with Sonia to lock down the details of the trip."

"Oh, right. The flights and all that," Patricia looked resigned. "Fine, we'll tell you all about it tomorrow night."

"Okay."

Patricia sighed.

"Alberto came home super late last night. Playing paddle tennis, he said." She waved over a waiter. "Could I have a *cortado*, please? And a *pincho*. Thank you. Obviously I didn't believe him, so I looked in his gym bag and…guess what I found?"

"A jockstrap?" Candela asked excitedly.

"Sweaty clothes. Really sweaty. Soaked like he had put them under a faucet. Do you think he could have gotten them wet on purpose? Except they did stink a bit. Do you think it's possible he wore his gym clothes to fuck his lover?"

"Sorry?" I asked.

"Yeah. So I wouldn't catch him. It would be a perfect alibi."

"Oy, oy, oy," Candela was laughing her head off.

I didn't even think about it. I grabbed my phone from the table, shoved it into my bag, and stood up.

"Where are you going?"

"I have to go."

"Now?"

"Where?"

"I just remembered that…I have to go."

Before I even realized what was happening, I found myself heading toward the florist.

~~~~

David was tying on his apron when I came in. Only one of the sisters was behind the counter, and she gave me a huge smile.

"Are you alone today?" I asked politely.

"My sister's at the doctor. She has a bad knee."

"I hope it gets better."

"Are you here for more flowers?" she asked.

"No," David declared, smiling at me and finishing the knot at the nape of his neck. He shook his hands and mockingly held out his right one to me. "She came to help me. Can she stay?"

I looked up at the woman, like she was David's mama and he was asking her if I could stay to play.

"Oh, you cad. Look at those little puppy eyes! Don't let anything happen to her because she's not insured and I don't want to go to jail. Ever since Pantoja got out, I have no desire to get thrown inside anymore."

I smiled, and we headed into the back of the store.

"David!" she yelled. "This isn't setting a precedent. And don't spend the whole afternoon yackety-yakking. Otherwise you'll have to pay me instead of me paying you."

"With a massage," he shot back. "Here."

He tossed me an apron that I tied on as I followed David to the back room, piled high with buckets, flowerpots, cloth, bows, and tissue paper.

"We have to make some arrangements for a wedding. Please, Margot focus."

He showed me a photo he had on the worktable of the final result, and with the same finger, he drew a path through all the flowers surrounding him.

"Watch me and then you can do a couple if you want."

"Okay."

He stretched his neck, cracked his knuckles, and got to it.

"Wait…aren't you going to ask me what I'm doing here?" I said, weirded out.

David looked at me out of the corner of his eye and smiled as he laced some flowers together by the stems surprisingly delicately for such rough hands.

"You came to be you for a little while. I get it. It feels good and… sucks you in."

The back room was quickly covered in small floral arrangements adorned with white bows and packaged into boxes. There were only a couple left to finish, and we chatted as we both worked. It was… relaxing.

"Then she said the thing about the gym clothes, and…I don't know, I just…I had to get out of there. I never do stuff like that. I always stay to listen, even if what they're saying takes years off my life. It's always been like this. I used to be a very polite person. What's happening to me?"

Explaining how my sister had ended up needing a private detective and the circumstances that led to her bringing it up when we saw each other had taken me longer than I thought, and surprisingly, I felt lighter after venting about all of it. More awake. Less responsible. It was so easy to talk to this near stranger.

"Nothing. It's completely normal. What wouldn't be normal is if you stayed to hear that horseshit. Your sister is paranoid."

"I don't get her either. Seriously. Where's all this coming from? Especially right now? Right after everything that…you know."

"*Maritus interruptus.*" He smiled.

"I have a theory that she's doing it so I don't think about Filippo and the INCIDENT too much, but…"

I turned to him with the last finished bouquet and handed it over. He studied it with a critical eye and then nodded his approval, gesturing for me to put it in a box.

"I'm boring you, right?" I asked him.

"Hmm? No, no, not at all. I was just thinking."

"About how boring I am?"

"Nooo." He laughed. "OMG. Exactly the opposite. This is like an IRL telenovela, like a choose-your-own adventure. The thing is… your sister seems like she's only thinking about herself."

"Maybe she spent so much time thinking about everyone else, fulfilling expectations, and now she just wants to focus on herself," I was making excuses for her, but deep down…I had just been talking shit about her a little.

"I'm not criticizing her," he clarified with a smile. "And I know you aren't either. Remember our rule: we don't judge each other."

"So?"

"So I think your sister is unhappy and she's looking for external causes. You have more in common than you think."

"You are judging!" I laughed.

"I'm giving you potential reasons so I don't have to say things like your sister is a jerk."

I let out a laugh, and he did too. He finished his arrangement and boxed it up.

"One thing I'm sure of is you were right to bounce." He stopped in front of me with his hands on his hips, and after a few seconds, he shifted them to my shoulders. "Seriously, don't feel bad."

"But that's exactly how I feel."

"Right now, you're into other things, Margot. Wild loop, remember?"

"Yeah, yeah, I remember, but…couldn't we make it a demure loop?"

"No, no," he teased. "OMG…we're going to have to make a list of things to accomplish on your trip to Greece."

"I really like checking things off lists."

"Great. Write it down while…Amparito!" he yelled. "The flower arrangements for the wedding are done! Ay…." He looked at me. "I didn't even think that maybe…this would be triggering for you."

"Why?"

"Wedding flowers."

"Oh, no. I don't even have a clue what mine looked like. Remember, I didn't even make it into the church."

"You're a brave little gangster," he roared with laughter. "I'm going to make dried flower bouquets now!"

"Great!" Amparito yelled from outside.

"As I was saying, you write while I make these bouquets. Go on."

I sat down at a worktable with my legs dangling and gestured for him to continue, but David went over to my bag, casually rummaged through it, and pulled out my phone.

"Hey! That's private property!"

"My head is too, and you fuck with it every time you give me one of your little advice things, so fucking deal with it."

"Advice you ask for, by the way."

"That I beg for desperately, true. Go on, write this down. If I have a notes app on my phone, you must too. Make the title 'Wild Loop.' Come on, I'm watching you."

He loomed over my shoulder as I manipulated the phone with both hands. I felt his unhurried breath on my skin, and I leaned to one side.

"You're breathing on top of me!"

"Sorry, so self-indulgent of me. What do I need oxygen for?"

Not only did he not move back, he stayed right there, centimeters from me despite my protests, while I tried to wriggle away and he laughed. David smelled like something that felt very familiar to me. Something I had smelled before, but it didn't really fit him.

"Hey, what do you smell like?"

"Me?" He looked at me. "Baby powder. I stole it from my friend's kid." He flashed his teeth at me in a weaselly smile.

"You're something else. You need to make a list too."

"Yours first."

I wrote Wild Loop on a note and hit enter. He nodded to himself and went back to his workstation.

"Eat moussaka."

"What?" I asked.

"Write down: *eat moussaka*."

"Jeez, this is going to be easier than I thought. Noted."

"Go topless."

I laughed and wrote it down, knowing there was no way in hell I'd do that.

"Skip out on paying at a restaurant. Skinny-dip. Get drunk. Sunbathe in the buff, of course. Drive a motorcycle. Have a wild night."

"What does *have a wild night* mean exactly?" I looked up at him and raised an eyebrow.

"Lady." He glanced at me and bit his lip as he cut some stems. "Make out with someone, at least. Ooh, look, you gave me an idea: make out with a girl. Moral obligation before you return."

"What about the wild night?"

"The wild night too. Write everything down. What else? Tell some lies. That's super fun. You have to spend a whole day telling lies. Everything that comes out of your mouth needs to be a whopper. And…did I already say skinny-dipping?"

"Yes."

"Then we're done. If I think of anything else, we'll add it to the list."

"You're realize you'll have no way of knowing if I do these or not?"

"Margot, you're a woman of your word." He winked. "Tell me you'll try at least."

"I'll try if you try too." I jumped up from the bench I was sitting on and grabbed my bag. "I'm leaving."

"Already?"

"I'm not going to spend the whole afternoon watching you work."

"What about my list?"

"I'll send it to you on WhatsApp."

He blew me a cheeky kiss, and I pretended to catch it and shove it into my bag.

"See you later. Bye, Amparito."

"Take care."

I hustled out of the florist, but with my phone in my hand. I dodged several passersby as I typed, alternating my gaze between traffic, people, and the screen. When I finished, I sent the message to David.

To Do List to Get a Modern Goddess Back:

- Stop saying *buddy*. You sound like a loser from the eighties.
- Wear clothes with no holes. Please, fabric is designed to be breathable already.
- Cut your hair/brush it. This is urgent.
- Put on a button-up shirt. Do this quickly.

- Change your scent. You don't count your age in months anymore.
- Get to know the noble art of eating in restaurants where everything isn't served in disposable containers. Do it for the ambiance at least.
- Find a room in an apartment with roommates. The whole couch-surfing thing gives girls the ick.
- Post photos where she can see them, where you're:
  › Having a lot of fun
  › Doing things you never did with her
  › With girls who aren't her
  › Not looking like you drink forties in the park while you eat seeds (no more sweatpants)
  › Working. The flower thing will get you laid

PS: We'll make you into a prince.
PPS: Scratch that.
PPPS: We'll make you into a god.

It didn't even take him two minutes to respond with:

Are we hanging tomorrow to go shopping?

When I caught my reflection in a store window...I was smiling.

When I got home...I smelled like flowers.

When I went to bed...I wasn't wondering anything. I had stopped worrying about pumping the brakes.

And now I wonder...how could we be the only ones who didn't see it coming?

21

~~~

SELF-CARE

We greeted each other with what had become our classic handshake, and he noticed that the afternoon before I had taken the time to go get a manicure and my nails were painted a soft pastel turquoise.

"Ooooh. So trendy!" he teased.

"Well, you're gonna freak out because I plan to buy super chic stuff."

"She-what?"

"Trendy, David, trendy."

He hadn't cut his hair, and of course he hadn't combed it. He was wearing faded jeans with a slightly dated cut and a black T-shirt that I held between my fingers and stretched as far as I could. On the left side, aha...a hole.

"What a fucking disaster." I laughed.

"Queen, since when does the wrapping matter when the gift is so great?"

We wandered down the street, not really knowing where to start. It was eleven in the morning, and stores were just starting to open, but Fuencarral Street was already teeming with people.

We walked without speaking, but I didn't feel the obligation to fill every silence. There was something about him that had made me feel that way from the very first day: comfortable.

"Why do we get along so well?" I made a face when the thought popped into my head.

"Because I'm weird, like you."

"Your weirdness and mine are like night and day."

"That's probably why." He tossed me a cheeky wink.

I thought there were a lot of curious things in his eyes, but I didn't know how to define any of them. Maybe because there are no words for the most beautiful things in life.

"I made a list of clothes that are essentials." I handed him a napkin I had scribbled on and noticed that, for some reason, I was blushing.

"You like your lists, eh?"

"A lot. I wrote it while I was eating breakfast."

David kept walking while he studied the napkin with a furrowed brow.

"Did you write this in Spanish or elvish?"

"Stop." I snatched it out of his hands and started to read out loud. "'Jeans. Black pants. A suit. A white button-up. A polo shirt.'"

"A polo shirt?"

A few passersby turned around after his cackles startled them. It was like watching a scene from *The Joker* live.

"What's going on?"

"A polo shirt? In your dreams. You're not going to dress me like some preppy *Cayetano*."

"Every man has a polo shirt."

"No. Every man should have socks that are mismatched or look like Swiss cheese and an ex who they would still fuck, but not a polo. Scratch the polo. And the suit."

"The suit?"

"Where do you want me to wear it? Walking the dogs?"

"There's always an occasion."

"I don't plan on getting married anytime soon, and no one is the right age to invite me to a funeral, so screw the polo and the suit. Go on."

"You didn't say anything about the white button-up, so I'm going to take that as a win."

"Scratch the white button-up. Not in a million years. I don't want to look like a waiter in Plaza Mayor."

I rolled my eyes. "Okay. Hmm…some new shoes."

"These are fine." He pointed to the ones he was wearing, which were battered and slightly faded.

I looked at his shoes and then at his face. I grabbed his arm to drive my message home.

"No, David. They're not fine, I promise."

"What's wrong with my jeans?"

"They're out of fashion."

"Did you come to that conclusion yourself, or did the girl who buys your clothes tell you?" he quipped like a smart-ass.

"Imagine how out of fashion they are if even I noticed."

"Touché. Anything else?"

"I assume you have decent underwear."

"Plain boxers. With no holes." He raised a solemn hand.

"Well, then I think we should take a look at the T-shirt section too…just in case you don't feel like walking around looking like a colander."

He cleared his throat and looked at me a little more seriously than usual. *Hmm, intense.* We already had things that were usual.

"Listen, Margot…I…I can't spend a lot of money."

"Oh…right." I suddenly felt a little thrown off. I had never had this problem before, so…I felt a little uncomfortable and superficial. Guilty about my privilege. "What's your budget?"

"If I say fifty euros, I'm going to sound stupid."

"No. You don't sound stupid. I'm sure with…I don't know… seventy? We could work miracles."

"What about you?"

"What about me?"

He shot me a strange look. "What about you? Because it's not fair if I don't write a list of essentials."

"I mean, go ahead then…"

"Gimme a couple minutes."

We kept strolling, peering into window displays on one side of the street and then the other, but David seemed much more focused on observing the people he was passing by than on the clothes. Every now and again he would take his phone out of his pocket, make a note of something with a playful look on his face, and then put it back. He was making his list.

We had almost reached the Tribunal metro stop when we realized that maybe it would be easier to go straight to Zara. It had clothes for both of us, its stuff was usually affordable, and it managed to provide options with personality that were stylish and fashionable. We turned around, and he kept mockingly writing things on the list.

Until we got to Gran Vía. And he handed me his phone.

Pleated skirt

Transparent stuff

Floral dress. Short

Converse shoes

Something with sequins

Very big earrings

Wide-legged pants

A band T-shirt

Something leopard print

A hat

Shorts

A super tight dress

A long dress

Something that shows your belly button

I stared at it. Right in front of me, dressed like a college kid with no concept of elegance, David had managed to localize the fashion trends of the summer just in a single stroll around Madrid.

"You might need to buy a fanny pack too," he said, side-eyeing all the girlies who had them slung across their chests.

"Not in a million years. I don't have enough swagger. And the ones about flaunting my belly button and running around in something super tight are vetoed too."

"We'll see."

When we got into Zara, we ended up dying of laughter, getting prepped for some kind of bizarre and demented competition where no one would win but there would definitely be a loser. Probably our wallets.

I would choose the things he had to try on, and he would choose mine. Taking turns, to make it more fun. I wanted to go first, of course, so I dragged him to the men's floor and demanded eagerly that he tell me all his sizes.

"No idea." He shrugged. "You look. I wear a size forty-four shoe, that I do know."

"What do you mean, *look*?"

"Well, I still haven't learned how to twist my head around and look at my back, but hey, doesn't Mr. Wonderful say nothing is impossible if you really put your mind to it?"

I grabbed his arm roughly, like he was a little boy, and spun him around, which must have seemed very funny to him because he burst into laughter. I peeked under the waist of his trousers and caught a glimpse of a tight butt in black boxers. I blushed a little and almost forgot what number I had read on the label, but I blinked a couple of times and then did the same with his shirt. His back was tan and wide, and there was an indentation down the middle. I noticed there was a whitish mark from a couple of scratches. Damn Idoia…or damn him, who knows?

I zoned out for a few seconds, then shook myself out of it, and planted myself in front of him.

"Ready."

"You enjoyed that, eh?"

And he said it with an arched eyebrow and a sly smile.

I had never noticed his eyebrows… They were messy, but they gave him a look…a something. Something. I couldn't put my finger on what it was.

He vetoed shorts that he said looked like a "politician who summers in Mallorca" (mental note, never introduce him to my uncle Luis) and sneakers that were "worse than wearing loafers made of gophers." I have no idea why he cracked up when he said that. But still, I got him to try on some skinny jeans, some black ankle-cropped chinos, some T-shirts, a patterned shirt, and…a white button-up! He didn't resist. He went into the changing room alone, weighed down by all the clothes.

"I'll wait for you here." I pointed to one of the racks of clothes.

"You're not coming in with me?"

"Me?"

"Of course. How am I going to know if they look good on me?"

"Trust your intuition." I gave him a few encouraging pats on the arm and moved away.

He stared after me like an abandoned puppy as I left, but I didn't give in. Digging around in his pants to find out his size had already been too far. What was I thinking?

He was quick. When I saw him come out, he was looking at the tags on the things he hadn't thrown onto the table outside the changing rooms. He looked disheveled, giving off "survivor of an accident in a wind tunnel" vibes.

"Let's see…I'll take these." Focused, he let his eyelids droop and piled clothes into my arms.

Two basic T-shirts; a patterned shirt with short sleeves, not too patterned; the jeans; and the black pants.

"What about the white button-up?"

"Fuck that shit."

"But I'm sure it looked great on you!"

"71.75 Euros," he replied very seriously, his eyes wide.

While we wandered around the women's floor and David eyed the clothes racks, I felt a minor panic attack. Nothing as bad as the day I sent my relationship and my discretion to hell, but similar to how I felt when I opened the clothes my mother had sent to boarding school for the days we didn't have to wear a uniform, but on the opposite end of the spectrum. Everything seemed so…small? Tight, of course. And low-cut. Risqué. Young.

"Size?"

I pretended to be deaf. I don't know why we, especially women, have so many hang-ups when it comes to saying our size out loud, whatever it may be. It's just a number sewn into a piece of cloth.

But David didn't have enough patience to give me time to realize I was going to have to tell him no matter what, so I felt myself being dragged behind a rack, where he studied the labels inside my clothes just like I had done to him.

"You've gotta be fucking with me," I heard him murmur.

"What?"

"You match your bra to the color of your shirt?"

"Leave me alone! You're having too much fun with this!"

"You say that like you didn't do the same."

He pushed past me and gave me a very smug wink.

"I didn't have that much fun," I justified myself.

"It doesn't matter, silly. If it scratches an itch, it doesn't matter to me. I know you're really lonely."

I didn't think twice before I grabbed an empty hanger and smacked him across the back with it. I don't think he was expecting my reaction, but…well, I don't think he thought I could be…spontaneous either. I was usually more rigid, a tough nut to crack, immovable.

David started wandering through the clothing racks with a scientific interest and specific protocol: first he did a long loop around the floor only to turn and retrace his steps all the way back. Just when I was starting to think nothing would satisfy him, he scooped up a black bodysuit and a pair of matching…shorts. He tossed them into my arms and darted toward a flowery ruffled skirt that another girl was clutching.

"Sorry, excuse me? Fashion emergency," he said, before snatching the hanger from her hands.

I had to hide behind the clothes he was tossing at me so she wouldn't see me laugh.

"This dress will give you a good pair," he said very certainly, looking at a very tight and colorful garment with a neckline cut down to the belly. "Can I say that without sounding sexist?"

"I'm not sure."

"I'm not objectifying you. Judging by the bra you're wearing, I get the impression you care how people see...you know, how they see your bust."

"How do you know what kind of bra I'm wearing just from the back, you troll?"

"Because the tag was sticking out, and even I can read 'Wonderbra.'"

"Eat shit."

"Not my fave, thanks."

Never, ever, had anyone acted so naturally with me, and...I still needed time to figure out if I liked it or not.

A leopard-print skirt and a silver-sequined miniskirt flew into my arms. I stared at them, flabbergasted.

"Do you remember where we saw those white pants...the crazy wide ones?"

"No," I answered in my best tough-guy voice.

"Ah, yes. Here they are."

Those pants and another tight, low-cut, ribbed white shirt joined the pile. Then a see-through top.

"Are you nuts?"

The snicker that escaped him sounded exactly like *mwahaha*.

He was getting cocky. Really cocky. I was scared I had created a monster, and I imagined him decked out in black, with a turtleneck and thick-framed glasses, sitting in the front row of New York Fashion Week, harshly critiquing the models for a major magazine. Well…at least that would be a successful future. Maybe it wouldn't be so bad.

"David, what does *success* mean to you?" I asked him.

"Winning the lottery without even buying a ticket?"

"No."

"Then being free."

"What do you mean *being free*?"

I could barely hold any more, but he still added a spaghetti-strap dress in a material I would guess was satin and a crop top to the teetering heap in my arms.

"You know. Time to do whatever I really want at any moment. I'm sure true luxury has nothing to do with money in a material way. Luxury, which is what money really buys, is time and freedom."

His scruffy eyebrows arched as he talked, and as he said the last word, he licked his lips, like his mouth was dry, like he had just given a speech where he revealed more about himself than he meant to.

"That's very wise."

"That short red romper'll be perfect for the 'kissing a girl' night in Greece," he said, pointing.

I was starting to discover that David swung between an interesting duality; on one hand, he made me roar with laughter, even when I didn't want to, and on the other…he made me think.

"This one with white Converse." He plucked a hanger with a short patterned skirt from the rail. "And this one." He grabbed another one with a white cropped shirt sure to show the midriff. "It'll be lit."

"Please tell me you're not copying Idoia's looks."

"What? No! Idoia loves lace, see-through stuff, and latex."

I made a face, which he answered with a purr.

"Chop, chop, into the changing room."

"You know you can only take in six items at a time, right?" I asked with a mountain of clothes in my arms.

"Well, then hurry…we have a lot of trips to make."

I didn't let him come in. That was the deal. He would stay outside the dressing room, and I would come out with the reject pile and get more clothes. And there were a lot of rejects: the see-through top was the first, the red romper the second, and the silk dress alongside it. Though I was pleasantly surprised by it, the sequin miniskirt still had the same fate, but he soon showed up with some wide-legged pants, cropped at the ankle, to fill that role. I decided to take everything else. Even those last ones. And, for the first time in a long time, I had the urge to walk out wearing some of the clothes, to rip off the tags and look at myself in the mirror after throwing a few of them together into funky outfits. I felt…playful? I don't know. Ready to take risks. Basically, I was definitely going to pack all of these for my trip. Nobody I knew would see me in them. It would be like the costume a superhero uses to disguise herself. It would be my new identity in the role of a spy. It would be what a teenager would hide in the bottom of her closet because Mama doesn't approve and she liked it more than her uniform.

When we paid and got out of there, I felt more gratitude toward the boy who was complaining about the price of jeans than for many of those lifelong friendships who…hadn't returned my calls since the wedding. The ones who knew exactly who I was, who invited me to their vacations on a yacht or who came to gossip at the events I attended. And I felt so indebted that…when we said goodbye at the metro so that he could drop all his new stuff off at home before he went to work, when I watched him trot down the stairs at the mouth of Gran Vía, getting lost among the people with the sound of a street saxophonist floating over them…I decided that we deserved to let our new friendship come to fruition. He had to get Idoia back if that was what he wanted, and in the meantime I would strive to tease as many smiles out of him as I could.

I passed a shoe store and bought three pairs of Converse, one white, one black, and another for him, which I sent to the bar with a messenger and a note: "I bought myself a matching pair. You deserve them."

I reread his reply at least four times, feeling thrilled and like I was doing something crazy each time.

I hope we wear the soles out walking around Madrid together. Thank you so much, Margot. Maybe sad people can do much more than understand each other.

22

NOTHING MAKES ME FEEL LIKE YOU DO

Apparently, the private detective industry was disappearing, but the few left standing seemed to make up for the lack of clients by hiking up their prices. Patricia didn't say the exact fee, just that it was going to cost a "small fortune."

"Is it worth it?"

"It'll be worth it during the divorce process," she declared, her tone hardened.

Poor Alberto. And I say, "Poor Alberto," because he had no idea what he'd done to make Patricia so convinced, hook, line, and sinker, that he was cheating on her. He adored her. Ever since they first got together, so many years ago, he had adored her. He always showered her with beautiful words that weren't just blowing smoke up her ass. Alberto demonstrated every day that he loved her with blind trust on every project she took on, like an enthusiastic and committed life partner, looking at her like she was a Marian apparition and he was a shepherd boy. They had always personified couple goals, the example for everyone to strive for.

"What if she's the one who wants to get separated and she's looking for a reason to back her up?" I asked Candela that night.

"That's super twisted even for you."

I shot her a side-eye. She'd been acting weird ever since she came home. Like she was suspicious or on the defensive.

"It's not twisted," I defended myself. "It's…a pretty feasible explanation."

"If she wanted to get separated, she would say so, right? People don't look for elaborate excuses to leave someone."

"Or maybe they do. The human mind…"

"The human mind is complicated, fine. But now you better tell me what you're doing when you're out all the time."

I was caught off guard, and I didn't know what to tell her; I swallowed and instinctively hid my phone under my thigh in case David texted me and replied, "What are you talking about?"

I mean, I had to buy some time.

"Did I stutter? I couldn't have been clearer. When you go out, when you tell us you 'have things to do' and you're talking about 'preparations for your trip,' like you're going to walk the Camino de Santiago or as if we live in the eighteenth century and you're going to traverse Africa in a horse carriage…tell me…what are you really doing?"

"I'm getting ready for the trip."

"Oh yeah? Can you show me any of those preparations?"

"Well…I don't have to."

"What do you mean you don't have to? Now you're getting cute with me?"

"I'm not getting cute. It just seems…like a lack of respect. A lack of privacy as an adult and as a woman." I was on a roll now. "Because nobody asks you when you're out there, in Nordic lands, what you're doing or what you're not doing. No one even asks you why you've colonized my guest room when you were supposed to be at Mama's house."

"Mama is a sphynx cat who drinks too much and even worse she doesn't want us. How long did you think I was going to last in the dandruff-covered, undiluted, diabolical version of the Barberini Palace? Why?" She looked at me with suspicion in her bulging eyes. "Am I bugging you while you 'prepare for your trip'?"

"I mean…" I feigned disappointment "Come on, Candela. What would I be hiding from you? Because if you're grilling me like this, you must suspect something."

It's better to make your enemy show their cards before you try to bluff.

"That you're seeing someone."

"Yes, of course. Why don't you ask the detective if you can get a two-for-one?"

"You're meeting up with someone."

"And I fled my wedding because I'm in love with someone else, of fucking course."

"You are?"

"Candela!" And I admit I raised my voice, but only to try to cover the noise of my phone vibrating as an endless stream of WhatsApps came in.

"What's that?"

"What's what?"

"That sound. Are you hiding your phone under your leg?"

"No." I made a surprised face. "What are you talking about? I have a Satisfyer for that. It's a good invention, the Satisfyer. Highly recommend it."

"Give me your phone."

"What?"

"Give me your phone. Are you deaf? Give me your phone right now."

"Under what authority?"

"Under the 'holy shit I'm going to kick the shit out of you if you don't.'"

I edged back a little. Candela was small, but she really could kick the shit out of me. I remembered too vividly how she whacked me with a paperback once because I borrowed a sweater. She was already starting to tussle with me.

I dug my nails into her hand. She didn't even flinch. I kicked out to stop her from grabbing my phone. She pinned me down by the neck like a kitten. She got the phone.

"Wait, who's sending you all these messages?"

"Someone from work. It's nothing. It's just work. I'm…okay, you caught me, I'm secretly working."

"And a dumbass. Who's David?"

"I already told you! Someone from work."

She took a couple of steps into the middle of the room, which didn't take long because, according to the decorator, these types of apartments used architecture instead of interior design and shouldn't have too much furniture. Idiots. The least cozy house in the world.

Candela looked at the screen, typed, and, to my surprise, unlocked the phone. Why would anyone think it was a good idea to use their birthday as their password?

"Let's see what could possibly be so important at work that they had to tell you at eleven on a Friday night. 'I'm wearing the shoes, they're awesome. They're so clean, they're glowing in the club. Okay, okay, I confess I'm also wearing the jeans. I realized they make my butt look really good. Watch out, I'm probably going to be snapped up by some scout from a major modeling agency and you'll be left without a friend.'"

Candela looked at me, and as I held her stare, she started to gape like a fish. Her mouth formed an O and an A at the speed of light, her eyes shooting out of their sockets.

"What?" I screamed, fully losing my shit.

"Wait, who the hell is this, and why is he texting these things to you?"

I don't know what came over me. All I know is that I couldn't hold in my pout, and before I realized it, I was crying. But it was a full-on meltdown…like a little kid when they get caught in a fib or you scold them for something they know is bad.

"It's just David!" I moaned between sobs.

"But…but…? No, for fuck's sake, Margot, don't cry. Come on…" She sat down next to me. "I'm not giving you shit. Well, I am. But only because…I don't know. You've never had a lot of guy friends. Girlfriends, yes, well, those snobs who you go on vacation with sometimes who pose next to their purses, but guy friends…no."

"He's just a friend," I blubbered. "And…I…I…I have a really good time with him."

"Okay, okay. Get a grip."

"Is it bad?" flew out of my mouth.

"Is what bad?"

"Having a new guy friend right now."

"But is he a new friend? When did you meet him?"

I gnawed on my nails.

"That's such a cool nail polish. So trendy."

"That's what he said."

Candela flipped her hair nervously.

"When did you meet him, Margot? Please tell me it's not a cyberfriend who you've never met from social media or… Look, there are always sketchballs who find a way to take advantage of people like you."

"It's not like that. I met him…the night we went out."

"Who?"

"Us. The day Patricia told us that Alberto has a lover."

Candela raised her eyebrows and sat back a little.

"That night? I didn't see you talking to anybody."

"The bartender…"

"The one with curly hair, blond, looked like a surfer?"

"No." I wiped my nose on the back of my hand. "The brunette. The one who gave us that last shot for free."

"Wait…the one who picked up all Patricia's shit after she threw it over the bar?" I nodded, and she kept talking. "But how the hell did you end up being such good friends in…I don't know, a week?"

"I don't know. Patricia lost her phone, and he found it. But don't tell her I told you… You know how weird she is. She always wants to be the perfect lady. She didn't want anyone to find out. That's why I didn't tell you. The next day, she made me go get it, and…he was super nice, and suddenly his ex showed up, and I wanted to do him a solid… Look, I don't know. The only thing I do know is he's the only person who makes me laugh lately."

"Thanks a lot." She crossed her arms.

"Don't be like that, Cande. It's just… He's a stranger. He doesn't judge me. He's fun. He doesn't treat me differently because of the money or my position in the business. And he's giving me good advice about how to get Filippo back."

"To get Filippo back?"

"Yes. He wants to get Idoia back, his ex. And we're helping each other."

"How?"

"Giving each other advice, talking. We went shopping." I smiled a little. "And we get each other."

Candela let out a frustrated sigh and then looked at me dead-on. "But you don't even know him."

"I mean. I know him a little."

"You don't know him, Margot. He could turn out to be a big letdown."

"Well…nobody can be trusted. Look what I did to Filippo."

"That was different. You…were… You had a panic attack. You've always been too hard on yourself, and you can't always be made of steel."

"Cande…he's a good guy."

"How do you know?"

"I know."

The phone, which Candela was still gripping fiercely in one hand, vibrated again. She looked at it, more out of habit than a desire to check.

"He says, 'Are you okay, it's weird you're not answering.' And, 'If you want to come have a drink, the club is dead.'"

"I'll answer him now."

Candela looked back and forth between me and the phone several times before she decided and started to type.

"What are you doing?"

"Take it." She handed the phone back to me. "Come on, get changed."

Her answer was still on the screen:

I'll be there soon. I'm bringing Candela.

I put on the skirt David had snatched from the girl in Zara and paired it with a black shirt and matching Converse. Anyone else probably would have been weirded out seeing me in such an obviously new look, but Candela didn't notice stuff like that. She was wearing baggy patchwork pants, and I prayed our mother hadn't seen them (or she'd be going on about them for months after Candela left) and a white tank top that made her look flat as a board. She looked like a formal dining room painting in a bohemian home.

The street was definitely quiet when we got there. It was early, to be fair. A few hours later, hordes of people from all the surrounding bars would probably pack the place, but when we went in, it was practically empty. Just the two other bartenders chatting to each other behind the bar right at the entrance and him in the back.

David smiled when he saw us, and I smiled back almost unconsciously. He did a drumroll on the bar with his fingers and shouted: "Ta-da!"

Candela side-eyed me, and I hid my smile with a surreptitious throat clearing.

"How's it going?" I said, pretending to be a completely sane person.

"Amazing! We're debuting the look!"

"As you can see."

He high-fived me when we got over to the bar and then gave me a thumbs-up.

"You look great. You've taken off…I don't know, at least two years and a stick up your ass."

"You're a dumbass," I exclaimed, embarrassed. "Do you remember Candela?"

"Of course. How's the private detective?"

"You told him?" she asked, shocked.

"I needed to vent."

"She told me the other day while we were making flower arrangements." He smiled at me. "But don't worry, your secret's safe with me. Anyway…when am I going to see Patricia again? I don't think she'll come back here. She didn't even want to come get her phone."

"She was probably embarrassed. Or too busy with her mental derangement," Candela muttered, sitting down on one of the stools flanking the bar.

"What can I get you?"

"I'll have a beer," I said.

Candela's second side-eye didn't go unnoticed.

"What?"

"Nothing. I don't remember you liking beer. I'll have one too."

"Where's Ivan?"

"He comes in a little later today. Domi gets off work at ten, and by the time she gets home and all that…" He looked at Candela. "Dominique is Ivan's girlfriend. They have a seven-month-old daughter so they have to switch off," he explained.

"Wow."

"Yeah."

He opened two bottles, cleaned their mouths with a napkin, and then passed them to us with another wrapped around them so our fingers wouldn't get wet from the dripping glass.

"What's new with you ladies?"

"What about you two?" my sister said before she took a sip of beer, looking back and forth threateningly between the two of us.

"Well, not much. We went shopping yesterday. Apparently, according to your sister, I've been going around looking like a bum. I'm trying to win my ex back, and Margot says she has to turn me into a god." He patted his chest softly through his bar shirt.

A smile spread across Candela's face. "Hey…what do you mean *flower arrangements*?"

"I work at a florist, and she came to see me the other day."

"Ah…that's why you have flowers in your room," she said, seeming very satisfied to have found clues about my secret friendship without even realizing.

I don't know why, but her mentioning that the flowers were in my bedroom made me blush. It made me embarrassed. As you can see. They were just flowers, and I didn't have them there because I liked David. I didn't like him, I swear. I just got along with him.

Right then, Ivan rushed in apologizing.

"Dude, sorry, sorry." He turned to the other bartenders. "Hey, girls."

"No worries, it's super dead in here tonight; there must be a soccer game on. Do you remember Margot?"

"Of course. Your new fake girlfriend."

David and I looked instinctively at Candela, who was polishing off her beer.

"This is Candela, her sister. She was here last week. I don't know if you remember."

"With all the people who pass through this bar…" He studied us for a second and raised his eyebrows in surprise. "Jeez, you two are like night and day."

"Yeah. I came from the non-Nordic branch of the family." I pointed at myself. "The regular Spanish half."

"The whole being blond and tall thing is overrated," David said, crinkling his nose.

"Of course, like Idoia."

"Idoia isn't a natural blond." He winked. "But I'm not going to tell you how I know."

"Subtle. Can't possibly imagine." I rolled my eyes.

"Your pants rock," Ivan said to my sister, going behind the bar.

"Hers? Have you seen mine? They give me an ass that could stop trucks!" David exclaimed, waving his hands over his back pockets.

The truth is, objectively speaking…they did look really good on him.

"I have similar ones for when I go surfing," Ivan was telling my sister, ignoring David.

"You surf?"

"Yes. Well, when I can. In September, I'm going to spend a week in Zarauz if I can swing it. My lady is getting some vacation time too, and we're gonna take our little girl. So she can breathe sea air when she's little."

"That's so cool," Candela said. And she meant it. She liked him. "I was in South Africa a few years ago, and I caught a few waves."

"You?" I gave her a puzzled look, but she ignored it.

"South Africa! That's awesome. I'm jealous. Tell me, what kind of board…?"

I tuned out the conversation because it was clear I wasn't going to understand a word and I didn't really care. When I looked up, David was staring at me.

"She caught you with your hands in the cookie jar, didn't she?" he whispered to me.

"Totally. She started screaming at me that I was hiding something."

"Are you hiding me?"

"Of course not." David raised his eyebrows and I smiled. "I mean, yes. I'm hiding you as much as I can. Candela will keep it secret for me."

"Oh, wow. I'm a secret. What exactly are you ashamed of? That we just met a week ago?"

"To be honest: yes. That and the fact that I made a new friend so soon after the INCIDENT. I should probably be—"

"Wearing a black veil when you go out on the street. Margot! Girl. We're in the twentieth century."

"We're in the twenty-first century, David."

"Don't change the subject." A hint of a wolfish smile played at his lips, but then he scratched the stubble on his cheeks and leaned on the bar with a serious look. "Give me the scoop. Have you heard anything from Filippo?"

"No."

"Hey…you've been crying." David jabbed a finger very close to my eyes.

"No. Leave me alone."

"What am I gonna do with you?" He sighed. "We have to figure out a good communication strategy for when you're away. That'll work magic. When I see that you've gone full Kerouac, backpack on your shoulder, hitchhiking on highways, finding yourself—"

"I'm surprised you know that literary reference, to tell the truth."

"And I'm surprised you're going to bring a backpack on your trip, but these are just empty words." He booped my nose. "Do you have a date set?"

"Monday."

"You're leaving on Monday?" he exclaimed.

"Nooo. On Monday, Sonia's going to give me all the details."

"Who's Sonia? Another sister?"

"No. She's...my assistant."

"Fucking hell...so fancy, you gazillionaire."

I suddenly felt tense. He did too, matching my energy. We both cleared our throats.

"You're going to have to get going with your Instagram feed so he can see you: super modern, superhot, tan, going topless on the beach..."

"I guess I'm gonna have to buy a selfie stick."

"You'll meet people, you'll see."

"Because I'm so charming..."

"Hey, look at us. Ten days ago we didn't even know each other."

"And now we're going shopping together."

"These jeans give me such a great little butt..." He waggled his head, smiling. "Wanna see it?"

"Immediately no. Hard pass. Have you heard anything from Idoia?"

"No. But it won't be long. I can feel it in my whole being."

I let out a cackle. The thing is...it wasn't even what he said anymore; it was...David. He was funny, natural; we were comfortable with each other. He had a beautiful smile with white teeth, the shadow of a still-scraggly beard on his chin, and deep eyes, like a well, like a night, like...

"Post a photo on your Insta. Does she follow you?" Candela asked.

I was surprised my sister joined in the conversation, shattering the silence that had enveloped us since we started looking at each other, but I actually thought it was a good suggestion. To be honest, I was annoyed I hadn't thought of it first.

"My Instagram isn't really like that. Plus, I barely use it."

"Let's see."

He took out his phone.

"Look, Candela, David has a calculator that makes phone calls."

"Look, Candela, your sister is so hilarious," he retorted, turning the phone toward us.

The screen's quality was terrible. I mean really bad. I wondered if there might be some spare phone at the business that an employee had given back. The kind that most would consider half obsolete already but was ten times better than his. But I didn't say anything, of course. It wasn't my place, and I looked like a superficial asshole every time I brought it up.

David's Instagram account had six photos. Not one more, not one less. The photos were varied, but he wasn't in any of them: a still from a movie, a girl's hands pouring wine into a glass, three guys (whose faces were cropped out) wearing the same classic shirt with the "I Heart NY" slogan, someone's legs walking down the street in front of a sign that said, "Turkey breasts on sale," a shelf full of bottles (definitely taken right in this spot), and the cliché sunrise taken from an airplane window. Each of them had six or seven comments from the same people, who called him "modern" or "artist" in a mocking tone. I imagined they must be the friends from the village he had told me about.

"You're planning to seduce her with that?" Candela asked.

"Of course. I'm more than just a perfect ass." He tapped his temple. "I'm going to get her back with my creativity and intellect."

"That's a crock of shit. Go off about your intellect as much as you want in person, but on social media it just seems like virtue signaling."

"So then what? I should take cringe shirtless photos?"

"No. Take good photos where you look hot. Look, come here. I'm going to take one. Margot, give me your phone."

"Listen to her," I said to David, handing my phone over to Candela. "She travels a lot, and she's an expert in photos that make other people jealous."

I watched them head toward the door arguing about whether posing with your hand on your beard made you look like a jerk or not. When I snapped out of it, I realized Ivan was looking at me.

"There he goes, the model," he quipped.

"The things people do for love."

"I'm more the type to make hot chocolate in August because she has a craving." He scratched his head.

"I bet you don't even have Instagram."

He shook his head, and we both smiled.

"Look, look, look," David ran back over with my phone in his hand. On his you would've just seen maddening pixels. "Send it to me. I'm gonna post it right now."

"No!" I said, grabbing his arm. "Tomorrow at like two in the afternoon. And in the caption put something that makes it clear someone sent it to you…someone you were with last night. The whole night."

"Whoa, you're such a witch! I love it!"

In the photo, he had his back turned, talking to the half of the bouncer's torso that was in the frame. It was candid, but it felt like a behind-the-scenes shot from a movie set. As if he was an actor and the photographer, a professional photographer, had caught him in such a human and quotidian moment. I noticed the name of the bar was on the back of his T-shirt too and…it was just a reflex; I didn't mean to look at his ass. It was just that…I saw the name of the club on his back and my eyes drifted down naturally to his behind (*jesus-fuckingchristwhatanass*). I swallowed. My sister was looking at me.

"You're so thirsty. Stop undressing me with your eyes." David pulled my phone away with a smile. "Should I take a few of you for your Insta?"

"How old is he?" Candela asked right in front of him.

"Twenty-seven. You can tell, right?"

"I thought he was younger."

"Come on, Margot, you look really pretty. I'm sure Felipe will die when he sees you."

"His name is Filippo, and I don't want him to die."

"I know, I know. Come on, you loon!"

"I don't think seeing me in the door of a nightclub will soothe him or seduce him much."

David's face fell, and he handed my phone back.

"Jeez, you're right. Your strategy and mine need to be completely different. We better meet up on Monday in a café I know. It's beautiful, full of flowers…and I'll take a classy photo of you. Reading or something like that. You could put…um…'My sisters, a coffee, and a book. Saying goodbye to Madrid and all my headaches for a few days.'"

"That's good." Candela nodded.

"It's not my amazing ass, but…"

I punched him in the shoulder, and we both burst out laughing. Candela kept staring at us.

~~~~~

"Be careful."

Candela spoke in such a small voice it barely reached me. I didn't want her to repeat it because I had actually heard her perfectly, though I didn't understand why she was saying it. I looked at her, walking next to me on the sidewalks of the Barrio de las Letras, and I furrowed my brow.

"But why? Didn't you see? He's a good guy. He has three jobs, he helps out in his friend's house, and…"

"Not because of that. I don't think he's trying to get anything out of you…economically speaking. But…"

"But what?"

"He's the kind of guy who makes you laugh, Margot."

"So? That's a good thing, isn't it?"

"No." She smiled sadly. "Those are the kind you never forget."

I stopped in the street, and she did too. We stared at each other; I was waiting for her to explain herself, and Candela seemed to be searching for the right words.

"Margot, you've only known each other for a week, and…look at you guys! Something's going to happen between you and that guy."

"What? No way!"

"No, not no way. I know it. And I'm not judging. When it happens, if you want to tell me, I won't judge, and I'll take the secret to my grave, but you need to be clear about what you're doing."

"He's just a friend. Men and women can be just friends."

"Yes, but you and that dude aren't going to be."

"Why are you saying this?" I chided her, overwhelmed. "You saw us together for what? An hour?"

"The first five minutes were enough. It's going to rear its head. It's already there, right under the surface. And it makes sense: you're a beautiful girl, a stunner, and he's a cutie. It's forbidden, I'm sure it's half-wild…It's tempting, I know."

"Cande, I'm really not following you."

"It's going to happen, and it's not the kind of thing where you'll have two romps in bed and then say goodbye. That guy makes you laugh, Margot. I've never seen you so bubbly and relaxed. There's something about him that awakens the person you want to be, and that…there's no going back from that. I'm not telling you not to do it, to be clear. I was the first one who supported you the day of the INCIDENT. I'm just asking you to do one thing: think it through."

"Nothing's going to happen."

"Do you want to get Filippo back?"

"More than anything in the world," I said right away, firm and convinced.

"Well then, get one thing straight: David is going to fall in love with you. And you with him. If you don't want that to happen, pump the brakes because I don't think it's going to be the usual story of a summer fling."

I didn't know what to say. She seemed like a total drama queen, and I was embarrassed. How could she have read anything between us except friendship? Okay, we had just met, but…

My phone buzzed in my bag, and I started walking again as I looked for it. I needed to get this out of my head. I had the urge to run away and never look back, to never text him or pick up his calls again. I didn't see him that way! I mean…I had looked at his ass for one second, but…what did that matter?

I looked at my phone screen and stopped dead.

"What's going on?" Candela asked.

"It's Filippo," I responded in a tiny voice. "He says his trip is working wonders to clear his head and think about what's important, and he misses me." I looked at my sister, my hopes soaring, with a lump in my throat. "He says he hopes I'm doing the same as him and that I'll realize I'm yearning for him too. That he hopes we're on the same page when the summer ends and we can restart our life together."

"Margot…" Candela smiled tenderly.

"He loves me." I clutched my chest, all smiles and excitement. "He loves me, Cande! He loves me!"

I launched myself onto her and held on tight. When her arms wrapped around me, I had to stifle an attempted sob, so I stayed there for a few more seconds, leaning on my sister's shoulder, happy and emotional. Hopeful.

"Jeez, Margot," I heard her say.

"What?"

"Don't listen to me. I'm babying you. Make friends with whoever you want, okay?"

23

DRUNKEN BENDER OF HOPE

DAVID

At two in the afternoon, I posted the photo Margot had sent me on my Instagram account and waited with my phone in hand for Idoia to show signs of life (and of interest). But after checking my phone every five minutes for a while, I finally got sick of it.

"This isn't love," crooned Domi, who had the day off and was finishing up making some yuca balls, a specialty from her country.

"It's called courtship, woman of little faith," I retorted.

Ada screamed from her baby bouncer, and I went over to scoop her up. Her mother gave me a stern look because she insisted her daughter would never learn to self-soothe if we picked her up all the time.

"Domi, I'm thinking I'm going to wait twenty years and just marry your daughter."

"Over my dead body."

I burst out laughing and went over to the tiny kitchen.

"First of all, I'm offended by how grossed out you are, and, second, it's obviously a joke. I love Ada like she was my niece."

"I'm not grossed out. It's just that…" She looked at me and smiled. "You're one of those guys, and that's not what I want for my daughter."

"What guys?"

"Ay, David, the kind who feel too much."

My phone started to buzz on the table, a stream of messages coming in, and I ran over to it with Ada in my arms. The sudden movement made her giggle.

"See, Domi? It's gotta be her! This is going great. You should buy a wedding hat because in twenty years, we're getting married."

Ada tried to grab my phone when I picked it up, but I kept it out of her reach. It was Margot.

> I saw your photo on Instagram and when I read the caption I thought: "Margot, the student has surpassed the master." I bow down to you. Now she's gonna think you have an amazing life without her. But if she doesn't text you today, don't worry. Some people boil over from a slow burn.

"Is it her?"

"No. It's just Margot gassing me up."

"Where did this Margot come from? You talk about her a lot."

"I met her at the club." I kissed Ada and popped her back in her bouncer. "You'd like her. She's a very strange girl, but not in a bad way."

"Your 'she's a very strange girl' scares me."

"No way." I said absentmindedly as I tried to focus on answering Margot's message.

"Well, you smile a lot when you talk about her."

"Yeah, because she cracks me up."

> What am I going to do without you when you're on vacation?

My sensei. And, more importantly, what are you going to
do without my sage advice?

"Why don't you invite her over for lunch?"

"What?" I asked, seeing that Margot was typing.

"I said, 'Why don't you invite her over for lunch?' There's plenty
of food."

"Today? It's pretty late notice."

"But I have work tomorrow."

"On Sunday?"

"They changed my shift."

Dominique was studying to be a nurse and simultaneously
working in an old folks' home, where she worked as a nurse's aide.

"Well, she's not going to be able to," I insisted.

"What about Monday for dinner?"

I looked up from my phone, puzzled, waiting for her to explain
why she was so into this idea, but she pretended not to see me.

"Why are you so hyped about this?"

"I want to meet her. You never introduce us to your friends."

"You know all my friends. You're practically part of the crew I've
known my whole life, Domi."

"You never introduce us to your *girlfriends*." She raised her
eyebrows with a little smirk.

My phone vibrated in my hands, but I ignored it for a second.

"Margot is not the kind of friend you're insinuating."

"Yeah, right."

"Yeah, right, yes. I don't get involved with all my friends, you know?"

"I know. There are at least three girls in the crew who would pay
you to."

I brushed her off with a gesture, but she tried again.

"Tell her to come for dinner, go on. I'll make *chicharrones* and *mangu*."

"Oh my god."

I looked at my phone, ready to formally invite Margot, but I was thrown off by her message.

MARGOT

Well, I think I'll be fine without your sage advice because...*(drum roll)* Filippo texted me last night. He said he missed me and that he hopes I'M ON VACATION too and that he hopes at the end of the summer we're ON THE SAME PAGE. Oh yeah.

DAVID

You're back together already? That's not gonna work! The motor that drives this advisory relationship is reciprocity. Now you're going to give me lazy advice because you'll be too busy giving him all your love. And I'll be here dying alone surrounded by rats.

MARGOT

It's supposed to be "dying alone surrounded by cats," isn't it?

DAVID

Cats are too cute. I wouldn't mind dying along surrounded by cats. But watch out for rats or pigeons...Sad endings follow wherever they are.

MARGOT

Don't be dramatic. We didn't get back together. We just...opened a window to reconciliation.

DAVID

You already had a window open to reconciliation, and it was the size of Bernabéu Stadium.

MARGOT

Be happy for me!

DAVID

No, I am happy for you. I'm just dying of jealousy. I want Idoia to text something like that to me too. Something like: "I saw your hot ass on Instagram and I thought, 'What am I doing with my life if I'm not digging my nails into that dude's butt?'"

MARGOT

Seriously, you have to explain to me how you hooked up with her because, from the little I know about her, I swear I don't get it.

DAVID

Well, actually I was going to make you an offer... Do you want to come over to have dinner on Monday? Domi really wants to meet you and she has the night off. She says she can make chicharrones and mangu, which you won't understand and I'm not going to explain them. All I can tell you is it's my wet dream and my favorite sexual position, all on the same plate. I dream about eating it all the time. If you don't come, she won't make it. So up to you. No pressure.

I stared at my phone. Margot wasn't typing, but she was still online.

"I think I went too far asking her to come over for dinner," I said to Dominique.

"Why, you twit?"

"For someone who's lived in Spain for twenty years, sometimes you talk funny," I teased her gently, like I always did when she repeated some expression she had heard her mother say all the time. "I don't know. Maybe it's too soon. I said it, and suddenly she stopped answering, but she didn't sign off or anything. She's just frozen."

"You sure she doesn't like you, David, my love?"

"No! She's trying to get her fiancé back. They almost got married..." But I shut myself up before I said anything that would allude to her dipping out on her wedding, because I wanted to keep her secret. "And it seems to be going pretty well."

"And how does that make you feel?"

"Me?" I smiled at her. "Terrible! Who's going to listen to me whine about Idoia when she gets her dude back?"

Dominique knew I was kidding. I'm not that selfish. Plus, I barely knew Margot. In that moment, I couldn't say, "I'm not happy," for any reason that made any sense. I didn't know if he was good for her or not; I didn't know if he made her be the Margot she dreamed of or if he turned her into the character she didn't want to be instead.

My phone vibrated in my hand, and I glanced quickly at her answer. But it wasn't her. It was a notification of a "like" on my Instagram post. Can anyone guess whose it was?

"Domi! She liked it!"

"Who, Margot?"

"No! Idoia! She liked it! The flame of love is still burning!"

Ada, who seemed pretty sleepy, let out a little peep of celebration.

"You're making me dizzy with all these girls," I heard Dominique mutter. "'Ooh, Idoia is the love of my life, ooh, Margot is supercool, ooh, the girlie from the corner store is making eyes at me.'"

"I've got it made now. I'm on the right path, Domi. In two months, mark my words, in two months...I'll be moving into Idoia's apartment."

"I'd say that's a shame, but I don't know if you doing all the laundry, ironing, and taking care of Ada sometimes is worth having to be silent while I get laid."

"Good luck with that, now that you're a mother." I gave her the finger with a flourish.

And I decided to text Margot, who was still online but still not responding.

DAVID

I'm going to ignore the fact that you haven't responded to my invitation even though you're online, and simp pathetically by messaging you twice in a row because...I need to tell you that... someone...pressed...like...on...my...ass.

MARGOT

Idoia?

DAVID

No. Someone from One Direction.
Of course!

MARGOT

Yeah, boy! We're flying off the shelves!

DAVID

We're on clearance.
Fine. So then?

MARGOT

So then what?

DAVID

Are you coming over for dinner on Monday?

Online, but Margot still didn't answer. I was about to tell her not to worry about it, to forget the invitation, when she finally responded.

MARGOT

What time? Should I bring wine?

DAVID

9:30. Bring whatever you want.

"Domi!" I yelled. "*Chicharrones* on Monday."

Then I did a little victory jig that completely horrified Dominique, who picked up her daughter and whisked her out of the room.

~~~~~

On Monday I went down to meet Margot at the door. I don't know why I waited for her there, but it seemed polite. I saw her climb out of a black car, which I figured was a Cabify, and say thank you to the driver by name.

"You're so sweet, Daisy," I said to her.

She hadn't noticed me, and when she heard my voice, it made her jump a little. She always did that when she was scared, and I found myself trying purposely to get that reaction, hiding around corners to watch her jump. It was as cute as watching Ada yawn.

She was carrying a bottle of red wine and a little box, probably with some kind of dessert, and she had forced herself not to get dressed up. I didn't know her well enough to know how she usually dressed, but from the way she tucked her hair behind her ear, I could tell she was insecure, nervous. She was wearing the jeans I had chosen for her, wide-legged and high-waisted, with a white tank top and a blazer and a bag that pulled the whole thing together slung across her chest.

"Hey, aren't you Jenny from the block?" I needled her.

"Aren't you Karl Lagerfeld?"

"Who?"

She came over, and I held out my hand to shake, which, as always, made her smile.

"When are you going to greet me the way God commands?"

I looked at her again as I opened the door. "How does God command I greet a girl like you?"

"With a bow."

I let out a chuckle that ricocheted around the hallway. "Are you nervous, sad eyes?"

"No, why?"

"Because you seem nervous."

"Well, I'm not." She flashed her teeth at me.

"Was that a smile, or is your vagina itchy?"

She sucked her teeth and pushed past me, heading toward the elevator and opening the door.

"What floor is it?"

"Third."

"Look at that, three, my lucky number."

"Maybe I'm your lucky number." I got in and stood in front of her. I noticed she took half a step back and, I don't know why, maybe to see what how she'd react, I took one forward.

She held her breath, and I pushed the button for the third floor.

"What's going on?"

"You're really close." She put her hand on my stomach and pushed. "And it's tiny in here."

"Do you think I'm hitting on you?"

"No. I just think you're annoying. Plus, I don't like small spaces."

I leaned against the opposite wall and held out my hand so she'd hand over the wine, but she shook her head. I was really enjoying seeing her lose her patience, get nervous, not know what to say. It was like having a box seat to the match between the official Margot and the real one.

I snatched the bottle and yanked it away from her.

"'Nebro, 2013,'" I read out loud.

"I looked up the food you mentioned, and I saw it was fried pork and mashed plantains, so I thought a red was the best option."

"Look how diligent you are. You were always top of your class, eh?"

"Well, no, smart-ass. My grades were never more than midrange. I'm the definition of *average*."

"You?" I cackled. "Are you serious?"

"I mean on tests." She pointed out with a grimace. "I don't stand out in anything. Not high or low, not skinny or fat, not pretty or ugly."

"That's not true," I mumbled, not sure why I was saying it.

"Yes it is." She smiled. "But it's fine. Not everyone has to shine."

I shrugged. I didn't agree, but I wasn't sure if Margot would want me to insist or if it would actually make her feel more uncomfortable hearing me say that I thought she was much more remarkable than her sisters, for example, with that helpless appearance and the inner strength. It was like one of those cookies where, when you bite into them, a filling you weren't expecting bursts on your tongue. Seriously, two big, round brown eyes had never said so much. She gave herself away when she blinked, but she probably didn't realize that, and I didn't want to reveal the secret.

We got the to the third floor before I could think of anything to say (*saved by the bell*), so I got out first and held the door open for her.

"Such a gentleman. You feeling okay?"

I took my keys out of my right pocket and wondered if she had noticed I was wearing my new clothes: the black chinos and an unwrinkled shirt in the same color. Everything chosen by her. But I didn't say anything about it; I just opened the door and announced our arrival.

"We're here. Domi, Ivan…"

Dominique rushed out first, elbowing Ivan out of the way so she could see Margot. She was really curious to meet her, even though I didn't really get why. She was just a friend. And, in theory, I only agreed to this to get her to cook *chicharrones*…and because I liked being with Margot and I would take any excuse.

"Hi, Margot." She pounced on her and planted a loud kiss on each cheek. "I was dying to meet you. David talks so much about you."

"Well, David talks a lot in general, I've noticed."

They shared a smile.

"I brought you some cakes for dessert."

"And wine." I held up the bottle.

"You didn't have to!"

"It was the least I could do… Something smells amazing!" Margot raved. "Did you cook all this yourself?"

"Yes, but it's nothing. Just a typical dish from my country that David loves."

"He told me. He said something a little more obscene. Hi, Ivan," she greeted him. "But…but wait! Who's this little person?"

Ivan came over with Ada in his arms, who was trembling like she was possessed.

"Is that beautiful smile for me?" Margot asked, leaning down to Ada. Ivan held her out, and, surprised, Margot took her skillfully. "Wow, what a little warrior. The world is your oyster."

And, ladies and gentlemen, she wasn't talking in a baby voice or talking like a cartoon character. Margot spoke to Ada just like she spoke to me. And I liked that. I liked it so much that she didn't call her "princess" or "pretty little thing" that I had to look away.

"She looks like both of you!" she said to them. "And she's super alert too. David told me she's seven months?"

Ivan gave me a slap on the back.

"Relax, dude," he whispered.

"I am relaxed."

"You look like you have a stick up your ass."

And he was right. I don't know why, but ever since Margot had set foot in the house, I was the one who was nervous. Maybe because I could tell from her manners that she had never lived on the couch in her best friends' apartment. Maybe because I felt…inferior in these conditions. But…to whom?

Domi showed her around the apartment while we chilled the wine and set the table. When they came back, we were both drinking beer from the bottle, leaning against the wall in the living room, hesitating, not knowing whether to sit down.

"What are you doing standing up?" Margot said startled, with a smile. She was still carrying Ada, and Ada seemed enchanted.

She held her hand out to me. Margot, not the baby. Well, actually to my beer. I passed her the bottle and took Ada while she took a sip straight from the bottle and then gave it back. When I drank again, she looked at me and laughed.

"Come on, let's go."

She ran her thumb over my lips a couple of times, roughly, and when she moved it away, I saw it was stained with lipstick. I hadn't even thought about it when I shared the bottle. Sorry...*did we just share a bottle?* So intimate, so soon.

I ducked my head and ran my hand over my mouth, and when I looked up, I saw Ivan and Domi smirking. And I was worried. I was worried for a moment that they would think my friendship with Margot was something more, that they would badger us or that they wouldn't understand our thing, whatever our thing was. We were probably the only ones who understood it. She said she wasn't special, and she didn't stand out? Well, I felt a peace with her that wasn't normal or mediocre.

We were just two very conspiratorial strangers. We were just two new friends, clumsy and strung out on feeling understood. Hasn't that ever happened to you? Suddenly you meet someone and you want them to be part of all your plans, and it seems unbelievable to you that you ever had fun without them. That's what was happening here. We were just a mountain of hope.

24

~~~

IN VINO VERITAS

MARGOT

The *chicharrones* were to die for, and the mashed plantain seemed simply divine to me. It was served with a delicious kind of cassava bread and fried yams. We were stuffed. It had been a long time since I'd eaten so much and so well. And the wine, which the boys had chilled a little even though it was red, slipped down and softened all my extremities until I was elastic and flexible. Enough to feel like I had stopped playing a role.

For dessert we ate the cakes I brought. Ivan left the table for a minute to put their daughter to bed, and Dominique and I made coffee while David made cocktails. We were having a good time, and even though I made noises about leaving a few times, the ones who had to be up at dawn the next morning didn't seem too worried about sleeping that night.

Ivan and Domi were a charming couple, and their apartment was small (tiny for three adults and a baby) but adorable. You could see affection in every corner; it smelled like family, and it was comfortable. David fit in, just one more member of the family, but even though I had just met him, I could still see he needed to open his wings and fly.

Dominique talked to me about her home country, the little she remembered and the lot she had learned through her mother, who lived a few blocks away and took care of the little girl when they (three) couldn't cover it.

"We can't abuse the grandparents," she justified.

And it all seemed wonderful to me. And the beer appetizer, the bottle of wine David and I split between us (Dominique was still breastfeeding, and Ivan was more into beer), and the "dessert" cocktail had me floating. I had a good vibe I hadn't felt in years. Which must be how my mouth ended up talking to them about the INCIDENT and my plan to get Filippo back. I talked about his blue eyes, how tall and strong he was; I told them how beautiful that sunset on Ponte Vecchio had been and the emotion in his deep voice when he asked me to marry him.

"That's such a beautiful story," Dominique whispered sincerely. "It's like a fairy tale."

"It was like a fairy tale," I sighed. "I fucked it all up. But David's going to help me get him back, right?"

"Right."

When he put his enormous hand on mine, on the table, I felt a tingle. A nice one. Because sometimes sad people can do much more than understand each other.

At one thirty in the morning, I left, but David insisted on walking me out. I didn't want him to, so I told him I could get the company chauffeur to pick me up. But he was so insistent that I changed my mind.

"I'll order a Cabify," I announced, as if he would know any difference.

"Already?" he asked. "Let's go smoke a cigarette on that bench."

He pointed to a solitary bench on the sidewalk, with stunning views of a wall, and it made me laugh. Him too.

"David, neither of us smoke."

"I do mentally. Get moving."

We sat down, and he stretched his arms along the back while I put my feet on his knees. It wasn't just a gesture of trust; that way I could make sure he kept a good distance. I hadn't liked feeling so nervous when he got close in the elevator.

"That was really lovely, thank you for inviting me," I said to him. "Ivan and Dominique are charming."

I caught the look he was giving me out of the corner of my eye.

"What?" I asked him.

"You talk like an ad for fancy chocolate." He smiled. "Tell me it was lit, that we're the shit and you'll be back."

"Do I have to talk like a Gen Z-er so you understand me?" I joked.

"Hey," he said, patting my leg, "the truth is you were…"

He nodded as if that completed the rest of his sentence. All he did was nod, but I understood.

"Thank you."

"No, no. Thank you. At this point in life, those two probably thought I would never hang out with anyone outside the gang. I think they were pleasantly surprised."

"That'd be because of the impeccable manners I learned in Swiss boarding school."

"You're such a pain in the ass." He laughed. "Are you always so proper?"

"Yes, but to make up for it, I always wear a hair tie on my wrist on the first date. Just in case."

He raised his eyebrows and then pretended to punch me in the side with a closed fist.

"Do you know what I liked the most?" he asked me.

"That I just mentioned how much I like giving blow jobs?"

Never. Ever. Give. Me. Wine.

"Apart from that." David wasn't shocked…or at least he didn't show any signs of being so. "That you said to Ada, 'The world is your oyster,' and not, 'What a princess.'"

"Princess?" I shot him a look. "Sabina already sang it, sweetie. 'Girls don't wanna be princesses anymore.'"

"'And boys have given up on chasing them…'"

"'…the sea inside a glass of gin,'" we sang the last line together.

"Hey! Speaking of the sea…when are you leaving?"

"Ah! Right. I never told you. I leave on Friday. Counting the day I arrive, I'll be in Athens for two days, a week in Santorini, and six days in Mykonos. Two weeks total." I sighed. "Even I'm excited now."

"Even you're excited? You say that like it's a punishment."

"No, but…it's weird. Have you ever traveled alone?"

"No." He shook his head. "But it's probably off the hook."

"Off the hook and boring. Two weeks without talking to anyone?"

"You'll talk to someone, girl. You have a lot of things to get done from the list I gave you."

"Yeah, yeah. A very realistic list."

"Hey, you have to send me photos," he said with his eyebrows raised. "If not, the jig will be up with Idoia."

"Okay, but promise me you're not going to Photoshop yourself out of another photo and stick yourself in mine with the ocean in the background and pretend you're there."

"I'll be more subtle. I promise."

David winked, and we shook hands to seal the deal. Then he didn't let go.

"Listen, Margot...can I call you while you're out there?"

"Of course." I pulled my hand away, a little uncomfortable, and to feign that it wasn't just to get away from his touch, I rested my chin on my fist, looking at him.

"I think I'm used to being with you and I'll feel like a blank page in a sea of words."

"A blank page in a sea of words? What are you, Rimbaud?"

"'It has been found again!/ What? Eternity. / It is the sea mingled with the sun.'"

I was stunned. Floored. I had never heard anyone recite Rimbaud, especially not by heart.

"Excuse me?"

"I don't like poetry, if that's what you're going to ask me." He tucked his legs under him on the bench and turned so we were facing each other. "I studied it in college, and those lines always stuck with me."

"You went to college?"

"Yup," he said, sighing. "I guess that surprises you coming from a waiter."

I tensed up.

"I didn't mean to offend you," I said.

"I'm not offended. That always happens."

"No, really, David. I never thought that...I don't know, that just because you work in hospitality means you're illiterate."

"There are people who didn't study and that doesn't mean they're illiterate, you snob."

"I know, I know. Fuck...I didn't mean that. I didn't mean to say illiterate like a bad thing. I just… Now I probably sound like a brat who went to a Swiss boarding school. What I meant is that…" I fluttered my hands nervously. "I don't know. I've never heard anyone recite Rimbaud from memory."

"It's internationally renowned." He rubbed one eyebrow and let his hands fall to his side.

"God…" I was mortified. "I insulted you. I'm an idiot. Forgive me, really. I'm just digging myself deeper."

"Margot." He gave me a half-smile. "Stop."

"No, I'm an imbecile! I'm sorry, really. I didn't mean to say anything bad. About you or about anyone. I just meant to express my admiration."

David lifted his chin and scratched his neck, looking up at the sky.

"See? You won't even look at me! I offended you!"

David tugged on my leg to pull me closer.

"Margarita." He smiled right into my face. "I'm not offended. If you had said, I don't know, 'You're a grouch and a whore,' then maybe I'd be thinking about poisoning you with a laxative, but that? Relax!"

"Sometimes I come off really stuck-up," I admitted.

"At this point, I already think of it as part of your charm."

"Well, excuse me for saying this, but you see me through rose-colored glasses."

"No glasses here." He pointed at his dark eyes. "Come on, tell me more stuff about your trip. Make me jealous."

"You don't get any time off?"

"I would if I quit that fucking club." He sighed and made a bored face. "I swear I'm only there for Ivan. I don't want him to be alone in that hole-in-the-wall dump."

"It's not that bad, dude. I've been to worse places."

"Oh, yeah?" he teased smugly. "Where?"

"In Thailand, once." I recollected as I took out my phone and opened the Cabify app. "After I closed a business deal, they took me to a ping-pong show. I'm not going to get into the details, but it was the worst night of my life."

"What the hell kind of business do you work in?" He laughed. "And why are there so many meatheads in the business world?"

"I often ask myself the same thing. It's late." I showed him the app, where I had already been assigned a driver who was three hundred meters away.

"Yes."

"And you have to walk the dogs tomorrow."

"Yes." He nodded. "They're all going on vacation like you, on Friday."

"What about the florist?"

"It's closed in August."

"Don't you have some vacation days saved up?"

"Vacation days? I'm a freelancer. Like everyone else under forty trying to figure out their lives. What's going on, lady?" He laughed. "You tryna take me with you to Greece? If you want to spot me a ticket, my full name is David Sánchez Rodrigo. My passport number is…"

"Can you imagine?" I laughed.

"What would it be like?"

"Terrible. I've never traveled with a stranger."

"I'm very tidy," he countered, stretching his legs and standing up. "And I've got a wicked sense of direction."

"Do you know how to haggle? If you know how to haggle, I'll bring you."

"You've got the wrong guy." He shrugged. "Haggling makes me feel a mix of cringey and sad. But give me another test. That can't be your only requirement."

"Can you carry suitcases?" I stood up, and he nudged me gently on the shoulder, leading me back to his door.

"I carry suitcases, open doors, I know how to rub sunscreen on backs," he said as if he were completely serious, "and I'm a great photographer."

"And you know Rimbaud by heart."

"Just that line. But I can recite it to you every time we see the sea."

"Maybe I should take you with me."

We both smiled, facing each other. The motor of a car turning the corner heralded my driver's arrival.

"I want to say goodbye to you the way God commands, since I never greet you that way," he said.

I swallowed.

"Go on then."

"Well, I can't be all bark and no bite."

He had to stoop a little, but suddenly we fit together. It was so natural, it was like we had always done it, like we had always known each other under our skin. I felt relief. Physical relief. From his heat, his smell, his breath. From that hug.

A hug is the first act of love, but it doesn't always go in that order. Sometimes you're only capable of really hugging after you've already broken up. But other times, like then, two people are capable of comforting a body they haven't loved yet.

I rested my cheek on his shoulder, and he kissed my hair while his hand slid down my back. The headlights of the car illuminated us, but neither of us moved.

"Good night," he whispered.

"Good night."

I took a step back. He did too. He smiled. I did too.

Right before the car pulled away, I lowered the window and called to him.

"David!"

"What?"

"Were you serious?"

"About what?" He shoved his hands into his pockets.

"About Greece. Would you come?"

"Are you nuts?" And his ever-present sad smile widened. "You're fucking with me, right?"

"No." I shook my head. "Would you come?"

I saw his Adam's apple bobbing up and down. I could almost see the words trampling under his messy hair, shooting in every direction and not finding a path out of his lips. He opened his mouth, and even though I saw hesitation in his eyes, I didn't feel embarrassed. Not for the rushed and inadequate style of the proposition. Not for offering something so conspiratorial and intimate to an almost stranger. Not even knowing that if Filippo did the same thing with another girl, it would kill me.

"I would go," he said finally, laughing his head off. "Of course I would go, for fuck's sake. But I can't. I don't have a dime. Well…I have something, but I can't blow it all on a trip."

"But you'd come if you could?"

"Fuck, if I went…" He shook his head gently, like deep down he wanted to banish the images that just the mere possibility were creating in his head.

"That's enough for me. Good night, David."

The car pulled out slowly, gliding over the asphalt on the tiny road, lit up by a single orange streetlight whose light made a pool on the ground, dappled with shadows from the trees that were planted here and there. It was a pretty, picturesque neighborhood street.

Someone whistled. A loud, dry whistle that made the car brake. I stuck my head out of the still-open window and saw David standing there, frozen.

"Margot!" he shouted, risking some neighbor complaining.

"What?"

"You do stand out. A lot."

I inhaled sharply.

"You're a dumbass." I laughed. "Oh, and…nice pants, by the way."

When I got home, I shouldn't have gone to my office.

I shouldn't have taken out my laptop or tapped in my password with nimble fingers.

I shouldn't have pulled up the airline website or reserved a flight in David Sánchez Rodrigo's name, pending providing more information when the ticket was confirmed.

No. I shouldn't have fallen asleep thinking about what that trip would be like or whether I would dare to confess to David the next day that I had bought him a plane ticket to Athens. In first class. Next to me.

25

~~~

WITHOUT A HANGOVER

With no hangover, it was difficult to tell myself the thing we normally say the morning after doing something stupid: *Blame it on the alcohol.* But…with no hangover…with no hangover there's not even any reliable proof that you went overboard with the drinks and you have no alibi to hide behind, just…shame. Because you fled from your wedding, okay, but you want to win your ex-future-husband back. And, suddenly, in the middle of your plan, you invited a guy you just met to come with you on the vacation where you're supposed to be finding yourself. And when you invited him, you meant it, because you wanted to. So much so that…you booked a flight for him.

Patricia found me at the breakfast bar pretending to check travel documents on my iPad. Actually, and I don't think this'll come as a shock to anyone, I was thinking about what it would be like to travel to all those places with David. Well, my head was splitting time between thinking about that and driving myself crazy.

"Who let you in?" I grumbled when she chucked her Louis Vuitton agenda onto the marble, alongside her laptop in a case and a pile of papers held together with a hair tie.

"You don't seem very happy to see me."

"I'm not happy because you're here to tell me about the private detective who's swindling you and I'm not in the mood. Because, like I already said, the Catholic church is looking for your mother-in-law's phone number to let her know they want to canonize your husband while he's still alive. Saint Alberto de Rascafría."

"Yes. Saint Alberto." Her lip curled in disgust, and…even that didn't make her look ugly.

"Genes are despicable."

"It could be worse. You could be Candela." She pointed to the aforementioned as she appeared in the kitchen dressed in…what the hell would you even call it? A towel? A towel with three holes: one for the head and two for the arms.

"Her problem isn't genetic. Her problem is that fashion matters as much to her as whatever your detective found does to me," I pointed out helpfully.

"Are you trying to get into it with me?" Candela helped herself to a cup of my coffee. "This is disgusting, Margot. What do you put in it?"

"Nothing."

"Look at her. She really is ugly," Patricia teased. "This is what you'd get from AliExpress when you order something like me."

"You smug whore." Candela laughed. "You're so fucking smug. Have you seen your knees? You have the ugliest knees I've ever seen in my life."

"You're both such losers."

I got up, ready to escape to my room, but Candela stopped me.

"Don't abandon me with this one. She doesn't look good. She's in an even worse mood than usual. What if it turned out to be true that Alberto's out there fucking like a rabbit?"

"Your mother is the one who put me in a bad mood," Patricia explained, opening the fridge. "She makes me want to eat carbs. But like, binge on carbs. She says she doesn't like that the kids go to summer school, that it's not a good look."

"So send them to her. Make her exercise her role as grandmother," I said slyly.

They both looked at me like I had suggested putting the kids up for adoption.

"The detective…" Candela pestered her. She wanted her piping-hot tea.

"Babe, for someone with your career, you're such a cunt," I muttered.

"I have to compensate somehow. Tell us, tell us."

Patricia sat down, grabbed her laptop, typed, and turned it toward us. In front of us were a bunch of pictures of my brother-in-law doing…things. Things like getting into a car with a lollipop in his mouth, going to work, having coffee and churros for breakfast, smoking a cigarette outside his office, eating a hamburger, picking up something from the dry cleaner for my sister (because it was definitely for my sister, I would go all in on that bet), eating a chocolate palmier, and getting back in the car.

"He ate all that on the same day?" Candela muttered.

"I mean, come on…is he a private detective or an obsessive nutritionist?" I asked.

"He can sweat if off later in the gym, Patri. With that huge amount of crap he eats. The poor guy does sweat, even if you refuse to believe that."

"This guy has anxiety…" I pointed out, waving toward the photos.

"I have anxiety. Why does he eat so much? Go on, explain it

to me. Because I can think of one thing that makes you really hungry."

"Do you think Alberto is cheating with churros?" Candela asked, bewildered. Considering how intelligent she was...

"Stop," I interrupted. "Because I can tell you that when someone's having an affair, they normally get a new look, they take better care of themselves and get hotter; they're not shoving everything they can find made with palm oil down their throats."

"He's hiding something."

"Oh, for God's sake."

I grabbed my iPad and headed toward my room.

"I can't wait to have you out of my sight," I snapped before I disappeared.

"Girl, what if Alberto realized he's being followed, confronted the detective, and offered him more money to give him an alibi? So he shows you this shit and not the truth, I mean," Candela threw out there, at the speed of light without drawing breath.

In the silence that fell after, I could hear the furious galloping of the four horsemen of the apocalypse.

As soon as I closed my bedroom door, my phone lit up with a message, but before I could see who it was from, a call came in from Sonia at the office.

"Hi, Sonia," I answered, immediately opening my email on the iPad. "Is everything okay?"

"Nothing new here. I won't bore you with the details, but when you get back from your vacation, you can read everything that's been covered. I'm calling about your trip." I could hear she sounded really excited. "When you have a minute, if you can, please have a look at your inbox."

"I have it open." I smiled. I knew her so well.

"I sent you the itinerary, a proposal of a plan for the days you're there, the hotel reservations and the information for the flight. As soon as you send me the registration information, I'll send you the tickets."

"What would I do without you? Die?"

"Not at all." She laughed. "I found good hotels from the chain, but nothing the Kardashians would choose, just like you told me. Five stars but nothing garish. And…by the way, as you can see, I booked you in using your first name and your second last name, so nobody will know you're the boss."

"I'm not the boss."

"Come on, you hold a thirty-seven percent stake in a very lucrative multinational. You're the boss."

"Thanks so much for the discretion. I don't want people to be sucking up to me wherever I go and monitoring my comings and goings."

"Done and done. Now they'll just think you're a single multimillionaire."

I bit my thumbnail. Fuck. That gave me kind of a lot of freedom, didn't it?

"Thank you, Sonia."

"I'll let you go. If anything comes up or you have any questions, call me."

I blew her a kiss, said thank you again, and hung up.

When I reopened WhatsApp, I saw that the message that had come in right before the call was, of course, from David. It was a photo. I don't know how he managed to pull it off on his phone, but the cackle it drew from me rang through the house.

The photo was the cliché you got when you Googled "Greek beach paradise," and, over that, he had scribbled a stick figure that was supposed to look like me. He had even drawn on the cross-body bag and my brown mane.

> To post on your Instagram. When you're traveling in style, everyone can see it. Speaking of seeing...am I going to see you before you leave?

I closed the app, searched for his contact, and called him. He picked up on the second ring.

"Amparito, relax, I can see your femoral artery from here," I heard him say to one of his bosses.

"Damn, Amparito must be very forward. The femoral is in the groin," I said.

"The jugular, the jugular, Amparito. I don't want to see your femoral," I heard him yell. Then I heard giggling. "She's on fire today... I think she had a few swigs of something strong after lunch. What's going on, princess?"

"Princess?"

"I'm just messing with you."

"I loved your Photoshop. It's super sophisticated. Barely noticeable."

"Imperceptible. Just...what NASA is missing."

"What does NASA have to do with anything?"

"I dunno. Mars, Princess Sad Eyes. You have two days left here in this swamp of horrors."

"Don't talk about my Madrid like that." I laughed.

"You haven't been outside yet today, have you? It stinks from the heat. The Sahara wind is blowing over us. As you can imagine…I'm wearing a cardigan right now."

"Well, at least we're going to Greece on Friday, right?" I tested the waters.

"Stop saying that, you witch," he whimpered. "Can you imagine? That would be the shit."

I fell silent, staring at the wall, biting my lip. My fingers had unconsciously opened the email with David's flight reservation.

"Margot? You still there?" he asked.

"I think I'm scared to go alone."

"You're shitting yourself, duh. But when you're there and you suddenly find yourself in a situation where you don't know what to do, just think, *What would David do?* Or even better, vividly imagine me there, in the jeans that make my ass look great, doing cool things. And then do them."

"You would do cool things?" I scoffed.

"Sure. I'd take you to Thermopylae…"

"There's not enough time."

"…where three hundred brave Spartans died…"

"There's not enough time."

"…led by Leonidas…"

"There's not enough time!"

"Hey, hey, you history fanatic, you have to calm down," he teased. "Do you guys hang out in plazas debating which was the coolest polis?"

I didn't answer. I was hallucinating David Sánchez Rodrigo's ticket standing in front of me. It was actually him disguised as a plane ticket, with a confused face and waving arms and legs.

"I think you're driving me crazy," I mumbled.

"Hey…" he spoke softly. "Why don't we have dinner tonight?"

Candela burst into my room.

"Hang up. Mama found out you're going to Greece alone and she's…" She shook her hand, like when we were little. "She wants us to go to dinner."

"To dinner?"

"I'm passing; the old lady isn't going to miss me. But Patri says she'll go with you… She's obviously the one who ratted you out, and she feels guilty."

"You're getting all this, right?" I said into the phone.

"Yes…how about tomorrow?"

"Okay."

"Okay. Well, don't make any plans tomorrow. And on Thursday I'll come over and help you pack."

I looked around me. My room, my room alone, was forty square meters, including the closet and the bathroom.

"No, that's okay, that won't be necessary."

"See you tomorrow. And whistle if you need a tamer for your mother."

"Thanks, David. You're the best."

"The best…" he repeated in a murmur. "Tell that to Idoia. No word from her since the other day."

"We're in the same boat." I sighed.

Candela sat on the bed next to me.

"Did Patricia leave yet?" I asked my sister.

"No way. She's in the kitchen making herself a grape and cheese sandwich."

"Please…she's lost it. David, I'll see you tomorrow."

"See you tomorrow, sad eyes."

"Not so sad anymore."

"Not anymore, no."

I hung up and stood up.

"What am I gonna wear so your mother doesn't call me a whore? Patricia!" I yelled. "What should I wear?"

"Better make it the dress the old lady likes the best," she yelled back. "Hang on, I'll be right there."

She was heading toward the door when Candela rushed forward and slammed it, leaving the two of us alone inside.

"What are you doing?" I asked.

"Yeah, I was about to ask you the same thing."

And in front of me, the email. The flight confirmation. David's.

26

IT'S NOT WHAT IT LOOKS LIKE

"What is this?" Candela's eyes, which were always slightly protruding, looked like they were about to pop out of their sockets.

"Nothing…"

"Please tell me you're not going with him."

"I'm not going with him."

"Tell me again and swear on your life because I'm considering having you committed."

"I'm. Not. Going. With. Him." I repeated slowly.

"Hey! What are you doing in there? Secrets, secrets are no fun!" Patricia yelled from the other side of the door.

"Swear to me," Candela whispered. "Swear to me you're going to Greece alone."

"I swear. I'm going to Greece alone."

"So then what's this?" She shook the iPad.

My mouth opened and closed soundlessly. I rested my forehead against the door. I couldn't say anything that would explain it away.

"Margot…"

"I thought about it, okay? He makes me feel so free, so capable…

so I briefly considered the possibility of going with him. It's not a crime," I whispered so Patricia wouldn't hear.

"I'm going to break this door down, seriously. And if you think I can't that's because neither of you have ever done Pilates in your life."

"I'm coming!" I shouted.

"We're going to talk about this later," Candela promised.

"I'm not going to talk about this now or later," I said, pressing my back against the door. "I thought about it. I did something stupid by reserving the flight, and I didn't even tell him because I felt ridiculous. So please do me the favor of not humiliating me anymore and leave me alone."

I opened the door. Patricia was wielding a piece of bread in her hand, and she showed it to me with indignance written all over her face.

"Bread! I'm eating bread! White bread! And it's after seven!"

"For fuck's sake."

~~~~

I have a lot to thank Patricia for. For example, she told me I shouldn't draw eyeliner inside my eye, and she once admitted that long hair looked terrible on me. She also brought bands, movies, and clothes into my life that were iconic in my teenage years. But, without a doubt, all those big-sisterly feats were nothing compared to the spectacle she put on at my mother's house that night. She really took one for the team. She told her that me going to Greece alone was the best decision I could have made. And that, besides how glamorous a retreat on deserted beaches in paradise would be (deserted my ass, it was the end of June, and it's not exactly an unknown destination), it was also the smartest thing to do.

"Scandals don't last forever. By the time she gets back, everyone will have forgotten about her running through the gardens of the hotel in a wedding dress."

If anyone was surprised that my mother would raise hell because I was going on vacation alone, well…they're probably lucky not to have a mother who is a strange mix between cat and human and who is more concerned about what her friends will think (even though she actually can't stand them) than what her daughters decide to do with their lives to be happy.

"I don't get it! You said the best thing to do would be to get away for a few days!" I exclaimed indignantly while my mother gripped her glass insolently.

"I meant you should go to your grandparents' manor house, not go traveling alone out there."

"I wouldn't really enjoy myself though, would I?"

"Do you deserve to?"

Of course I deserved to, but…even I didn't know that yet. Sometimes our sin meter gets broken when we're judging ourselves.

I kept quiet, of course, because I had learned to weather my mother's semialcoholic hysteria. I kept quiet because I didn't want to get into another fight or more of a mess. And because at that point, it was worth swallowing my bile along with the words I wanted to say, to nod and go home where, well, sometimes my anger swallowed me alive, but I didn't have to give explanations to anyone.

I didn't even want to talk to David when I got home that night. Or to Candela, who offered me ice cream (which was completely forbidden in my mother's house) while I told her how it went and we roasted Lady Meow (as an excuse to bring up the David thing again, of course). I just wanted to shut myself in my room, not see anyone, not talk to anyone, and sleep. I took off my Max Mara dress, left it crumpled in a ball in a corner, and climbed into bed in underwear and a bra without taking off my makeup. I didn't even take my phone out of my bag. Only a mother can make you feel so disappointed in yourself.

~~~

David believed the story that the reason I didn't answer the message he sent before he went to sleep was because I fell asleep on the couch after a feast at my mother's house. Of course, he didn't know my mother, so he didn't think it was weird when I told him I had eaten too much. Plus, he was pretty excited about our plans for tonight. Maybe he had heard from Idoia or some exciting plans for the summer had come up, but he refused to answer any of my questions until we met up that night; he was being very mysterious.

I was going to wait for him at the door of the florist, but it seemed very rude not to go in and say hi to Amparito and Asuncion. I found them balancing the register.

"Good evening," I said shyly. "Sorry, I came to collect David and I felt bad not saying...hi!" I lifted my hand stupidly.

"Look how lovely this child is," one said to the other, as if I weren't there.

"Come in, come in, don't loiter in the doorway like that."

"Oh, I don't mind. I can see you're busy and..."

"Don't be silly. David'll be right out. Wait until you see how spruced up he is tonight."

"Can you shut up?" I heard him bellow from the back room. "You screwed up my surprise, you biddies!"

"I don't know how you keep him here, with all the terrible things he says to you." I laughed.

"Ah, well, only because he can lift the flowerpots two at a time." One of them made an excuse for him.

"And he's cute too," the other added.

"He really is. I would've been head over heels for him if I were twenty years younger..." Asuncion nodded.

"Love has no age."

The beaded curtain that separated the more private storeroom parted as his fingers pushed through it. And he was there. Fuck, he was definitely there. Spotless Converse, tight black ankle-cropped pants, a patterned shirt, and...a new haircut. He still had the messy spirit of before, with a few long locks here and there, but with a little more order, mostly combed to one side. He looked...he looked really hot.

"Jesus Christ. You clean up well." I smiled at him, making a gesture of approval that allowed me to simultaneously disguise the fact that I liked what I saw a little too much.

"Well, I'm just getting started."

He stood in front of me and offered me his arm. He was good, really good. OMG.

"What do you want us to do, walk arm in arm?"

"Like two old ladies," he said with a fake seductive air. "My queen."

I burst out laughing. So did he.

"You two are always giggling," one of his bosses commented slyly.

"Don't get jealous. I love you the most, Asuncion, from the bottom of my heart."

"Get out of here before I take my shoe off."

He blew them a kiss and forced me to take his arm, and we left.

"You didn't have to get so dolled up." I smiled.

"Yes, I did. I'm practicing." He winked. "And just wait and see because there are more surprises."

~~~~~

We walked along the cobblestoned streets, hopping over broken cobbles and cigarette butts in our new shoes, arm in arm, until we got to Malasaña, where we meandered through its arteries, veins, and capillaries. We passed by a man walking a dog that looked like him, a little girl with a pacifier that made it look like she had a mustache, and a hipster in a super cool hat…and we gabbed about all of it, everything surprised us, everything was wonderful. With David, the world was full of treasures to dig up.

David stopped suddenly, and I tried to tug his arm so we could keep walking.

"Come on! I'm hungry!" I complained. "What's it gonna be today? Hot dogs, pizza, calamari sandwiches?"

"What if we go nuts today and sit down somewhere, with tables and everything?"

My eyes widened, and my mouth fell open. I realized we had stopped at the door of a restaurant called 80 Grados.

"You made a reservation here?"

"Yes, little lady."

"Hey!" I nudged him with my shoulder. "This keeps getting better!"

We sat at a small table, miniscule really, crammed in right between two others, but it wasn't David's fault he had chosen a restaurant that seemed to be very hot right now. We ordered *tinto de verano* to drink and a few small plates to share. The waiter insisted we order more, and we picked a few randomly, giggling hysterically, pointing at dishes on the menu without even knowing what we were ordering. Another great thing about David is that I never went hungry with him.

Tintos were dangerous…cold, sweet, smooth… We ordered two more because they came in tiny glasses.

"This is nice," I said, looking around while we were waiting for our food.

"Pretty noisy, no?"

"True, maybe you better not bring her here."

"I'll bring her in the beginning, when I have to play hard to get. That way it'll seem like I'm not really interested in what she has to say."

"Is that how it is?" I teased, but was slightly offended.

"What? No! But you're my sensei. Everything that comes out of your mouth is pure wisdom."

I pretended to punch him, and he told me to get out my phone.

"Let's take a picture?" he suggested.

"Why not with yours?"

"Because it has such low resolution it would look more like an abstract interpretation of us in a restaurant."

I nodded and pulled out my phone. "I need to ask the business if they have any extra phones from the renewal we did a few months ago."

"Sounds like charity."

"Would it wound your little masculine ego?" I asked, taking another sip of my tinto.

"Bah, no way. My little ego, as you call it, is rock solid. When a man is happy with the size of his penis, he doesn't worry about that stuff."

I almost snorted wine out of my nose, but I caught it just in time.

"Come on, picture."

"Wait, come here," he said.

"Come where?"

"Here. We both have to be in it, right?"

"Well then you get up," I whined.

"Come here, silly."

I tutted and stood up. As I clambered over, slowly so I wouldn't stick my ass in any of our neighbors' faces, David grabbed my wrist and pulled me into his lap.

"What are you doing?" I asked, bewildered.

"A photo. Come on. So they can see how affectionate we are with each other."

"Wait! This is for your Instagram?"

"Of course!" He laughed. "I'm following your list point by point."

I furrowed my brow and studied his expression. "Are you messing with me?"

"Of course not, woman. Come on, pose."

He grabbed my phone and flipped it around to the front camera, and we showed up on the screen. We smiled. He took a few pictures. I turned back to him again.

"What do you smell like?"

"Like a macho man," he said, and he pretended to growl.

"Idiot." I cackled. "What are you wearing, I mean."

"Cologne."

"You got a new one?"

"Maybe." He made a face like he was playing hard to get.

"Well, I guess you are listening to me."

"Of course."

"There's something fishy going on here…" I looked at my camera roll again, and suddenly my qualms reappeared. "Hey, if this is for your Instagram, I don't want you to show my face. It wouldn't be that crazy of a coincidence if someone I know saw it and it got back to Filippo."

"Yeah, true. That would be pretty hard to explain. Well…um… how should we do it?"

I sat on his lap. His knee was digging into the bones of my ass. I moved and let my legs dangle between his. The table next to us was watching everything happening at ours intently. They seemed to be on a pretty boring date.

"What if I sit like this, like I'm hugging you?"

"Ah! Great idea! Let's see?"

I hid in his neck, and I felt him moving his arm, looking for the best angle.

"It's good, but move a little that way, you can see the table behind us and they're eating *salmorejo* soup; it's not very sexy."

I laughed, and he shivered from my breath on his neck.

"Sorry."

We rearranged ourselves, and I clung to him again. I buried my nose in his skin, and he rubbed me affectionately. He smelled really good. Fresh, clean, masculine. I felt both his arms around me, and I lifted my head.

"Did you get it? Lemme see!"

He showed me the screen of my phone. It had turned out really, I mean, really well. We looked like a couple whispering sweet nothings, and…it must have looked that way to the waiter too when he arrived with a few plates.

"Should I wrap it up for you to take home, lovebirds?"

I jumped up like a spring. "We're not a couple. We're just... We were..."

"Yeah, yeah." The waiter laughed. "I'll leave the croquettes here for you, okay? Careful, they're hot...like it's getting in here."

I felt a wave of heat on my cheeks. David pressed his lips together so he wouldn't burst out laughing.

"David!" I whimpered when he left. "Don't put me in these predicaments in public!"

"He was being a dick." He nearly pissed himself laughing.

I took a croquette, put another on his plate, and then split mine open so it would cool down a little. And as I watched the steam pour out, it suddenly occurred to me that...

"Hey! I know what you're trying to do!"

"Me?" He pointed at his chest, pretending to be offended.

"Yes, you! You haven't called me *buddy* all night, you bring me to a restaurant, you cut your hair, you changed your cologne, you put on a button-up shirt, you're going to post a photo with a girl who's not Idoia, doing something you probably never did with her, having a good time and dressed to the nines..."

"I already told you I'm doing my assignments. You made a list, and I'm simply following your advice to the letter, my sensei."

"Yeah, okay, but what are your intentions?"

"I don't have any."

"None? Ha! I'll tell you your intentions: you want me to go to Greece knowing that you've checked off your whole list...so that I have to check off my list too."

He put his hands up like he had been found out.

"That's so devious! So you want me to feel guilty if I don't finish your list from hell!" I insisted.

"I'm wearing a button-up shirt. Whose list is from hell?"

"Yours!" I laughed.

"Asun took a photo of me working, surrounded by flowers, to post with a retro filter. Wanna see it?"

"Stop!"

He shoved a croquette in his mouth and waggled his eyebrows.

"You look really pretty today," he said with his mouth full. "What did you do?"

"Nothing." I shrugged.

"Yeah, you did. You curled your hair, didn't you?"

"I just…" I flattened it down. "I didn't straighten it today. My mother always says straight hair is more elegant, and…I mean, I don't know, I got tired of having to waste fifteen minutes using a hair straightener every day. But don't change the subject."

"I'm not changing the subject; there's just not much more to say. It's not that weird that I want to make sure you're gonna try to let loose, go a little crazy, and have a good time in a place where there won't be anyone you know to hold you back."

I stared at him as I chewed. He raised his eyebrows.

"Or not?"

"Why are you worried about what I do? You barely know me," I retorted, suddenly serious.

"Because I like you." He took a deep breath, his chest puffing out. "I just mean…we get along, I'm starting to feel affectionate toward you. I like how you are when we're together, and something tells me you like me too, but…you're not normally like this."

I grabbed my drink and downed it. David waved at the waiter and pointed to my empty glass to order another.

"Go a little crazy, Margot." He smiled. "Listen to yourself."

"I never said—"

"No, but at some point in the last two weeks, you said that we could give each other good advice, that we could help each other. I'm holding up my end of the bargain, and you are too, but…now that you're going—"

"David," I cut him off.

"What'd I say?" He made a face. "I said something; I fucked it up. You've gotten all weird."

"It's not that. It's just that…the other day I did something…"

"Touching yourself is normal. Being curious about your own body and experimenting. It's called masturbation," he quipped.

"David…"

"What?" He laughed, grabbing another croquette from the plate.

"I bought you a ticket."

He put his fork and knife down slowly, one at a time. His tongue moved around his mouth while his chest filled with air…and he was slow to meet my gaze.

"What?" he repeated.

"I bought you a ticket."

"A ticket to where?" And he was suddenly so serious that I was scared to keep talking.

I hung my head and put my hands in my lap.

"Forget it."

"You bought a ticket for me to…go with you?"

"Yes, but I know that was completely out of line, okay? I just…I don't know. I don't even know why I told you."

"But…what did you do with the ticket?"

"It's pending confirmation." I shrugged.

The waiter brought over my drink, and I seized it as soon as it landed on the table.

"Margot, look at me."

"I don't want to. I'm dying, I'm so fucking embarrassed. I'm such a blabbermouth." I took a gulp. Then another.

I put the glass down. I looked around us, as if everyone knew how stupid I had just been and they were silently laughing at me. I grabbed my bag, stuck my hand into it, and dug around for my wallet.

"Don't even think about it," David intoned, half-standing to stop me with his hand.

"I'd like to leave."

"Don't even think about it. Please look at me."

I glanced at his face. He didn't seem angry. Or scared. Just a little overwhelmed, treading very carefully.

"I went a little nuts, okay?" I said to him.

"No. You're going a little nuts now. Put your bag down and look at me."

His lips were curved into a smile, and as always, I felt like I could relax with him.

"You bought me a ticket to Athens."

"I wasn't thinking. If I had thought about it, I would have realized that you need connecting tickets to the islands too."

"That would be on a boat, wouldn't it?"

"Yes. But I already have the tickets."

"Your assistant is very diligent."

"How do you know...? Anyway, it doesn't matter."

"You said you had an assistant. I'm just putting two and two together. So you bought me a ticket to go with you to Greece."

"Can you stop repeating it?"

"No." He grabbed his glass and studied its contents. "I just want you to tell me why you did it."

"I mean…" I sucked in air. "I don't really want to keep talking about this, to be honest."

"Please…"

I threw my hands up in despair and hyperventilated. The neighboring table was living for this.

"I'm comfortable with you. I feel…I guess I feel a little indebted to you for making me feel good these last two weeks. It would have been hard without you. And I think…well, that you make me feel free and understood, and I'm not so scared when I'm with you, and I never do anything rash, so…"

"You know I can't pay you back for this ticket, right?"

"I never wanted you to pay me back."

We stared at each other.

"So you really want me to go?"

"I wanted. I had a moment…" I looked at the ceiling and pulled a face. "In a trial, a forensic psychiatrist would determine it was temporary insanity."

"Wow," he said, with a joking face. "A trial."

"Yes. Over time it will become known as the iconic case Sánchez v. Ortega"

"Margot Ortega? I didn't even know your last name."

"See, that's how crazy I am. You didn't even know my last name, and I bought you a plane ticket."

"You're such a weirdo."

"No." I shook my head. "I'm a dull girl. Boring."

"Yeah, yeah…mediocre, eh?"

"*Chi.*" I nodded.

"Have you ever listened to Carlos Sadness?"

"What are you talking about now?" I was baffled.

"Have you ever heard 'Te Quiero un Poco'?"

"No."

"I'll play it for you later. On my iPod. Because I'm the kind of guy who still has an iPod."

"You're the weirdo."

"I can't pay you back for the ticket," he said again.

"This is a nightmare." I covered my face. "The croquettes are making me feel sick."

"Hey, Margot…how long would a forensic psychiatrist determine temporary insanity lasts for?"

"I don't know," I replied, my face still in my hands.

"Do you think it'd be good for another two weeks?"

I peeked through my fingers at him. "What are you saying?"

"Do you want me to go? I want to go."

"But…?"

"I want to be by your side while you feel free, you're not scared, and you go crazy. I want you to come back to Madrid knowing what you want and how you want it, and I won't settle for anything less. I don't want you to be lonely on your vacation. I don't want you to have a bad time, thinking about whether Filippo this or Filippo that. I want you to drink Greek liquor, jump off something high into the ocean, dance, lose your voice from laughing and singing, stroll along the beach with a bottle of wine in your hand, your new dresses greeting the dawn filled with sand and…"

I stood up and covered his mouth.

"Enough," I whispered slowly.

He raised a hand, asking permission to speak, and I pulled my palm off his lips. I sat down gingerly.

"There are rules."

"Of course there are," I repeated. "Nobody can know."

"Nobody." He nodded.

"You can take photos, but you can never show my face."

"Okay. We'll share costs. Hostels and all that…"

"Hostels? Oh, sweetie…" I laughed. "Don't worry about that."

"Well, you have to let me treat you to things. I'll rent a motorcycle and…"

"Okay, okay."

"And if you change your mind, even in the middle of the trip, I'll come back. And if you get home and think better of it, you just have to send me a message and say: 'I was out of my mind, David.' But you better not be hoping I'll be the one to impose sanity on the plans because…I'm no good at that, angel."

I smiled. "This is fucking crazy."

"Yes." He nodded, looking like a little kid. "Nuts."

"We don't even know each other."

"Not well enough." He nodded.

"It could go terribly."

"Terribly." He stopped a waiter who was passing by our table just then. "Could you bring us the wine list? We need to make a toast."

~~~~~

At two o'clock in the morning, the breeze woke up and tiptoed around Madrid, over all the wild people who were out on a random Wednesday at the end of June on one of the hottest nights of the year. It went around cooling necks, mussing hair, and dragging empty beer cans in its wake. It found David and me sitting on a bench in the Plaza del Dos de Mayo, with a beer we bought on the street, sharing headphones. Carlos Sadness was playing, and David and I looked at each other, as if the lyrics of the song were actually a conversation.

"Twirl, twirl, sad girl. Twirl faster."

And that sentence David uttered when we said goodbye was forevermore engraved in the song, and I could never listen to it without twirling, twirling, twirling faster.

27

MAYBE WE SHOULDN'T

I woke up with Candela sitting on my bed. It wasn't pleasant. At first I thought she was a fucking hallucination, then that I had one of those sleep guardians watching over me, but my sister's obviously terrible mood dispelled my doubts immediately.

"What time did you get home?" And the tone she said it in didn't sound like a sister encouraging me to feel free.

"Sorry?"

"I said what time did you get home?"

"I think around three thirty."

"On a Wednesday."

"I'm on vacation. Leave me alone."

"You're in lost-your-head land. Who were you with?"

"Like you don't know." I turned over in bed and curled up in the hopes that she would leave me alone. "I don't know if you've noticed, but I have no desire to talk to you. That's why I'm avoiding you, you know?"

"Margot, you can't go on vacation with him."

My heart was pounding, but I ignored her.

"I'm serious. And I know you."

"Can't you just leave me alone?" I insisted.

"No." She tugged on my arm. "You know I always encourage you to do stuff, but this…I am not cool with this. He's charming and fun, but you don't know him at all. You don't know where he comes from. He could be a pervert. He could get you into a real fucking mess. What if he's violent? What if he's in a cult? What if he steals from you? What if he tries to blackmail you?"

I shoved a pillow over my head.

"Margot, I mean it. Text him right now, in front of me, and tell him you went crazy and you just realized you shouldn't go together."

"I already told you…" I started to say, muffled by the pillow, which made it much easier to lie, but she yanked it off me. "I already told you I'm going alone."

She stood up and pulled the blanket off my bed, rolling me over in the process.

"I'm really worried," she said in a small voice.

"You should get back to your job already," I suggested. "You don't know how to do nothing, and you've been here for so many days…"

"That's not the problem. You're about to go on a vacation with a dude you just met, and your older sister is forcing me to spend tomorrow trailing the private detective she hired to trail her husband. I'm not leaving here until you can guarantee both my sisters aren't going to show up on the news."

I sucked my teeth and closed my eyes. This was a fucking nightmare. I was the first person who knew that going to Greece with David for two weeks was, without a doubt, the craziest thing I had ever done. But it's what I wanted! I wanted to feel alive, crazy, young…to find out what all those things even meant because lately they had lost all meaning. I wanted excitement to drench my skin, warm it under the sun, and I wanted David by my side because... he was my catalyst.

"Candela, I mean it... I'm going alone, but even so, I want you to butt out of my life. And if Patricia wants to investigate the detective and it doesn't seem like a good idea to you...stop sucking up to her! Stop feeding her paranoia and she'll get tired of it. Like I am of you trying to control everything I do."

Candela's mood seemed to shift suddenly, and I inwardly declared victory. I had sounded really firm, and I was proud of myself, even though lying is bad. But in that same moment, just when I was thinking my sister would leave me alone, an alert popped up on my phone saying I had a new WhatsApp. Candela and I stared at it in silence for a second and then both pounced on it at exactly the same moment; we both knew whom the message was from.

"I'm not fourteen years old! What are you doing?" I yelled, trying to pry the phone out of her grip. "Stop butting into my life, you twatwaffle!"

"What are you hiding? Hey! What are you hiding? If you weren't hiding anything, you wouldn't be making such a big deal out of this."

"Have you ever heard of the concept of privacy?"

She dug her nails into my hand in a maneuver that any judge, even an MMA referee, would have called illegal, and scurried away from my bed with the phone.

"Aha! Guess who it is?" she said to me.

"Well, of course I can guess who it is! Give me back my fucking phone!"

"'Hi, sad eyes,'" she started to read, putting on a ridiculous voice. "'I still can't believe we're going to do this. Everything's all set. I found a friend to cover my shifts at both my jobs and the dog owners had no problem giving me the morning off because it was going to be the last day of dog walking anyway."" She stopped, and her mouth fell open. "You lying whore!"

"Let me live!"

"Let you go on vacation with a stranger? Text him right now and tell him you changed your mind."

"Are you listening to yourself?" I interrogated her, trying to calm my tone down. "You sound like Mama."

"Don't say that, Margot. I'm doing this for your own good."

"She also sent us to boarding school because she thought it was for our own good."

"She sent us to boarding school so she could live *la vida loca* with her mushroom. Don't try to gaslight me."

"Well, maybe I want to live *la vida loca* with my mushroom."

"Yours isn't a mushroom, he's a perpetual Lost Boy."

I let out a howl of impotence and threw myself back on the bed.

"He's not going to kill me. He's not going to traffic me. He's not going to use me as a mule to move drug packages through Europe. He doesn't even have any romantic or sexual intentions toward me."

"Ha." Candela sat on my bed again and crossed her arms, turning her back to me.

"I just want to have fun."

She turned back and gave me puppy dog eyes.

"I know he's not going to kill you or traffic you or make you move drugs. That dude doesn't even know what drugs are, that's for sure. I'm not even scared he's scamming you to get a free vacation and then ditch you."

"So?"

"So...I'm scared you'll fall in love, you'll do something stupid, you'll fuck up your life. I know you really want to get Filippo back, and after this fling, you won't be able to. I'm scared you'll screw him in a drunken haze and he'll come inside you and then you'll get pregnant. I'm scared you'll get dickmatized, and then he won't want anything to do with you. I don't know what I'm afraid of, and maybe I'm not being rational because I've done worse things, but that's exactly why I'm in the position to tell you that this could turn your whole life upside down. Because you're going on vacation with some guy you just met!"

She lobbed the phone onto me and stood up. Mentioning Filippo had been out of pocket. Filippo. My Filippo. He wouldn't understand it. No. He wouldn't understand the trip with David if he ever found out. What Candela was asking me was did I want to start our life together with a lie?

"My advice would be to tell him you had second thoughts, that it's crazy, and that—"

"For fuck's sake." I grabbed my phone, typed, and stood up.

The phone landed in my sister's lap.

"There. Done. Now, please, leave me alone and go to hell."

Candela grabbed the phone and read the message.

I think we made a mistake making this decision.
Sorry. See you when I get back if you still want to.

"Margot..." she mumbled.

"I'm serious. Leave me alone."

~~~~~

I went out to buy a few things. Sunscreen, some bikinis, and some other clothes. I was dragging my feet, disappointed because no one seemed to understand that this was my life and only I could make a final decision. So what if it was crazy? So what if everything went wrong? Wasn't that something to experience?

It was nonsense, but…I felt more alone that day than the day I fled my wedding.

David didn't answer. No, he didn't answer. I discovered that later that night when I found Candela at home, where I had purposely left my phone. She was sitting at the breakfast bar, her face ashen. She felt guilty. I guess no matter how scared she was of someone like David, a crazy near stranger who I suddenly felt more at home with than home, she'd had all day to think about how she would've felt in his shoes. Bad. Terrible. Shitty. And I wanted her to feel that way.

"He didn't answer." She pointed to the phone, which was sitting in front of her on the bar.

"I bet. What could you possibly answer to that?"

"Call him."

"I don't feel like it."

"Message him," she insisted.

"I said I don't feel like it, Candela. Didn't you get what you wanted? Stop bugging me. I'm going to go finish packing."

"I don't want you to leave angry with me. Imagine if the plane crashes and you die. It'd be so shitty if your last words to your favorite sister were an angry *go to hell*."

"You're not my favorite sister," I lied. "And thanks so much for always giving me calming visions of my life."

"Jeez, Margarita." She kicked the floor, her eyes welling up. "Don't be mad."

I sighed, put my bags down, and flipped my hair.

"I don't know what's going on with me. I have no fucking clue why I ran out on my wedding to the man of my dreams. I don't know why I feel so comfortable and so myself with David. But I want to find out. How I discover these things is up to me and me alone. I would've expected this from Mama or from Patricia. I thought you would keep my secret and be my ride or die. But now...what? I don't even have you."

"It's not like that." She covered her face. "Seriously. If you want to go with him, I get it. But we're all capable of making really stupid decisions just so we can feel happy for a minute. It's like drugs. I'm your sister; I would never let you get addicted to drugs, even if you swore they made you feel amazing. So...sometimes we need someone else to help us decide."

I stared at her in shock, but after a few seconds, I realized I didn't have any interest in debating with her, so I headed to my room, saying over my shoulder:

"David isn't some designer drug. He's a person, and I'm not a child."

"Margot..." she pleaded.

"I'm not leaving angry." I gripped the doorframe of my room. "Just in case the plane crashes, now you know. I'm not angry. I just... wish you would trust me more. Good night."

I barely slept a wink that night.

~~~~~

I had always liked the Adolfo Suárez Madrid Barajas airport. Even though, as a child, I always experienced a kind of anxiety on the way back to school, huge suitcase in hand, bound for Switzerland. But over time I converted those memories until they ceased to hold water compared to everything else that happens in an airport. They're so full of emotion: school trips, honeymoons, getaways, starting life anew somewhere else, dreams fulfilled, vacations, responsibilities, and work. There's a little of everything. I always find goodbyes emotional, but…this time I had no one to say goodbye to because I went alone, in a taxi, seizing my chance when Candela was in the shower.

I was tired, that was true, but as I dragged my suitcase through the terminal to security, I realized I wasn't sad. That meant that somehow I was gradually finding peace with the decisions I had made. I did miss Filippo, but even he had started to forgive me for ruining our day. I was suddenly filled with certainty that going on this trip was the right thing to do.

I got through the fast-track security in just a few minutes, with my carry-on suitcase, dressed in black baggy pants, a short-sleeved colorfully embroidered shirt by Kenzo, and a denim jacket thrown over my shoulders. Besides my carry-on suitcase, I also had a bag full of all the "just in case" stuff that anyone could possibly imagine for a flight that wasn't even four hours long, plus a few magazines I had bought in the terminal. When I arrived in the waiting lounge, as a rather handsome boy let me in, I caught a glimpse of my reflection in the glass, and for the first time in a long time, I liked what I saw. Everything. It wasn't just about my skin or my clothes. I was proud of myself that day, and the image I projected made me feel confident.

I got a coffee and a sandwich in the VIP lounge while I thumbed through magazines. Candela messaged to guilt-trip me for not waiting for her to take me to the airport. And, while she was at it, she wished me bon voyage.

Text me and call me whenever you want.
I'll text you too, but remember I don't want to bug you.
It's your trip. And you'll come back knowing what's what,
I'm sure.

I rolled my eyes. I was a little pissed off, I'm not going to deny it.

David messaged me too, but he just said a curt have a good trip that made me choke on my coffee a little. Patricia probably didn't even remember. Launching a line of jewelry in an important and impressive retail chain while she followed the guy she had hired to follow her husband, on top of raising her three children, already took up a lot of her life and headspace.

In case you're wondering…no. I didn't answer any of those messages.

Sonia had bought me a business class ticket, as she always did when I traveled for work and the business didn't charter a jet, a detail that made me nervous because, honestly, it wasn't necessary. My seat was wide and comfortable, and I put my stuff down on it while I grabbed my suitcase and tried to put it up in the overhead compartment. A man asked me if I needed help.

"That's okay. I can do it myself."

I can do it myself was a sentence I wasn't used to believing, but it was time to change that.

I put it in the luggage rack, rearranged the stuff in my bag so I just had what I needed for the flight, and finally sat down to sip a glass of champagne while I waited for takeoff.

Someone sat in the seat next to me, and I glanced up. I smiled. He smiled back, leaving his book on the tray table and accepting the glass offered by a flight attendant.

"Have a good flight," he whispered lifting his drink toward me.

"Same to you."

We each took a sip. I smiled, looked down, and bit my lip. And I had an idea… I took out my phone and snapped a photo before I turned it off. After I gave it my seal of approval, I sent it to Candela along with a terse text:

From now on, I'll be deciding on my own life.

But thank you. I know you had good intentions.

And David and I looked great in the photo, smiling, raising our glasses, and promising ourselves the best vacation of our lives.

Candela, sweetie… you're very intelligent, but as the youngest of the three sisters, I'm obligated to be a little wicked sometimes.

28

~~~

THE AIR IS OURS

DAVID

When I saw her going through security, I couldn't believe it. What exactly? I don't know. I felt lucky and stupid. Those sad eyes, the saddest in the club, were shining, and...I felt like I had something to do with it. For someone who had never done anything important, it was very refreshing.

She was wearing low-waist black pants, a black shirt with colorful embroidery, huge sunglasses that she had definitely forgotten she still had on, a jean jacket, and a bag whose logo I didn't recognize but I would bet cost more than rent on a place I could never afford anyway. But that was part of her charm. She didn't care how much what she was wearing cost; it wasn't important to her. What was important to her was looking into your eyes and asking you what songs you would listen to on a desert island. I had never met anyone who wanted to fade into the crowd more than her, and she wasn't even aware of it.

When I got her message telling me she had changed her mind, all I could do was smile. The night before, just as I was falling asleep, she texted me and said that might happen.

My sister smells a rat. Send me a message when you
have everything figured out, and if I answer that it'd be
better to let it be, ignore it. I'd never say that through
text. It'll just be so Candela leaves me alone, okay?

Margot said she wasn't pretty enough or smart enough, but it
seemed to me that she didn't even know what she was capable of.
She was convinced that what everyone else said was true and that her
opinion should lie dormant, but something was starting to wake up.

Domi and Ivan lost their minds when I said I was going to
Greece with her. Ivan got a little freaked out and warned me, pretty
awkwardly, that accepting things in exchange for sex was prosti-
tution. The guffaw that slipped out made him blink, taken aback.
Domi, on the other hand, seemed excited.

"Is it bad that I accepted?" I asked her, a little worried.

"She can afford it, David."

"But how do we know that? I mean…"

"She has a Louis Vuitton bag, Chanel sandals, and a six-figure
engagement ring. David, whoever this girl is, she can afford it."

"But I probably shouldn't have accepted, right?"

"Money can't buy everything." She smiled sadly. "What if she
needs someone who helps her feel like you make her feel? What
if this trip doesn't make sense on her own? What if she convinced
herself that she matters for what she has and not who she is? Go to
Greece and enjoy it."

At the risk of being a boy toy. At the risk of turning into the
temporary plaything for a loaded girl. At the risk that I might be
wrong about Margot and she might turn out to be an insane whore…
yeah, I would go. And I would enjoy it. And yet…for now I didn't

want to announce it on the WhatsApp group chat from the village because I didn't know how to explain it without sounding too off-the-wall.

During the flight, while she drank champagne, I glanced over a guide she had downloaded on her iPad, and she told me how we were going to arrange everything in the hotels so we didn't "raise suspicions." I found myself thinking this wasn't so bad. I will say, though I would deny it in front of anyone, that she was beautiful in a way that only those who are beautiful both inside and out can be. Her huge brown, slightly sad eyes were a reflection of the little girl still curled up inside her, waiting for a hug. Her lips, tiny and soft, looked even prettier when she smiled. Her body, which, despite its somewhat helpless appearance, revealed the anatomy of a woman whose weapons I didn't yet know, was starting to catch my attention a little too. She had a super tiny waist, which launched out into round hips, and two breasts that weren't very large but were proud and perky.

"Are you listening to me?" she asked, punching me on the arm.

No, I was thinking about her topless.

But don't get it twisted. I respected her. Fuck, I really respected her. I didn't know what that girl had done to me, but she made me serve her my life on a silver platter so she could organize it and transform it into what she would consider more satisfactory. I trusted her blindly... Is there more honest proof of respect?

~~~~~

When we got there, I was surprised by the Athens cityscape; I hadn't been expecting something so...Mediterranean. Pretty stupid of me. Well, not that or the uniformed guy who greeted us, taking charge of our luggage.

"Margot…" I whispered. She was looking at her phone.

"Candela is flipping out."

"Margot…" I repeated. "All this must be pretty expensive."

She looked at me, surprised. "Why are you thinking about that? Don't worry about money. It's all paid for already, and, anyway, it's not important."

"But Margot…a private transfer and everything?"

She sucked her teeth, sighed, put a hand on her hip, and said: "Well…it's a company car. They didn't pay for the trip, but…let's just say I have access to certain perks, okay? In reality, it's…let's say free."

"It's not free, don't lie. Someone has to pay this gentleman…"

"David." She put her hand on my face. "It's a business expense, and don't worry because I already handed over my whole life to pay it back."

I don't know if she convinced me. All I know is I wanted to stop thinking about it. I wasn't in it for the luxury, just the experience, and I should have focused on that, right?

When we went into the hotel, a bellhop ran out to grab our bags. But separately, of course. We pretended not to know each other despite the fact that we had just gotten out of the same car. Why? Well, I didn't know much about Margot's life at the time, so I thought it was just pure paranoia. One more cute quirk. We stood at the reception desk with our passports, side by side, and snuck each other smiles as they helped us.

I got the feeling we had the best rooms in the whole hotel. Especially when staff saw our reservation and then changed their behavior, suddenly becoming downright obsequious. I don't know if I felt uncomfortable because these people deduced they should behave like this with guests like us or because I was actually a guest like us. I was reassured by the fact that Margot didn't look delighted either.

"It's just a formality," she whispered in a muffled and discreet way.

"Girl…what the hell do you do for a living?"

She didn't answer; she just hung her head while they made out the key to her room to the name of one Ana Ortiz. I was completely lost. I would have bet I had gone on a trip with the daughter of a fucking mob boss…

The hotel seemed typical to me: the kind of typical they always showed in movies, where people with money come and go, the types people like me normally opened doors for. As we walked through the corridor in silence, all the words Idoia had said to me in our breakup were echoing in my head. And everything that could be extrapolated from them: *mediocre, starving, thrown away, no future*. Maybe she was right. I couldn't afford any of this, and let's face it, Idoia liked luxury. She wasn't like Margot, who seemed to come by it naturally. Idoia always said she liked expensive things. Every two months or so, she would make what she called "an investment," which boiled down to her buying a bag with a price tag I found offensive.

"Are you okay?" Margot asked softly.

"Yes, but I feel like…like I'm scamming someone. I didn't earn this. I don't know if that makes sense."

"Of course it makes sense." She smiled at me. "I feel like that every day."

"I never thought I'd travel like this."

Margot stopped at the door to her room, the door next to mine. She looked around us in case our luggage was already being brought up, but there was nobody in the carpeted hall. She held her hand out to me, and I grabbed her fingers.

"Who cares how we do it? The destination is all that matters."

"And the company," I added.

"I don't want you to judge me based on the details of this trip."

"I won't."

"We're not what we have. We're just what we feel."

"And what we do."

I went over and kissed her forehead, putting my hands on her head. It was a slow movement. Somehow it felt intimate, very intimate.

We opened our respective doors just as footsteps announced the bellhop's arrival.

The room had hidden treasures. Money doesn't just pay for gold and luxury finishes but also air and views, judging by what you could see from the small balcony; the majestic and imposing Acropolis was right there. I got a lump in my throat and had to swallow it, I admit it. Well, actually I had to stifle a huge desire to cry that made me feel embarrassed. I clung to the railing, took a deep breath, and took out my shitty phone to take a picture, though, just like the moon, the photos could never do it justice.

I only unpacked three or four things from my suitcase before I snuck down the hallway to Margot's room. She opened the door with her phone pressed to her ear, in what seemed like a work call, one of those tense and cold ones you want to hang up from as soon as possible. But I soon found out it was actually a mother-daughter chat.

"It's nobody, they're just bringing in my suitcases." She took a deep breath, and I closed the door carefully. "Yes, yes. The flight was good. The hotel too." She paused. Rolled her eyes. "Okay, Mother. Goodbye."

"You guys have such a sweet relationship," I said sarcastically after she threw the phone on the bed.

"My mother is a hemorrhoid."

I let out a chortle and sat on her bed. The room was exactly like mine: huge, a little tasteless, but gleaming and with incredible views. I glanced at the opulent white-marble bathroom, where Margot had already unpacked a few toiletry bags.

"I know we're going to wander around the city now, but…all I can think about is getting in there," I said, pointing to one of those rain showers.

"David…you want to take a shower? Take one!" She smiled. "This is a vacation, and on vacation you can eat breakfast at three in the afternoon and drink wine at eleven in the morning."

I imagined how her face would look if, following her advice, I stripped naked right there and jumped into the shower. I laughed.

She laughed too, and I thought her laughter was just a reflex, but she quickly made it clear that she knew me better than I thought: "I was talking about yours, you sketchball. Don't even think about it."

We ate moussaka, drank beer, and had ice cream for dessert, lost in the alleys of a city that didn't belong to us and that seemed chaotic and full to the brim with people like us, who usurped the place for photos, toasts, and souvenirs. I hate how tourists stain every place we tread with compulsive footprints, even if we don't realize it. Even though we link arms with the person walking next to us, following their ankles and feet in those black Converse that were already getting a little dirty. Margot's.

It was hot…very hot. We walked a lot, checking which ruins we were stumbling over on our phones. And as much as I have tried to conjure the memory of what we did or what we talked about, I can't. The only things that come to mind are the image of Margot laughing, complaining about the heat, pointing at something with awe, chugging a whole bottle of water in one go, holding my arm so she wouldn't trip. I think I was overwhelmed. No one had ever given me something so big. And I don't mean luxuries, though it's good to realize you never needed to be picked up in a nice car at the airport or have your bags carried for you. I mean what money really buys: time. But for yourself.

The next day, very early, we had planned to visit the Acropolis, and between walks and pit stops for a drink, we had already seen a good chunk of everything Margot had written down for the first day. We would only be in Athens for one more day before we left for Santorini, but she turned to me, smiling, and proposed: "Why don't we go back to the hotel and go for a swim?"

Maybe we should have forced ourselves to be good tourists and consult the guidebook, but all the places they proposed on lists of "what to see in one day" fell by the wayside because Margot and I wanted to go for a swim.

The rooftop had a restaurant and a pool surrounded by sun loungers, but they were all taken when we arrived, so we left our stuff in a corner and peeled off our clothes. We had stopped by the room to change, and I was already wearing my bathing suit, a slightly faded red one, so all I had to do was take off my shirt. She had put on a simple black dress like a long T-shirt, and when she took it off, I understood why she had laughed at the sight of my bathing suit: hers was the same color. We hurled ourselves into the glass-walled pool and let out a yelp that was covered by a couple of children who were racing and ducking down. The water was weirdly freezing considering how hot the city was.

"Hello?" Margot said with her eyes wide. "Can you explain this frostbite?"

I felt weird looking away, but her nipples were showing through her bathing suit, and it was hard for me to look at her face. I felt like a dick for noticing them…small and dark, crowning two breasts that seemed to have shrunk in the cold water.

"Two free chairs!" I exclaimed, looking behind her.

I backed away with the excuse of grabbing them before anyone else saw them, but really I had to get away because I didn't want to look at her like that. No. I just wanted to look at Idoia like that, and thinking about Margot like that would be dirty.

She ordered a bottle of cold white wine without even looking at the price list, and we lay down while the sun set over the city. In silence. Occasionally tossing peanuts to annoy each other.

I watched her settle in her lounger, close her eyes, sigh…and I wondered what her life was really like. Was she used to these luxuries? How could I feel so comfortable with someone so different than me? What were we, Lady and the Tramp? Maybe I shouldn't have accepted this trip.

Then Margot turned back toward me and looked at me. I don't mean she glanced over at me. No. I mean she *looked at me*. Like I was glass and she could see through my skin. Like my thoughts had traveled to her lips in the form of a question: "Do you regret coming?"

"No," I said quickly, but for the moment I wasn't ready to say anything else.

"No, but…?"

"But it scares me," I added.

She sat up a little, holding her wineglass, and a worried look appeared on her face.

"What scares you? Me? It's not about…the money?"

I shook my head, even though the cost of the trip definitely worried me.

"You're scaring me," she whispered. "If you don't want to be here…I mean…if you're bored and you think traveling together wasn't a good idea, it's fine. I'll give you your tickets, the name of the hotels, and everything else. You can keep traveling on your own, David."

"Margot." I stretched my hand out toward her. "Dummy. That's not it."

"So?"

"I don't know." I shrugged. "Maybe I'm scared of going back to real life when this trip ends."

"That's not it either." She raised an eyebrow but with a smile. She seemed relieved suddenly. "It's something you're embarrassed to tell me."

And…yes. It was something I was embarrassed to even accept myself: I was scared of not being enough, of my presence there not making up for the money she had invested. Fuck. We only met… what, two weeks ago? What happened if she realized I was just a mediocre, poor, scatterbrained dude, like Idoia said? Idoia was such a bitch, for fuck's sake. But seriously, what a bitch. I don't think I had ever stopped to think about it until that moment. How could she refuse to give me a chance just for being broke as a joke when I loved her so much?

I turned back to Margot, who was waiting impatiently for my answer, and I did what I knew best, pretended everything going on inside me was the symptom of a very basic need.

"I'm hungry. Actually, I'm always hungry."

"And you think that's going to be a problem on this trip?"

I nodded, shoving all the peanuts that were left into my mouth while she laughed and climbed off the sun lounger.

"I'm going to take one last little 'ice' dip. Then we can go watch the changing of the guard at the Syntagma Square and have dinner. Sound good?"

"Sounds good."

She took a few steps toward the pool, but at the last second, she turned back to me. She twisted her fingers in my hair in a way she never had treated me before that moment. I looked at her, pushing the hair off my forehead, and she said with a smile: "I'm scared too, but I feel better when you're with me. You don't need to hide things from me. Ever."

"I don't know if I'm worth all this money," I confessed. "I'm scared I'm not up to scratch."

She sat opposite me, her hand still in my hair, but now stroking my temples. I did the same. I stroked her hair too. I wondered what we must look like to the other guests. I wondered what Margot saw in me when she looked at me. I wondered if she had realized that ever since I had met her, I had separation anxiety when we were apart.

"Two fools," she whispered. I guess we were. I guess she knew.

29

CONFESSIONS

MARGOT

"What was Filippo like as a partner?"

"What do you mean?"

David and I were lying on his bed after a massive consumption of cheese, tzatziki, and gyros in pita bread. Both of us were staring at the ceiling with our hands on our stomachs. We felt tired and stuffed, but we weren't sleepy yet.

He turned to me again. "Was he fun, affectionate, good in bed…?"

"David!" I groaned with a smile. "I'm not going to discuss my sex life with Filippo."

"Why not?" He shrugged. "That's silly. Sex is just one part of a relationship."

I kept quiet, looking at the ceiling.

"Come on…" He elbowed me, egging me on to speak.

"Filippo is very pleasant, but I wouldn't say he's fun. I mean…in the sense that he doesn't pull pranks or tell jokes or…"

"I don't tell jokes, and I'm fun."

"The thing about you is you have a laughing face," I justified. I wasn't sure why, but I felt like my comments had been an attack on Filippo. "He's a man of few words. He speaks little, but he does a lot."

"Are you about to get dirty?"

"No!" I cackled. "I mean he… I don't know. He's a man of few words, but sometimes he can be kind of an old-fashioned romantic," I bantered affectionately. "He can be a little dry, but then he kneels down in the middle of a park full of deer to propose."

"You're still wearing the ring." He pointed to my hand.

"Yeah. So stupid." I sighed sadly.

"It's not stupid to keep wearing something so valuable to you. And by valuable I mean sentimentally valuable, though I bet you could buy me and half of the Cuenca province with what it cost."

"Don't be like that," I moaned, and I rolled toward him so we were lying face-to-face. "I love our routines, you know? That's what I miss the most."

"What do you mean?"

"I don't know. Getting home from work and Filippo being there, reading, with a glass of wine in his hand, listening to Italian music. Every Thursday we'd order Vietnamese food, and on Saturdays we'd cook together… We got into making fancy stuff… Half the time the food ended up in the trash because we didn't make anything that would pass as edible."

"Well, that sounds fun."

"Ah, no." I smiled. "Filippo gets really angry if something doesn't turn out well. He's very proud, and I always suspected he was kind of a perfectionist."

"Dude, with those genes…" David muttered.

"I didn't fall in love with him because of his genes." I smiled.

"It had nothing to do with how broad his chest is or the fact that he is nine feet tall?"

"Well, it caught my eye, I'm not gonna lie. But he was, I don't know…Filippo is…"

"What do you like most about him?"

I turned onto my back and bit my lip, looking for the right words. David leaned on his elbow, and I saw his face appear above mine, greedy for information.

"He made me feel like a ten."

He raised an eyebrow. That didn't seem like the right answer.

"Wait, let me get this straight." He straightened up into a sitting position. "You're telling me Filippo made you feel better? Like a better woman, I mean?"

"Yes." I nodded. "I felt like I grew by his side."

"He's a man, not yeast," he said insolently.

"What did I say?" I sat up too, so we were level.

"I mean I don't understand what you're saying. How are you going to base your opinion of yourself on another person? That's like if I said…I don't know, that I'm funny because you laugh."

I squinted, confused.

"I'm already funny, whether you laugh or not!"

"Let's see, considering you're not funny, but you have a jokey face, I think I get what you're trying to say."

"Okay, what am I trying to say?"

"That I'm valid and I'm a ten outside of him."

He nodded raising his eyebrows excitedly. "Yes, you are."

"Tell that to my mother. Watch how she argues with you."

"How would you argue it?"

"Ah, my mother doesn't understand arguments, David. She's a human cat hooked on pain pills and champagne."

"So do you really care what she thinks?"

"I mean, she's my mother." I wanted to change the subject, and I put a finger on the end of his upturned nose. "Now drop my mother and tell me...what did you like most about Idoia?"

"Well..." He bit the inside of his cheek, his gaze wandering around the room. "I don't want to make you uncomfortable."

"Why would it make me uncomfortable?"

"Because I'm probably going to get raunchy." He smiled roguishly.

"I think I can handle it."

"Well, in the beginning Idoia and I were just sleeping together," he said kind of timidly. "It was the typical fuck buddy relationship: 'I'll call you, and if you're around, great, and if not, that's great too.'"

"And what made it turn into something more?"

"I snuck in." He smiled sheepishly. "Little by little, it started to bother me when she would blow me off. I started coming on strong."

I raised an eyebrow.

"What?" he asked me.

"So basically, you came on strong because she ignored you."

"Not exactly."

"So then what exactly?"

"Well, I don't know. I liked her a lot. She would show me cool music, we did awesome stuff, she drove me crazy...seriously, literally crazy. She was...is a force of nature."

I made a face like I didn't believe him.

"What? You should've seen us in bed! Well, I don't mean 'you should've seen us' literally; I don't think you're into live porn. But we were the shit. Seriously."

"Okay," I said, a little uncomfortable. It was impossible not to imagine him with that beautiful blond knockout really going at it. "But did you really talk?"

"Come on, girl, we didn't use smoke signals."

"I mean, did you guys really talk about your relationship, about books or movies, death, the future, if happiness exists, or if there's life on other planets?"

"About books, yes." He nodded. "And movies. Music, too."

"You're repeating yourself," I teased.

"The thing is, Idoia isn't very communicative, you know?" He shrugged. "And she never really liked the idea of getting together with my friends. We fought about that a lot or about…I don't know, because sometimes it seemed like I wasn't enough. It's possible I really wasn't and that's why she left me, but…but we always made up in the end…hard." He widened his eyes, making sure I understood which body parts did the making up.

"Well, it sounds like a pretty toxic relationship."

"I could say the same about yours, babe."

"I guess we're both screwed."

I let myself flop back, and David's face loomed above mine again.

"But this time we'll do it right," he assured me. "When we get them back, we'll do it right."

"Yes," I said, not quite as sure as he sounded. "We'll be the shit."

David lay down next to me and sighed.

"Fuck. I miss her."

"Did you post the photo you took in the Athens airport?"

"Yes." He nodded. "She liked it, but nothing else."

"You didn't tell me."

"It didn't really matter. It's just a 'like,' like last time. It's not progressing."

"What do you miss about her?" Now I was curious.

"Now? Well, you're not going to like the answer."

"Try me."

"I miss how she panted when we fucked," he said, his voice much lower suddenly. "I never managed to get a single word out of her, but she moaned in this way... She would dig her nails into my back or my chest and moan like my body was melting into her."

I swallowed audibly. He looked at me.

"Sorry."

"Don't worry about it." I sat up. "I think I'm going to go to bed."

"You can sleep here if you want," he offered.

"Ah, no, no. I'll let you have your privacy. I think you need it."

He started laughing, and I got up. As I gathered up my bag and my phone, David reached out and grabbed my wrist.

"Now I feel bad."

"Bad why?" I asked.

"Because I turned into a gross bro, went full hard-core porn, and you didn't let loose at all, which makes me think it makes you uncomfortable and..."

I leaned down until my lips were almost brushing against his ear and, before he could finish, said, "You have no idea how much I miss his cock in my mouth."

When I stood up, David was grinning from ear to ear, his eyes even wider.

"You're filthy!" he cackled.

"Well, then what does that make you?"

"Your soulmate."

30

~~

A TEACHER

To my left, there were three girls in their twenties: pretty, trendy, well- dressed, the kind who take perfect photos in perfect settings of their perfect bodies. The Parthenon was right in front of me, impressive and incredible, but suddenly the three girls were undressing David with their eyes.

"So rude," I complained. "What if you were my boyfriend? Don't people have any respect anymore?"

"They're just looking," he teased. "Don't be jealous. Looking is free."

He glanced back and winked at them. Their giggles echoed through the whole Acropolis.

"Go over there, go on. I'm going to take a photo of you," I said brusquely.

He stood in front of me. A lock of hair fell against his slightly sweaty forehead. It was really hot, and his black T-shirt was sticking to his chest. He crossed his arms, probably to hide the sweat stains on the fabric. I was surprised to see my own reflection gaping in his sunglasses. Fuck. He had woken up much more attractive that morning.

"What's taking so long? Come on!" he hurried me.

"Wait. Push your hair off your forehead," I said as a cover-up.

"Like this?" he messed it up even more.

"No. Stop."

"Come on, Margot, people can't get by, and they're all jostling me."

It made me laugh that he was whining like a little kid, and I went over to fix his hair. The girls who were eye-fucking him seemed to hold their breath.

"Are you going to make out with me to teach them a lesson?" David asked sarcastically.

"You wish. I'm going to fix your hair a little because it looks like a rat's nest."

I smoothed his hair a little to one side, and he tried to push his messy hair behind his ear, as if he could. Then he grabbed my waist.

"Make me look hot, okay?"

"Let go of me. It's sweltering."

I pulled away and took one, two, three photos. Spectacular. Had he always been this hot? It must be the sunglasses. I looked at him and then the screen of my phone. I wasn't just an amazing photographer, he was a good subject. That image could have been on the cover of any music magazine and he could be the teen idol of the moment. Fuck...

David snatched my phone to see how the photos came out and then glanced over at me with a super confused look.

"Margot!"

"What?"

"You can't even see the Parthenon!"

"Ay, shut up." I covered my eyes with my hands, and he burst out laughing.

"What the fuck! Wait. Hey…" He called one of the girls over, but she looked petrified. He called her again, this time in English. The girl came over. He asked in Spanish: "Do you speak Spanish? No? Well, it doesn't matter. Will you take a photo of us?"

He handed her the phone with the camera app open and mimed to make her understand. I asked her in English, and it made us laugh.

It was a really good picture. On our right, the building, standing for so many centuries, and the two of us looking at each other, laughing like two assholes. Before he returned the phone, I turned my back, hugged David a little, and told him it was time to take one for his Instagram. I was surprised when he lifted me off the ground and spun around with me in his arms. The poor lady I inadvertently kicked was surprised too.

The girls hung their heads and pushed past us as we headed to see the remains of the Erechtheion.

"Look at them. They're so bummed now that they think you're off the market."

"They gave me a pretty good eye-fucking," he needled me. "I'm worn out. Three is too much even for me."

I side-eyed him and grinned. "Do you know you're shameless?"

"Do you know the Erechtheion was erected in honor of Athena, Poseidon, and Erechtheus, who, according to mythology, was the king of the city? It's famous for the portico of Caryatids."

"Apparently I booked the private tour."

"And it comes with an erotic show. Later, I'll show you the peach." He winked.

David liked history. He understood art too, but when I had asked him what he studied, he just said nothing that would help him make a living. He sounded disheartened when he said it, and I thought it was a pretty weak-sauce argument. He just used it as an excuse for not graduating. I didn't bring it up anymore. He seemed insecure whenever we talked about his studies. I clung to his arm, I listened to him talk about Pericles, Phidias, the battle of Plataea, the wet drapery technique, Ionic and Doric capitals, polychromes lost over time, the Parthenon being smashed to pieces during one of the Ottoman-Venetian wars…

We weren't planning on buying souvenirs, but as we walked through the Plaka, in the shadow of the Acropolis, we were immediately drawn to the shops proudly displaying hundreds of penises. They came in all shapes and sizes and were very detailed.

"Wait…are cocks a Greek specialty or something?" David asked smoothly.

"Well, I don't know, but some of these are so big they're scary."

He raised an eyebrow and firmly grabbed an enormous one hanging from the wall.

"Filippo's size?"

"He's almost six foot five, and everything else matches. You do the math."

"Show-off." He laughed. "Wait, I'm going to find one that looks like mine, and I'm going to give it to you so you have something to remember me by."

"I don't want a replica of your peewee!"

"Come on, dummy."

I got the giggles. He did too. The shopkeeper looked at us wearily. He must have been sick of hearing the same jokes day in and day out.

In the end we bought four, but tiny ones, key chain–sized: for Asuncion, Amparito, Candela, and Patricia. We thought it was the perfect gift.

~~~~

The bougainvillea was blooming beautifully, creeping up the street walls and draped over terraces. Here and there, men in T-shirts with the name of their restaurants emblazoned on them approached to offer you a table in their establishments. But we were sticking to the travel blog of a Spanish girl who had lived there for five years and looking for a hidden place that few tourists made it to. And when we found it, we sat under the tiny magenta flowers on a shady terrace.

We drank a few beers and nibbled on whatever the waiter recommended. He spoke better Spanish than we did. And while we chatted, David got a message.

"I can't believe it," he muttered, his eyes glued to the screen.

"What?"

"It's Idoia."

My heart leaped into my throat, pounding furiously. Why hadn't Filippo texted me?

"What did she say?"

Hi David. I just wanted to say I've been seeing your photos on Instagram and it's so nice to see you so happy. Life is funny...you never know what's gonna make you smile, right? Or who you're going to fall in love with. I never would have thought you liked girls like her, but I have to be honest with myself and admit that you never smiled like that with me. But we can still be friends, right? Call me whenever you want. I'd love to talk to you for a little bit.

David lifted his eyes from the screen and looked at me, confused.

"What the hell is this? Now she wants to be my friend? Margot, girl, we're doing this all wrong."

"No, idiot! She's smarter than a fox." I pointed out angrily. "And she has zero scruples, that's for sure. If she's so happy to see you like this, why is she trying to play the role of 'ghost from the past'?"

"I mean, we only broke up a month ago."

"A month ago is the past. Don't contradict me." I snatched his phone and read the message again.

"Don't get pissy with me," he groaned. "Sometimes I swear you don't understand love at all."

"This isn't love," I spluttered. "This is ego."

"Thanks, Margot, I feel so much better now."

I looked up from the phone quickly.

"No, David! I didn't mean that. Well, I did. It's ego, but it's good. Good for you. Ego is what made her emerge from her lair, but you can use it to your advantage."

"You think so?"

"Of course." I nodded. "She already regrets letting you go."

"She didn't let me go. She gave me a verbal beating, and I went off to cower and lick my balls where she kicked them."

I raised my eyebrows. "You sound hurt."

"No." He sucked his teeth and rubbed his eyes. Then he pulled his sunglasses down over them. "I just don't understand what the fuck this girl is doing. Deep down, I know you're right; she's so egotistical."

"But that's the reaction you were hoping for, right?"

"Yeah, I guess so."

I handed him back his phone and took a sip of water. What if Filippo didn't…?

"You haven't heard from him?" he asked.

"Not since the message he sent me, nothing."

"Text him," he said in a small voice. "Send him one of the photos you took today and tell him…I dunno, thank him for encouraging you to take this trip. Tell him it's been very illuminating."

"What if he asks me if I figured out what caused the panic attack that made me flee our wedding?"

"Then tell him the truth."

"That I have no idea? That doesn't sound like progress."

"No. Tell him that you're not thinking about that right now. That you only care about what the future holds."

I grabbed his hand off the table and squeezed it.

"Thank you."

"Tell me the truth…" He got very serious and turned my hand over so our palms were touching.

"About what?"

"Do you think Idoia is an idiot?"

I made a face. "That's not it."

"So what is it?"

"I think you think you're not good enough for her, but, actually, Idoia is the one who doesn't deserve you."

"I don't even have my own house."

"Who really cares about that stuff when we fall in love?"

He pouted and looked up at the sky. It was stiflingly hot even in the shade. "If it had been the other way around, I would have asked her to move in with me."

"Well, I wouldn't have," I said, tugging on one of his fingers a little, to make sure he was paying attention. "Because love isn't about creating dependency, it's about making you grow wings. And you're still growing your feathers, little chicken."

David smiled.

"You wouldn't have left me for being mediocre and a pariah. It seems like fun to you."

"You don't seem like a pariah or mediocre to me…"

"What do I seem like to you?"

A cute and scared little boy. A free soul. Someone who's scared to go more than skin-deep. A fuck-boy. A guy who definitely wants her to take the lead. Funny. Outrageous. A little crazy. A man in the making. A misunderstood man. A dreamer.

"You shouldn't depend on anyone's opinion except your own."

David's smile spread until it filled his whole face. He laced his fingers through mine, and he gave my hand a little jerk.

"Such a good student."

"Such a good teacher."

31

~~~

THIS IS WHERE THE
TRIP REALLY BEGINS

The first thing I did when I woke up was check my phone. At the time I dragged around this fixation, which since the INCIDENT had become an obsession. Even worse, it always left me feeling disappointed because usually all I found were work emails where I was cc'd with an FYI. But that morning it wasn't like that.

Following David's advice, I had texted Filippo before I went to bed. It was a colorful photo where the shadows gave depth to the flowers and cobblestones. My own shadow was projected on the ground, elongated and solid, in one piece, without features or detail. Next to me, a few steps back, you could make out what I knew was David's shadow, but in Filippo's eyes, it could be anyone's.

I texted:

Athens in July. Thank you for encouraging me to do this.

Yeah, I know I didn't say much. I know I could have sent that message to Filippo, my mother, Sonia, or Candela. Even to David. Well, I would've written a longer one to David, to be honest. The reason I was so concise was…I couldn't think of anything else that wouldn't put me on blast. And, I mean, it turned out well.

In his message, Filippo said:

> You don't know how happy it makes me that you were finally brave enough to do this. I'm sure you're having a tough time eating alone every night and that you still haven't dared to ask a stranger to take a photo of you, but you'll learn. And I'm sure this trip will help you mature. I miss your lips.

I took a shower, and even though we had planned to meet up at breakfast, I ran to David's room as soon as I was ready. When he opened the door, disheveled, in shorts and a shirt in a color I don't even think was in the Pantone catalog, the first thing that met him was my phone.

"Read it!" I screamed.

"Unlock it, you doofus. The screen turned off," he said, rubbing his eye with his fist.

"Were you still sleeping?"

"We weren't supposed to meet up for another forty-five minutes. Of course I was sleeping."

"Look! Filippo texted back last night!"

David let me in, and I tossed him my now-unlocked phone so he could read the message. I was excited. Really excited. He missed my lips! Our kisses…ay, how I yearned to feel his.

I sat on the bed waiting to hear him gush about my tactics (which were actually his), but instead his brow wrinkled a little.

"You don't think he sounds a little patronizing?" David asked.

"Patronizing?"

"Yes. Kinda like a know-it-all."

"A know-it-all? I don't understand you."

"You know." He stretched, and his shirt rode up a little, giving a glimpse of his belly button and a strip of hair that ended under the waistband of his pants…pants that made it obvious he didn't bring underwear.

I looked away, a little uncomfortable. "What am I supposed to know?"

"What's going on with you? You look like you saw a ghost."

Yeah, the ghost of your penis.

"What were you saying?"

"That he sounds patronizing to me. Like he knows everything and you're just a little dog who's learning the tricks her master teaches her."

I shot him a horrified look.

"How about you go to hell?" I responded when I could muster a word.

"Well, as soon as you get out of my room, I'll try." He smiled sarcastically. "Seriously, Margot, does he always talk to you like that?"

"Like what?"

"I don't know. He says he's sure you're going to mature, like you're a teenager who's on a foreign exchange trip or…or…a turnip."

I made a grumpy face.

"Thanks for the encouragement, eh?"

"Listen." He scratched his chest and yawned. "It's just I don't know how excited I am to see you run back into the arms of a guy who thinks he's your dad. By the way, you look great. What did you do?"

"Me?" I pointed right above my sternum. "Nothing. I didn't even brush my hair."

"Well, you look great. It must be love. Turns you into a wild thing." He moved like he was dancing. "I'm going to take a shower. You coming?"

I raised an eyebrow, and he smiled slyly.

"If I did…" I joked.

"If you did, what?"

I pressed my lips together in a smile, unable to add anything. After my silence, he tugged his shirt over his head and sauntered toward the shower.

"I called it," I heard him say.

"I'm only brave enough to get halfway through a threat."

"Go get ready, go on. This disheveled version of you seems dangerous."

"Hey! But what do I do about Filippo?" I moaned.

He turned halfway. The light in the bathroom cut off his silhouette, and I wanted him to turn all the way around so I could see him better. But honestly even like this he seemed like he had just been yanked out of the pages of a fucking ad for a perfume where suddenly a guttural voice would come out of nowhere speaking French.

"Do?" he took an interest.

"Of course. What do I do now? Do I respond to him? Do I send him a tit pic?"

"Better to stay quiet." He smiled. "The ball is in his court. He needs to win you back too."

~~~~~

David had a sandwich, an omelet, two coffees, three glasses of orange juice, and two sweet rolls for breakfast. He was always like this, and normally I found it entertaining to watch someone eat so much and so happily, but this time it seemed risky to me: in a couple of hours, we were catching a boat to Santorini, and it was a four-hour trip.

"Do you get seasick on ferries?"

"Me?" he responded, surprised as he bolted down his second very milky coffee. "How would I get sick? They're like buildings gliding through the ocean."

"Fine, well, I do get a little seasick," I confessed.

"Then why didn't you book a flight for this leg instead?"

"Because I'm sick of airplanes. You waste so much time in airports. I travel a lot for work, so Sonia knows that if I can get there any other way, I'd rather do that."

"So considerate, your Sonia." He smiled.

"I have two Dramamines left. If you want, we can each take one," I offered.

"Save them both for you."

I guess he remembered that "both for you" during the journey, especially when he started to change color. His regular shade morphed to a burning red on his cheeks about half an hour into the trip. He told me he was hot, but the truth is, it was colder than a witch's teat because of the mall-style air-conditioning. We hadn't even made it an hour when he went from crimson to yellow. Then to white in a matter of minutes.

Filippo never got seasick. I hadn't even seen him get sick at all. Maybe a dry cough or a sneeze. I vaguely remember a "My head hurts," but I never, ever saw him vomit. And much less as intensely as David ended up doing it with two hours still to go. I don't even remember how I ended up with my legs spread, straddling his back, clutching the strands of hair on his forehead while he vomited like a real animal. I just know he ran away with what seemed to be his last breath of life and that I followed him without thinking into the men's bathroom and no one stopped me.

When the deed (which wasn't pretty to look at) was done, he couldn't even get up. He stayed there on his knees until I figured out how to unwedge my body from the cubicle, clamber out, and then wrench him out.

He looked in the mirror. He pushed his hair off his forehead. He retched again. He vomited in the trash can. I splashed the nape of his neck with cold water. He vomited a little more into the trash can. I dragged him to the sink, forced him to bend over it, like I was going to peg him, and then I shoved his whole head under the faucet. At least, as much as I could because the bathrooms on the ferry weren't exactly the Four Seasons.

He was resurrected and pressed both hands into the counter where he had just been underwater for a couple of minutes. His hair dripped down his neck and clothes, but he only seemed able to focus on his breathing. The way he gasped with his eyes closed…I have to admit that even though I had just seen him puke like a Guinness World Record holder, the image was kind of erotic.

When he managed to open his eyes and look at me, the only thing that came out was an "I'm sorry" so sincere that it almost hurt me.

"It doesn't matter." I smiled at him. "Shit happens."

"Is there puke on my shirt? Puke is my kryptonite, Margot. Please tell me there's no puke on me."

I looked him up and down. Not a trace. Then I cracked up, and as much as he possibly could, he did too.

"I'm not gonna lie," he panted. "I made an ass of myself, sad eyes."

"I'll take care of you."

I bought a bottle of cold water, and he drank a few sips when he was back in his seat, with his head back and his feet up on the empty seats in front (on both of them, manspreading). At first, I didn't dare get too close. I just held the bottle of water out to him every once in a while; I would have done that the rest of the journey if he hadn't curled up in my lap. He let himself fall sideways, resting his cheek on my thigh, and put his arms around me so his hands were interlocked between my legs, under my skirt. I don't think he even realized. I did. I was very conscious of rough hands touching very smooth and sensitive skin.

"David…"

I was going to tell him, in a tactful and friendly way, to get his hands out of there. I didn't want anyone to discover me in that predicament. What if I bumped into someone I knew? What if some friend of Filippo's had picked the same destination? Eating breakfast with him in the hotel had been risky enough, so having him there, clinging to me, seemed like too much.

But…I couldn't because right when I was about to say it, he smiled and said, "Never stop."

He fell asleep. Right there, huddled and clutching me like I was his only chance for salvation. When David slept, it took years off his shoulders, as if with each inhale and exhale, he traveled backward, dreaming of his childhood and returning to it. If it weren't for that shadow of a beard blooming across his cheeks, you could forget that he was already a man.

I woke him up by sliding my fingers through the longest parts of his hair and stroking his earlobe. He became laser focused on collecting the luggage, and I felt like maybe I had been too affectionate.

～～～

The transfer to the hotel took about ten minutes. To be honest, I expected it to have sea views, but it was about a ten-minute drive from Fira, where I feared that the Ortega Group didn't have any hotels. Or maybe Sonia had followed my request and just restricted herself to finding our best hotel that wasn't a five-star luxury hotel. It was impossible to know them all by heart.

Why would we even think about buying this desert? I wondered when we got there. But the truth is, even though it wasn't exactly near the ocean, the chain knew how to make this hotel a slice of paradise. I just didn't know that yet.

The girl at reception seemed much sharper than the ones in Athens and handled both reservations at the same time. We had arrived in the same car from the port, and she could see from a mile away that we weren't strangers, so she found it all very odd.

"I'm afraid there must have been an error when we confirmed your reservation," she said to me in very formal English.

"What's she saying?" David asked.

"I'm showing two separate reservations," she apologized quickly, looking back and forth between us, as if David could understand her.

"You have to get your act together with English, you savage," I said to him. Then I turned back to her with a smile. "It's not a mistake. We have two reservations. One made through an agency"— the one the Ortega Group always used—"and the other directly through your website."

She looked at me, furrowing her brow, confused. "But…"

"Um…we're friends. Not a couple," I clarified.

"Right. Well…" she insisted, "I'm not asking for explanations, by any means. It's just that the room we have you in is a private villa with two bedrooms. Four in total…for two people."

I made a face. Sonia must have chosen the best room, not worrying about it having two rooms. And then I just duplicated her reservations for David without looking at the details.

"Maybe there was some misunderstanding," I finally said.

"That must be it. I see the reservation made in the gentleman's name was made just a few days ago. You'll be here…seven days?"

"Yes."

"Well…let me see." She looked at the computer and typed. "I can cancel it, but starting from tomorrow. You'll be charged for tonight."

"Ah. Well…great. That's no problem."

"Perfect. Sign here for me then, Ms. Ortiz."

"Why do they call you Ortiz?" David asked me.

"Because my assistant must've made the reservation wrong. Ortiz is my second last name. Thank you," I said, returning the signed bill to the receptionist.

"They'll bring your luggage up in just a moment. My colleague will show you to your room."

When I looked at David, he didn't seem to buy my explanation.

"What?"

"What happened?" he asked, sliding our suitcases and putting them on the bell cart himself.

"I didn't want anyone to know we were coming together, so I reserved your rooms for the whole trip, but I didn't realize that the one Sonia chose for me is a villa with two bedrooms. She was just handling the cancellation for the room I booked for you."

"What about the last name thing?"

"I already told you. Sometimes the agency mixes things up."

He wanted to believe it. I could tell just by looking at him. He wanted to believe it and not question anything.

The room was beautiful. As soon as you went in, you were in the middle of a living room with a round table and four chairs, an armchair, and a sofa. To the right and left there were open doors that led to our bedrooms, and opposite, behind a curtain, there was an impressive terrace with a private pool, a solarium, and another table with chairs. David's mouth hung open.

"What are you talking about?" David asked me suddenly, when I was thanking the boy with the suitcases with a tip. "This is for us? They made a mistake."

"No. They didn't make a mistake." I smiled.

"Impossible," I heard him murmur, peeking out onto the terrace.

"Well…what do you think? It's not near the ocean, but…it's nice, right? Do you like it?"

David widened his eyes until they were like plates.

"Do I like it? Margot, I thought we were going to campsites!"

"Oh, come on. Like you didn't know me better than that."

I didn't even notice him coming over, but suddenly he was grabbing my waist, smiling, excited.

"Dear Margarita…you're a snob."

I offered to call room service and order something to eat. I figured he'd be hungry after all that vomiting. Starving. Hungry and probably not in the mood to go out and explore considering how hot it was. He thought it was a great idea, but he asked me to please let him take care of the stuff we charged to the room. I said yes to make him happy, but I knew it would all go to the expense account associated with my card.

"Do you mind if I leave you alone for a moment?" he asked me. "I want to call Ivan and my parents. I didn't even tell my parents I was going on a trip, and I just remembered."

"Of course. No rush. I'll just be here unpacking my suitcase."

The cicadas enveloped the whole hotel with their summery sound, and although there was nothing but yellowish fields as far as the eye could see, it had its charm. I opened the windows overlooking the pool and played music as I took the wrinkled clothes out of my suitcase and put them in the closet, neat and hung up. The bathroom was slightly gloomy because the window was pretty small, but it was beautiful: white marble, open space, a large shower, and a huge bathtub plated with small iridescent tesserae that changed color as the light sparkled across them.

As I unpacked my toiletry bags, a certain sense of loneliness hovered over me. I reflected on how even David, who looked like one of those happy stray dogs who didn't want an owner, felt the need to call someone who wasn't there. And I didn't. I know it was part of the process I was going through, but in that moment, I didn't try to rationalize it. David was constantly sending photos and friendly voice notes to his friends from the village, and I...I didn't have anyone to do that with.

I hesitated a little, but I ended up calling Candela. The truth is I had ignored a bunch of her messages while we were in Athens.

"You're alive?" she asked as soon as she picked up.

"No. I'm calling you through a Ouija board. I'm going to kill you."

"That's not funny. I was about to call Interpol. How's the experiment going?"

"Really great," I answered cheerfully. "Honestly, really great."

"Did you fall in love yet?"

"What are you talking about, you nutjob? I'm in love with Filippo, who, by the way, sent me the sweetest message last night."

"Ay, so you're still sane? Not brainwashed from traveling with that dude?"

"Not at all."

"Great news. You're not doing anything dirty then?"

"Who, me and David? No way! Well, unless you count me holding his head up while he vomited on a ferry as dirty."

"No. Probably for some sicko out there, yes, but thank God, not for me. Where are you guys now?"

"In Santorini. We'll be here for a week. Then we're going to spend six days in Mykonos."

"So fucking jelly."

"Don't be. I thought the hotel was right by the ocean, but it's in the middle of a desert. I guess land must be really sought after on the island. But it's nice, you know? We have a private pool and—"

"Does he look hot in a bathing suit?" she cut me off.

"Really good," I answered without stopping to think about it. "I mean…if he was my type."

"What type is he?"

"You know. The kind that could be a skater, a Vans model, or a rapper."

"David doesn't look like a rapper. A rapper would have a toothpick."

"You're right." I laughed. "He's like a little boy, right?"

"Not really. He's just skinny, but…does he have a six-pack?"

"He has a hint of a six-pack, yes."

"What about the other package?"

"Candela, girl. I'm not looking at his package." I feigned

indignation. And I was feigning it because I actually had looked as much as I could get away with.

"Men's bathing suits are very clingy when they get out of the water. You must've seen something."

"How's it going back there?" I changed the subject.

"Here? I don't wanna make you feel bad but…all I wanna do is get back to the real world and do something useful for humanity. Your sister is wearing me out. She didn't text you?"

"Not yet. But come on…I'm sure it won't be long."

"Oof. We've been wandering around Madrid with an English newspaper in hand. One of those huge ones. You can't even imagine what my hands look like…they're black!"

"A newspaper? What for?"

"Well, you know…she got it in her head that the detective is conspiring with Alberto and that's why he only sends pictures of her husband eating fritters and churros, so now we're following him…"

"Alberto?"

"No! The detective. We told you that already! She wants to catch him red-handed so she can get her money back. We're following him and hiding behind a newspaper."

I perched on the edge of my bathtub and covered my eyes.

"I probably tried to erase it from my memory so I could cope. I'm so fucking embarrassed to share genes with you guys," I muttered.

"Told you so."

"Margot?" David called out as soon as he came back into the villa. "Where are you?"

"I'm on the phone. Order anything you want from room service."

"Language barrier," he said succinctly.

"I'm going to order food," I informed Candela. "Please keep me posted on that…I don't even know what to call that mess."

"It's like the plot of a shitty movie. Basically. I'll call you if we end up in a pyramid scheme or something."

David nudged open the bathroom door just as I let the hand holding my phone fall to my lap. He had swapped his jean shorts and wrinkled shirt for a bathing suit that looked new. An acquisition I hadn't mediated, but I would bet my right hand he had procured it after our morning of shopping. It was black, a little shorter than the one he had worn in the hotel pool in Athens, and…ugh, fine… it was pretty sexy. He was shirtless and barefoot. And as he leaned against the bathroom door like that…I realized that I did find those kinds of guys attractive.

"Let's drink beer in the pool?" he proposed, handing me a cold bottle.

It was curious. According to my mother, I should have been going through a kind of penance to repent for my sins (you know, the INCIDENT), but I felt like I was in paradise.

32

SURPRISE: YOU'RE FREE

A month and a week without sex. That was totally why I was starting to find David attractive. I mean. I'm lying. I always found him attractive, but in the way you can appreciate someone's beauty without any real interest. But now…in that moment, in the pool with the fucking little black bathing suit (it was short and gave him a scandalous ass), David was turning me into a little slut.

Compared to Filippo, David was tiny. Filippo was six foot four; he had a wide back, big strong arms, basically a ridiculously impressive dude. I had said it many times…going out to dinner with Filippo was like having dinner with a movie star: he got all the attention.

David, on the other hand, how tall was he? Five foot nine at most. And he was skinny. His shoulders were toned, and his arms were sinewy, definitely the result of hauling cases of bottles and heavy flowerpots, but he was skinny. Not scrawny, but…

But he did have a pert ass that, damn, made him look like a snack. And his face. He had a nice face: brown eyes that shone with their own light, a soft mouth, a cute nose…

"Are you listening to me?" I heard him shout.

Gotcha.

"What?"

"Earth to Margot?" he teased. "I was saying I have a surprise for you."

"A surprise? What kind?"

Stop thinking with what's throbbing right now, please, Margot.

"A surprise. But it's for later. I bet you're gonna scream and everything!"

Margot. Stop thinking with your clamshell.

"You're going to burn." I changed the subject.

"You are too."

"I put on sunscreen."

Don't ask me to put sunscreen on you, please.

"I did too." He pointed to his shoulders. "Here." Then to his nose and cheekbones. "And here."

"You know that's not enough?"

"It's enough if you're going to take a nap." He shot me a saintly smile.

What did I do to deserve all this temptation? Fuck.

"You already took a nap on the boat!"

"But we're on vacation, remember?"

He swam over to me with a teasing expression on his face, and I yanked my legs out of the water before he could tug on them and pull me back into the water. My mistake. I left room for him to hoist himself up where my legs had been and climb out.

Shit.

"Let's go?"

And why was David suddenly taking it as a given that we would take a nap together?

The plates with our leftovers were still on the table on the terrace, next to the pool. We went into our respective bedrooms to get changed. I stayed there, with the door closed, sitting, hoping David would get into his bed and fall asleep. I mean, it's not like anything would happen just from lying on the bed to take a nap or…chat. We had already done that. In his room in Athens, we had talked for a long time every night before we went to sleep, and we had even touched on sexual topics, but…

But back when we did that, I wasn't feeling the call of the jungle, that was obvious.

I had to focus. It was all because of Filippo's message and that "I miss your lips," which could simply mean "I want you to kiss me" or "I want to see them wrapped around my cock again." I liked his cock. I mean, he was my fiancé. I was going to marry him…makes sense I liked it, right? He was an elegant Italian with the body of a fucking Viking. Of course he got me wet, and…I wondered how big David's cock was. He didn't have small dick energy at all. Maybe a little thin. I didn't like skinny dicks…they were like…puff. No. He said once he was happy with his size, so…it wouldn't be outrageously huge, like Filippo's (fucking perfect fairy-tale prince), but it was still a good sausage. Girthy. Erect. A show-off…the kind that turned into a chorizo, a grower, not a shower. The kind that got really hard in your mouth…

"Margot…" David whispered, opening the door.

"What, you can't sleep alone?" I snapped, a bundle of nerves.

"Hey!" he complained, surprised. "What's up with you, you loon?"

I leaned back and whimpered. Please…I didn't know what it was like to be horny without having Filippo on hand. Well, I did, before Filippo, but I didn't remember anymore.

"Hey…" David lay down beside me, looking at me. "What's going on?"

"Nothing."

"No, not nothing. Something's up."

I turned my head and looked at him. How could I ever explain this to him? "I'm a little worried," I confessed.

"About Filippo?"

The last time we fucked had been a quickie in the kitchen, I remembered. It wasn't bad, but it wouldn't have won any medals. I remember I had said so to him, giggling. We had been in a hurry because Filippo was going on a work trip to Barcelona and his train was leaving in an hour.

"Yes." I nodded. Being horny because you hadn't gotten laid in a month and a week counted as being worried about your partner, right? That wasn't a lie.

"What's going on? Tell me."

I took a minute to organize my thoughts. I didn't know what to tell him without mentioning the fact that I had been mooning around for quite a while. I didn't think it was a consequence of being with him, more like being all riled up with him next to me forced me to find him attractive suddenly.

"Do you think he's sleeping with other girls?" I asked abruptly.

"Um.." He made a face. "Ask me something else."

Oy. What a strange reaction.

"No. Answer me."

"I have no idea," he replied, settling his head on the cushions.

I propped myself up on the pillows so we were the same height.

"Don't front. You do have an idea."

"I have no idea what Filippo might be doing because I don't know him at all."

"But…?"

"I know what I would do."

"Develop this further."

"I'm not taking an exam," he defended himself.

"Oh, yes. Yes, you are," I insisted.

"Fuck…" He pushed his hair from one side to another. "If my girlfriend had left me at the altar and I had proposed a summer apart to figure out whether we should fix it…I wouldn't be shy about sleeping with other women if the opportunity arose."

"Imagine if the one who had left you at the altar had been Idoia."

"Then I would make an even bigger effort to sleep with anyone I could. Plus, I would try to seduce all her friends, her sister, her cousin, and probably some of her younger aunts." He smiled. "Revenge sex isn't as much fun, but…"

I grabbed a pillow and turned my back to him. Great. At least I wasn't horny anymore.

"Margot…" I noticed the warmth of David's body coming closer. "Idoia is kind of a witch. Honestly, I don't think I would feel the same if I had gone through that with you instead of with her." He put his hand on my waist. "Come on…Filippo knows you. He knows you much better than I do. He knows you didn't do it to hurt him or because you were being immature. You must have gone through something really terrible to dip out like that. You weren't disregarding anyone or humiliating him. Just…escaping. You were scared. You don't have revenge sex because the person who you love was really scared."

I turned around. He was very close. Did Filippo really know all those things? I wasn't even very clear on them.

"I'm going to ask you one more time. Do you think he's sleeping with other people this summer?"

"Honestly?"

"Yes," I responded.

"I think you shouldn't base your actions on what you think he's doing, because this summer, like, it's for you. And it's an incredible gift. Do and don't do like you don't have to explain it to anyone but yourself. I think he's doing the same."

He could've just said no. That's definitely what my sisters would've said, but David preferred the truth, the whole truth, baked into an explanation that softened the information that could have hurt me, but still the truth when all was said and done. I put my hand on his cheek.

"Fuck, David."

"Do you hate me?" He smiled timidly.

"No, but when I met you, I didn't think you had such a good head on your shoulders under that scruffy hair."

I gave him a kiss on the forehead. I took a deep breath. I turned around and stared at the wall. He stayed there, behind me, with his arm on my waist.

"David…"

"Hmm?"

"Can you do me a favor?"

"Of course."

"Go to your room."

There was still no point carrying out illogical experiments.

~~~~~

David told me his surprise was outside the hotel. I didn't understand what he was saying. Seriously. It was like he was speaking ancient Aramaic. What did he mean, *outside the hotel*? I couldn't even think of an idea or suspect anything because…what the hell? When had he had time to organize anything? And, above all, what kind of surprise could I expect outside a hotel where we ate, we swam, we took a nap, we showered, we got dressed and left?

"Wait a second, David. I'm going to ask how we get to Fira. The hotel probably has a shuttle or something."

"No! Wait! Surprise first!"

"Give me a second, David."

He tugged on my arm, pulled me closer, and then covered my eyes with his hand, leading me to the exit.

"Let go of me, you stupid ass!" I moaned.

The evening breeze greeted me when I assumed we were heading out into the parking lot. I didn't even have time to think before he let go and yelled, "Surprise!"

The surprise had two wheels and the appearance of not being able to handle both of us on steep slopes. The surprise was white; it had an English name (Twister? Storm? something like that) etched onto one side and two wing mirrors with thousands of mosquitoes plastered on them. It was a surprise that looked terrible, but…I loved it.

"Wait, this is so cool!" I shrieked.

So yeah, in the end he did get me to scream.

He opened the seat with a key he had hidden in his pocket and took out two helmets…well, they looked like two eggshells split in half. Hideous. They made me feel sorry for them.

"So you can check it off your list!" he said, exhilarated.

"Do you know how many people have worn those helmets before?"

"What?" He looked at the helmets. "Don't think about that. Come on, get on."

"You get on first, and then I'll climb on."

He waggled his eyebrows and tucked his chin down. "No, no. You're driving, sad eyes."

"What are you talking about?"

"You heard me."

"I've never driven a motorcycle in my life. We're gonna get killed."

"Well, you better learn because you and I"—he pointed at the motorcycle—"are not going to die on a moped with an engine that size, my love."

The negotiation lasted minutes. Many. I ended up huffily sitting on the wall with my legs dangling down to prove he wasn't going to convince me.

"Not today," I repeated in English over and over, feeling like I was Arya Stark, courageously insisting that today was not the day...to die or even rehearse it.

David proved to be quite stubborn, but...I'm even more stubborn, so we had to find a compromise. He would drive that evening, and I would have to check it off my to-do list starting the next morning.

He hopped on easily, and I gathered up my skirt, not really knowing how to get on.

"I looked at Google Maps for directions. It's only ten minutes away," he said, putting his phone in his pocket with the helmet still hanging from his elbow.

"Hey," I said timidly. "I don't know how to tell you this, but...I don't know how to do it."

"Don't know how to do what?"

"I don't know how to get on."

"You've never ridden a motorcycle?"

"No. Only a horse that hated me."

"Come on, snobby! You've definitely ridden something else." He winked.

"Now's not the time, David."

"Hey, I'm not just being stupid." He patted the seat behind him. "It's just like climbing onto a dude. You straddle it. You know? Grab my shoulders, throw one leg over the other side, and then put your feet up on the stirrups."

"What stirrups? Do motorcycles have stirrups too?" I asked, confused.

"OMG."

He bent over the handlebars, dying of laughter.

"What's going on here? Are you one of those Hell's Angels and I never noticed?"

"Who's never ridden a motorcycle at thirty-two?"

"Me, I guess. Shut up."

I grabbed his arm and threw my leg over the saddle with the agility of a retired gymnast. My calculations were inaccurate. I think I even got some momentum, so when I landed, I hurt myself in the…well, in the crotch, where all my weight landed with nothing to cushion the fall. I dug my fingers into his arm and rested my forehead on his back.

"I think I broke something."

"What?" He turned back to me.

"I think I broke my pussy."

"It comes from the factory with a slit in it, don't worry."

I jabbed him a few times while he cackled, and then I settled in as much as I could.

"Ready or should I call an ambulance?"

"We're going to miss the fucking sunset, you jerk," I groaned.

"OMG, you're so romantic today. Hold on to something."

"What do you mean something?"

"Well, me, the saddle, the part on the back…I don't know. I don't want to accelerate and leave you sitting on the road."

"Oh, god. Be careful, for fuck's sake," I whimpered.

My body jerked when he started the bike and accelerated, so I ended up plastered to him. I went to hold on to his waist, but I was a little embarrassed, so I gripped a piece of cloth from his T-shirt in my fist as we headed straight toward Fira. It didn't take long for him to release the handlebars one by one to put my hands on his belly.

"It's better this way. This piece of junk doesn't go very fast, but just in case."

Have you ever ridden a motorcycle? What am I talking about? Of course you have. I'm the only one here who's missed out on the experience. And even though I spent a few anxious moments thinking about all the bad things that could happen and how unsafe the helmets looked, in the end I felt safe with David. He was a good driver. He took it easy. The wind snuck down the collar of his shirt, and his scent wafted toward me. And if I shifted a little, I could see his smile in the rearview mirror.

I had spent my whole life listening to my mother say people envied people like me because we have a personal driver, because we travel in first class, and because, sometimes, we even charter private jets and…how sad to realize the real truth. The only thing worth envying in the world is the feeling I experienced riding on that piece of junk, and it took me thirty-two years to feel it; out there you can be free, regardless of what you have or who you are.

33

~~~~

WOULD YOU DO IT?

The sunset in Fira was beautiful. A girl was playing a hang drum sitting next to the facade of what looked like a church. People were chattering endlessly, and children were screaming. I don't know about David, but, sitting on that little wall, with my legs dangling and the sea in front of us, all I could hear was the melody emitting from that strange instrument.

The sky was changing color. I looked over at David, whose eyes were also changing as the sun plunged into the distance, becoming somehow even warmer, glowing with the reflection of the orange light.

"So many colors," he said, when he noticed I was looking at him.

"Just like your face on the boat."

"Shut it, you rat."

He put his arm around and me, and I took a breath. I closed my eyes. I felt at peace. There was something about David…something, something that me feel this way. Especially when he wasn't wearing that sexy black bathing suit.

We had dinner, as night drew in over our heads, in one of those restaurants for tourists teetering on the steep slope of the cliff that was Fira. We were well taken care of, but it seemed like everything tasted the same. A Greek salad, which was exactly the same in every restaurant, a little chicken, an undercooked pizza... The wine tasted like shit to me, so David finished it. It always tasted fine to him.

Then we bought ice cream cones at one of those places that stayed open well past midnight and strolled around. You could hear the bells of the poor donkeys who had to traipse around the city weighed down by tourists who had no concept of animal welfare. The sidewalks of the city were slippery, and we walked with our arms linked, like two old ladies. I was thinking about what we must look like to other people, and I felt a certain envy of that image that didn't really exist, of the funny and calm couple they probably imagined us to be. I was envious of a Margot who felt, at last, like she had arrived in the port with someone who would never demand the impossible from her beyond the unconscious demand to be happy.

~~~

"Have you heard anything from Idoia?" I asked once we were back at the hotel.

I had gone to my room to put on my pajamas (a spaghetti-strap, ankle-length, cotton nightgown, nothing special) and I found him sitting on the edge of the pool, looking at the sky.

"No," he replied, without looking at me.

"You responded to her, right?"

"Yes." He nodded. "I left my phone on the table. Read it and tell me what you think."

I padded barefoot over to the table and picked up his phone, which didn't need a security code to unlock it. Idoia must be an idiot; he was one of those honest guys…

I opened WhatsApp, and I didn't mean to snoop, but before I read his reply to Idoia, something caught my eye in the conversation still open on the screen. It was with Ivan:

…one of those girls who doesn't know what they're worth. Some jerk made her believe she wasn't enough. It's a bummer. She's beautiful…

I looked at it, fleetingly. Was he talking about me?

"Did you find it?" He looked at me and raised his eyebrows.

"Yes. Sorry." I opened it and read it hastily. "I was digesting it." I read it out loud: "'We can be friends, of course, but I seem to remember you saying that the last thing you'd want is to be friends with someone who isn't living up to his potential. So think it through carefully because maybe it's not such a good idea.'"

"Do you think I went too far?" A half-smile spread across his face…a beautiful one.

"No." I swallowed. "That's going to piss her off. Idoia is one of those girls who only want what they can't have."

"And when they have it, they lose interest." He took a deep breath and diverted his gaze to the glowing pool.

"Maybe this time will teach her a lesson."

"Maybe," he repeated, still not looking at me.

"Do you want a drink?"

"For a million and a half yen from the minibar? No thanks."

I went over to the living room between our bedrooms and took two beers out of the mini-fridge under the counter. I waved them at him and smiled.

"I guess I can allow myself one."

"David, you should stop worrying about money."

"No."

I sat next to him and held out his beer.

"I can't, Margot. You're talking from the privilege that assumes it isn't your problem, but…it is mine. Please don't feel judged."

"No. Well…I meant during this trip. I invited you, remember?"

"And I accepted. But I'm not your little plaything, okay? So I have to pay for my own stuff. Deep down, it pisses me off, but…Idoia was right. I have to get my life together or I won't be able to fix it."

"So where do you wanna start?" We clinked the butts of our beer bottles together.

"With an apartment." He made a face. "I'll look for a shared apartment near Ivan and Domi. I want to keep helping with Ada."

"You're so sweet, David," I said without thinking.

He turned to me with eyebrows raised. Anyone would think *sweet* was an insult in his language. I had probably gone too far. Maybe I was losing it with so much David everywhere.

"Me? Sweet? No way!" He laughed. "That's because you're only seeing that part of me, but I promise it's not the main part."

"Are you hiding something from me?"

He looked at me, raising his eyebrows meaningfully, and a very cunning smile spread across his face.

"So much…"

"Like what?"

"I'm not falling for that," he retorted.

"I don't know what you're talking about." I took a sip of beer.

"You're being silly, sweetie."

David jumped up, yanked off his shirt, and tossed it behind him without looking. It landed hanging off the back of one of the chairs on the terrace.

"What are you doing?"

"I'm going to go for a swim."

"Hey, hey…" I laughed. "Don't go full rogue just because I said you're sweet."

"I can't go for a swim?" He unbuttoned his pants and had them off in two tugs.

Okay. David in his underwear in front of me. At least he was backlit and he didn't delay in falling into the water with his arms crossed. The huge wave reached me, splattering my nightgown in drops of water.

"David!" I groaned.

Before his intentions even crossed my mind, he yanked my legs and I ended up in the water in my nightgown, between two arms pulling me into the middle of the pool.

"You jerk!" I roared with laughter, trying to wriggle free.

"Didn't you just say I was sweet?"

I was grateful my nightgown was long and wouldn't let me wrap my legs around his waist. I swam as far away as I could.

"What about that part?"

"What part?" he asked, floating in the middle.

"The one you're hiding from me…is that what Idoia likes?"

"I have no idea what Idoia likes about me. I mean…she never complained about the intimate parts, but it seemed like she was bored outside the bedroom."

"You could never bore anyone, David."

"That's probably because I'm very creative in bed and I set a precedent that I can't maintain when I'm not fucking."

I could tell you I hid my surprise well, but…I didn't. My mouth fell open, and I gaped like a guppy until David burst into laughter.

"Wait, what's that face you're making?"

"Leave me alone! I wasn't expecting you to start talking about your sexual prowess."

"Liar, you started it. Listen…how long were you and Filippo together?"

"Don't talk in the past tense," I started stressing. "We've been together three years."

"Is that your longest relationship?"

"Yes." I nodded. "Before him nothing ever really stuck."

"Oh, wow. A femme fatale over here."

"Fatale, yes. Fatally waxed. What about you?"

"I don't wax, as you can see." He stroked the patchy hair on his chest.

"I mean, how long were you with Idoia?"

"Nine months."

"Wow," I teased. "And I bet that was your longest relationship."

"No, smart-ass."

"Were you with your high school sweetheart for a year? No, no, wait…eleven months."

"I was with my ex for five years."

I opened my eyes wide, leaning against the edge of the pool.

"Excuse me? Five years?"

"Yes. I was crazy in love with her."

"And what happened?"

"We loved each other like what we were: little kids." He shrugged.

"We were twenty-two when we broke up, you know. But I'm sure that if I'd met her now, I would marry her."

I turned around, looking into the lit-up villa. I didn't want him to see that it rankled me a little. I didn't want him to notice because I didn't even understand why I felt this way.

"So go find her."

"It's too late now," he said, coming a little closer. "We fucked it all up."

"You don't believe in second chances?"

"No."

He appeared next to me and gripped the edge like I was, crossing his arms in front of him. We held eye contact for a few seconds.

"Can I ask you something private?" he said.

"I held your head while you vomited…I think so."

"How many guys have you fucked?"

I swallowed and looked straight ahead. "Jesus fucking Christ, what a question. I mean…I don't keep a list."

"Come on…give me a number. A range at least. Less than five?"

"More."

"Five to ten?"

I made a face.

"More than ten?"

I covered my mouth. His eyes were very wide.

"Can you leave me alone now?" I took my hand away.

"You're a treasure chest of surprises, Margarita."

"What, a woman can't have a sexual past? Guys are the only ones who show off everything you know and we're left with one singular experience in life?"

"Ah, no, no. You're telling me you've slept with more than fifteen dudes…"

"I didn't say that…"

"But I guessed it. I like that."

"Why?"

"Well, because it gives me hope. You have a free soul…"

"It's not about having a free soul. It's just that every time I thought it was the last one, and then I would see that it…it wasn't."

"Don't talk about love to try to hide the fact that you felt like doing it. And you did it. Bravo to you, little Margot."

I made a face.

"Six," I confessed. "What about you?"

"Well…six too."

We both smiled as we looked at each other.

"Seven is a lucky number," he said pushing off the edge. "What if your crazy night in Greece ends up being the love of your life?"

"Or the biggest cock of my life. Come on, David…"

"What?"

"What kind of crazy night am I going to have?"

"Oy! What do you mean what kind of crazy night are you going to have? You think it's all going to be as chill as this? Wait 'til we get to Mykonos. Maybe even before. You're going to eat—"

"Don't finish that sentence!" I warned him. "And what are you going to be doing in the meantime? Cheering me on?"

"Ah, no. I like to participate." He winked. "I'll probably make my own plans and I'll be recreating your moans from my room."

"Would you do it?" I let go of the edge too and floated over to him.

"Do what? Moan? Yeah, I'm pretty expressive."

"No, idiot. Fuck some stranger in your room."

He pouted and scrunched his mouth up to his nose, making an ugly face.

"I thought you were going to ask if I would have a threesome with you and another dude."

"Where did that come from?"

"Nowhere, nowhere…"

He swam away, laughing, and as soon as he got to the edge, he jumped out of the pool.

"Hey!" I yelled from the pool.

He tossed a dry towel near the edge and wrapped another around his waist.

"What?" he asked, sweeping his hair back.

"Would you do it?"

He bit his bottom lip and laughed.

"Get out of the water or you'll turn into a raisin."

"You didn't answer me!"

"Good night, Margot."

"Hey!"

I watched him go into the living room, turn off all the lights except a floor lamp, and switch on the one in his bedroom.

"Good night, David."

34

~~~~~

THE MOTORCYCLE BRAKE

"Okay. Give it a little juice." David sounded serious. His hand was on mine. "You don't need to squeeze it that hard, come on."

"I'm not sure this is a good idea."

"Let yourself go. Stop overthinking it."

"Like this?"

"Hey, hey, hey! Hold on! Not so hard."

"See? I don't know what I'm doing."

David sighed and pressed his forehead against my shoulder.

"Please, Margot. Driving a car is much harder." I felt his breath on my shoulder. "This is just a bicycle with an engine."

The sun was beating down on the long, deserted road where we had stopped. David was wearing a backpack holding everything we needed for the beach, but we'd never get there if I didn't get a grip because clearly I was going to be the one to drive there.

I hit the accelerator again, this time more gently. David let go of my hand and dropped his to my thigh.

"Okay. You're getting there."

We moved slowly. My white Converse were still grazing the ground.

"Lift up your feet," he told me.

"Put on your helmet," I told him.

"You know it's not mandatory here? That's why they give you these shitty ones."

"Put on your helmet," I insisted, accelerating a little more.

"Lift up your feet."

I saw his shadow put on his helmet, and then his hand returned to my thigh, gently squeezing to soothe me. Fuck. My horniness hadn't gone away after all.

"Good, good, good. Lift up your feet and accelerate."

I lifted my feet; I accelerated. David clutched my short black romper.

"Margot, take it easy…"

"Look, look! I'm doing it all on my own! David! I'm driving! Ay, ay. A curve. There's a curve up there."

I slammed on the front brake, and David smacked into my back.

"Sorry!" I yelled.

"Use both brakes, Margot, we're gonna get killed."

"Sorry, sorry."

I accelerated again.

"Okay. Follow the road. You don't have to turn for another five kilometers," he said, looking at his phone.

I juddered over a pothole. I whimpered.

"I wanna stop, I wanna stop! I'm scared."

"Don't brake, Margot."

I braked with the front wheel again, and David was hurled against my body once more.

"Ah, ah, ah," I moaned.

"Come on, girl, don't lose your nerve."

"What?"

"Nothing."

I accelerated. I saw a pebble. I braked badly again. David's chest ended up crushed against my back.

"Margot, please."

"Ah! Ah! Ah! There's a car coming behind us!"

"So they'll pass us. You stick to the right, and that's it, but stop making those sounds, please."

"Ah! Ahhh! David, David, I hate this."

A car passed us, and I braked again. David smashed into me again. I braked. He smashed. I heard him groan.

"Sorry, sorry!"

"Margot, are you doing this on purpose?"

"What? No! I'm super overwhelmed!"

A bigger motorcycle passed us with a dude without a helmet. He yelled something, and I braked.

"What's happening? Why did he yell?"

"Margot, please, because he's an idiot. Stop braking."

"Can I stop?"

"No, but seriously, accelerate. Just accelerate."

His mouth was pressed against my shoulder. I glanced back, confused.

"David...are you getting sick? Am I that bad? Should I stop?"

I braked.

"Margot!" he yelled.

"I know, I know. Sorry."

"Do you know why you're saying sorry?"

"For slamming on the brakes," I answered, confused. "What... what's going on with you? I don't get it."

"Every time you brake, my dick thumps against your ass, Margot. And fucking hell, girl, I respect you, but I'm not made of stone."

I stared straight ahead, freaked out. A little angel, sitting formally on my shoulder, asked me to brake as gently as possible. The devil, with my sister Candela's face, God knows why, squeezed my fingers against the brake again.

"Go ahead and keep braking." I heard him laugh. "But don't worry, the thing you feel is my phone in my pocket."

"What pocket? It's in your hand!"

"My phone," he insisted. "You keep braking like this, when we get there, I'm going to need a cigarette afterward."

I bit my lip, hiding my smile.

"I'm watching you, you minx."

And I would swear he was getting used to it, slamming into my butt again.

~~~~

Kamari Beach was pretty crowded, but we had gotten up early and found a couple of free beach chairs. David was apathetic about this kind of "summering." He wanted us to go to Red Beach, which was much more hippy-ish; he wanted us to go to a supermarket, grab some snacks and drinks, and spend the day lying there, swimming and diving with goggles that he showed me proudly. We played rock, paper, scissors, and…everyone knows I have a gift for that game. I won and decided it would be better to start with something more "commercial." Now that we had started ticking off the to-do list he had written back when he didn't know he was coming with me, I was afraid he would say it was topless time. At least I'd have an excuse there: too many people.

"What?"

"I like it."

"That's just because of the beating I gave you on the way here," I said sarcastically as I tugged my bikini bottom back in place.

He rolled up his red bathing suit and smiled slyly.

He passed over two hotel towels, which we spread over our chairs, always watching the other's movements. Then he handed over the spray bottle of sunscreen. I spread it over my arms, my neckline, my tummy, my legs on the front and back, my butt, and…I asked him again to put it on my back. He was looking at me.

"You're getting really silly, eh…" I warned him jokingly.

"Has Filippo seen you in that bikini?" he asked me, grabbing the sunscreen and spraying it on my back.

"Yes."

"It drives him crazy, right?"

"Nothing drives Filippo crazy."

"What a boring dude," he muttered.

"It's just a bikini."

David rubbed my cream into his chest. I looked, I admit it. I looked harder when he went for his belly, where the line of hair disappeared into his bathing suit.

"Has Idoia seen you in that bathing suit?" I shot back.

"She's seen me naked, which is better."

"Hey! Wait, what's going on here?"

"During that little ride on the motorcycle, you gave me an excuse for the whole day." He raised his palms, defending himself. "Only you know what's going on with you. If…you find that this"—he patted his chest and his belly and finally discreetly grabbed his crotch—"makes you very nervous, I'll turn around."

Excuse me. Did he just grab his Lambrusco right in front of me? I blinked to try to get the image out of my head.

"You're an idiot," I said.

David moved the loungers, strategically positioning them so our bodies were in the sun but our heads were in the shade, and flopped down to read. He was holding a well-thumbed book, and I had forgotten my magazines and my book in the hotel, so I leaned over to snoop at the title because, I admit, a dude reading had the same effect on me as one with a baby. It made me drool.

"*The Color of Milk.*" I read on the cover.

"Uh-huh." He nodded. "You seem surprised. What'd you think? That I'd whip out a *Playboy*?"

"What's it about?" I asked.

"It's about a girl who…wait…no spoilers so all I'll tell you is she has a really hard road in life. We think we've found a way to be more free, but we end up being even more enslaved than before."

I raised my eyebrows.

"Sounds sad."

"Less sad than that motorcycle ride left me," he muttered and then looked at me slyly.

"Read me a little," I asked.

"Come here… Put some sunscreen on my back. I can't reach. But use my stuff. That shit is cold, and it makes my skin crawl."

He took out his bottle, and I sighed. Here I was thinking I was done with touching him…I squirted a little into my hand and then spread it on a broad, unblemished back, just a couple of small moles here and there, which created a beautiful constellation on his cinnamon skin. David flipped through the pages of the book until he came across a specific passage and began to read aloud:

"'But at other times your memory will keep things you would rather never know again and no matter how hard you try to get them out of your head…they come back.'"

He turned and looked at me over his shoulder as I rubbed his back.

"So true," I said.

"What do you wish you had never known, Margot?"

How far my cowardice goes popped into my head, but it was a pretty novel thought. I'd have to mull it over for a few more weeks to really parse the idea.

"Nothing in particular," I said. "I still have a lot to learn."

"Well, knowledge doesn't free us. It just makes us more aware of our own limitations."

"How do you go from grabbing your package so crudely to philosophizing like that, David?"

"It's innate. I have a talent…"

I stopped his hand when he tried to grab his package again.

"Let's go in the water." I tugged on him.

"What about our stuff?" he asked.

"Excuse me," I said in English to a woman in her seventies who was playing Sudoku in the chair next to us. "Would you mind keeping an eye on our stuff while we go for a dip?"

"Of course!" She smiled at me. "Would you like to leave your bag under my chair?"

"Thanks so much!"

I put everything valuable in my bag and slid it under the lady's chair.

"We'll be quick."

"No rush. I'm planning on spending the whole day right here."

I don't know why David and I held hands as we ran to the sea. Maybe because Kamari Beach was a pebble beach. They were small and round but stones after all. It would have been easy to trip or hurt ourselves…or at least that was a good excuse, I don't know. We let go when the first small gentle wave, hardly even worth calling a wave, hit our knees. The sea was a perfect temperature, not too cold or too hot. My nipples got hard when they touched the water as I pulled my hair back. When I looked for David, I found him suddenly pressed against my back, grabbing my waist. We smiled at each other.

"Let me take a photo when we get out," he said to me. "Filippo has to see this."

"Okay, quit laughing at me."

"At you?" He turned me around. "I'm laughing at him, who nothing drives crazy."

I raised an eyebrow. "I know what this is all about. You're trying to raise my self-esteem."

"Me? No way! It's no good if someone on the outside raises your self-esteem. It has to happen inside." He pointed to his chest. "Like when I tried on those jeans you made me buy and I saw the ass they gave me."

"They probably need to be confiscated for the good of humanity."

"Seriously, let me take a picture of you later. You have to see yourself the way I see you."

We waded further into the water until it was up to our necks. I let myself be rocked there, with my arms open and my eyes closed. I couldn't remember the last time I felt so…detached from everything that pulled me. For years I had always traveled with my laptop, and even on my trips with Filippo, I would make time to read emails, return calls, and review Excel documents. But here, nothing. I couldn't say I felt relaxed exactly, but at least my head had stopped being an asylum for that nest of anxieties with no beginning and no end.

"Look at those two…" I heard David say.

I bobbed back up. About twenty meters away, a couple was kissing…but they were kissing how you kiss when you're the kind of horny that will only be solved by fucking. I couldn't take my eyes off them once I spotted them.

"Fuck…"

"Do you think they're fucking?"

I looked at David. A few drops of water were running down his neck. He looked like a snack.

"Well…" I looked back at the couple and saw they were moving, I don't know if it was because of the waves or because of what we couldn't see under the water. "I would say so."

"Have you ever done that?"

"In the ocean? Yeah. It's not that great. It stings."

"So you do like doing it in weird places, eh?"

"The ocean isn't a weird place. It's weird that you've never done it there."

"Once I did it on the stairs of a metro station."

I turned to look at him again, stunned.

"On the stairs of the metro?"

"Yes." He nodded. "The last train of the night, a corner where there was unquenchable horniness and no cameras."

"Wasn't it uncomfortable?"

"Well, I sleep on a sofa bed. The metro stairs felt like the lap of luxury. What about you? The weirdest place…"

"The Italian Embassy."

"This girl, so fancy." He smiled. "And did you like it?"

"Not really. I don't like having to hurry."

"How do you like it?" David came round in front of me and looked at my mouth.

"What about you?"

Whoa, whoa, whoa.

I never thought a boy like David would look at my mouth that way. And I definitely didn't think I would feel butterflies when I discovered him looking at me like that.

"Hey, angel…" I warned him. "You're getting pretty riled up."

"Riled up? We're getting down with that plan of yours to start a 'wild loop.' We've been soooo good that even your mother would approve of this trip."

"My mother would commit hara-kiri if she saw me with a boy like you." I regretted it as soon as I said it. "I mean…like this, like a bad boy."

"A bad boy? I'm not David the sweet anymore?"

I raised an eyebrow.

"I know what's happening to you," I said.

"What's happening to me?"

"How long have you gone without sex?"

"Without sex or without sleeping with a girl?"

"What do you mean?"

"I mean, I masturbate sometimes. You should try it."

"We're getting a little intimate, aren't we?"

"We should probably stop, right?" he played around.

"Well, yes. We're friends."

"You've never fucked a friend?"

"Who said anything about fucking?" I was shocked.

"No one. If you'd prefer, you could blow me."

I let out a cackle, and he joined in. We howled with laughter like two idiots.

"I'm not going to blow you, not in a million years," I added.

"Your loss." He shrugged.

This all seemed hilarious to me.

"Is yours skinny? I hate skinny cocks."

"Before you start making predictions…why don't you try it for yourself?"

"Because it's one thing to judge a play and another to get on the pitch yourself."

"Oh, okay, okay. I get it. This is like a podcast."

"Yes." I smiled, looking into his eyes.

"Well, mine is normal, darling." And a smile appeared on his face that melted the poles a little more. "And if you want more information, it's been three weeks since the last time I had sex. When Idoia dumped me, we had just been to her house to fuck like animals."

"Do you do it that badly?"

"Terribly." He smiled. "They cry and everything when they come. Now it's my turn to ask, right?"

"You're not going to ask me what my nether regions are like."

"No," he said, shaking his head. "I'd rather ask if you touched yourself last night."

"What kind of question is that, you monster?"

"You asked me what my cock was like, and I even offered you the chance to take it for a test drive, but you didn't want to. Come on, answer. Did you touch yourself?"

I smiled as an answer.

"I bet you touched yourself thinking about having a threesome with me and a stranger."

My jaw dropped wider and wider, and then I burst into giggles. "You're shameless!"

"They're shameless." He pointed at the couple who were really going at it now. "You shouldn't feast in front of hungry people."

"On the way back, you'd better drive. I don't know if I'll be able to brake less, and it obviously puts you in a bad way."

"That damn brake," he teased.

"I'm going to get out. I can see a waiter walking among the chairs, and I want a beer. You coming?"

"Um…order one for me, I'll be right out."

I did a couple of strokes toward the shore before I stopped. I hesitated. I waved at him, and when he looked at me, I confirmed that David was getting cuter every day.

"I was just thinking maybe you need that crazy night out more than me," I pointed out.

"Well, then we better organize it."

35

JUST IN TIME

DAVID

I didn't like that she said I was a very sweet boy. I felt like when my grandmother bribed me to behave and my brothers made fun of me. I felt like when Idoia gave me some of her condescending advice and said, "You're so young. One day you'll understand." I felt more like a child and less of a man. I think that's why I put on that whole show of *I'm going to get naked and throw myself into the pool* and the subsequent *Come here, girly, I'm going to make you get a little crazy*. I think I did get her to a little, but I didn't even know why, and besides, I didn't count on the fact that I'm not made of stone.

Ay, the braking as she moaned.

Ay, the black bikini and her hips.

Ay, her butt, and her fingers sliding over it to spread the sunscreen. Ay.

I took a bunch of pictures of her. She wanted Filippo to think she was capable of asking a stranger to take a photograph of her, even if that was a lie, and I wanted her to see herself the way I saw her: incredibly powerful. Sitting on the lounger. In the sand, with her hands sunk into it. Sitting on the shore, not looking at the camera.

Please…I had a great time; I felt like a photographer on a *Playboy* shoot. It was incredible, even if she did pout when she saw herself.

"You can see my muffin top," she complained.

"What's a muffin top?" I asked, pretty baffled.

"The doughy bits." She smiled. "The pudge."

I slung my arm around her shoulder and kissed her hair. For fuck's sake. How could this woman not feel comfortable in her skin? The only thing her skin needed was to be touched a little more.

"Idoia doesn't have that, huh?" she made fun of herself.

No. Idoia had nothing on her back but soft, freckled skin. She was thin, with large round perfect breasts. She also had thin smooth, athletic thighs. She was tall. She liked heels, and her blond hair was always almost white. Idoia was delicious, like those girls who star in movies and then walk the red carpets in designer dresses. She was very good in the kind of "very good" decreed by society as a whole. When we were in bed, I never stopped feeling like I had won the fucking lottery. But I never thought about her the way I did when I saw the picture of Margot on the shore. The thought was kinda cringe: if the earth had a body, if nature had a body, it would be like Margot.

Who the fuck thinks like that when they see a hot woman? A very sweet boy.

God…I had turned into a very sweet boy.

After we spent the day on the beach, I drove the bike back to the hotel. I didn't want any more little brakes and moans because maybe Margot was right and the lack of sex had made me too hungry to stay on a diet. But that didn't work either. Clinging to my waist, with her hair tossed to one side, wavy and disheveled, with her legs spread so I fit between her thighs…Margot was a fucking temptation. And

I couldn't help it, I drove for as long as I could with one hand while the other rested on her leg.

We stopped at a supermarket relatively close to the hotel, on the way to Fira. The idea was to buy food for the next day because we were going to spend it at Red Beach, but when we were in the alcohol aisle, Margot pulled my shirt, hugged a bottle, and proposed: "What if we get wasted in the hotel tonight?"

"You think…? Wouldn't you rather see the sunset?"

"Who are you, and what have you done with David?"

"Shut up, clown; I'm doing it for you. Or do you want to wake up naked in bed tomorrow?"

"Well…that doesn't sound so bad. Aren't you the one who was saying we were losing sight of the 'wild loop' plan? I don't want you to get bored," she said, surprised I wasn't jumping at the idea.

"I'm not bored. And…I'm not really the kind who gets wasted."

"I'm not either!" She smiled from ear to ear. "That's the fun part! Plus, it was on the list."

"So was going topless…and I still haven't seen your tits." *For the love of God, David.* "See? It's better if we don't drink."

"Come on! What's the worst that could happen?"

I looked at the hair tie around her wrist and remembered her telling me, cheeks flushed from the wine, how much she loved giving blow jobs. She looked so wild with her hair all messy. She had such a nice mouth. I had never noticed her lips.

Did I like her?

No. I just found her attractive. And she was charming. She could be very sweet. And very fun. She was cute too. Could she be naughty? I got along with her… I felt comfortable with her… I enjoyed every minute so much…

I liked her.

God! I liked her!

I swallowed. I grabbed the bottle she was holding out and headed to the cash register.

~~~~~

We took a long shower…separately. If we had taken one together, I probably would have come. Coming in the shower is not really my thing, I have to admit, but I tried, without luck, to relieve some of the built-up tension. There was no way. It's very difficult to enjoy sexual pleasure when you're so scared. The last thing I wanted was to be irresponsible because I was horny, screw it all up by letting myself go with someone who was so hurt. I was too. I didn't want to revenge fuck some stranger…how could I want to do that to Margot?

Before I got dressed, I sat wrapped in a towel on the bed and decided to write a message to Domi. I could have chosen any of my friends from the village, but they didn't know Margot. They would have made a whole thing out of it, and they would have been bugging me the rest of the trip. Domi, she would help me find the answer. I wrote:

I think I like Margot a little.

But in the end I had second thoughts, and I changed some of the words to soften it:

I think I'm a little attracted to Margot.

I made a face when I saw her sign on and the app told me she was typing. She was going to come down hard on me, I knew it.

DOMINIQUE

And? You say that like it's weird.

DAVID

I don't get it.

DOMINIQUE

You were already attracted to Margot before you even left.

DAVID

That's not true.

DOMINIQUE

Ah, of course not...
But it's fine. Margot likes you. You like spending time with her, you are on a trip to Greece with her when you barely know her.

DAVID

We have a connection. That's different. I'm probably just getting horny because I'm human and that's it. It probably has nothing to do with her.

DOMINIQUE

Okay. You got horny...just like that?
She wasn't involved in the horniness at all? You weren't looking at her or touching her?

DAVID

That's nothing more than circumstantial evidence.

DOMINIQUE

Please...you guys went to Greece together, I'll say it again.
What did you think was going to happen? I'm not telling you to be irresponsible with the first thing

that gives you a boner, but…if something happens,
why stop it?

DAVID

What are you talking about? No way! We want to
get our partners back, remember? She told you
at dinner. She's crazy about her ex. Even I'm crazy
about her ex; he's amazing. And what did I tell you
about Idoia? She's a goddess, Domi. I want Idoia.

DOMINIQUE

Prrrrrrr.

DAVID

I know you don't get along with her, but…I like
Idoia. I love Idoia. I can't go out with someone
like Margot, not in a million years. She's such…a
princess. I'm a street dog. Please. It wouldn't even
work in a movie. I don't like good girls. You've
said that yourself a million times: I always fuck it up
because I go for the bad girls. The evil ones. The
ones who rip my heart out and eat it.

DOMINIQUE

Who said anything about a relationship? You know
you can have a fling with someone and you don't
have to get married after?
You texted me hoping I would say, "You're crazy!"
and I don't know why you're so scared to sleep with
someone who's not like Idoia, but…I don't plan on
acting like a Victorian mother. Get laid. Once? 25
times!! You're in paradise and my idea of heaven
includes fucking like a rabbit.

I left the room worse off than I had gone in. What a mess. What a huge fucking mess. And she was there, completely unaware, with her hair wet, barefoot, and in that innocent little black dress, buttons up the front and…basically backless. I wished I could lick her back.

"I ordered dinner. They said it might take a while," she said to me smiling, twirling around. "While you were showering, they brought up an ice bucket. Want a drink? I think the wine is pretty much cold now."

"Um…okay."

We looked at each other. Well, I looked at her a little more, but only for scientific analysis: Was there something about her I really liked, or was I just horny?

"So handsome," she mumbled as she glanced at me.

"Me?"

"No, some guy from college I just remembered." She shot me a perplexed look. "You! Of course you! You're being such a weirdo."

"You are too! You're definitely being a weirdo."

"I'm the same as always. It's you. You're the one who's been weird ever since this morning."

She fumbled with the wine, trying to get the foil off. She was so clumsy.

"Here, leave it to me. You're very accustomed to being served, it seems."

I went over, and when I took the bottle, I accidentally brushed her fingers. I had held her hand a bunch of times… I didn't understand why there was an electric spark now. I yanked off the foil in one go, looking at her. She handed over the opener without a word, and I shoved the corkscrew into the cork and then twisted. The cork came out with a muffled *glup*, and I gave her the bottle.

"That was sexy," she confessed.

"Opening the bottle?" I furrowed my brow.

"Yes. Open bottles when you're with Idoia. She'll like it."

"I don't know if all girls are as weird as you."

"I don't know if you're always such a jerk, but try not to be one with her."

I made a face.

"Sorry." I rubbed my forehead, looking down at the ground.

"What's going on with you? Tell me." She came over and put her hand on my arm. Her fingers caressed my skin, playing gently with the hair on it. "Come on…"

"Get two glasses, please."

I tried to keep my eyes off her and concentrate on, I don't know, on the short mint-green vases on the table. What were they made of?

To hell with it. I looked at her again while she poured the wine. I imagined wrapping myself around her from behind, kissing her neck and whispering something like I was sick of seeing that mouth touching things that weren't my body.

Her smile widened when she passed me the glass, which was pretty full, by the way.

"Cheers to our planets of origin, out there, beyond the Milky Way."

A vein was throbbing in her neck. In her long, beautiful neck, a vein was throbbing, and I imagined sliding my tongue over it. I took a deep breath and…

Downed my wine in one gulp.

"What are you doing?" She pissed herself laughing.

"Go on, your turn. Weren't you the one who wanted to get wasted?"

Margot made a horrified face and fumbled behind her back for a chair, but I grabbed the fabric of her dress, tugged her toward me, and shook my head. She looked at the glass, at me, and then, after a few seconds of uncertainty, chugged it. She coughed and gagged, and I poured more wine.

"To honesty," I proposed.

"David, are you high?"

I knocked back the wine in one gulp again. She watched me with wide eyes, and when I put my glass down on the table, she drank hers.

"God, it's not very good," she complained while a few drops slid down her chin.

You are good, I thought. *No, I don't know if you're good, but I'd like to find out. I'd like to discover what you taste like and show you what I taste like.*

"David, is this because you're bored? Or you want to go home? Because it seems like you want to tell me something and you can't decide. Don't worry about me, do you hear me? If you need to go out, to meet more people, I get it. Maybe we should, I don't know…"

I stretched my hand out to her, and Margot instinctively did the same. Her fingertips, cold from the glass, stroked my palm and… before she could react, I pulled her over until she was a few scarce millimeters from my mouth. I wanted to kiss her, but, more importantly, I wanted her to want me to.

I heard her take a deep breath, looking at me so close. I parted my lips, offering myself, and she did the same.

"This is crazy," she whispered.

"Do you want to or not?"

The gentle brush of the tip of her nose against mine felt like an invitation, and…I stopped thinking. When I collided with her lips, they were half-open and wet. I could taste the softer notes of the wine as I nibbled them. The glass Margot was holding tumbled gently onto the table, and then her fingers were in my hair, pulling me closer against her. My left arm wrapped around her waist, and my right hand had intertwined fingers with hers as we kissed. We were kissing.

Wait… What the fuck?

It was my tongue that took the initiative, but Margot's danced so slowly and so sexually that I moaned and…I let go of her waist so I could slide my open hand over her ass. She let go of my hand to do the same, grabbing mine eagerly. Really eagerly.

I slammed her into the TV cabinet and then turned her again and hoisted her up onto the table with a burst of glass shattering that we ignored. Our tongues licked each other with a shamelessness I had never known. She bit my lip. I bit her chin. She wrapped her legs around my ass. I pressed her hips against the edge of the table and rubbed my bulging zipper against her black panties, which were starting to get wet.

We were panting. I knew we were panting when I put my tongue back in her mouth, desperately because a kiss had never made me so thirsty. I wanted to pull her hair, stroke her tits, rip off her panties, rub my cock between the wet lips of her pussy, and wait for her to beg me to penetrate her. I wanted to stroke her head, kiss her neck, embrace her, smell her, promise her I would never hurt her, that with me she would be free. I wanted too many things to be able to settle for just one.

I grabbed her thighs, lifted her up onto me, and stumbled to the door of her room, where her feet touched the ground again and we looked at each other, panting, as we stroked each other's chests. It was the moment of truth, the moment of consent, which came in the form of a tug on my shirt, a clear signal for us to go into the bedroom. There was no turning back now.

Two days in Santorini and we were already running around like this. When I lay on top of her, in bed, part of me almost couldn't believe it. Half of that part of me was outraged by my reluctance and the other half was beside itself, excited, crazy, as if after years of effort I had just reached fucking nirvana.

The way she arched under me. The way she opened her mouth hungrily to lick my mouth, to bite my neck, to moan when I pressed against her pussy with the bulge of my pants.

She pulled off my shirt, and I fumbled awkwardly with the buttons on her dress. As I had seen from her bare back, she wasn't wearing a bra, and despite the faltering light coming in from the terrace, I exposed both her breasts. They weren't very big, but I thought they were perfect. I lowered my head, leaving a trail of kisses down her neck and cleavage until I closed my lips around her left nipple. She arched unendingly; it felt like her hips were asking for attention to a part of her that was throbbing as much as my cock.

I put my thumb in her mouth and kept sucking, pulling, licking, biting, blowing on her nipple. She took it into her mouth with her eyes closed, going crazy on it. If I liked the Margot who jumped when she was scared, if I drove myself stupid when she stuttered nervously…this Margot who went crazy was my favorite.

I pulled my thumb out from between her teeth and lowered my hand to her stomach as she looked to see how to open my pants. I was distracted for a second from my goal of making her scream by sitting up and making it easier for her to get to my boxers. I knelt and unbuttoned my pants and then let her grope me, with my eyes closed and my head falling back, first on top of my boxers and then directly on my cock, stroking it firmly but gently.

I think I said something. Something like, "Keep going," or "Like that," or "I like it," but I know myself, and when I lose myself in bed, I could say anything; maybe I told her I wanted to stick my cock in her until I covered her in cum down to her ankles or maybe that I wanted her. Who knows? All I know is that, whatever I said, she liked it because her hand started moving faster. And I was coming.

"Wait, wait," I whispered. "I haven't even touched you yet."

I kissed her again. She told me, through kisses, licks, nibbles, and moans, that she was really horny. Ah…so little Margot liked talking during sex, eh?

"How much?" I asked her, bringing my lips closer to and farther from her mouth to provoke her.

"More than I've ever been in my entire fucking life."

I slid my hand down her body as I kissed her passionately. To borrow the expression, never in my fucking life had I ever felt so many parts of my body kissed. Not even the first time a girl stuck her tongue in my mouth and I thought I came on the spot.

I slid my hand under the elastic of her panties and noticed that she was wet. Really wet. So wet that…I admit, I was surprised.

"Margot," I moaned, kissing her neck between each word. "Do you always get this wet?"

"What?" she asked, confused.

"You're really wet. But like, really."

I found her clitoris, and I rubbed. It was sloshing, I swear. The room filled with sounds.

"No," she moaned.

"No what? You want me to stop?"

"No. No. I'm not usually this wet."

"You like it…" I left it hanging in the air, almost more a question than a statement.

She didn't answer, and…it occurred to me to take my hand out of her panties and look at my fingers. I don't know why I thought of that. It was instinctive, maybe. But under the fading light that, like I said, was filtering in from the terrace through the half-open curtains, I understood.

I let my head fall onto her shoulder with a frustrated sigh.

"Margot…"

"What? What's going on?"

"I don't care at all, but…you're bleeding."

The light suddenly blazed in like lightning had struck the bed, and we both struggled to see. When we did, it was a scene. A real scene. My right hand, the bedcovers, the sheets, a little bit of the pillow, my jeans, her thighs…all streaked with blood.

"Are you fucking kidding me right now!" she exclaimed.

She had gotten her period. She had gotten her period! She looked at herself; she looked at me.

"It doesn't matter," I whispered. "Really. It's nothing."

"So fucking embarrassing."

"What? No!"

But I couldn't add anything else because she jumped out of bed and, with a slam, shut herself in the bathroom.

When she came out, I had washed myself off, put on pajamas, and done what I could to fix her bed, though there wasn't much that could be done. Margot came out a little pale, ruffling her hair, looking at me from the doorway to her room with an expression…

the kind you make when you have no fucking clue what face to make.

"God…" she scoffed and looked at the ground.

"It doesn't matter, Margot."

"I know that, for fuck's sake," she groaned. "I got my period, I didn't send a letter full of anthrax to your whole family."

I smiled. "So?"

"So…" She smiled too, but timidly. "It's just that it's a fucking sign."

"A sign?"

"A sign that what we were doing was really fun…"

"Very," I finished off.

"But messy."

I licked my lips, took a deep breath, and looked away.

"We're here to find ourselves, right?" she went on. "To find the reasons why it didn't work with our partners and fix them. Throwing ourselves into this doesn't make any sense."

"It could also mean that we're here to have fun and that's all."

Can you tell I still really wanted to do it?

"We were friends."

"We are friends," I insisted, scared.

"I don't sleep with my friends."

"Neither do I."

"See? I want to fix it with Filippo, and you want to get Idoia back. What the fuck were we doing? It's better if we don't continue down that path."

I didn't want to insist, but in my head, I couldn't stop thinking that, maybe, we weren't like everyone else and that everything we felt couldn't just be folded back into our suitcases, squished in next to our clothes, waiting to be diluted by time.

"Do you agree?"

"No." I laughed. "But maybe that's my peanut talking."

"That's much more than a peanut." She raised her eyebrows. "That's a cucumber."

I bit my upper lip. Fuck. Why did I tell her? A little blood didn't scare me. I could have taken a condom out of my box and had the fuck of our lives and she would've discovered the blood later, after everything was over.

"I told you because I think you have the right to decide if you want to continue when the circumstances have changed, not because it matters to me, okay?"

"Okay." She nodded. "But it's better this way."

"Okay." I nodded too. "How are you feeling? My friends always tell me it hurts like hell."

"No, I'm fine. That was the dirty trick: zero symptoms."

"Good."

"We fucked it all up, didn't we? We're going to be awkward for the rest of the trip," she asked me, her face filled with terror.

"Don't worry, sad eyes." I smiled at her. "We're going to force ourselves to. Like nothing happened."

"I don't know what you're talking about. Like what happened?" she joked.

"Exactly. Come here."

She came over hesitantly, and I hugged her. I wanted her to change her mind, but I also wanted to change my own mind. It was a mess. I knew it was for the best, even though it bugged the shit out of me.

"I'm sorry," I said.

"There's nothing to be sorry about. We both did it. The brakes on the motorcycle and PMS. We're victims of circumstance."

Someone knocked on the door, and at the same time, Margot's phone beeped from the bedside table.

"That must be dinner," she said.

"I'll get it. Do you want me to ask them to change the sheets?"

"Ay, no. Too embarrassing." She laughed. "Tomorrow's fine. I'm going to…" She gestured to the bedside table, where her phone was charging.

"Yeah, yeah. I'll go answer the door…"

A boy came in with a cart, and when he saw the broken glass on the table, he stared at me, not knowing what to do.

"Outside?" I raised my eyebrows and made a face, hoping he would understand me.

He nodded and pulled the cart to the terrace. Margot appeared resolutely, with her phone in her hand, and leaned out to say something to him, while I bent down to collect the larger pieces of glass scattered across the floor.

"Leave it. You're going to cut yourself. I asked the guy to take them. He's wearing gloves."

I left the pieces on the table. We looked at each other.

"It was Filippo, right?"

"Yes." She nodded.

"And what did he say?" I tried to sound unbothered.

"He sent me one of our songs. He says he can't stop listening to it and thinking about me."

We held each other's gaze. I wanted her. I wanted all of her. I would have been content just to make out all night, stroke her slowly…and she wanted me too. I knew it.

"Good thing we stopped," she said to me.

"Yeah, good thing."

The room service guy appeared at that exact moment, and I sloped off and went outside, where I could more easily hide that it bugged me. What exactly? Everything. From stopping to her wanting to pretend it never happened. And that guy. That guy too. That guy wanting to come back into her life felt like a kick in the stomach.

Shit.

36

~~~

EVERYTHING NEW
UNDER THE SUN

MARGOT

I was woken up, as I had been for the last two days, by the sounds and light flooding into the room. I was tormented by the thought of the days when the alarm clock would once again rule over all those sensations: the light, the touch of the cold sheets under my feet, the deliciously lazy feeling that all time is mine. But, also, everything was better there; the world was calmly awake, the water in the pool was dancing, twirling, twirling, twirling in swirls caused by the filter, the birds were calling happily over the leftovers of some breakfast momentarily forgotten on the restaurant terrace. I remember thinking it was going to be hard for me to get back into my routine.

I tried to reach out for the bedside table, but I felt a little disoriented when I didn't feel my phone on it. Then David moved behind me, and I remembered.

I remembered that he kissed me the night before. I remembered that "Do you want it or not?" that turned me on so much. And the bites, the licks, the hands touching everything until we got to the bed. I remembered his cock in my hand, hard, thick, warm, and his fingers rubbing between my legs. I remembered the blood, the shame, and the dinner, trying to act like nothing had happened. I remembered his offer.

"You can sleep in my bed if you want."

The sheets were stained, and, well, I don't know if I just wanted an excuse, but not sleeping there seemed like the most logical thing to do. We fell asleep cuddled up in his bed, after talking for a couple of hours, about his friends from the village, his mother, mine, my year in America; any topic was good enough to distract us from what we had done. And after we fell asleep spooning, we woke up in the same position because the damn air-conditioning in that hotel could never be turned off, only moved up or down by a degree or two, and it created the kind of cold that makes you seek out the heat of another body.

"Good morning," David's voice mumbled into my back.

I turned to look at him. He always woke up a little dozy and very disheveled. He was cute, even with bags under his eyes, messy hair, and swollen lips. And I wanted to kiss him, as if instead of forgetting what happened, as we agreed, I had forgotten our agreement.

"Nice hair," I teased.

"Well, you look like you just came out of the salon, girl."

I don't know if I was relieved or felt sorry for myself that what had happened last night didn't seem to exist for him anymore.

"My back hurts," he complained, rolling over onto his back with a moan.

"Because of the mattress?"

"No. I think it's because I'm not used to sleeping with someone and I spent the night curled around you, like Gollum. It was cold."

"Don't worry, I'll ask for an extra blanket from reception for you." I smiled. "Anyway, luckily they'll change my sheets today and I won't bother you for the rest of the trip."

I propped my head on my hand and my elbow on the pillow. He looked at me and smiled. For a few seconds, nothing was said in the room…at least not out loud, but our eyes spoke volumes.

"What?" I tried my luck.

"Oh, no. Don't do that."

"Do what?"

"Poke me so I'm the first one to break the promise."

"I have no idea what you're talking about," I said coyly.

"Of course you do, but here we go: for me, there would be no better bed from here to Madrid."

I covered his mouth. He kissed my palm. It didn't look like we were going to act like nothing happened, and…I was relieved.

But…what about Filippo, Margot? What about Filippo?

I got up and checked the time.

"We missed breakfast."

"We can grab a couple of coffees from the bakery on the way to the highway," he suggested, luxuriating in the sheets.

Everything was so easy with him. Okay, we were on vacation, but David always had an answer for everything, a solution, or the opposite, a fun flight forward. I took a look at the bed. He was lying there, with his arm under the back of his neck, shirtless, disheveled, between such white sheets…

"What are you looking at?"

"You look like you're in a shroud. Uncover yourself a little, dude." I pushed it as far as I could.

"Do you want to see something in particular?"

"Do you have qualms about me seeing something in particular?"

He threw the blanket and the sheets to one side with an expression of superiority, and I quickly understood why. *Good morning to you too, dear David's cock, that's a very happy greeting.* Fuck...I really wanted to get back in bed.

"I have to go to the supermarket." I made a face, dragging my eyes away from his erection, which he had not hesitated to show me. "I forgot to pack tampons. I found a few in my toiletry bag, but I'm going to need more."

"Of course. We can go now. Are you driving?"

"I am pretty good at braking."

"I'm not going to keep slamming you into furniture while I shove my tongue down your throat."

I scurried off to my bathroom.

~~~~~

He was the one who went into the supermarket. When he came out, he had a box of tampons for me and something else he shoved into his backpack very mysteriously. I considered the possibility that it could be a box of condoms to use with someone else as soon as he had the opportunity, and I got angry like a little girl for two reasons: one, I didn't want any lucky tourist to squirm with pleasure with David on top (or below or next to or behind or in front), and two, because point number one was not at all consistent with what, with great wisdom and maturity, I had told him the night before. What was happening to me? I kept remembering what we did and fantasizing about a thousand different endings. No one had ever kissed me like him, and even though I knew it was wrong...I felt so alive... like when I was fifteen and still harbored the hope of being free.

The journey to Red Beach took about fifteen minutes, and when we arrived, we found there were way fewer people than we had expected.

"Did we just luck out?"

Pretty much. It was late, and because there was only a crappy snack bar, people had gone to eat lunch, leaving their spots mostly free. We threw our towels down on the sand, and David seemed so happy I didn't even miss renting a chair.

"They're all taken," he said, looking over to where we could get them. "But if you want to later…"

"No. We're fine here."

And as I said it, I put my arm around his waist from behind, resting my chin on his shoulder.

He was wearing the black bathing suit again, short and pretty tight. I was wearing a bikini printed with drawings of lemons; the bottoms had a very cute ruffle that he seemed to like.

"You're dressed perfectly to keep completing the to-do list, right?" he said as he put on sunscreen.

"The topless one, you mean?"

He nodded and turned his back to me so I would put sunscreen there. I enjoyed myself, I'll admit it.

"As far as I'm concerned"—I took advantage of the fact he couldn't see my face—"I can already scratch off the crazy night one, right?"

"Um…I don't think so."

"Why?"

"Because you have to be satisfied, don't you think?" He looked at me over his shoulder with a wolfish smile.

"I wasn't suffering."

"In my opinion, it's like scratching *eating* off the list because you got some cutlery."

I gave him a pat to let him know he was all finished and focused on putting sunscreen on myself.

"Want me to do your back?" he offered.

"Yes."

"Should I untie your bikini top?" He raised his eyebrows, joking.
I laughed. I looked around and then at him.

"Can you imagine?"

"Ooooh," he teased. "So wild! How are you going to take off
your bikini top like…at least, at least…two dozen other girls on
this beach?"

"But I'm not one of those two dozen girls." I pushed my hair off
my face. "I grew up listening to a mother recite all the things that
are considered vulgar for women to do, and it turns out that encom-
passes almost everything fun."

"That's your mother's concept of what's vulgar. What's yours?"

"Showing my tits on a beach is not part of that concept, I know
that much."

I looked at David over my shoulder and smiled a little wickedly.

"Go on." I moved my arm. "Untie it."

He raised his eyebrows.

"Seriously?"

"But I think the time has come to tell you that I don't know if I
see myself kissing another woman."

The strap on my back disappeared between his fingers, and I bent
down to grab the highest SPF sunscreen I had, a stick of it, to put
on my boobs. David was looking at me in awe when I dropped the
bikini top and concentrated on the task.

"If you keep looking…" I warned him, not looking up at him.

"I'll piss the bed."

"The pissing-in-the-bed thing is when you stare at fire for too
long, I think."

"Exactly…"

I looked at him. He was smiling at me and pulling the hair on his forehead apart with his fingers.

"It's super creepy and gross that you're ogling my tits," I insisted.

"I'm not ogling," he replied, his eyes clamped on mine. "But they're beautiful. And now, if you'll excuse me, I'm going to get in the water."

A family with children laughed and built sandcastles. Two boys were talking, very close, about something that made them laugh. A dog was barking, running up and down the shore and splashing the swimmers who were getting out and going in.

"Lights Up" by Harry Styles was playing in my headphones while I tried to focus on reading a book on the use of new technologies in internationalization, updating, and branding strategies. A few drops fell on my back.

"That book sucks, and you know it." David lay down next to me and, with his still-wet fingers, drew a couple of figures on my skin, joining the drops that had fallen from his hair.

He had put on his sunglasses. *Fuck. Those damn sunglasses.* I closed the book and took the opportunity to pull them off when he lay on his back.

"Hey!" he complained. "Give them back. The sun is hot as hell."

"Let's keep the peace, David. You look too cute in these," I warned him.

I lay on my side, and he did the same, propping his head up on his forearm.

"You're half naked next to me. I deserve my sunglasses."

"Here's what we'll do. I'll put my bikini top back on, and you forget the Ray-Bans; then we'll be on equal footing."

"No." He snatched them from me and put them on. "We're fine like this. You do your list, and I make up for it."

"Now I can't see where you're looking."

"At your tits. Don't doubt it for one second."

I wanted to sit on top of him, comb his wet hair with my fingers... maybe talk about the night before. If it had been any other guy, I wouldn't have dared to even think about bringing it up, but it was him, and I always felt comfortable with him. Peaceful. Comfortable in my own skin.

I opened my mouth to say his name and leave a few ellipses in the air, hoping he would help me bring it up, but my phone started ringing.

"You're fucking kidding me, dude," I muttered. "There shouldn't be any service here."

"It's probably Filippo. He probably changed his mind and is coming to get you in a helicopter."

"Go to hell."

I tried to sit up as elegantly as possible and reached for my phone from the pocket of David's backpack.

"Oh, God," I muttered when I saw who the call was from.

"Work?"

"Worse. My sister Candela. I'm going to go over there, okay?"

"Okay." He nodded. "That way I won't hear anything when you tell her about last night."

I didn't even answer. It was hard enough putting my feet on the soft, uneven sand and moving away without looking like an ex-soldier holding a grenade.

"What?" I answered.

"You're not going to believe it."

"I'm fine too. Yes, the break to think about myself and my priorities is going great, thanks for asking."

"Fuuuuck, such an attitude, diva."

"I'm sick of this shit!" I whined, looking over my shoulder at David settling down to read his book.

"Is there something you want to tell me?"

"No," I said emphatically. "What happened now?"

"Patricia got more photos from the detective. I sent them to you. You have to see them."

"What the fuck are you saying?" I got scared.

I took the phone off my ear and looked for some shade under some rocks at the foot of the hillside where we had climbed down to the beach and sat down so I could open the email Candela had just sent me. And she was right. I couldn't believe it. In the photos, two tall blond girlies were watching, hiding behind a recycling bin, peering out from behind a huge newspaper (standing in the middle of a crowded street...that's what I call *discretion* in capital letters), using a baby stroller to sneak around "without being seen." I looked at the sky, flipped my hair, and asked the universe for strength.

"But what does all this shit mean?" I asked her.

"Well, to start with, the detective wasn't as bad as we thought. He spotted us following him."

A camouflaged laugh came out of my nose.

"You wouldn't believe the scene he caused with Patricia. He said he'd give her money back, but she had to swear never to contact him again. He felt harassed. Harassed. Apparently, your older sister told him at least once, 'I was so lucky to find such an attractive detective.' The gentleman thought Patricia was a nutjob who was obsessed with him."

"Your sister has lost her mind. Tell me he's not going to report her or anything."

"No, no. In the end, he just refunded most of her money in exchange for the promise he would never see her again."

"I hope that punishment was enough and she's learned her lesson," I answered, dead serious. "Harassment isn't funny, Candela."

"You don't have to tell me. Your sister is the one being disgusting."

I looked over at David. He was opening a can of beer. I wanted to be all the drops of water flying off him when he did it.

"She hired another guy," Candela announced.

"What are you talking about?" I turned back to the sea again. "Seriously?"

"Yeah, but this one is an old bag. He must be two hundred years old. I think they found him in the Egyptian pyramids."

I burst into laughter, covering my eyes.

"Is there anyone normal in this family?" I threw the question out into the air.

"I think Papa was normal."

"I don't think so. Why would he have married Mama then?"

"Um…I never looked at it that way. Well, what about you?"

"Me?"

I glanced back. Fucking sunglasses.

"Yes, you."

Silence. I was debating whether sharing some information would make me feel better or worse.

"You guys have hooked up, right?"

I let out a whimper of incomprehension, and she sucked her teeth.

"Have you slept together?"

"No! Well…we were about to."

"But?"

"I'd love to tell you that in a fierce struggle between my reasoning and what my clamshell wanted, common sense won…but no. Have you seen *Carrie*?"

"The new one or the old one? Doesn't matter, I like the book better anyway."

"Do you remember the scene at the dance, almost at the end?"

"When she ends up covered in pig blood? Wait!"

"Yes. The bed ended up looking like a prop from *The Texas Chainsaw Massacre*."

"That must've been a mess, right?"

"Well, to tell the truth? No. More like a letdown because you don't know how he touches, how he kisses, how—"

"Okay, okay, okay. Simmer down. What about now?"

"Now? Well…" I looked over my shoulder. "We're going to pretend like nothing happened."

"Wait, when did this happen?"

"Last night."

"And you're going to pretend it didn't happen."

"Yes."

"You don't even believe that yourself." She laughed.

I pushed my hair out of my face, overwhelmed.

"I love Filippo," I declared.

"Okay."

"This isn't fair."

Candela didn't say anything.

"I want to get him back."

"Okay," my sister repeated.

"Do you think he's slept with anyone? I mean…he was very angry with me, he's on vacation with his friends, and…"

"Hit the brakes. I have no idea what Filippo is doing; what I'm interested in is what you're doing. If he had slept with someone, what would that change for you?"

"Well…señora, it changes the map of the situation a little…"

"You wouldn't want to get him back?"

"I want to get him back," I repeated. "In September, when we see each other, we have to see what went wrong and try to fix it…but I want to be with him."

"What about David?"

"David is a friend."

"You don't fuck friends."

"Well, *you* don't fuck friends, but David probably does."

"Would you go out with David?" she asked. "Could you have a relationship with him?"

"No. No way. That dude is a hot mess." I felt bad and looked at him. Poor guy. He didn't deserve that. He was just going through a complicated time. Like me. "Well, I mean, *a mess* isn't really fair, but the thing is, no, I couldn't be with anyone like him."

"Why?"

"What do you mean why? Because…no. It hasn't even crossed my mind."

"You're playing with fire." She sighed. "Margot…that guy makes you laugh."

"Fuck laughing. Dani Rovira makes me laugh too, and I wouldn't leave it all behind for him."

"Come on, girl, you know what I'm saying."

I stared at some boats in the distance that were heading toward the beach. Out there where the sea seemed to blur into the horizon, the water rippled with golds and turquoises.

"Margot? You still there?"

"I'm here, Candela. I'm…I'm on an incredible beach with red sand and crystal clear water and my tits out…"

"Your tits out? You?"

"Tits out. Me. The same me who's going to hang up the phone and stop overanalyzing. Do you hear me, Candela? Because I'm going to hang up the phone and live. But live like I'm going to die the second I land in Madrid. And I'll live everything I want to in secret. If I feel like blowing him, I'll leave it raw. If I feel like taking it up the ass, welcome to the back door. And you know what? No one will know. Just like no one knows what the fuck Filippo is doing. When was the last time I was selfish? Hey? Because I ran away from my wedding, I know; how fucking embarrassing for the cat mother's family, but that's it! I'm going to enjoy myself, and that's that. Let's go."

I hung up the phone and stared at it like it had just fallen out of a flying saucer. Next to me, a family was looking at me a little stunned. I guess because of my tone. I prayed they didn't speak Spanish, but I didn't have time to find out. As far as the phone, that started buzzing in my hand with a WhatsApp notification from Patricia.

You're online. Call me. I'm not okay.

I went over to where David was waiting and sunbathing.

"Everything okay? You took a while," he asked when he felt my shadow move over him.

I chucked my phone on top of the towel and went back to the shore, where I threw myself into the sea without looking back.

The water cooled my sun-reddened skin, and my ideas hardened, like lava, when they touched the sea. Firmer, colder, immovable.

I was aware that an affair always hurts someone. I wanted to fix it with Filippo, and...I also wanted to keep getting to know the Margot who bloomed when David touched me. No. The Margot that emerged when she felt completely free, when no one was going to judge her. I wanted to know what it felt like to make decisions just for myself.

When I got back to where David was lying, I took the book out of his hands without a word and left it on my towel face down. I straddled his thighs, a little farther down than the area that I had been handling the night before, mind you. Breaking free is one thing, and a canoodling session on a public beach quite another. I thought he would sit up like a spring, but he stayed still, staring at me. My hair, tossed to one side, was swaying, drying in the sun. Drops fell from my nipples and dappled his chest, where I placed a hand as I bent down.

"Yes." He nodded seriously.

"Yes, what?"

"To what you're asking, yes."

There was no kiss, but the way he trailed his thumb down my back said much more.

Problems.

37

~~~~

A PERFECT PLAN

If I tell you that, actually, nothing big changed between us after making that decision, you probably won't believe it. But it was true. Nothing changed. We were still David and Margot, and for a good part of that day, we were just the same David and Margot as always, which made me think that there had been something from the beginning…something tacit, intimate, only ours.

We took pictures (and how gorgeous is that one where we're lying down, hiding my breasts with his arm, both laughing in the reddish sand); we dived in search of little fishes, taking turns with his goggles. We each guarded the bathroom door while the other peed and we ate some sandwiches, which we both filled with tzatziki, turkey slices, and chips. There were no rules by his side. Any imposition could be challenged with a "Why?" If my mother had seen me this happy, she would have died.

The room was freezing when we got back, maybe because they had left us a plate of fruit and they didn't want it to rot.

"The energy waste at this hotel is bordering on irresponsible," he muttered. "I'm gonna snitch to Greta Thunberg." He popped a grape in his mouth and smiled as he chewed. "I'm going to take a shower."

"Me too."

"With me?" He raised his eyebrows.

"Ask me in a few days."

I headed toward my bathroom, but David ran over, caught me in his arms, and spun me around.

"Stop!" I screamed playfully.

David tried to open the door onto the patio with me on his back, a pretty hard job since I was wriggling, trying to get away.

"David, seriously, I have to go to the bathroom," I complained.

"Quiet for a sec."

I kicked him and accidentally hit the door, which finally opened wide. David grabbed me tightly and ran to the pool without thinking twice: still wearing his shirt, his sunglasses, and his flip-flops. I remember the fabric of my dress floating around me, surrounded by bubbles, and David in front of me holding his breath, his sunglasses still on. I remember those seconds underwater almost more clearly than many of the memories that theoretically should have been my core memories. The light bounced off the blue tiles on the bottom of the pool, and instead of letting go, David's hands grabbed me tighter so we emerged together, tangled in my legs and panting. Those five or six seconds lasted hours. Sometimes, at the very moment you're living something, you know you will spend years wishing to live lost in that memory.

And it's a pity life isn't a movie where we can choose the soundtrack we deserve at all times. Because right then we deserved to listen to one of those shitty and amazing songs that show you that you're lucky to be alive and feeling things and even if the timing is off and you're with someone you shouldn't be experiencing these things with. You can't choose to hoard emotions to live them later with the person who everything points to being the right one.

And there, soaked, clinging to each other, smiling, happy…I couldn't stop looking at him and wondering how it was possible that two conflicting needs coexisted in me: to have Filippo close to me, and David. David in general.

"What?" he asked.

"What song would you choose right now?"

"Does your insurance cover psychiatric needs abroad?" He smiled.

"I mean it."

"'Never Tear Us Apart' by INXS," he answered firmly, in pretty stiff English.

I took off his sunglasses and put my arms around his neck.

"I don't know it."

"Sorry. I'm a sucker for the eighties," he said, looking at my lips.

"You weren't even born back then."

"When they wrote that song, you weren't either."

"Stop looking at me like that."

"I can't."

David's voice came out of his throat a little strangled. I stroked his hair at his temples, and he put his mouth on my chin.

"Let's take a shower and go to Oia for dinner. Do you want to? We can make it in time for the sunset, and they say it's the best place on the island to see it. But you drive, okay? I looked it up, and it's like half an hour on the bike."

"Can I ask for something in exchange?"

"Try me."

We looked at each other silently, and like always, we smiled immediately.

"I'll hold on to that as an ace up my sleeve," he whispered. "Come on, let's go or we won't make the sunset. It's a date."

For someone who wanted to get back the fiancé she lost when she ran out in a wedding dress in the opposite direction of the church, I tried way too hard to get dressed for that "date." I wore a short fringed skirt (very short, when did I even buy this? Oh, right, at some point after I went shopping with David and he gave me wings), and a plain black T-shirt. Simple sandals in black too, with a little wedge. I even put on lipstick. And eyeliner. And I straightened my hair. Yes...I made too much effort for that date, but the thing is...I really wanted it to be a perfect night. Maybe it had something to do with how disastrously the night before had ended. Maybe it had something to do with my stupid need to make everything flawless enough to justify its existence.

When we met in the villa's little living room, David seemed surprised.

"Wow...you look so pretty." He pointed at himself awkwardly. "Should I change?"

I looked him up and down. Some pretty worn jeans and a black T-shirt. I went over, pulled on it, and found the ever-present hole, which made me smile.

"No. The whole grunge thing looks good on you."

And I meant it. I didn't care if he wore a perfect white button-up and tight pants. I didn't care that I could see the band of his boxers because the waist of his jeans drooped down even though he was wearing a belt. I didn't care.

The plan seemed idyllic. I couldn't think of anything more

perfect than watching the sun go down at the northwest end of the island, sitting in some restaurant embedded in the cliff itself, holding a drink, looking at each other...but the thing about plans is that they rarely go as expected. The first thing was the skirt...which was not stretchy and gave me a lot of trouble getting onto the bike. A lot. So much that either I had to go back and change or ride pillion in my panties, or I would have to drive. I wasn't prepared for half an hour of driving, but...I wanted to wear that skirt. It was the outfit that went best with the idea of the evening I had in my head.

The second problem, besides the nightmare I had with that infernal rattletrap, was that I'd forgotten David and I weren't the only two people on the face of the earth after all. I had never traveled like this, to a place like Greece in the middle of high season, so I wasn't used to having to elbow through to get a glimpse, in the distance, of a tiny corner of the sea. So I didn't even think about the possibility that Oia would be crammed with people who had come with exactly the same intention as us.

The entrance into the town was already pretty backed up, but when we finally managed to get through, there wasn't a single restaurant, bar, or terrace with a free table. Not even a stool to sit on to watch the sunset. The streets were full of tourists (which we were too, by the way), and the only place we found to watch the sunset was in the parking lot where we left the motorcycle when we arrived. And to cap it all off, we'd have to find a gap through hundreds of heads. And I better not even mention how hot the evening was. The backs of my legs were dripping sweat, my upper lip, my forehead, my neck, between my boobs, and even my underboob.

"This is unbelievable," I muttered, disappointed, patting my upper lip with the back of my hand, trying to dry the drops of sweat on my mustache. "Where'd all these people come from?"

"Princess…" David laughed. "I know it's hard to believe, but we're not the only people on the face of the earth."

"I know that," I grumbled.

"Margot…this is normal. This village is probably in every guidebook, and tourists aren't exactly known for being the most original."

I shot him a side-eye and felt ridiculous when I thought about the fact that I had come up with this plan after seeing it on an influencer's Instagram. I had constructed an image of this date that I was dying to have with David entirely from a stranger's photo, which was probably incredibly posed.

"Well, this sucks." I stamped my feet grumpily.

"Just because you're used to seeing everything from the seat of honor. Here's what we can do…"

I turned back to him.

"Let's go back. We'll go through Fira, pick up a pizza, and we'll go back to the room. We'll listen to music, chat… We've barely used the terrace in the room."

"We spent half an hour getting here," I grumbled.

"Margot…there are two types of people in the world: the kind who complain and the kind who look for a solution. Which do you wanna be?"

"Right now, the kind who complains."

David cracked up, drawing looks from everyone around us. He was so cute when he laughed. He was so cute at golden hour, when the shimmering light started to tinge everything. He made me feel so free.

"You wanted to see the sunset," he said, babying me.

"Yes."

"Well, it's a good thing the sunset happens every day. Come on, my little baby, come with your doggy; he's hungry."

I pulled his arm, resisting.

"A pizza and Spotify isn't my idea of a perfect evening." I was still whining.

"Why does it have to be perfect?"

I blushed. I felt stupid. Maybe he just wanted to drink a beer and go to sleep, and I…I had taken the whole "date" thing very literally, just because we had kissed the night before. And talked. And almost…

"Hey…" David hooked his right arm around my waist and jiggled me until I smiled. "Things can't be perfect just because you want them to be. There are a lot of factors, and we're just two humans."

"But—"

"I don't need everything to be perfect. I only have one request for tonight, and that's to spend it with you. There'll be many more, and maybe, if we're lucky, one of them will be completely perfect. We won't have to plan it."

I smiled reluctantly.

"You look beautiful," he whispered. "But not because of the skirt or the lipstick. You're beautiful when you're free, and when you get angry and you want everything to go the way you hoped…"

I covered his mouth and saw him smile.

"Don't say things like that to me."

"Okay," I heard him say, his voice muffled by the palm of my hand, and I let go. "Let's do something. Unzip your skirt."

"What are you talking about?" I exclaimed.

"Come here." He pulled me over to where the motorcycle was, opened the seat, took out the two helmets, and got on.

He threw his hips forward and kicked up the kickstand. Needless to say, that move with his hips made me like one of those monkeys who snatch things from tourists: crazy.

"Unzip your skirt and get on behind me," he insisted. "I'm sure the fabric will give and you'll be more comfortable."

"I'm going to flash everyone and their mother."

"That'll make it even more refreshing."

I undid the zip on my skirt and shimmied it down my thighs. He was right, that way I could sit behind him, open my legs a little and snuggle into his body without having to show my ass the whole time.

"Ready? Think about what you want on your pizza, babe, because tonight I'm paying."

And with the laughter he stole from me, he set off, and while we were going as fast as the rented motorcycle allowed, we left behind hundreds of people and a trail of giggles.

The sunset discovered us in the curves on the main road that led to Fira. We didn't see the sun sink into the sea, and we didn't toast with a good cold wine in a place with air-conditioning. But I wouldn't trade that moment for anything in the world. The feeling I had leaving there and realizing that we could make the ordinary something special. Oh, David's scent wafting into my face and both of my hands around his belly…

~~~~~

We bought a pizza and a couple of diet sodas and some cookies. We had dinner sitting on the sun loungers, quickly and hungrily, bolting it down before the pizza got cold and wiping our oily fingers on toilet paper. The part of Margot that I had built from romantic speeches and rom-coms died when I realized that, in the end, that part's existence wasn't sustained by anything real. Perfection is romantic by pure chance, and the most beautiful things are always ephemeral. And in that imperfect scene, actually, I didn't miss anything. Not cloth napkins or duck magret. Well, maybe the napkins.

When we finished, we lay on the loungers and looked up at the starry sky. I had never been that into astronomy. But maybe that's only because no one had told me, the way David told me, with a slow but passionate voice, the myth of Andromeda.

"Andromeda was the daughter of Aethiopian royalty. Her mother, who had a pretty big ego, declared that both were more beautiful than the Nereids, the nymphs of the sea. They were very offended and went straight to Poseidon to complain: 'Come on, either you do something or we'll go out and explain it to these narcissists ourselves.'"

I giggled like a kid.

And he told me more and more things about a monster; about Perseus, who later became a king; about the withering love he felt when he saw Andromeda chained to a rock, ready to be devoured. And I was gobsmacked...by the history, by his lips conjugating every verb, by the way he narrated all of it, like he had it all stored in his head, alongside those names of plants and flowers, all coming together to make him the perfect person he seemed to be.

"And that one there, follow my finger...is Andromeda's constellation."

And, leaning against his chest, I pretended to find the stars that made the group while I thought about how luxury sometimes had nothing to do with stuff.

I hated every single one of the mosquitoes buzzing around our ears that forced us inside so we wouldn't be bitten. I was having so much fun I didn't want the night to end. I felt stupidly disappointed because, well, in the end, the "date" had gone great, but subconsciously I had been expecting more. It's interesting the capacity humans have to say one thing and do exactly the opposite.

It seemed like we were going to say goodbye in the living room, but when I went to close my door, David blocked it.

"Wanna come listen to music in my room?" he asked. "It's still early."

I nodded. I couldn't even speak. In my mind, I was grinding on him with a talent I can promise you I don't actually possess. Please, we're so cool in our imaginations.

"Give me a second, okay? I'll be right there."

I took off my makeup, put on my creams, ran a comb through my hair, put on perfume, brushed my teeth, put on a different, shorter nightgown, and took a few deep breaths before I went out. Ten steps separated his room from mine, and I never walked more certainly despite being barefoot.

I found him lying on his bed, fiddling with his ancient iPod. He smiled when I went over and offered me a headphone.

"Welcome to Nostalgic Music 101 In this class, we'll be studying the themes present in the best songs of all time written twenty or thirty years ago. Ready?"

"Ready." I lay down next to him and put the earbud in my ear.

"This is the one I was telling you about this afternoon," he said, lying opposite me. "It's called 'Never Tear Us Apart,' and it's by an Australian group called INXS."

David, a kid who was closer to twenty-five than thirty, who poured drinks on the weekend in a dive where ninety percent of what they played was reggaeton, listened to songs from the eighties on his dated iPod, ballads that would never go out of style but that hardly anyone knew anymore. I stroked his rough cheek, and he moved closer, chasing the caress.

God. Wasn't he so handsome? He was. How had I not found him cute the first time I saw him? With that enfant terrible air, the bad boy who makes any honorable daughter fail a couple of subjects, a bartender who elicits sighs and doesn't even care about the age of the mouths expelling them.

I don't know if David understood enough English to know that the song had a lot of us in it…or the us that the romantic part of me wanted to imagine, but it made me excited. A kind of teenage excitement and nothing mature on my part? Obvs. An excitement that made me feel really alive? That too.

He edged a little closer. I did too. We smiled, like two fools.

"This is called, 'I Want to Know What Love Is,' and it's by Foreigner," he whispered, not moving away.

"English is your first language, right?" I laughed.

"Are you making fun of me?"

"A little."

I admit, I was the one who started it. I nuzzled my nose against his, begging silently for him to kiss me. He put his hand on my cheek and brushed his nose against my chin, my lips, and my nose again, but he didn't kiss me.

"Sorry…" I mumbled.

"Why are you sorry?"

He looked into my eyes, and our mouths were centimeters apart again.

"I think I'm too close," I answered.

"It seems like you want to get a little closer."

I pulled away a little, feeling rejected, but he eliminated the distance, coming closer.

"You clearly want to do it, so why are you putting the ball in my court?" And when he spoke, his mouth was almost brushing against mine.

"You're a dick."

"I'm not. Just…"

I didn't let him finish. He tasted like mint when I put my tongue in his mouth, and he responded more passionately than I was expecting. He moaned, and it seemed to be out of relief, at the same time as he slapped his iPod aside to press himself against me; in one of each of our ears, we still had the headphones plugged in, and the music was still playing.

I slung my left leg over his hips, and suddenly David let gravity and desire overcome him and rolled on top of me.

"Oof…" he panted, looking at me, before he pressed his mouth against mine again.

His tongue was moving so slowly in my mouth, it felt like he was unraveling me. The way he kissed was mind-blowing. David was still kissing as passionately as he had at fifteen, I knew it. For him, kisses hadn't lost their power, as often happens once you try sex. For him kissing was erotic, sensual, sexual, a carnal act. He somehow confirmed this by the way he kissed my neck and his hands seemed to come alive as they reached for my breasts.

The song changed in our ears, and he balanced on his arms over me, smiling slyly.

"Wanna know what this one is?"

"I don't give a shit." I laughed. "But you're going to tell me anyway."

"'Love Bites.'" And suddenly, he was biting my bottom lip. "Did I say it right, professor?"

"Terribly. Kiss me," I demanded.

He buried his mouth in my neck again, and his right hand, finally, reached my left breast. His fingers dug into me, rubbing his palm against the thin fabric of my nightgown, and then he lowered his mouth to it, until he was blowing against the outline of my hard nipple.

"This song is weird as hell." I smiled, while he spread my thighs apart and pushed his erection against my *monte de Venus*.

"Yeah, like me."

"You like fucking to this music?"

"Yes, but tonight…" He leaned down until his nose was brushing against mine again. "Tonight all I want to do is kiss you."

"Nobody believes that."

"Well, you should because I'm just going to kiss you. Well…I might touch you a little."

"And what are you going to do with that?" I lifted my hips and brushed against his hard cock.

"Grin and bear it." He smiled. "There's much more to life than instant gratification."

"You're going to drench the bed."

"I'm going to make out with you until it hurts. I'm going to stroke your breasts until I memorize them. I'm going to rub myself between your legs. And when we can't take it anymore, we'll probably find some way to make ourselves feel better within those boundaries."

My lip was trapped between his teeth, and he slowly let it free, as his hips moved back and forth between my legs. I went crazy, and as I moaned to show him, he kept doing exactly the same thing for a whole song until I thought I was dying. My skin was burning, my mouth was stinging, and my clit was throbbing so hard it was already unbearable. Then, in our headphones, The Police were playing "Every Breath You Take," and without realizing it, our kisses and movements were in step with the beat.

David knew afternoons lying in the park watching clouds go by. David moved like someone who loses hope of stopping time. David took me back to a time in my life where everything that didn't matter mattered a little less.

It was inevitable that we lost more clothes because we were getting more and more heated. We were feverish, like those first few times you let someone touch you like you touched yourself secretly, dying of shame. He took off my nightgown, and I pulled off his shorts, but we kept my underwear from the waist down. By the time he placed my arms on top of the pillow, grabbed them with one hand, and put his heart and soul into rubbing against my panties, I had already lost track of the songs that had passed through our ears. Then one came on that I knew: "Nothing Compares 2 U" by Sinead O'Connor. I had to admit this was the best playlist of throwbacks I had ever heard. The best to make us feel like we were fifteen again.

We kept going with one of his hands clasping both wrists and the other's fingers digging into one of my butt cheeks, where he had found the perfect point of support to trigger an orgasm.

"Do you think you could come like this?" he asked me.

"I don't know."

"You do know. Could you?"

"No," I confessed.

His mouth found mine again, which was waiting hungrily, and he found a way to let go of my wrist and slip that hand between us.

There, right there. My eyes rolled back and then I let go, closing them. I had never even touched myself in such a perfect spot.

"Give me a warning," he whispered, pulling away from my mouth for just a second.

I slipped one of my hands in and joined the party. I helped him. He smiled into my lips, and his hip found that point to rub himself again. The rhythm started to go faster, faster…and we lost each other's kisses to give in to the moans and pants that were misting up the windows and gliding across the floor.

I felt my whole body devastated by pleasure. My toes, one by one, from right to left and left to right. The skin on my legs, which were wrapped around his. My cunt, my clitoris. My monte de Venus. The fuzz covering it. My belly button. My nipples. My fingertips… they were all overcome by it: five buried in David's hair, three slowly watching how everything was unfolding and two rubbing, rubbing, rubbing.

"I'm coming…" I managed to say.

"Can I come?" he asked.

"Yes."

"On you?"

I nodded, and he whispered for me to watch. My eyes fluttered shut a few times while I came, but I managed to return them to the lighthouse of his eyes until the final thrust, which pulled a suffocated scream out of me. David blinked slowly. Very slowly. Almost as slowly as he had moved his tongue during those first kisses. Then he bit his bottom lip, gyrated between my legs, and buried the fingers of his left hand in my hair.

"Ah…ah…ah…" he moaned thickly.

He moved a little more over me, clumsier every time, until he let go of me and leaned on two arms with a growl. He looked at his cock, he looked at me, in my panties underneath him, and then... he kissed me.

He kissed me until we were both moaning again.

I have no idea what song was playing then, but I felt like dancing.

38

~~~

WITH YOU, YES

David whispered and stroked me gently to wake me up. I opened my eyes and saw him dressed and smiling.

"It's not even seven yet, but you have to get up."

"What are you talking about?" I moaned, letting my eyes droop shut again.

"Hey, hey…Margot. Trust me…please."

I sat up in bed. I was still in my panties, and the sheet draped over my waist left my tits in plain sight, but I covered them up, embarrassed.

"My girl…" He laughed. "That's not necessary. All I need is another half hour and I'll have them memorized."

"That's not very gentlemanly on your part."

"That's good because I don't believe in that stuff."

"What do you believe in?"

"In a relationship between equals. Get up, please."

When he winked at me, I thought of Filippo…who opened the door for me in every restaurant, who closed my car door, who sent flowers with beautiful notes, who paid the bill and once proclaimed himself the alpha in the relationship. Did I need it? Did I need chivalry? Did I really know what that term implied? In fairy tales, it's always a given that the princes are always gentlemen and the princesses…little ladies.

"What's your favorite Disney movie?" I asked him, expecting him to tell me he hadn't seen any.

"*Brave*." He came over and leaned over me with an arched brow. "Are you getting up, darling?"

I snorted, pushed off the sheets, and, with one boob in each hand, hurried into my bathroom, where someone had left a bikini and a beachy dress.

"These don't go together!" I called out.

"Do you think I care?"

I started to laugh.

After a quick shower, I came out dressed but with a sleepy face, and I bumped into him with his backpack hanging from his shoulder and my beach bag packed at his feet.

"Where are we going?"

"You're going to have to wait and see. But don't worry. I packed everything you need. And forgive me, I had to go through some of your stuff. But this way…it's a surprise."

A surge of affection. The urge to kiss him. The urge to scream. The feeling of being able to fly. A catapult landing a ball of regrets in my stomach.

"Have fun!" the girl from reception waved us off when she saw us going out.

"Thank you," I mumbled, surprised.

"What did she say?" David asked me, taking out the keys to the bike.

"Does she know where we're going?"

"Ah, yes."

"When...?"

"I got out of bed at five thirty, and when I came to look for help, she was already there. You won't believe it, but we managed to understand each other. We have to leave her a good review so her boss can see."

He climbed on, put my bag between his legs, and gave me the backpack to put on my back. Then he patted the back of the bike.

"Come on, Margot, adventures don't live themselves."

~~~

I was pretty slow to recognize the direction we were heading in when we were already in the last turns leading down to the port. When we got there, David locked the bike and waved me into an old building, where we went straight into a line.

"Wait, where are we going?"

"Take this." He pulled a box of Dramamine out of the outer pocket of his backpack and a bottle of water from the hotel out of the main pocket.

"What's this for?"

"Do you know they sell them in supermarkets?" He smiled. "The one from the other day had a pharmacy section."

"You bought this?"

"Yes. I guessed we were going to take another boat before we left, and I didn't want to become a human piñata again."

"You know, I thought you bought condoms?" I laughed.

"Oh, those too. Dramamine, condoms, and a box of tampons. You can imagine the checkout guy's face, right?"

He smiled like a saint. I swallowed my two pills, drank a little water, praying I wouldn't choke on everything (the surprise, the condoms, his attention), and handed over the bottle so he could take his.

"Where are we going?"

"It's a surprise, sad eyes." He came a little closer to me, and his innocent smile was wrapped in that kind of complicity you only have after you know each other's skin.

He didn't kiss me, but he left me wishing he would.

We got on a ferry, still yawning, but I still had no idea where we were going, since this same boat made stops on many surrounding islands before going to Athens.

Unlike on our journey there, we were tourists this time, but at that hour the deck was practically empty. He bought me a latte and a bun, and we had breakfast while we played a game: I was trying to guess our destination by asking him yes or no questions. No, I never guessed it.

We got off at the first stop: Ios, another island more or less the same size as Santorini, an hour-and-twenty-minute ferry ride away. I was freaking out that he had organized all this.

We walked about two minutes under the morning sun until we reached a two-star hotel that was above one of those old-fashioned travel agencies where tourists hired excursions and maritime activities. We were given only one room (of course) on the second floor, small but clean, everything in its place, but it had a monastic modesty: a double bed with a heavy wooden headboard, flanked by a small table, two chairs, and two bedside tables. We also had a terrace where two plastic beach chairs and a table held court. The railing on the terrace was painted a blue that stood out because everything else was whitewashed and almost blended into the dark sea in the port opposite the room.

David put our stuff in the room and the bathroom while I watched the boats swaying. I didn't hear him come back in, and I jumped when I saw him.

"It's not very nice, but…"

I went over and hugged him. I hugged him the way two people who have much more than friendship hug, true, but I didn't want him to see it as a couple-y gesture. Just a thank-you.

"It's beautiful. Thank you."

"Don't thank me, please. It was the least I could do…"

I pulled out of the hug to look at him. Sometimes, eyes can tinge words with emotions that wouldn't fit in any sentence. He had incredible eyes…two brown eyes had never held so much inside them…galaxies hidden in tiny golden streaks. Doubts. Emotion. An imperfect story.

No. He didn't kiss me then either.

"Come on…" he said, taking my hand, taking a step back and tugging me along. "I'm going to take you somewhere incredible, you'll see."

We walked over to one of those seedy rent-a-car places you see in every beach town, and David tried every which way to get the guy working there to understand him, but I had to step in when it became obvious he had no desire to understand.

"Tell him, please, that we need a small car for the day."

"Wait, where are you taking me?"

"To kill you in some remote corner of this island, where I'll take photos of your body and abandon you in the trunk. Come on, please…" He pointed at the attendant.

It was the first time I had seen David get exasperated.

He insisted on paying, but as he did so, he launched into a speech about the reasons he was doing it, which had nothing to do with the patriarchy.

"You see, it doesn't matter to me if you're a woman, a man, Medusa, or a tropical cockatoo, when it comes to paying. But I can't let you pay for everything."

"Do you feel like a whore?" I teased.

"No. I feel like a freeloader. And I haven't been working since I was sixteen to end up feeling like that with you."

"You know I have too much, right?"

"Nobody has too much money." He waved his hand scornfully toward me as we headed over to the white C2 we had been assigned. "You just have more than you can spend."

"No, David. I have too much," I insisted.

He stopped walking toward the car and looked at me with a furrowed brow.

"And why are you telling me that now?"

"Because I don't want you to worry about that when you're with me."

"And I don't want you to think everything has to be how you want it and what you're accustomed to just because you have too much money." He smiled teasingly. "Your millions can blow me, queen. Tonight you're going to sleep in an inn."

I couldn't do anything but laugh.

He didn't give me the option to drive, and...I would have liked to because watching him do it was actual torture. Why was a cute guy so much cuter behind the wheel? Every time he changed gear, my head filled with his expression when he came while his fingers rubbed me. I liked that he wasn't one of those guys who treated you like you had Ebola or you were dying when you had your period. I don't think Filippo and I had had sex of any kind when I was on my period. Was that weird? Was it normal? With Idoia, did he…?

"What?" he asked, taking his eyes off the road for a second. "Your face looks like you're doing calculations."

"You're such hot stuff."

He smiled, but then his smile faded slowly. "I'm actually pretty cold stuff."

Should I say it? Or not say it? *Come on, we came here to play.* "You didn't seem cold at all to me last night."

I studied David's reaction, intrigued. His eyebrows moved almost imperceptibly, and then he licked his lips.

"You didn't seem like it either."

Silence.

I felt a surge of violence. What if David wanted to forget what happened in his bed last night? I turned to look out my window.

"Did you reply to the message?" he asked.

"What?"

I looked at him, but he wouldn't look anywhere but straight ahead.

"Filippo. Did you reply to his message?"

A slap in the face would have had a less devastating effect. I felt completely wounded. Yeah, I know just a second ago I was thinking about Filippo myself, but to hear it coming out of David's mouth…I didn't like it. I didn't like it at all. I might not have had the most mature reaction in the world.

"Ah…" I bit my lip and turned my eyes back to the window. "So that's how we're gonna play…"

"What the…? What do you think I'm playing?"

"I already know last night meant nothing. You don't need to bring Filippo into it."

"Seriously?" He looked at me with a furrowed brow. "Margot, I have zero passive-aggressive tendencies. I promise you if that were the plan, you would already know."

"Hey, aren't you getting pretty cocky?"

"Me?" His eyes widened. "I just wanted to know if you replied to the message from a dude who, up until two days ago, you wanted to get back."

"Exactly," I declared.

He let out a sigh.

"Do you feel bad?" I asked him. "Is that it?"

"I have nothing to feel bad about. I'm single, and as far as I know, so are you."

I opened my mouth, but I had no idea what to say to that because he was right, though I didn't exactly agree with the nuances.

"I don't know this side of you," I muttered finally.

"I guess there are a lot of sides of me you don't know."

I couldn't believe the audacity, and I scoffed to let him know.

"Hey, Margot. What do you think I'm saying to you? Seriously."

"Well, you sound like a typical misogynist running your mouth. Next you'll have your dick in your hand telling me to calm down, to not get all hysterical, that this means nothing."

He raised an eyebrow. It was the first time I had seen that expression. He was very serious.

"A misogynist running his mouth. Uh-huh. It could also be read as genuine interest about how you're planning to do things with your ex-fiancé now that I'm implicated in this mess in one way or another, but fine…why not just assume I'm being hostile?"

"I don't know, David. We were talking about last night, and suddenly you bring up Filippo."

"Well, sorry if it seemed inappropriate to you, but it made sense in my head, okay?"

"Well, explain to me how it made sense at least."

"For fuck's sake…" He sniffed.

"Don't worry about it, David. It's easy enough to include what happened last night in the temporary insanity that made me invite you."

"You're really starting to piss me off." He shot me a side-eye.

"I'm really starting to piss *you* off?"

"Now, on top of pretending that nothing happened, you're saying bringing me on this trip was a fuckup, right?"

"I'm not saying that."

"What are you saying then?"

"How would I know! I don't understand shit!"

David pulled over to the side of the road (which couldn't be called a highway), where the tall yellow grasses seemed to provide a reprieve for the landscape, and slammed on the brakes. It scared the shit out of me.

"What are you doing?"

"I can't argue and drive at the same time. I'm not that good of a driver."

"That's enough, David. It doesn't matter. Everything's very clear."

"What's going on with you?"

"With me?" I yelled.

"With you, of course with you. If you had asked me about Idoia, would you understand if I reacted like this?"

"That's the whole point: I didn't mention Idoia."

"Wanna know what I think is happening? You feel bad, right? About what happened yesterday, for running off with me. When you think about it, you're like what was I thinking?"

"What are you talking about?" I raised my voice.

"I know that compared to Filippo I seem like a little schoolkid, that's pretty clear, but if you feel bad, it's better if you just tell me. What happened to the trust we had?"

"I mean, you're the one who probably feels bad. Because Idoia and I aren't exactly even from the same species. But don't worry, you never have to do it again. You can go back to Madrid and you'll have her eating out of your hand, which is what you wanted, right?"

"Yeah." He nodded. "And don't you worry either, as soon as you set foot in Madrid, your prince will sweep you up in a horse-drawn carriage. So in the end, look, we can both get a grip, right? Everything's going to be fine. You'll get back with Filippo, and I will with Idoia. And it doesn't matter because we just got caught up in the heat of the moment. It was just a momentary attraction." David looked at my mouth, almost panting. "A summer fling that…"

I tugged on his shirt, and he had the wisdom to unbuckle his seat belt before he pounced on me with his mouth already half-open. We moaned in relief again as David reached down between my legs and pulled the lever that threw my seat back, and I turned the little wheel that tilted it back even farther. He climbed on top of me. I have no idea how he managed it in such a small car or how we contorted ourselves, I just know he got himself between my two legs as easily as two puzzle pieces fitting together. In less than two minutes, our hands were under each other's clothes and our mouths were drenched.

"You get on top," he ordered.

We turned over, and in the process, I banged into the hand brake and the gear stick and hit my head on the roof. But I liked it. I liked having him under me, looking up at me with his mouth open, panting, touching everywhere he could. He struggled with my dress until he left the straps slumped around my arms and managed to pull both breasts out of my bikini, while I gave him a hand job with my hand folded into his swimsuit. Just like that. Very prim and proper, huh?

We weren't comfortable, but…we were hot. Very.

"Fuck…" he started to moan. "Fuck…keep going, keep going…"

His cock was throbbing in my hand and his fingers were gliding all over the place, unrhythmically between my legs, over my bikini. I was about to tell him where and how he could do better in that position, when we heard skidding and suddenly, we could hear honking and two kids yelling God knows what out of another car in who knows what language. And I was sitting there with both tits out.

~~~~~

Leaning against the hood of the car, we silently smoked a mental cigarette, with our clothes back in place and our eyes lost in the sea of parched grasses stretching out in front of us. He was the first to speak.

"I'm sorry," he mumbled.

"Me too."

"Seriously, I didn't have bad intentions when I did it. I didn't even think about it. You said that thing about being hot while I was driving, and I thought about Filippo and…" He rubbed his eyebrows. "That guy is like the Iron Man of fiancés."

I went around to stand in front of him and pressed my stomach against his. He sighed.

"I don't want to pretend nothing happened," he confessed to me. "It doesn't work for me."

"Me either." I shook my head.

"But I want to get back together with Idoia."

I felt a pang of anguish that I didn't understand.

"And I want to with Filippo," I declared honestly.

"So?"

I shrugged, and he tucked my hair behind one ear.

"We're jerks." He sighed, looking at the skin on my neck that his fingertips were grazing.

"Maybe we just want to have fun, like you said the other day."

"Or maybe we're hurt as hell and we want to get revenge."

"It's not a good plan," I admitted. "But, honestly, I don't think that's it in my case. I'm not hurt by Filippo. He's the one who should be. I just…I don't know. I'm opening my wings."

He looked at me and bit the inside of his cheek.

"Well, you should feel free to fly," he insisted.

"You too."

"What if…?" he proposed.

"If…what?"

"If we let ourselves get swept up in it." He raised his eyebrows. "Just stop thinking. Like two friends who like each other. Because… it's obvious I like you, but I don't want to lose you."

"I don't want to lose you either. But I don't know if what we want to do is possible."

"I don't feel like worrying about that right now." He made a face.

I shot him a side-eye.

"Me either."

I watched him close his eyes when he leaned in to kiss me. It was a good kiss…the kind that happens when you want to get out of your own head.

"Eh, eh, eh…" I stopped him, drawing back.

"What if we don't worry about this?"

"How would we do that?"

"You want to get back with Filippo and I do with Idoia, right? Fine. These things aren't mutually exclusive…they're not here."

"David…"

"When we met…well, we saw something in each other that hasn't disappeared just because something happened between us."

"You sound exactly like you're offering to take me on a quest to find the philosopher's stone."

"It's not that deep, Margot. Think about it. Let's do it, and then we'll see." He tried to smile and put his arm around my waist. "We'll talk about them when it comes up, and we'll try to find a natural way to let what's happening between us and what's happening between them happen in parallel."

"You're just saying that because you have blue balls." I pressed my hips against his, and he nodded, grinning.

"You don't want to?"

"I don't want to what?"

"Repeat last night, have a roll in the hay, find out what it would be like to fuck each other…"

"Seems complicated." I wanted to play, even though I yearned for it as much as he did.

"What if we put an expiration date on it? Knowing beforehand will make it easier, right?"

"Are we going to be lovers?" I teased.

"Love-friends, for vacation." He smiled. "Until we get back to Madrid."

"Well, when we get back...we'll have to have some time apart to get back to normal, right?"

"Okay. When we get back, we'll focus on getting our partners back, and we'll see each other when that's done. Then we can be friends and nothing more."

"I've never been friends with an ex."

"Well...there are always arguments with exes, but if we already have a breakup date set, it'll be easier, right?"

I nodded. I don't think either of us believed what we were putting out there, but human beings are curious when it comes to finding excuses to justify what they feel like doing in that moment.

"Do you want to?" he asked.

"Just sex?"

"Intimacy."

We smiled. I wanted to say that ever since we had met all we had done was be accomplices in an intimacy I had never felt with anyone, but that thought scared me. Intimacy, he said, and I feared I knew what would happen: the day we got back to Madrid, it would break my heart a little because, in some way I couldn't explain, I had already begun to love David. We'd say goodbye at the airport, and I'd get in a car and cry all the way home, where I'd have to get a grip and do something about my fucking life, which seemed to be going down the drain by the minute. I was there to find myself, but I ended up finding something else. I wasn't sure what it was, but I never wanted to lose it.

Even so, we sealed the deal and...we didn't exactly do it with a handshake. We made out for fifteen minutes until we forced ourselves to stop and give the agreement the go-ahead.

~~~~~

We arrived at Magganari Beach about twenty-five minutes later. That was the surprise destination. The beach was practically empty, and I wasn't surprised because the road to get there was winding and stomach-turning. It was a long beach, with fine sand (very fine) and crystal clear water. The beach was divided into two sections by an invisible line: an untouched side, where a few couples had put down their junk, which was like a hidden paradise, and the part farthest away from us, which had chairs for rent and the Christos Taverna bar, where there still weren't many people but there was movement. David asked if I wanted to rent a chair. I replied that all I really wanted to do was canoodle with him in the sand.

That's basically how we spent the whole day. Lying in the sun, we always found some excuse to come closer to each other and silently nibble on each other's mouths. I loved kissing David. Suddenly, as if I had been bewitched, he seemed like the most desirable man in the world to me, given that he was just some twenty-something guy. A handsome one, with a good body, a clear and sincere smile, and a great cock. Can't argue with that.

But we did much more than kiss, of course. That's the problem. As well as the kissing, touching, rubbing, whispering in each other's ears the things we wanted to do to each other, we talked. And there was so much calm between us when we talked, it was the closest thing to being at home.

"I shared an apartment with a guy and a girl, near Tirso de Molina. The landlord suddenly told us he'd sold the house and we had a month to get out. My roommates looked for another apartment," he told me, stretched out beside me, playing with the sand, "and they found one with three rooms in Lavapiés, but…I told them no."

"When was that?"

"A little over six months ago. I had been with Idoia for nearly four months, and I was so hung up on her that I thought that, if I moved into that apartment, it might close the door on the possibility of encouraging her to let me live with her. Ivan and Domi had just had a baby, and I was already helping them out every once in a while, so Dominique offered me their couch for as long as I needed. And time flew by."

"So it's not really about freedom, is it?" I asked.

"I guess not. It was pretty clingy of me, to tell the truth. I wanted to be free so I could run after Idoia whenever she asked me to. But I've been thinking…you made me think, actually, and I think September is a good month to move." A lopsided grin spread across his face, as he convinced himself.

"What if Idoia offers to let you move in?"

"Ah, well…" He shook his head. "It's clear now we have to wait to do that. Our thing is still…"

"On thin ice," I said in English. He raised an eyebrow. I translated for him.

"Exactly. Such a know-it-all," he teased.

I lay back and sighed.

"Why are you sighing?" he asked.

"Yes, I replied," I confessed. "To Filippo."

"I figured."

"I answered him secretly, I don't know why. I was embarrassed, I guess."

"And what did you say?"

"That this summer apart was the best thing we ever could have done for us, and…I sent him back a song."

"What song?"

"'Sola Con la Luna' by Anni B Sweet."

He sat up and furrowed his brow.

"What?" I asked when I saw his reaction.

"Nothing."

"No. What happened?"

"It's just that…" He flopped back, face up, letting himself fall next to me, and this time I was the one who sat up so I could see his face. "The night we met, when I saw you, I thought of that song. Your eyes were screaming it."

I straddled him and whipped off his sunglasses, and he wrapped his arms around my hips.

"What are they singing now?" I asked him.

"'True' by Spandau Ballet." And a teasing smile spread across his face. "Uh, uh, uh, uhhhhh," he crooned.

I leaned on his chest and jabbed my fingers into his side as I cursed him out. He was laughing out loud and raising his knees to playfully tap my ass and distract me from tickling him when someone's shadow drifted over us and momentarily blocked our sun.

"David?" a feminine voice mumbled.

Both our heads shot up, surprised. We had spent so many days immersed in that liberating feeling of not being tied to anything around us, and we didn't expect to find anyone familiar there. But there she was. Tall, thin, wearing a beautiful bathing suit, trendy, tattooed.

"Ruth?" David asked, stupefied.

I climbed off him, and he sat up, uncomfortable, smoothing his bathing suit, probably so his half chub would be less obvious. They greeted each other with two kisses, but she threw an arm around his back and hugged him. You guys will know how dumb this is, I had so little information they could even be family, but I was seething with jealousy. With Idoia, fine, but…now there was a new one?

"What are you doing here?"

"I was going to ask you the same thing. I saw you from afar, and I thought…it can't be him."

"Well…uh…yeah. It's me."

"What are you doing so far from Madrid?" The girl looked at me with obvious suspicion.

"Vacation." David glanced back, looking for me, and reached out his hand to me. "Ruth, this is Margot…"

Dunn-dunn, dunn-dunn, dunn-dunn. Tense, suspenseful, and terrifying music played in the pause after my name, leaving his friend to deduce my title.

"Margot," David stuttered, clearly uncomfortable. "My girl?"

We'll overlook the semiquestioning tone.

"Ohm." She smiled, also seeming awkward.

"Hi, Ruth. Nice to meet you." I waved when I saw she had no intention of giving me two kisses.

"I guess she didn't tell you," David mumbled, playing discreetly with my fingers.

"No. Not a word," this Ruth girl replied.

"We broke up last month. Well…she broke up with me."

Mystery solved: she was Idoia's friend.

"I had no idea. I called it. You never seemed like a bastard." She smiled a little sadly. "Too bad. I mean…" She looked at me, holding her palms out toward me, like she was apologizing. "It's not too bad because I can see you're doing fine and…you know, you guys…"

"Yeah, right." David scratched his neck.

"But I liked you for Idoia. You calmed her down. Weird…I thought she was crazy about you."

"Well, now you see: she wasn't."

I could see David's Adam's apple bobbing up and down as he let go of my hand and crossed his arms over his chest, visibly unnerved.

"I don't get it," she muttered.

"It's Idoia. Who knows what's going on in her head?"

"Sometimes she loses it." It seemed like this girl genuinely appreciated David or, at least, what he meant for her friend, but…she was pretty tactless. "Maybe she went all in and…she lost the hand."

"More like the whole game." David cleared his throat.

She stared at us for a few seconds and finally tutted.

"Well, I won't keep bothering you. Have a great time. Both of you. And good luck with each other."

"Thanks. Send my love to everyone."

"Everyone except her, I guess."

"We're still in touch," David explained nervously. "It didn't end badly."

"I'm glad. Hope to see you soon."

"Yeah."

As the girl walked away, David seemed to deflate. I stroked his back and perched my chin on his shoulder.

"Are you okay?"

"Yes." He turned back toward me and his eyes roved my face before he wrapped me in his arms and snuggled me against his naked chest. "With you, yes."

39

~~~

PERFECTION IS PERFECT BECAUSE IT'S WITH THE RIGHT PERSON

We didn't go back to the hotel until the sun went down, although I'm not sure a hundred percent of David returned with us. Some part of him was left behind in that conversation with Idoia's friend. And, I'm not gonna lie, it gave me the ick, having her there, almost like she was sitting in the back seat because of the muteness that had descended over David. Tucked into the car, traveling down a smaller road, submerged in the blue light with the windows down, there was too much silence.

"Is this because of that girl?" I asked him.

"What?" He pretended not to understand me, like he was trying to buy a little time to come up with an adequate response.

"You've been weird all afternoon… I'm guessing running into Idoia's friend turned you upside down."

He ran his hand over his chin and then put it back on the steering wheel. It wasn't fair. Silent, so handsome, so worried about another girl…even though that shouldn't matter to me.

"Of course it got me thinking."

"And what are you thinking about?"

His face pinched into a grimace.

"Did we travel back in time and erase the whole conversation we had this morning?" I said. "Seriously, David. We've been over all this."

He shot me a look loaded with meaning, like he wanted to send me a ton of information through brain waves, things like: *Don't go there, Danger of annoyance imminent.*

"Tell me," I insisted.

"I'm kinda scared to talk to you about this. I don't want to make you feel bad."

"Who says it would make me feel bad?" I felt uncomfortable. "We promised we would still talk about Idoia and Filippo when it came up."

"Yeah, but…"

"But, what?"

"Margot, my sweet." He glanced over at me with his lopsided smile. "Human beings are made up of seventy percent water and thirty percent ego. I don't want you to think I'm not enjoying the time I'm spending with you or that I'm thinking about Idoia when I have you in my arms and…"

"But that's just how it is sometimes," I stopped him, feeling pretty bad but believing I was acting…normal. "The clearer things are, the better. You know that."

He sighed, throwing in the towel, but he still didn't say anything for a few seconds. When he saw that I was squirming in my seat, he burst out talking.

"I want to think carefully about the words I'm going to say; I don't want you to misunderstand me." He was such a good guy; that fucking Idoia had been so lucky. "The thing is…I don't know.

I'm super confused. As far as I know, Ruth is one of Idoia's best friends. And she didn't tell her we broke up? I don't get it at all. What's going through her head? Does she not even care a little bit? Or is it that Ruth was right and she was bluffing and I didn't understand? Maybe…maybe she's just batshit and that's all there is to it."

Of course she was crazy. Knowing David, a girl would have to be crazy to dump him and tell him he was a nobody, a pariah, a dude with no talent and no future. I didn't know what to say, so I went off in a different direction.

"Well, now that girl is going to tell her that she found you on a beach in Greece rolling around in the sand with some chick. And she's going to go crazy."

"I know. Dammit…what possessed me to get involved in schemes and setups? I mess up when I'm just trying to follow the steps in a cake recipe. Anyone could see this coming."

I smiled at the tenderness aroused by the mental image of David in an apron, making a mess while he was measuring sugar or flour, but I snapped back immediately and focused again: he was very cute, he kissed like a fiend, but he was trying to get his ex back.

"You have to be prepared, David, because…she's going to react. You know that. Idoia seems like the type who can't stand being jealous. I'm not saying you need to upset yourself trying to predict what's going to happen, but I think you need to contemplate what you want to do when she makes a move."

"The thing is I don't know. One part of me would love to look her in the eye and say: 'Idoia, fuck off.' But the other part of me…I don't know, Margot. The other side of me I think would almost feel grateful."

"Grateful?" I said in a slightly shriller voice than I meant to.

"Yes. Grateful." He hesitated for a moment. "Idoia always made me feel…it's hard to put it into words. But with her I felt, for the first time in a long time, like I had something that was valuable, like I was so lucky… She made me feel like a winner."

"You're already a winner in a lot of ways. First of all, because you're an upstanding guy. You're true to yourself. Do you know how hard that is?"

"Come on, Margot…I sleep on my best friends' couch, I'm underemployed, and I have three jobs that aren't exactly working miracles, plus a collection of T-shirts full of holes."

"You're intelligent, witty, unique, magic… You're so stinking handsome!"

"God." He sighed exasperatedly. "Don't say that. I'm not handsome. At best, I'm cute."

"You're stinking handsome. Say it with me."

"I'm not gonna say it," he griped with a smile.

"You're handsome, and you have an ass that begs to be nibbled." I put my hand on his knee and slid it up to his crotch.

"Hey!" He yelped, giggling. "I'm driving!"

"Let's see…handsome, witty, fun, super cute, hardworking, thoughtful, great ass, and…" I tried to squeeze him a little through his bathing suit. "My hand doesn't close when I give you a hand job."

"That's because you have tiny hands."

There he was again, the boy who masked his fear and insecurity with a joke…but he couldn't fool me. I was an expert in recognizing someone who was too used to hearing his own voice distorting his self-image, trapped under the yoke of being too hard on himself that didn't even align with his own values. I saw it every day in the mirror.

"Repeat after me: *I'm a gift.*"

David looked at me for a second. He only took his eyes off the road for a second, but it was enough for me to feel the sudden peace that flooded him hearing someone tell him all those things. I hardly knew him, but, it was interesting, I already wanted to love him well and beautifully. But I tried to camouflage that flush of tenderness when he answered: "I am, dear Margot, the best thing that's going to happen to you tonight."

But he didn't succeed in throwing me off because he accompanied the answer by taking my hand, moving it away from his crotch, and interlacing his fingers with mine on his thigh. That gesture held much scarier things than the promise of sex.

~~~~~

After forty-five minutes in the car and all day at the beach, I was looking forward to getting in the shower and washing off the stickiness of the sun, the sand, the sea salt, and the feelings of the afternoon.

We had agreed to go out and find somewhere to have dinner and, making the most of the fact that we wouldn't have to take the moped (or the car in this case) to get back to the hotel, drink a bottle of wine. Or a cocktail. Or both. Go nuts.

I left David on the terrace chewing on his thoughts like they were tobacco and got in the shower, a little nervous about what he had chosen from my bag. I suspected it might just be a pair of panties. Filippo would never have been able to pack for me, no matter how short a trip; not because he didn't know how but because I would have been too worried about not taking the right thing. I couldn't imagine David being more organized...especially at five thirty in the morning. So I was worried about getting by with what he had chosen.

I was rinsing off my hair when David came into the bathroom.

"Did you say something?" he asked.

"What?"

"Did you call me?"

Good thing he couldn't see the face I was making.

"I didn't call you," I clarified.

"Oh, sorry. Hey, this curtain is pretty opaque, right?"

"Did you really think I called you or was that just an excuse? By the way, I'm showering in flip-flops. I suggest you do the same."

He fell silent, but I didn't hear the door close again.

"Are you still there?"

"Yes."

"Can you leave?"

There was no answer, just the sound of stealthy movements muffled by the shower.

"David!"

"What's up."

"You're not pissing, are you?"

"No, babe."

"Then what are you doing standing out there silently?"

"Nothing."

"Get out of here! You're such a creep!" I complained in English. No sound.

"Seriously, you're driving me nuts. If I slip in the shower and kill myself, it will be on your conscience until your dying day. I'll probably even come back as a ghost wrapped in this shower curtain and drag you back to the underworld with me."

The curtain opened, and he stuck his head in.

"David!" I yelped, covering myself up...well, the important bits anyway.

"What?" He smiled.

"Wait...are you naked?"

"Just like my mother brought me into the world, but with more hair. Can we both fit in there?"

"No," I snapped.

"I think we can."

"Well, I'm telling you we can't."

He squinted, like he was weighing his possibilities...or calculating the cubic meters of the shower.

"Don't even think about it." I smiled at him.

And because of the smile, the message must not have come through very clearly because...with a little hop he was suddenly in the shower with me. I turned around immediately. It made more sense to me for him to see my ass than anything else, although... out of that "anything else," he was already familiar with a few things.

"Ah! It's chilly. Turn up the heat, you little minx, the cold water is gonna make my peanut disappear."

"Well, then let it disappear! Get out of here!"

I felt his cock, happy but not euphoric, pressing strategically against my butt cheeks and the vibration of his laughter.

"If you're thinking about shower sex, think again. If I touch any of these tiles with my bare skin, I'll have to disinfect myself with bleach."

"You think I want our first time to be in the shower? For God's sake, so cheesy...that's a teenager's wank bank fantasy."

"So that's what you want, a hand job in the shower."

"I mean...if you insist."

I couldn't help laughing.

"You better not make the clichéd joke about me dropping the soap," I insisted.

"Course not, darling. After the foreplay we've had, we can't do it fast and badly. We're gonna need a big bed, and while you're at it, I'm gonna need to spend a good while with you sitting on my face."

"Could you be more vulgar?"

"I could, but I'm not going to exert myself. Can I help you lather up?"

"I'm already lathered."

"What's left? I want to help you."

I looked over my shoulder. God. How could anyone look that good wet? I didn't think there was anything sexier, more sensual, than David with his wet hair pushed to one side, smiling, pretending to be a good boy, but with that wicked glint in his eye.

"Conditioner." I played along.

"I love your ass," he groaned, almost grimacing. "Now I want to bite it too."

"Conditioner. Focus."

He sighed sadly and grabbed the mini bottle I was pointing to.

"I didn't get any pats on the head for remembering to bring all your toiletries," he murmured. "You use more stuff in the shower than all the people who live in my house combined."

"I use the right stuff," I complained. "I'm sure you use the same stuff for everything."

"One bar of soap, I'm not even fucking with you," he mocked himself. "All I worry about is not drying my face with the same part of the towel I dried my ass with yesterday."

"For the love of God," I stammered, concerned.

"Whoa, so bougie. Let's see…where does this stuff go?"

"On my hair, from the midpoint to the tips."

"In layman's terms, please?"

"The tips, David, the bottom part."

I glanced back and saw him laughing malevolently.

"I mean of my head. Otherwise you're going to give my nether regions a Japanese straightener treatment."

"Don't tempt me. Let's see…like this?"

He lifted a lock of hair very carefully and rubbed the product into the tip.

"Yes. Very good." And I was grateful to have my back turned on him so he couldn't see how much I was enjoying this. "But you don't have to be so meticulous."

"I'm a very diligent boy, sad eyes."

He painstakingly divided my shoulder-length hair into segments and rubbed the conditioner into them carefully.

"Are you going to be one of those dads who French braids his daughter's hair?"

"I'm gonna be the kind who tries at least."

And I was smiling, but I was paralyzed by the pang of sadness that filled me when I imagined him carefully combing the hair of a sweet blond girl about six years old with her papa's laugh and her mother Idoia's ruthless eyes. I was about to ask him if he wanted children when he started speaking:

"I…actually wanted to talk to you," he said.

"You didn't come in here to condition my hair?" I tried to lighten the mood.

"No. I wanted to thank you."

"Thank me? What are you thanking me for now?"

"The thing in the car."

"I just touched you for a second…"

"I invented the strategy of throwing off your opponent by

bullshitting. You know exactly what I'm talking about. Thank you for helping me with the shitty self-esteem this breakup left me with."

"According to your own words, you should never base your value of yourself on other people's opinions."

"And I was right because I'm pretty fucking wise, but something's better than nothing, and you know that better than anyone. So thank you. Especially for the part about your hand not fitting around my cock. That was key for lifting my spirits."

I turned, and he put his arms around my waist, pressing against him. He tilted my head back and carefully rinsed my hair, having fun running his fingers through the ends. It was, without a doubt, the most romantic thing anyone had ever done in my life, but it wasn't until a couple of months later that I could appreciate all the tenderness, intimacy, and complicity held in the act.

"You're so handsome."

"Shh, hush…it's my turn now."

"No," I whimpered.

"You're incredible, Margot."

"Shut up!" I writhed, trying unsuccessfully to wriggle away.

"I don't know who made you believe you have to constantly strive to be more or be something different, but you need to know that you don't need anything or anyone to complete or empower you. You complain that you're mediocre and dull, and you unconsciously seek to blend into the crowd until you disappear because you know, deep down in your being, that as soon as someone really sees you, they won't be able to see anything else."

"Come on…" I tried to wave off the gravity of what he was saying.

"No. Listen to me. You're funny, intelligent, pretty, generous, free of the prejudices that anyone else in your situation would have.

You're a flash of light so powerful that when you're around, nothing else in the world exists."

"David, seriously…" I begged him much more urgently.

"Nothing, Margot. Nothing in the world matters more. That's the reality, as much as we try to avoid it. When you're here, all I want is to hear you telling me things, to learn every shade of your voice while you tell me them, to look at me like only you do. I've never met anyone who holds so much truth. But the thing is…the thing is, when you sleep on your stomach, I would do anything to live in the curve between your back and your ass."

I pressed my cheek against his chest, my eyes darting away from his that were shining as he spoke, but he ducked a little so he could make eye contact again. He smiled. What a smile…

"I would spend my whole life making out with you when you moan. Seriously…your mouth is like a strawberry. And if I could choose how I die, I'd choose to suffocate in your tiny tits."

We both cracked up.

"I want to be inside you," he murmured as his smile shifted into something more intimate and conspiratorial. "And it will be perfect."

I wanted to tell him that nothing is perfect, but deep down, I knew he was right. We would do it. He would penetrate me, he would pause between my thighs, and it would be perfect, like the fucking Disney magic we all hope to see appear when we first get together with someone. And I was scared because it would be perfect for so little time that nothing, not us or time, could ever ruin it.

"I wanna spend a whole night between your legs, mounting all the furniture in the room," he added. "I want to destroy everything while you beg for more. And to make the world spin in whatever direction you want."

For a few seconds, I couldn't even make a sound. The only thing I could do was look at him. Look at him pretty hungrily, I confess.

"What?" His lopsided smile was back.

I bit my lip so I wouldn't say what I really felt.

"I don't think anyone has ever said anything like that to me."

"Yeah…well, I'm pretty deep." He raised his eyebrows. "Wanna blow me?"

I punched him on the arm, and before he could grab me, I hopped out and wrapped myself in a towel.

"Hey!"

"Come on, I'm hungry." I wrapped another, smaller towel around my head. I needed to catch my breath away from him. Words were filling the bathroom, ricocheting off the damp tiles, and it was too much for me. "I mean…did you need to invade my shower? Couldn't we have talked after?"

"I wanted to see you naked at least once before I make love to you."

"Make love to me? Don't you mean fuck me?"

"Sometimes the verb *fuck* makes me uncomfortable because it doesn't sound reciprocal. I don't like to imagine 'fucking you.' It has bad vibes. I want it to be mutual. I don't know if that makes sense. Now, in the context of 'us fucking,' I'll say fucking is fine, but when it comes to making love, I'm the best."

David was every good thing in this world.

When I emerged, I found my toiletry bag and my clothes laid out on the bed: some panties (the cutest ones—he obviously had an eye for this), a low-cut dress printed with little flowers that I had bought with him, and black sandals. I leaned against the table and sighed. I sighed with something in my chest that was very bad luck if we took a minute to assess it through the lens of the promises we had made to each other.

~~~~~

I remember that night as flashes of light, of life. That night has ended up becoming one of those images that nourish the memory, that are what nostalgia is made of, and that make us feel that one day, far away, we can live in that memory on top of existing.

I remember the surprise. The feeling of my stomach flipping and the excitement when I finished drying my hair and found him tucking a white shirt into his jeans. He was cursing, pouting, like a child whose plans have not gone exactly as he expected.

"Do I tuck this in or leave it out?" he asked me, frustrated.

I took the chance to look him up and down: the Converse, the ankle-cropped jeans, the worn belt, the white shirt that fit him like a glove. He looked incredible.

"I seem to remember you refusing to buy this."

"Well…" He looked up at me and raised an eyebrow with a smug look. "I might have gone back for it. In or out?"

"In."

He managed to tuck it in, and I covered my mouth so I wouldn't laugh.

"What? I look awful, don't I? Does it look like I'm going to celebrate my dad buying me a golf course?"

I went over to him.

"You look so handsome I think I'm gonna scream."

"That sounds good."

"Good thing it's nighttime because if you added your sunglasses, you'd have to make love to me on top of the reception desk."

"I gotta warn you, I don't have any hang-ups, so as soon as I get the go-ahead, I just go wild." He raised his eyebrows and, in a flash, grabbed his sunglasses from where he had left them on the table and shoved them on.

I had no option but to kiss him.

I remember that he hid to scare me, and on top of the little jump I usually gave when that happened, I let out a scream that made us both crack up. And there were few things more beautiful than his eyes when he was laughing hard.

I remember the way the street smelled, a mix of jasmine, the sea, the food from the restaurants all around, David's cologne and his skin.

I remember walking hand in hand and feeling like I had never, ever, in my entire life, felt so alive.

"Why is your hand so sweaty?" he teased.

"I feel like I'm fifteen again."

I remember the kissing. The kisses were like a first kiss. Like the last ones before you went to sleep. Like the ones you use to say goodbye to someone you never want to leave.

The streets were riddled with gangs of boys between eighteen and twenty-five who were drinking straight from bottles clearly freshly bought from the supermarket. The ground looked like it was dappled with lights and night, which we tread on as we talked and talked about anything. About the flowers growing on the balconies of the houses, about Amparito and Asuncion, about how my sisters were doing with their paranoia and how I had ignored another message from Patricia…everything was easy with David. Even being his girlfriend just for a few days.

We had dinner in a restaurant with views of the sea and a fountain on the terrace. First we had a few glasses of very sweet Greek wine, and between toast after toast ("Kiss me every time we toast," he said. "You just kiss me because when you're not kissing me, I can't feel my mouth,"), we cracked up imagining our clumsiness would land us in the fountain. When we finished the wine, we were left with no choice but to order another bottle of the same wine because, apparently, it had a side effect of making you have nice dreams.

I don't even know what we ate, but I know everything tasted delicious, and David let me try his dinner and I let him try mine, and we finished the wine quickly, and we laughed. Oh, how we laughed. Even tales about boarding school seemed funny with him.

I remember thinking that maybe with David by my side, I'd be able to turn struggles into strengths.

When we finished dinner, we sat on the part of the terrace closest to the railing, where the sea stretched out in front of us, and ordered cocktails.

"Wine and a cocktail…I'm going to fall into bed tonight and sleep like a baby," David warned me.

But no. He didn't sleep like a baby. Quite the contrary, it seemed to awaken a hungry man in him. When I sat on his lap and tasted the alcohol on his tongue, I got drunk…drunk with desires, promises, the life we were playing at that seemed like ours. When his hand started running up and down my thighs through the slit of the dress, the waiter brought over our bill and a recommendation that doubled as an invitation to leave:

"Maybe you'd like to continue your night somewhere else?"

He told us about a club where we could grab a few drinks and have fun, and we piled out of there laughing, convinced he had sent us to a swingers' club or something. When we got to the address he had told us, after five pit stops to make out in dark corners, lick each other's necks, and fondle each other over our clothes, we discovered it was a disco. Well, not a disco, a huge club. David glanced at me when he saw the deal: hundreds of young tourists (very young) bopping to the rhythm of electronic music, turning the air into a current, the whole place shrouded in smoke and bright lights. I guess it was the last place he thought I would feel comfortable.

"Should we get another drink?" I asked, pulling him toward the door.

And it's strange, I really wanted to be alone with David, but I also wanted the night to last forever. I felt…free.

Getting the drink was easy thanks to David, who slipped through groups of people too drunk to realize that they were being passed with a smile and catlike movements. Using the same method, getting to the middle of the dance floor was easy too.

I remember the feeling. Of dancing, the kind that makes everything else drift away. In a crowd of people dancing like the world would explode tomorrow, it was easy to feel eternal.

We drank. We embraced. We kissed like everyone else, with tongue, groans, and, deep down, an almost adolescent desire. And between making out and making out, David danced uninhibitedly; I later learned that he only danced like this when he was drunk. He had the gift of rhythm installed somewhere between his waist and his chest and moved smoothly because he didn't need much to let himself be carried away by the mercy of music. And I clung to him and followed his lead until the rhythm heated our tongues.

The crowd of people filling the dance floor moved as one, like a huge insect with thousands of limbs, and we felt like its heart. I recognized a Drake song featuring Rihanna, "Too Good," and I closed my eyes and melded with its tribal rhythm, forgetting that people were watching, what people thought, that I had to prove that I deserved what I had and all those things instilled in me as a child. When I opened them, David was smiling at me, his gaze hazy and sex on his lips.

"What?"

"If you keep…"

"If I keep what?" I asked, expecting a spicy answer.

"Singing, dancing…I'll fall in love." He pulled me closer to him. "I swear."

"Well, that's messy."

"That is messy."

I remember the heat clinging to us, both dripping wet, which just showed how good we felt in our own skin.

David whispered thick, dirty words into my ear, sometimes poured into my ear between gasps and sometimes accompanied by laughter and a hand sneaking up under my dress. The good thing about dancing right in the middle of a bonfire is that nobody cares about anything but their own flame.

I remember his voice, my back on his chest, his hand gliding up my inner thigh until it slipped between my legs over my underwear, hovering over my clit until it sent a shiver down my spine.

"I'm going to need a lot of time…" he was saying to me. "Just give me time because I want to spend an hour licking every inch of your skin…" His fingers were exploring every corner of my flesh. "Until you come and come and come…"

"I won't last an hour."

"Well, half an hour then. I need half an hour with my mouth on your cunt. If you can't last, I'll hold on for you."

And that boy with the dirty mouth, who loved eighties music, who served drinks in a rowdy dive club and knew about flowers… that boy who dreamed of finding something that would give meaning to his life and was convinced that it didn't have meaning already, forgot everything and closed his eyes when I kissed him.

Another drink. More music, please…don't stop twirling.

"I love this song!" he yelled, after downing the drink and getting rid of the glass with a kid who was walking around with a tray. "Do you have Shazam? Margot, Shazam it. This song is so fucking good!"

I took my phone out of my bag, and while I was opening the app, his arms wrapped around my hips and lifted me up. Suddenly I was flying over all the heads, I was flying, I was flying…and when he held me up there, I felt…ethereal. The breeze up there cooled my skin, and the music swayed more forcefully. I raised my arms, and for a few seconds, there was nothing. Not the board or my sister Patricia or my mother or frustration or sorrow or world hunger. Up there, in David's arms, I surfed a wave of puberty that I hadn't experienced when I was supposed to, feeling fragile and invincible all at once, on the edge of death and immortal. Flesh and blood…at last.

When he put me down, his eyes were smiling. For me.

"Half an hour," he whispered, looking at my mouth.

"Dreamboat."

"You're right about that: I would die for you and spend the rest of eternity haunting your dreams."

The song was "Ride It" by DJ Regard, by the way. And I felt just like the lyrics: riding everything, losing control…

If I hadn't drunk so much, I think I would have realized that night that I was already feeling something for him that went way beyond what we could justify. Maybe I had already fallen in love with him and hadn't even needed one night of true passion. So later there's no debate when I say that fucking is overrated.

Well...it's not like I would try that hard to convince you.

Dawn broke at 6:10, and we watched the sunrise sitting on a beach near the hotel, in happy silence, after joking all the way back from the club that someone must have laced our drinks with drugs to make us stay up all night. Maybe we were right. Maybe not. It was true. We were high as hell, intoxicated, deranged...but we were the only ones to blame: we were as high as you can feel when you're falling in love and you haven't asked yourselves the questions that scare you yet.

David sat hugging his legs, the orange of the horizon reflected in his eyes, and whispered his second declaration of love without looking at me:

"Margot, never stop."

But the last thing he said before we passed out fully clothed, on top of the bed, was: "Half an hour. Give me half an hour and I swear I'll make you go crazy."

40

<del>~~~~~</del>

NEVER STOP

DAVID

I would've liked to wake up with Margot on top of me, straddling me, dressed only in the white nightgown I packed from her stuff. I imagined her with the fabric riding up around her waist and one strap drooping off her shoulder while her hips sailed nonexistent waves on top of me. And then, because I'm weak, I would kiss her nipples; I would whisper the kinds of loving words that don't hurt and use caresses to ask permission to enter her and live forever inside her in the form of a moan. And the light reflected in the sea, the breeze, and freedom would applaud us as we made love.

Sounds good, huh? Well, nothing could've been further from the truth because I was startled awake by a chair crashing to the floor that almost gave me a heart attack. And when I sat up, I found Margot disheveled and with makeup running down her face, snatching things off the floor.

"What the…?" I managed to say.

"The ferry! We're gonna miss the ferry back!"

Running with a hangover is not cool. Running with a hangover when it's 110 degrees in the shade is even less cool. Running with a hangover, in 110-degree heat, to catch a boat…could only be a sign from destiny to wake me up and show me that something was wrong. A sign I missed, by the way.

The Dramamine took so long to take effect that I felt sick the whole way. Margot was no better off. She didn't even wash her face before we ran out. We looked like summery, desolate versions of the Joker and didn't speak a word to each other until we arrived in Santorini.

I was about to ask her to drive the bike back to the hotel, but I took pity when, after I unlocked the massive bike lock, I turned around and looked at her. I couldn't help but smile.

"What are you laughing at?"

"You look terrible," I teased.

"You should talk…"

"Me? The grunge look works on me, aren't you the one who said that? But you…you look like a junkie who survived an orgy with a bunch of chainsaws."

"Your hair is plastered to your head," she informed me, making it crystal clear I was grossing her out too.

I touched it. Fuck. I always got so grimy when I went out to party, especially in dives where you could smoke. She was right.

"But we're going to get in the shower now and you're going to wash it for me, so it doesn't matter."

She rolled her eyes, I climbed on the bike and kicked the kickstand, and she clambered on.

"Half an hour," I whispered before she put on her helmet.

I earned a punch on the arm. Some things are probably better not to say out loud when you're not wasted.

We stopped at a bakery on the road back to the hotel, and along with two coffees the size of our heads, we bought everything... anything soaked in cheese and as greasy as possible. Then we went into our villa and hung the "Do not disturb" sign, taking shelter in a room we darkened by lowering the blinds. We turned the room into an artificial and refrigerated womb where we could hide out with the expectation (and hope) that we'd become human again.

The truth is, after the previous night and being startled awake so abruptly, my body couldn't take any more partying, and I wasn't thinking about sex at that point, although I was still convinced I needed thirty minutes with my tongue buried between Margot's lips...and I don't mean the ones covering her teeth. What I'm trying to say is that, at least consciously, when I got into the shower with Margot, I didn't have erotic intentions. I wanted her to wash my hair.

"David!" she screamed, beside herself, like she had repeated something hundreds of times and I had ignored her again.

"Don't scream, you loon, my head's going to explode!"

"Out of my goddamn shower, for fuck's sake!"

"Why?" And I swear I asked her that because I really didn't understand the reason I couldn't take a shower with her. For fuck's sake, I wanted her to wash my hair.

"Because I want to shower in peace!"

"Okay, babe. So shower then."

I turned around and focused on soaping my body fastidiously.

"If you're doing this to seduce me, I have to tell you it's not working. I swear watching you wash yourself reminds me of a documentary I saw about monks in India. They wash themselves just like that. Exactly the same."

I glanced over my shoulder. Her hair was plastered to her head, and her makeup was even more streaked down her face, not even a hint of a smile.

"Whatever you say, but I want to be nice and clean in case you want to suck on my balls for a bit."

"When you're hungover, you're the gnarliest dude I've ever met in my life, you know that?"

"Will you wash my hair?" I asked.

"Yeah right, because you've been so nice, you've earned it."

"I'm charming, and you know it. Come on…wash my hair, please…"

"What do I get out of it?"

"You're a fucking capitalist," I teased. "Come on. I'll wash yours after."

"But the whole deal like in a salon. With a head massage."

"Fine."

Margot's fingers on my scalp, spreading the shampoo and rubbing gently, all the way to my temples…was the most relaxing thing I had ever felt in my life. I had never gotten a massage, and I promise the barber in my neighborhood didn't massage my head when he cut my hair. Anyway, I decided I wasn't made for so much pampering when I noticed my cock was starting to get hard. I looked at it sideways. Poor thing…it was so optimistic.

"Rinse now," I asked Margot.

"Whatever you say, but I want you to rub me more than that."

I bit my tongue so I wouldn't say something dirty.

I guess she noticed the state of my cock when I started washing her hair because it kept knocking against her butt. It was driving me up the wall. But she said nothing, and I kept adding shampoo and sliding my hands over her head and neck. After a while of her moaning with pleasure and saying, "There, right there," which almost made me lose it, she rinsed off under the tap and worked in the conditioner herself. I took the opportunity to fill my hand with soap suds again with the worst of intentions.

I pulled her against my body, her back turned, and shoved my hands unceremoniously between her thighs. She must have been thinking something along the same lines because she received my attentions with a moan and apparently without any surprise.

"Should I rub like this or harder?" I asked her slyly.

"Rub until we fill the bathroom with foam."

I slid my middle finger between her pussy lips and rubbed in circles while she grabbed my forearms hard, like she was scared I would stop and leave her hanging.

"Can I spend the next hour keeping my promises?"

"No," she moaned in my arms. "I'm still spotting a little."

"What does that mean, you're 'spotting'?" I asked, intrigued.

"That I'm still bleeding a little. It should be okay by tomorrow."

"So what do I do now? I want to pleasure you," I complained.

She directed my hand a little farther down and made me press my finger into her.

"This isn't good enough for me," I announced.

"It is for me. Keep going…"

Her hand found a way between us and stroked my cock, which responded harder than I ever remember it doing before. I moaned with my mouth close to her neck because I wanted her to hear the pleasure I felt when she touched me, and with the hand that wasn't between her legs, I clasped her left breast. Margot was moaning too, telling me what movements she liked best, and when I was about to offer to get out of the shower to lie on the bed and get comfortable, she surprised me by asking something I wasn't expecting.

"Do you think I'm being unfaithful?"

"What?"

She squeezed my cock between her fingers, and I let out a moan.

"For the love of God, don't ask me that right now."

"Do you think so or not?"

"No…" I moaned again, let go of her boob, and wrapped my hand around hers touching my cock, to stroke it faster. "He ran off for the whole summer, right? Well, this is your summer, Margot." A groan slipped out of me. "Don't stop now… Keep going."

She let go of me. *Fuckingstupidregrets*, I muttered without opening my lips, in a kind of roar contained in my throat. *But that dude can't even love you right, Margot, because you don't have to tell me much about your relationship for me to know that he didn't even try to get to know the part of you that's hidden way down below your outward appearance. Fuck my life, Margot. And you feel bad? He should feel bad for not being able to see that the love of his life was terrified on the day of her own wedding.*

I didn't say anything. Margot looked into my eyes.

"Really?"

"Really." I nodded.

"You're not just saying that because you want me to finish what I started?"

"I want this hand job, and I want to come on your tits, Margot, but more importantly, I want you to understand he's free and you are too. And I don't care if he hasn't been with anyone because, in the end, he's not with you, right?"

She smiled. "Fine. Then a blow job can't be any worse than a hand job, right?"

I blinked. I couldn't believe it. Even my cock smiled. Memorizing

Margot was impossible. How many different women lived inside her?

But she got out. She got out of the fucking shower before I even got to feel her mouth around me. I watched her, stunned, as she wrapped herself in a towel and then pulled me over and wrapped another one around my waist.

"Don't worry," she whispered.

When I sat on the edge of the bed, the towel fell open, leaving in sight, very clearly, the fact that I hadn't forgotten her promise.

"You know you have a beautiful cock?" she said, tossing a pillow onto the floor and kneeling on it, in front of me.

"I never stopped to think about it. Do you think it would win a beauty contest?"

"Let's see…" She grabbed it and…magic: she made it disappear.

I yelled. I don't know what I said, probably something rude because she was looking at me with very wide eyes. I think I made reference to where I wanted to put what was filling her mouth.

I laced my fingers through her hair and pushed her down a little onto me, following the rhythm she was making by pulling my cock in and out of her lips.

I stroked her forehead with my thumb, and she looked at me. I nodded, as if that was enough to tell her everything I was thinking and didn't even understand myself: to keep going, that I wanted to come in her throat, that I didn't want the trip to ever end, that I didn't know if I'd ever be able to leave her, that Idoia had no idea how to give blow jobs, if a blow job was what she was doing, which was more like a supernova of pleasure. I couldn't stop staring at her. It was the best blow job of my life, but also…she was so pretty…

She helped herself with her right hand, and I laughed. Laughter! I threw out a couple of pitiful laughs because it was unfair that I liked her so much, and she smiled. With her mouth full, with her eyes, swallowing my fucking soul.

I didn't have time to warn her. I opened my mouth to say something, I swear, but the words stuck until they were nothing more than a stupid gurgle, like a teenager, as I emptied myself completely (of semen, worries, and fears) inside her mouth. I didn't last ten minutes, but Margot didn't seem surprised; she just stopped, wiped the corner of her mouth, and then licked me again before kissing the fleshy head of my cock and standing up.

She straddled me, took off her towel, and said to me with a serious, hot, unsettled, look on her face… "Now me."

I fingered her with all the desire bursting from my body. All of it. The desire I had for her and all the desire I had ever felt in my life for any other girl. All of them. The entire universe folded in until it only fit Margot, like a cruel goddess who fed on whatever I gave her. And she came in spasms over me, but I knew that pleasuring her like that no longer satisfied me. It wasn't enough anymore.

~~~~~

We forgot to eat. We didn't even try the coffee. I couldn't help it. As soon as I could, after I recovered from coming, I wanted to make love to her. And she wanted to make love to me.

I rummaged in my bag, which I had tossed onto the dresser in her room, and I found the box of condoms I bought in the supermarket a few days before; I tore one open with my teeth. Badly done, I know, but I needed my eyes to ask her if she needed it as much as I did.

She was writhing naked on the bed, squeezing her thighs, trying to relieve, I imagine, that throbbing need.

We both fumbled to get the condom on me while we kissed with our eyes closed, and then she lay back on the bed with her legs spread. I got on top of her and directed my cock inside her; she was so wet I glided in almost without thrusting. We looked at each other with open mouths, surprised by the sensation, and I pulled out to push back in; her knee fell to one side, next to her ass, and she let out a shriek.

"Did I hurt you?"

"I'm a virgin," she said.

I swear I was paralyzed; I tried to swallow, but I couldn't. A smile spread across her face and then evolved into a cackle.

"You're an idiot!" I complained.

She dug her fingers into my ass, pushing me deeper, and smiled slyly.

"You should've seen your face. How could I be a virgin?"

"You're an idiot, you know that?" I leaned in to kiss her.

"Don't stop, stupid. Don't stop."

And I didn't. I didn't stop.

And now, just between us, listen up because I'm going to say something I probably shouldn't. Something very ugly, because feelings, emotions, and women…should never be compared to each other. But…I had gotten used to fucking Idoia, and it was always like being in one of those porn movies that are filmed like your eyes are the camera. Everything. The moans, the positions, the requests, even the aesthetics…it all looked like well-edited and highly polished porn. That only meant one thing: that everything was perfect, pristine, without ifs, ands, or buts, and that…it never felt real. I was always telling myself I wasn't up to the performance, so when Idoia and I fucked, it felt like a competition. I had to be the one who pushed it furthest, the one who pushed the hardest, the one who could get it in the fastest without coming, the one who made it, and the one who gave the best ass slaps, when to me…actually those slaps lowered my spirits quite a bit. All this coupled with the fact that I've never been a huge fan of the porn approach… It made me frustrated because I didn't enjoy it as much as I knew I could, and I kept telling myself it was my fault.

Well…doing it with Margot made me forget I had to be "the most" because I wasn't worried that she would vanish before I had my fill. Doing it with Margot showed me that I had never even thought about myself with Idoia. I just wanted to make her happy. Her. And with Margot it was just naturally for both of us. Both.

I made love to her, but I left space between us for her to make love to me too. And so much intimacy was breathed in the sounds of our bodies, in the gasps, in the smells of sex, in the smiles we shared. If someone ever tells me again that laughter is the enemy of passion, I'll tell them they should've been there watching Margot laugh.

Margot, full of light. Margot, still moving under my body, begging for the next thrust. Margot, with her horny face. Margot, who whispered that she was coming while she rubbed herself and I thrust in, out, in, out. Margot, riding on top of me, leaning on my left knee with one arm thrown back behind her. Margot swallowing fears and turning them into a sigh of pleasure.

Margot.

And there, in plain sight, the connection, the thing that united us: her body open to me, allowing me to give her pleasure. I was grateful for so much truth. For a porn director, that truth would be nothing more than imperfections, sounds, hair, wetness (not the good kind), interruptions, laughter, and words that were so much better than the absurd dialogue in porn. But it was perfect. It was real sex. Even the "take your hand out of there, that hurts" or the pause to take a sip of water from the bottle on the bedside table because, let me say something, a small truth: What good is perfect if it can never really make it out into the real world?

I hated myself when she started to let out her delirious moan of pleasure and I moaned hoarsely, almost growling. Why? Well, because I was losing it too, because I was exploding, because I never wanted it to end.

I don't think denying it made sense anymore because you can't hide what's in plain sight: I had already split my soul so it could grow between the two halves. Falling in love was the only logical consequence.

She came twice, and both times she had to help finish herself with her hand, but I didn't care at all, and it didn't make me feel any less of a man; her pleasure was hers. When I came, lying between her thighs this time, I needed more help…the help of seeking refuge and intimacy to confront and swallow so many things. I sank down between her breasts, biting back my urge to cry, and pushed it down my throat alongside a certainty that appeared out of nowhere, and I didn't share with Margot that what we had just done would be more important in my life than I wanted to believe.

I came. I filled the condom, and when I finished, I stayed there, inside her, panting, accepting. Not understanding a single thing.

When I could, I looked at her. Two eyes with a woeful gleam were waiting for me. Maybe I was comforted by the thought that she felt more overwhelmed than I was, but it gave me a moral kick that was hard to forget.

"Fuckkkkk…you dirty dog! That was incredible!"

Ah, shit. Ah, shit, shit, shit. She laughed. She cracked up, writhing…adding trust to our relationship, subtracting that awkwardness that comes the first time two bodies interact, multiplying what I felt when I came, and dividing until the barriers were left at zero.

"Incredible?" I asked. "You're incredible."

We melted into a kiss, and I prayed. Prayed that Margot would never stop.

By the way, that afternoon, after a nap, I woke up with Margot on top of me, straddling me, dressed only in the white nightgown I had packed from her stuff. She had the fabric riding up around her waist and one strap drooping off her shoulder while her voluptuous hips sailed nonexistent waves on top of me. And then, because I'm weak, I kissed her nipples; I whispered the kinds of loving that don't hurt and used caresses to ask permission to enter her and live forever inside her in the form of a moan.

And the light flickering on the pool, the damn air-conditioning, and freedom applauded us as we made love.

41

THE RULES

MARGOT

David complained when I didn't want to shower with him, but I needed a second. I wanted to call Candela and confess: "Bless me, Candela, for I have sinned...three times in the last night. Five times in my thoughts, but I understand the kid needs to rest."

I grabbed my phone from my bag that I had tossed aside when we got into the room the day before, and I was shocked to find it was turned off. I mean, I get that device's batteries aren't infinite, duh, but in the last four years, I had never had my phone turned off for more than an hour.

I found the charger, plugged my phone in, and called room service on the landline.

"Sorry, I know we missed breakfast, but would it be possible to bring something up to our room? Maybe some fruit or bread or something sweet...and coffee. A vat of coffee."

Then I went over to the bathroom door, which David's singing voice was floating through.

"David…"

"What?"

I went in and stuck my head around the curtain. He looked spectacular in there, drenched and half-covered in foam. My resolve almost faltered.

"Did you change your mind?"

"No." I smiled. "I ordered breakfast. I'm as hungry as a dog. Can you listen for the door in case room service shows up? I have to make a work call."

"Okay. Leave the door open. I'll just rinse off and jump out."

My phone vibrated as it turned on, and after I put my PIN in, it vibrated a bunch more. I swallowed when I saw some of the notifications and crashed back down to earth.

My mother. A missed call and a voicemail. "A little lady doesn't just have to be one, she also has to appear like one. Remember that and be discreet on this damn vacation of yours. All it takes is one person taking a photo of you in a bikini. Although, of course, with your obsession with not doing interviews or photo shoots and all those things someone in your position should be fulfilling, it would be difficult for anyone to recognize you, but…just in case. Always wear a one-piece bathing suit. I dreamed that you were in one of those trashy magazines that aren't ¡Hola! and…"

I hung up on my voicemail. What a horrible woman.

Candela. Seven missed calls. A WhatsApp:

I understand you're caught up in your little fling, but don't turn off your phone, for fuck's sake, it freaks me out. I'm dying to talk to you. I swear it's not about the detective who's older than the Ten Commandment tablets. I just want to know how you're doing.

I smiled. Candela could be very clumsy with her emotions, but she was my sister.

Patricia. A WhatsApp:

Enough already. Seriously. Can you connect with the real world and call me? It's going fucking terribly with the detective, okay?

If I weren't so relaxed and well fucked, I would have thought my sister was one of the most narcissistic people on the face of the earth.

Filippo. Two missed calls. Two WhatsApps:

Hi, Margot. I called you because I wanted to hear your voice. Well...and probably because I've had a few too many drinks, and you know how that goes. They say when you get drunk you always call your ex. Call me when you read this.

Excuse me? Your ex?

You haven't returned my call and your phone is still off.
I'm worried about you.
Please, call me.

I scoffed and looked over my shoulder when I heard David whistling through the villa. I texted with nimble fingers.

Hi, Filippo. Sorry...I went on one of those multiday excursions and I left my charger at the hotel. But...you know what? I think it's better if we keep our distance for a few more weeks. We'll both be a lot more clear about things when we do see each other again.

He logged on immediately.

FILIPPO

Thank goodness, Margot. I was so worried about you I was actually mulling over the possibility of calling your mother to see if she had heard anything from you.
Are you okay?
I...have also been thinking a lot about what happened. I'll be back in Madrid in two weeks.
What do you think about us meeting up?

MARGOT

Of course. We'll keep in touch.

FILIPPO

I love you.

MARGOT

Typing...
Typing...
Typing...
I love you too.

I can't describe the pang of emptiness I felt then. He loved me. And I was pretending to be meditating on my life while I was actually fucking a twenty-seven-year-old dude. Please...I had even pressured him to tell me he didn't think it was infidelity...while I was touching his cock. But did I regret it?

Candela answered right when David stuck his head in, so I did the first thing that popped into my head: I spoke to her in English.

"Hi, this is Margot. What's up?"

"Margot?" my sister answered, completely baffled.

"Yep."

"Sorry, Margot..." David whispered. What was he wearing? The hotel robe? Oh my god, he was so tan. "Breakfast is here, okay?"

"Okay, thanks. I'll be right there, David. I just need to sort out a few things and..."

"Ah!" Candela exclaimed in Spanish. "You're speaking English so he can't understand you!"

"Exactly. Just follow my lead, okay? Are you alone?"

"Yes. I'm on your couch, eating leftover KFC from yesterday. Did you know they can't call it Kentucky Fried Chicken anymore because of some lawsuit?"

I sat down on one of the lounge chairs, the one farthest from the villa, and whispered in my own language again.

"It's just sex." I looked sidelong at David organizing the breakfast on the table. Fuck, he was so cute.

"What's that?" my sister replied.

"I said it's just sex. It's...animal, passionate, fucking insanity that's going to completely knock me out, but it's just sex. And it's not infidelity because Filippo and I are taking some time apart."

"Jeez. When you left Madrid, it was just a friendship. Then just a few kisses...and now?"

"Well...we stuck our friendship in a ziplock bag for now, and we're dedicated to fucking like rabbits."

"I knew it. I have all the brain cells in this family."

"And Great Uncle Rogelio's bulging eyes."

"Great Uncle Rogelio was a sex symbol and you know it. And since when did you start fucking?"

"That doesn't matter. I just need you to understand that it's an agreement between friends who need to let off some emotional steam. I think…" I bit my nails. "I think this might even be good for my relationship with Filippo. I'll come back…more centered. It's going to clear my head."

"How? With a giant cock? That's bullshit! First of all, it's not true… Nothing you've said is. Second of all, you don't need *me* to understand anything because you're just trying to convince yourself. *Yourself.*"

David pushed his hair off his forehead right as he passed by the window, not looking at me.

"Probably," I mumbled.

"Did you fall in love? Tell me you didn't fall in love."

"No! It's just sex," I repeated.

David poked his head out.

"Is everything okay?" he asked in a low voice, but projecting enough that I could hear him from there. "You seem upset."

"There's a disaster at work. I'll be right there. I just need a coffee."

"And to close your legs," Candela added.

"Shut up, asshole!" I shot back in English.

"That sounded bad." David made a face. "I'll leave you."

"Margot, listen to me. Sometimes, women…well, everyone, but especially women…we fall in love with our vadge. We go crazy and the next day we think we're in love with the guy, the girl, or the clitoral vibrator we spent such a fun night with. But those feelings aren't real."

"Aren't you the one who encouraged me to do this the day I ran out on my wedding?"

"It's one thing to not want you to get married when I can see that just thinking about it is making you have a psychotic break and another very different thing to push you into the arms of the first dude who strolls through your life. He's very fun, very cute, he makes you laugh, and I *think*, I repeat, I *think* he doesn't have bad intentions, but…Margot, girl…you're still too weak to make important decisions. You have to give yourself time."

"Well…that's what I'm doing. Giving myself time…while I fuck."

"That's one way of looking at it, but you're not fooling me. For you that dude is…"

"I really like him." I cleared my throat. "I don't know. I like him, but this wasn't part of my plan. And my plans are important. It's not…it's not like I decided to get hooked on crack and let myself die or fill myself with Botox like Mama until I look like a hairless cat or…"

"Chill out. Take a deep breath. By the way, just so I know…have you guys talked about it?"

"A little."

"And?"

"Well…we decided it would be over the day we get back to Madrid. End of story."

"Okay. Um…well, I think you should make a few rules."

"Rules, okay. I like rules."

"Propose something that you think'll make it easier for both of you in the long run, even if it'll be hard to pull off when you get home. Have you thought about…?"

"About what?" I asked, scared. "We're using condoms, I swear."

"Yeah, bitch, I don't think you're insane. I meant have you thought about what you're going to do with Filippo when you get back?"

"What do you mean what am I going to do with Filippo? Filippo wants to get back together. We were just messaging right before I called you."

"Filippo wants to get back together, uh-huh…"

"He does," I insisted. "He's making it super clear. Problem solved."

"Margot, you giant moron…" I was surprised by the sudden fit of rage, but this was Candela after all… "What do you want?"

"Me? I mean, I want to forget this whole disaster once and for fucking all and get back to the life I had before."

"The same one? The life you had? Because let me just say you didn't seem very happy. You spent fourteen hours a day in the office. You ate like shit, you slept like shit, you disguised yourself as a serious office worker, trying to prove yourself to a bunch of dudes who have no desire to give you a reason that you deserve what you have. You're an Ortega, Margot, but that doesn't make you any less valid."

"Tell that to the board." I rubbed my temples.

"Don't make any important decisions right now."

"But can I keep fucking?"

"What do I know? For the love of God, Margot. I swear sometimes I regret even giving you advice."

"It's just that you're scaring me."

"It's just that it's your fucking life and I might not even be right! I'm just saying whatever pops into my head. You're my sister and I'm worried, but that doesn't make my opinion more valid than yours. Stick up for yourself a little, girl."

"I fight a lot," I complained. "I spend the whole day fighting at work."

"Work can eat my cooter right now. Every single hotel in the Ortega Group can eat my cooter; I'm so glad to have cut ties with all of them. Right now all I want is for you to think for a minute...a second...and tell me what you're actually feeling. As if I just hung up. I'm going to forget this whole conversation and all I'm going to remember is what you tell me right now. Come on...think."

I took a deep breath. I slowly crept back over to the villa again and saw David sitting at the table drinking coffee. He always put so much milk in... I'd bet my right hand he didn't even like coffee but he was ashamed to admit it. I smiled.

"Candela, I slept with David, and I know I should feel awful and be really scared, but I'm rediscovering a Margot who I like, so I think I'm going to keep fucking him across the whole Aegean Sea like I've lost my mind, and when I get back to Madrid, I'll say goodbye to the whole affair so I can mature as a person and, above all, as a woman."

"Women are people too."

"I'll let you go. The service is getting patchy."

I hung up, went inside, turned off my phone again, and left it on the credenza in the living room.

"Everything okay?" David asked, grabbing a croissant.

"Umm...yes. Nothing important."

"Fuck me, the way you speak English...you're so fluent, girl."

"Not really." I shrugged. "My French is better."

"How many languages do you speak?"

"English, French, and German, but German isn't really my strong suit."

He looked at me with a half-smile, his mouth covered in croissant crumbs.

"Well, you know, seeing you like that is so hot."

"You want to role-play with me as the boss, right?"

"What? No!" He licked his lips. "Fuck...seriously. We're not always thinking about cock. I just meant I didn't know that side of you, and…I'm sure you're an awesome boss. It was…" He looked at me, furrowed his brow, and started the sentence again. "I'm sure Filippo is very proud to share his life with a woman like you. You have it all."

I sat down sideways on his knees and brushed the crumbs off his face. I could have told him that I had messaged Filippo or even that when it came to the pride he was referring to, my *ex* (as Filippo had referred to me in his message) was full of it. But what did I do instead? I kissed him because it was the only thing I felt like doing. French kissing. I opened his bathrobe a little. Nibbled his neck. Let him put his hand between my legs. Fucked wordlessly on the bench in the bathroom and came while I screamed, "Yes."

"We should establish some rules," I said.

I was lying on top of him, my head resting on his naked chest, one of his legs between mine. It must have been twenty minutes since we finished doing it…for the second time. I knew that the second round had been a little tricky for him, but after having a little more breakfast and getting his strength back…

Okay, fine, I admit it: I couldn't stop. I felt like when I lost my virginity; I didn't want to do anything else for the rest of my life. The attack of regret after the exchange with Filippo had vanished completely, even from my memory, with the first kiss on the neck. That wasn't right, but dwelling on it now…bah. It was going to be over soon. We'd forget all about it. Nobody would get hurt.

"We should establish some rules," I repeated when I saw he wasn't responding.

David stroked my back and looked at the ceiling. He didn't move a muscle when he answered: "Rules? For what?"

"For when this ends."

"Do we have to talk about this right now?" he complained, slightly mockingly. "Leave me in my postcoital bliss. I'm in heaven. The way you move your ass, for the love of God."

"If I notice you responding to encouragement, I swear I'm going to want to do it again."

"You're going to kill me." He sighed. "In my eulogy, I want you to praise my resistance, my persistence, and my capacity to ignore that I was starting to chafe, because all I wanted was to satisfy you."

"The rules."

"The rules," he repeated, though he sounded pretty weary, like this didn't interest him at all. "Go on then…"

"When we say goodbye, when this is over for real…"

"…for real, for real…"

"I'm being serious."

"Okaaaay." He tucked his arm under his head and looked at me. "When this is over…what?"

"Neither of us will try to contact the other for a month. WhatsApp will be allowed after a month, but nothing else."

"Uh-huh."

"And…we can't kiss goodbye. I don't believe in goodbye sex either, even though I'll probably beg you for it. I'm an addict."

"Okay. No kissing, no sex. What else?"

"We say goodbye in a neutral place. Somewhere that's not going to make us have bad memories when we end up being friends."

"Sounds good." He took a deep breath.

"And we're not going to cry. Or complain. Or…"

"Got it."

"Now, repeat the rules." I wanted to test him.

"One: no contacting each other; after a month, we can WhatsApp. Two: there will be no goodbye kissing or sex. Three: it will be in neutral territory. Four: there will be no tears."

"Five," I added. "We won't hurry. None of that meeting up too soon."

"Six: we won't tell lies."

I looked at him and nodded.

"And we should start that one now," he said.

"Start being honest? I thought we already were."

"I'm the type who believes you can lie by omission too, so I'd prefer you not to keep things from me."

He rolled me over until we swapped positions and held himself over me with both arms.

"Margarita…my daisy…little flower…" he teased, "nobody has ever made me feel the way you do."

"And how do I make you feel?"

"Like I could do anything."

I reached up to kiss him again, but he pulled away.

"Please, if you're going to want to do it again, now's the time I should tell you I have some meager savings in a philosophy book in Ivan's house. The Hume one. Do something nice with it when I die on top of you. And remember: talk about how good I was, and don't forget the part about your hand not closing around my cock."

"I'll make sure of it."

42

MYKONOS.
CONTRADICTIONS.

Complicated stories are always like that. I don't know why someone made us believe that love fixes everything. It's not true. We're much more than two halves of an orange. The majority of time, love doesn't fix anything, just like getting married doesn't fix an engagement that doesn't work and kids don't revive a broken marriage. Love puts us to the test. It almost always demands something from us: more maturity, less egoism, more courage. I won't say that love is complicated; it's exactly the opposite. Love is simple, it's easy, it's fun…but life isn't always. And I don't know if you know this, but the head and the heart are old enemies. They sound the alarm, ignore each other, throw each other into the unknown. And somewhere between the head and the heart is where the painful part happens. It's always there.

Always.

The hotel in Mykonos was really impressive. Secretly, I felt proud it was part of the company. It felt like an oasis, like you had built your own custom paradise. Besides the bed, my room had a big, wide, and luminous living room, with windows looking out over the sea. Pops of bright color were dotted throughout the mostly white decor, and they made the place warmer, along with all the wood and details like dusty-rose armchairs, a jar full of fresh flowers displayed proudly on the center table, and the turquoise cushions scattered across the large white corner sofa. The bed was huge and had simple lines and nothing elaborate, but it had a canopy draped over it. I remember thinking when I saw it, with its white, almost translucent curtains hanging from the posts, that a Disney princess would definitely lose her virginity in a bed like this. Next to it, there was a walk-in closet that led into the huge bathroom, all white, gold, and emerald. My room, I repeat, because we never even set foot in his.

Between the floor-to-ceiling windows on the wall across from the bed, there was a sliding door that led out to the private terrace, with two very large loungers and a midsize infinity pool that was level with the floor and seemed to flow out into the sea. High walls covered with bright strawberry-colored bougainvillea protected us from the eyes of the guests in the neighboring rooms. It was the perfect refuge for those days. Our arrival in Mykonos was the starting gunshot for our looming goodbye. Maybe that's why we didn't get out of bed at all the first day. I opened my suitcase. He opened his. We looked at each other. Before I even realized, I had my back against the wall, my legs around his hips, and his hand trying to push my underwear aside.

"Now can I invest that half hour of my life between your thighs?" he asked.

I nodded while his tongue slid down my neck, and I flew. Literally, he threw me onto the bed in a perfect maneuver where I fell exactly where I should so all he had to do was take off my panties and kneel on the edge of the bed.

"How do you like it?" He lifted my left thigh up on his shoulder. "Fine, if you refuse to talk, I'll have to figure it out myself. Moan when I get it."

I dug my fingers into his hair when he unfurled his tongue between my pussy lips, and he groaned. That groan did a lot. He groaned like an animal who liked being stroked. It was his human purr but deeper, sexier, and dirtier.

David was the most passionate person I had met in my life. And the most curious. And the most generous. He was selfless to the point of madness when it came to pleasure, and proof of this was discovering that I would be more likely to abandon oral sex than he was to get tired of it. Half an hour, he said, right? Well, I think he did a few extra minutes. And as someone who had always thought guys just did it to fulfill their obligations, this seemed like the fucking best. Seriously…he was incredible at seeking pleasure with his tongue, his fingers, blowing, kissing, licking…

From day one, sex with David was a place to take refuge from everything bad in the world. A space where once you entered, you let go of shame, fears, and any sensation that threatened to diminish pleasure. I wasn't fucking David, even though I was. I fucked, laughed, explored, discovered, shouted, traveled, growled, and asked for two minutes to catch my breath in positions I had always wanted to try and had never dared. And it made his mouth water just hearing me whisper, with a mischievous look, "Stay still. I've always wanted to try this."

And I tried it. Sitting on his chest, with his hair between my fingers, I tugged his locks as he devoured me calmly, slowly, looking at me as I soaked his mouth. And it didn't matter if I fell asleep after I came. When I woke up, he climbed on top of me and, without a word, entered me until our voices melted again into a chorus that only knew how to conjugate the verb *enjoy.*

But in the end, what definitely changed my (our) life were not the sex marathons that we started back in Santorini, and which felt like we were trying to break a world record, but how selfless and generous David was when it came to opening up for me. I guess that started from day one too, but it wasn't until that night in Mykonos, when we stayed in bed all day, that I felt he had opened his life so wide that I could find myself in whatever corner I most wanted to occupy.

And between orgasm after orgasm, I didn't miss the marvelous beaches of the Aegean or the incredibly famous party scene on the island, but I learned a lot about him. Wrapped in the same sheets where we made each other sweat, David seemed to make me, somehow, part of who he really was.

David grew up in a tiny village in the Avila province, in his grandparents' house, where three generations all lived together. His older brother was born when his parents were still very young, and the maternal grandparents stepped up and gave them a place to live. There were three siblings: Ernesto, Clara and him. None of them lived in the village anymore.

He told me about his childhood, a childhood like the one all eighties babies had, even though he was a nineties baby. Scraped knees, mouths full of chocolate, games in the street, "regulation" balls so dusty that when it rained they became heavier than corpses. Games of basketball, soccer, pogs, pants torn every week and patched until they were nothing more than a seam with legs.

"My mother always said to my brother and me that raising two pigs instead of two sons was worth the trouble because at least she'd have four hams by now. We were rougher than a box of rocks. We both had heads full of holes; we were always falling out of trees and stuff like that."

His first kiss, hidden behind the church wall. His first girlfriend, the daughter of a mayor his parents hated because they said he was a reactionary. His first real love, Marina, who smelled like flowers, was a redhead and cheated on him many times in their five-year relationship. The breakup and the subsequent heartbreak. And here it seemed that the true essence of the little boy who had fallen on his knees in front of a woman like Idoia emerged, mixed with oxygen and the smell of sex.

"Look…my mother said my life fell apart when the thing with Marina happened." He sighed.

"Why?"

"I guess she says that because I left school right after, but I have to give it to her that I think I threw my life into free fall at that point."

"You left university because you were lovesick?" I asked, surprised.

"No. It felt pointless that I had picked humanities. That's not what my mother thinks, of course; she says that I'm sensitive and when Marina left me, I thought that people's dreams were just fantasy; I was disillusioned. I say I had a screwup attack and got overwhelmed thinking that a conventional life was awaiting me, with a conventional schedule and a conventional love." He turned and looked at me. "I thought, *Am I really going to spend my whole life complaining about the alarm clock, never finding a job that I like, looking for 'a good girl' who won't hurt me again, wishing I had made other choices?* I don't know. I got obsessed with the idea of freedom."

"And you threw everything away."

"Everything." He nodded, not looking at me. "Even my dreams."

David turned his gaze back on me and smiled, emerging from his memories.

"Do you know my mother never wanted to meet any of my girlfriends?"

"Seriously?"

"Seriously. Same with my siblings. She told us: 'Live however you want, kiss who you want, and enjoy it however you want, but don't bring any of it into my house.' She hopes that when one of our partners comes to her house they will be the last one."

"And you wanted to bring Idoia?"

David seemed to look deeply into one of my eyes and then the other, like he was looking for the reason I asked that question. Or maybe interrogating himself about the truth.

"Yes, I wanted to," he admitted. "It's possible I still want to."

Did it hurt me? In a way, yes; in another way, no. Did I do myself a favor by asking that? In a way, yes; in a way, no.

"Will you forget how much she hurt you?"

"Don't you want Filippo to forget?"

I was stunned, and I didn't know what to say. He noticed and closed his eyes.

I tried to gather my thoughts. "I'm sorry. I know it's not the same. You and Idoia…well, you're very different from each other. But the thing is…I don't want a conventional love. I understand you want that, and…the truth is I get it, but…conventional love doesn't fill me."

"Right."

"Don't listen to me…my head is all mixed up." I took a deep breath and stared intently at the ceiling. Suddenly I didn't want him to see my expression.

"What about your family? Are they all like your sisters?" he asked.

"Worse."

"Maybe you were adopted?"

"No way. I'm exactly like my father."

"Well, he must have been a very 'dashing' man."

I burst out laughing, partly to hide the claws that were digging into my stomach and not because I had just mentioned my father. It was…I don't know. The thing about conventional love had made a mark on me. Had I ever really asked myself what kind of love I wanted?

"I didn't know him. I mean…he died when I was really little. He had a heart attack." I shrugged. "People say he was a nice guy; that's why he was so good at closing deals. From the few photos my mother kept, I'd say he had a pretty androgynous beauty."

He smiled and stroked my hair. With that caress and the look he gave me, maybe understanding, maybe compassionate, David opened a dam in my chest too.

It was probably because he had told me everything about his life or maybe because I had never told anyone about mine in the terms I wanted to with him. Deep down, the reasons escaped me, but the truth is I talked. I talked about my mother…absent, preoccupied by her life of magazines and appearances. I talked about boarding school, the feeling of drowning. About my sisters, who had been father, mother, teacher, example, and hug. I talked to him about my first love, how I realized that I had never really loved him. And the perverse and obsessive passion I felt for one of my professors at university, who broke up with me because he had gotten another student pregnant. I told him how I had never dreamed of being anything really, that the only thing that ever existed in my head was the image of a better me that I was forever reaching for and a feeling of emptiness when I failed.

"Until Filippo showed up," I confessed.

"Why until he showed up?"

"Because then I didn't want anything more from life than what his love promised."

Have you ever heard yourself say something that, a minute before, you believed to the tips of your toes, and suddenly it doesn't mean anything to you besides a bunch of words all piled up in a certain order?

David made a face. I did too.

"Silly fairy tales, little girl," he muttered.

"Silly."

The next thing he did was something that princess stories don't end with, something that doesn't come before the "happily ever after" and that I don't think the Prince Charming we know would ever do: he pushed the sheet away, got on his knees between my thighs, naked, and grabbed his cock with his right hand to caress my clit with it, never taking his eyes off me.

"I don't believe in fairy tales," he whispered.

"Me neither."

"We both need something else to lull us to sleep. None of that 'once upon a time' or promises. Just moans. Making love until we fall asleep."

And it sounded like a plea.

A few minutes later, when the only thing separating us was a thin layer of sweat and latex, when I felt like I needed more, I wanted him closer and the emotion turned to weakness, it was my turn to beg.

"Call it sex, David. Never say 'making love' again."

And he nodded without a word because he understood, like I did, that we couldn't keep making things more complicated.

The countdown had started. For both of us.

Had the spell broken?

~~~~~

I startled awake, but I didn't know why. I turned toward my bedside table in a daze and checked the time on my phone: 2:30 in the morning. When I turned back over, I realized I had probably woken up because David wasn't in the bed.

I got up in the dark, while my eyes were slowly getting used to the dimly lit room, and walked to the bathroom, but the door was open and nobody was in there. I crossed the room again and…stuck my head out onto the terrace.

I found him sitting on one of the lounge chairs, his fingers buried in his hair, looking crestfallen. His left hand was holding his phone to his ear.

"No. Of course not," I heard him whisper. "It's just that… Did you check the time before you called, Idoia?"

My heart did a flip. I didn't know what to do. He hadn't noticed me standing in the open sliding door.

"I know you always called at these hours, and it never used to be a problem, but the thing is circumstances have changed. First of all, you know perfectly well that I'm not working right now and I'm on vacation. And second, I'm on vacation…with another girl."

He fell silent, and I heard the muffled sound of a girl answering, but I couldn't make out a word of her spiel. I thought about going inside, getting back in bed, pretending to be asleep, and never bringing this up unless he told me about it the next day, but he kept talking, and…human beings are curious by nature.

What did they say killed the cat?

"It's not that we can't talk as friends; it's just that it's the middle of the night. And I don't understand the urgency."

I heard him suck his teeth and her responding. And her answer was long and elicited two soft sighs from him.

"No." And his tone lowered and became more intimate. "You know what I think, Idoia? I think you miss me. You miss me a lot. And you got to thinking about this trip, and it made your blood boil. Am I wrong?" A pause. "Right. Well, you have to learn to say it how it is. You can't expect to just drunk-dial me…Yes, yes, you are drunk, Idoia. And I don't know if you've taken anything stronger." A deep breath. "Come on, please! Do you seriously think I'm that stupid?"

I took a step back, not to go back to bed but to hide behind the curtain in case he suddenly stood up and found me there, like an idiot.

"No, don't say that. You're saying that because you're drunk and jealous. And tomorrow, when you sober up, you'll act like nothing happened and I… What am I gonna do with all this 'David, you and I are so awesome together'? I'm with another girl. Idoia… I'm sleeping with another girl, and when I do, I'm not thinking about you."

My heart was pounding so fast I thought he was going to hear it from the terrace.

"You know what she doesn't make me feel like? A pariah. I'm not mediocre to her, and when I'm with her, I don't feel like I am. She gives me wings, Idoia. And you clip them."

In his eyes, there was no one else when we fucked. When we laughed, it sounded like water running over a riverbed of smooth round stones. I gave him wings. He felt capable. Together we were worthy of anything that shined in life and we didn't always see. The patina of magic we insisted on not believing was there, on our sweaty skin and in the last moan—a hoarse whimper coming out of David's throat—mixed with the desperate gasp for oxygen. What if…? What if we weren't crazy? What if life had brought us together for a reason? I clutched my chest over my nightgown. Terrified.

But David kept talking. And…I felt like such an idiot.

"That's not it. Of course I'm not falling in love with her. You know damn well that this thing with Margot isn't love, just like you know how much I miss you. And I think about you. I can't just cut that off overnight. I love you, Idoia, but that's always been the big problem: I love you, and that scares you a lot."

I love you, Idoia. I swallowed.

"Let's leave it for today, really. I…need to think. Give me time. I'm here and…" A pause. She was talking, suddenly, much lower. I could barely hear the sound of her muffled voice. "You know. Don't make me say it." He thought it. He looked up, searching for the moon. He weakened. "I still love you. And that's it, Idoia. I'll text you. I don't want… We'll talk when I'm back, but…I don't want to make her feel bad." She asked something, and he pulled the phone away to sigh deeply, like he needed to get out a ghost dwelling in his chest. "I can't promise that, Idoia. I'm not going to promise I won't touch her again. I'm not going to do it. And I'm hanging up on you now because…I don't feel like being reminded how egotistical you are. Good night."

When he threw the phone down next to him, I went back to bed. Worried. Anxious. Wanting to cry. Feeling like shit. Apparently completely forgetting all the things we thought were so clear.

He didn't come straight to bed. He took long enough for my

head to turn all that information into a bullet with my name on it, embedded in my gut. And also gave me time, accordingly, to send a message to Filippo:

I miss you. I'll never feel as safe as I do in your arms. I can't wait for you to hold me again.

43

~~~~

THE TRUTH ISN'T
ALWAYS COHERENT

I missed the moped, but I didn't ask if he wanted to rent another one. I was kind of pissed off. I felt extremely disappointed. Almost betrayed. Even though I hadn't told him that Filippo had texted me when we were still in Santorini and told me, among other things, that he loved me.

I felt almost betrayed and kind of like a traitor myself. When I woke up, the fact that I had texted Filippo after listening to David's conversation with Idoia made me feel uncomfortable. But his answer provoked a strange mixture of hope and terror in me. He said:

> You were always the love of my life, even before I met
> you. We'll be holding each other again soon and, when
> we do, this whole summer will disappear.

And in that moment, I felt like I'd never wanted anything more than I wanted him to be right and like when I sank into Filippo's strong arms, my head would erase everything that I had lived through since I ran out in my wedding dress, like a kind of magic.

I guess I still had a lot of inner work to do to understand why not forgetting scared me so much. New things that demand more strength, more passion, less control…are always terrifying at first.

Usually, when I woke up, the ghosts of the night before were gone. But this time they were still sitting at the end of the bed, and they seemed even scarier in the light of day.

And the fact that David didn't tell me about his conversation with Idoia as soon as he opened his eyes felt like him stabbing me in the back.

I gave him an extension, at least until breakfast. I thought maybe he needed coffee or to stuff two dozen buns into his gut to build up his strength. But it didn't happen. Of course not. David didn't want to tell me about his conversation with Idoia because it was private and special and had nothing to do with me.

When he cleaned his last plate and was talking to me about something else, I absent-mindedly asked myself what exactly I wanted him to say: "Last night Idoia called; she wanted to get back together and she made me promise that I don't love you." Fuck. It wasn't a crime. It was, simply, reliable and tangible proof that our plan had worked. Why did it hurt me so much when Filippo's message taking our reconciliation for granted had felt like a salve on an open wound?

We went to Panormos, a very pretty beach that, according to the girl in reception, wasn't usually as crowded as all the others. We went in a shuttle from the hotel, in silence, listening to foreign versions of Luis Fonsi's hits on the radio and looking out the little window. In my head, which was prone to turning any minor discomfort into World War III, I tried to accept that soon David would no longer be in my life.

"What's up with you?" he asked when I went straight to put my stuff on an empty lounger without even checking with him. "You're very quiet this morning."

"Nothing. What about you?"

He raised an eyebrow. My tone was pretty hostile.

"You have big bags under your eyes." I softened.

"I have big bags. And, well…I didn't get much sleep."

"Why not?"

He bit his lip and diverted his gaze over to the bar.

Please, David, I need to hear it, whatever it is you want to tell me.

"No reason. Listen…how 'bout I grab a couple beers? Come on, I'll be right back."

"I hope you get diarrhea, you bastard," I muttered resentfully as he walked away.

When he came back, he was holding something for me to eat. He told me, with a soft and attentive tone, that he thought I might be hungry. He had noticed, it seemed, that I hadn't been able to have anything but coffee and everything else on my plate had made me queasy. Being sad made me hungry, but being angry felt like my stomach was being clenched with an iron fist. And even though it was a kind gesture on his part, I couldn't help but stand firm in my silent hostility. Perhaps because I knew I was wrong and I'd rather keep quiet than say something I would regret and that I was sure even I wouldn't understand. So for the next two hours (yes, I said two hours…I'm a very stubborn woman), I pretended to be super engrossed in reading my book, turning the pages randomly every few minutes, not really absorbing anything. But he spent the whole time staring out at the sea with his headphones on under the umbrella. We were the living image of the cliché couple who organize a trip hoping it'll fix everything. The cliché couple both in love with someone who wasn't there.

And I grew angrier with every passing minute. And he seemed less honest.

My book flew onto the sand, between the two loungers, after he snatched it from me.

"Hey!" I grumbled.

"Enough already."

I looked him in the face. He wasn't angry. No. He was worried.

"Can you give me back my book?"

"No."

"What do you want?"

David gaped, but he didn't say anything. Words wouldn't come out. They were clogging up his throat the same way and in the same place as my emotions. Forming a ball, causing a jumble of incoherence and contradictions that hurt and burned.

He sighed.

"Can I play a song for you?" he asked.

"You threw my book in the sand so you can play a song?"

"No. But who cares? You weren't even reading it."

He dangled a headphone in front of me, jiggling it until I took it and put it in my ear. He looked at me for a few seconds and pressed play. I recognized the song right away. Like the other times, I found myself wondering how much he understood the lyrics of the songs he was sharing with me. If you've ever heard "Sacrifice" by Elton John, you'll understand why I'm pretty sure it's the only song that could have softened my mood right then.

Even though it might tell a specific story that happened before I was born, it speaks of things not going well, jealousy, infidelity, a misunderstanding when things are already done, being at sea somehow…

I listened to it like it was the first time. I listened as I watched David's expression with a trace of anxiety on the surface of his features. We didn't get angry. And if we got angry, we kissed four times in a car and that was that. At least, that was how it had been in our only fight. But maybe…maybe in just a couple of days everything had changed too much. And in the coming weeks, even more would change.

His brown eyes were lightened by the reflection of the sea, and his eyebrows were mussed. I had to hold myself back from using my fingertip to comb them. I wondered if he knew how handsome he was, if he used it, if one day his beard would grow in evenly, if he had lied in his conversation with Idoia, if he felt something for me. Something real. Something I was scared to ask myself if I felt for him.

When the song ended, he surprised me by playing it again. The whole story sounded in my ears again from the beginning. And he was there, in front of me, trying to hide the lump in his throat, the twin of the one I had. I couldn't take it anymore and yanked the earphone cable out of my ear. He did the same and pushed the iPod away.

A couple of seconds of silence, hesitation, and, finally, the elephant in the corner that was filling the whole room but no one was mentioning barreled into the conversation:

"You heard me talking to her, is that it?"

"Yes," I admitted, no energy left to lie.

"And what bothered you? That I didn't tell you or what you heard me say?"

"Both."

"I didn't say anything that could have offended you, Margot."

"Can you summarize your conversation? So I can confirm you remember what you said."

"It was a conversation between two people who aren't ready to give up on their relationship. Nothing you didn't already know."

"Her not being ready to give up is a surprise, to be honest," I pointed out viciously.

"That was harsh."

"Well, that was exactly what I thought when I was listening to you last night. That you sounded pretty harsh," I retorted.

"I don't understand why."

"Because it sounded like you were using me and I felt like a toy. No, even worse: I felt like a warm hole in the mattress where you can put your dick until Idoia wakes up and comes back."

"You're taking it out of context. You know the role I had to play to her and how I had to represent our relationship to her. I am using you." He nodded. "Of course I'm using you. That was the deal. You were using me to have fun and I was using you to make Idoia jealous, right?"

"What's going on with you?" I asked him, hurt. "Why are you talking like this?"

"Nothing's going on with me, Margot, but...I mean...this is ending, right? We're going to go back to our lives and..."

"Fuck." I looked away and pressed on my temples. "This shit isn't like you. Don't even try it."

"What shit, Margot? Maybe *using* isn't the right word, but...you and I are two friends, and everything I said to Idoia about us fits with that perfectly. If you don't agree, that's where your problem is."

"Do you know what this looks like?"

"Surprise me."

"Don't use that tone with me," I demanded.

"I'm not using any tone."

"Of course you are... What are you trying to do? Seem more sure of the things you're saying?"

"I'm very sure about what I'm saying to you." He furrowed his brow. "What I'm not sure of is what the hell you're understanding."

"Can I tell you something? You told Idoia you love her and that she was always scared of that, right? Well, I think there's something about this trip that scares you."

"Nothing scares me." He shook his head.

"You're a terrible liar."

"Well, you are too, if we're gonna go there," he said, jabbing his index finger at me.

"What are you talking about?"

He rubbed his face and then pushed his hair off his forehead.

"It's been five days since you've even mentioned Filippo."

"So?" I swallowed.

"This is getting really messy, Margot," he warned, his voice trembling.

"Because I didn't mention Filippo? How is that messy?"

"That might work for you at your job, where people are scared of you and everyone shuts up because they don't want to argue with the boss, but not with me. You haven't heard from him?"

I bit my cheek.

"Yes."

"Yes, what?" He tightened.

"Yes, I've heard from him, but you already knew that."

"Of course, because I'm not as big an idiot as you think. Turning your phone off and putting it face down on the bedside table doesn't make things disappear."

Uh-oh.

"Better to remain silent and be thought a fool than to speak and remove all doubt," I muttered, looking down at the sand.

"Ah, fucking great." He laughed ironically. "So that's why you suddenly stopped telling me you've been talking to him?"

"We had just fucked, David. Maybe I don't feel that comfortable telling you how romantic the message from my ex was when I'm still wiping your semen off my tits."

I felt like I had been punched in the gut by newly discovered feelings. The memory of his mouth hanging open, panting, as he came on me, with his eyes locked on my face. The pleasure of feeling capable of enjoying so much. The smile, the kiss, the stroking my hair, my back, my left thigh, while we spooned naked afterward.

David made me look at him again.

"You're allowed to feel uncomfortable and keep things quiet, but I have to tell you about the thing with Idoia even though I could still taste you in my mouth, right? 'Listen, Margot, I know right before we fell asleep we were fucking like dogs, I was eating your cunt, and I came on your tits while I was saying filthy things to you, but…wake up, my ex called and she says she misses me.'"

"If it's all as clear as we want to pretend, we shouldn't have any problem talking about this stuff, right?"

"I don't know, ask yourself. You were the first one to hide information," he spat.

"You're pissed off," I said in an informative tone.

"Yeah." He nodded. "Of course I am!"

"Your anger has nothing to do with me. You're angry with yourself and your own shit."

"Oh, but your anger has everything to do with me, right?" He threw his hands up in disbelief.

"Yes."

"Fuck outta here," he thundered through clenched teeth. "I'd bet my right hand you can't give me a logical explanation for all this rage."

"What about yours? You can't either."

"Yes, I can. I'm angry because we haven't been honest with each other. And I'm pissed off for being so naive to think that fucking you wouldn't ruin everything."

He jumped up, threw his iPod aside, and marched straight into the sea. Oh, no. We weren't going to leave it like that. I followed him.

"Wait…what the hell are you talking about?" I screamed. "Now you're worrying about it? Now? When we've already done it in every position on the planet! You insisted! 'Come on, Margot, let's live life, let's be free!'" I added in the worst imitation of my life. "And now your ex calls because she wants you back, you realize that we fucked it up by fucking like rabbits, right?"

"No. Not now that my ex calls, now that we're lying to each other, we're hiding things from each other and…"

"And what? What else?"

"Now that you're all jealous like this, Margot. Look at yourself, for fuck's sake." He gestured at me disdainfully. "You're rabid!"

"I'm not jealous!" I lied.

"Of course you are! You're jealous because I told Idoia I miss her and I think about her!"

"I'm confused. Not jealous or rabid, David. Confused because you say one thing and you do another and…"

"Me? What about you? I have no idea where you're at with Filippo. At this point, I can only think of two options: Either everything is fixed with him but you don't want to mention it so you can keep enjoying the little toy you brought on vacation who's a good lay. Or this means something to you that isn't really there between us."

"And what is there between us?"

"A friendship," he answered firmly.

"It's time to accept that friends don't fuck, you know?"

"And while you're at it, it's time to accept that just because you fuck someone doesn't mean you have to have feelings for them. It's an exercise in physical needs, not emotional."

I took the hit with dignity.

"You're not even making sense anymore. How would anyone even know what you're saying?" I sniped back, feigning levelheadedness. "Can you figure it out with yourself and then give me the official version? Did we fuck it up by sleeping with each other, or are we just friends with benefits so it doesn't even matter?"

"I don't know!" he yelled.

"So?"

"So it bugs me that you didn't tell me about Filippo and it would bug me if you did too. It bugs me that you care that we fucked and it would bug me if you didn't. And you know what else? It bugs me that you're acting like this just because you heard me talk to my fucking girlfriend."

"She's not your girlfriend," I pointed out.

"You know exactly what I mean!" He snorted and pushed his hair off his face.

"What the fuck is going on with you?" I screamed back. "Are you scared? Do you think I'm going to stalk you or follow you around when we get back? Like I'm going to be crying at your door for love?"

"No, don't worry, it's very clear that if you're groveling for anyone, it'll be him because that's the easy way out."

"Now who's jealous?"

"I'm not jealous. I'm just pointing out the obvious. A girl like you only chases someone with a pretty full wallet."

I raised my eyebrows, surprised.

"You're asking if I'm afraid you're going to chase me," he continued, "but I'm not worried because boys like me are only good for sticking their cocks in you, eating you out, and making you feel wild for a few weeks until you return to the arms of the magnates you deserve."

"I never thought you'd say something so sexist."

"Sexist? You're not understanding me. I'm not talking about you as a woman. I'm talking about you as a class."

"I can buy Filippo and his whole family with the loose change in my bank account," I spat, enraged. "You think I need him to get the life I deserve? I don't need him or anyone else. My love can't be bought."

"Don't get off topic, Margot, or try to make me think that money doesn't make an insurmountable difference. Not even everything you have can paper over the fact that I'm a street dog and you're a little purebred lady."

I furrowed my brow. I didn't understand anything, especially not the turn this conversation had taken.

"Are you aware of how screwed up your head is, David? You're accusing me of being jealous, of giving our relationship more importance than it has, and now you're accusing me of not wanting you because I'm a snob. What do you want?"

"And do you know what you want, Margot? Tell me. Because the life you deserve has absolutely nothing to do with what you can or can't buy. And you know what you can't buy at the end of the day? Dignity."

"You're talking to me about dignity? You?" I thrust my finger into his chest. "You're the one who wants to get back together with a girl who says you're not enough for her, and you're a poor slob, and you have no future, and you're mediocre. You're so dignified, you're dying from lack of affection, but you're so used to the beatings your bitch of an ex gave you that you think love is having some clown make you feel important."

"Go to hell," he spat ragefully.

"Why don't you? But not to hell, David. Why don't you go back to Madrid and get your life together instead of staying here scared that I'm falling in love with you? Or that I'm using you. I can't even keep track of what you're accusing me of anymore. Go!" I shrugged. "Go already! I'm not going to die without you, you know? I've known you for about five fucking minutes. You have absolutely nothing to do with me or with my life. Go and bark up her tree. She's more your type."

David nodded, swallowed, and licked his lips. He took a few steps back toward our chairs, but he changed his mind and turned back to face me.

"I'm going. And I'll be the bad guy, but you're a poor little rich girl, and you're so lonely that you had to spend your vacation with someone you just met. Your advice is really worth a lot…and I don't give a shit what happens in your life, princess."

I watched him walk away, unable to move a muscle. I think I even stopped breathing.

When he disappeared from sight, it felt like flowers and other things that no longer existed were appearing in the sand.

44

MAGIC DOESN'T EXIST BECAUSE PEOPLE DON'T BELIEVE IN IT

I spent the rest of the day on the beach he left me on, crying. I didn't even know why I was crying. I mean, I did. Because I knew that everything we had said was true, even though it was a horrible truth and, even worse, contradictory and incongruent. Yes, I did feel more than I said I felt. Yes, I did want to run back to the refuge of the familiar and I was probably blinded by Filippo's pedigree. In a way, I respected him more than David, and that wasn't fair. I was dying of fear and rage, and the only thing that soothed it was throwing myself into the ocean and sobbing. It's a miracle no one stole all the stuff I left on my chair.

When I got back to the hotel on the shuttle that did a loop every couple of hours to the same spot it had dropped us on the way there, I was starving, tired, covered in sand, and completely fucking messed up. I pictured the empty room, and I knew that when I opened the door and didn't find him or his stuff, the trip would be as good as over for me too. A lot of things were over. I still held on to the hope that he wouldn't have left, even though I wasn't prepared to find him there or to face everything our discussion really meant. It was...it was like when you wish for something as hard as you can but you don't prepare yourself for it because if you don't get it, it'll somehow hurt less that way.

But of course, as you can imagine, I should have prepared myself to open the door and find him there in front of me, with no painkillers. There he was. Sitting on an armchair, with his suitcase zipped up next to him. He had just taken a shower and was dressed and his hair was combed. He looked like he was about to leave for the airport, so I assumed he was waiting for a taxi or something like that and passed by him without a word. I barely even looked at him. I didn't want to watch him leave the room, the island, my life.

I stripped in the bathroom, leaving all my clothes crumpled on the floor, and I got in the shower, where I waited under the water for him to leave. I took a long time. I cried again. I thought between the sobs and the water I wouldn't hear the door closing when he left and it would be better that way. A girl has to protect her heart.

When I got out of the shower, I pulled on the nightgown I had left hanging on the back of the bathroom door. I dried my hair with a towel. I combed it out and walked out barefoot. Maybe Sonia was still in the office and I could ask her to move my ticket home up to the next day.

David had his forearms resting on his knees, and he looked up at me, still sitting in the same chair where I had found him when I came in. The ever-present bags under his eyes were bigger than ever. His mouth was swollen from anxiously biting his lips so much. He stood up, and I stopped dead in the middle of the room.

I turned so he wouldn't see me cry, like an ashamed little girl, and he wrapped me in his arms from behind, slowly, like deep down he was expecting me to pull away. I felt his uneven beard bristling against my shoulder and his breath when he stroked my neck with his nose.

"I'm sorry," he moaned with a trembling voice. "I'm so sorry."

I didn't answer. I wanted to bite my hand to stem my tears and muffle my sobs, but his arms were holding me tight.

"This is so shitty, Margot. So shitty." He pressed his forehead against my damp hair. "This isn't what we planned. Forgive me."

I didn't answer.

"I don't think you're a poor little rich girl," he insisted.

"You do think so, and you're probably right."

"I never wanted to hurt you."

I put my left hand over his on my belly.

"I don't even know what I said to you on the beach." He sighed, overwhelmed.

"Let's forget it, David. We fucked it all up."

"I should've told you. I wanted to wake you up and ask you to hold me, but I was scared."

"Why?"

"I guess for the same reason you didn't tell me about Filippo."

I turned around, and we both had understanding expressions while he put his arms around my waist.

"We should have talked," I said.

"Yes."

I swallowed.

"I was jealous," I admitted.

"Okay. I was angry."

"At yourself, at me, or at her?"

"Mostly at myself, that I'm going to go crawling back to her with my tail between my legs."

"Don't think like that." I looked him in the eyes and pushed some hair back from his temples. "If that's what you want to do, think more like you're returning victorious. In the end, she followed wherever you wanted. Rabid with jealousy."

"And you. And me," he said wiping my tears away with his thumb. "We were both rabid with jealousy too."

"You?"

He nodded.

"You were scared I might fall in love with you," I said, my throat dry.

"Yes. And that I might fall in love with you. And the truth is, Margot, I think if we don't leave it here, that's what'll end up happening."

He stroked my cheeks.

"And I'm terrified of falling in love with someone like you," he insisted, tilting toward my mouth.

"Why?"

"Because if I'm a disappointment to Idoia, my love…imagine what I'll be to you."

"Let me decide that."

"No," he said, looking at my lips. "That can't happen."

"David, we can't claim we experience these things and then forget them…"

"Yes, we can." He smiled sadly. "We can leave it here. We can keep going with what we planned and…not fuck up our lives. Otherwise, I'll hurt you and you'll hurt me."

I stroked his lips.

"You deserve a perfect story, a princess story, and I don't believe in magic. We'd love each other sweetly for how long? A few years? At most. Then, little by little, you'd realize that I'm just a dream deferred. And you'd hate me for not accomplishing anything. And I'd hate you for being too good for me."

"Isn't Idoia?"

He half-smiled, but he didn't answer.

"Once upon a time, the saddest eyes ever in a bar…" he said, "who recognized each other through a crowd of people."

"And they went to Greece." I smiled sadly.

"And they fell in love with what could have been…" he went on.

"…until the sea swallowed them up…"

"There's a flight at nine thirty tonight." He wet his lips. "Do you want me to buy the ticket?"

"The sea is still hungry."

I guess there's nothing love likes more than impossible stories. And there's nothing more impossible than the things nobody believes in. Even ghosts, they say, are able to keep their existence a secret because people don't believe. And David was right: we were impossible. Two strangers, really, who had only seen the good in each other, who had scooped each other up from the street and cured each other's wounds, but…even if you cure the wound, the scar will never be yours.

When he kissed me, I understood that he was scared I would fall in love with him. I was scared too. You never find the warmth of home in something new, even if the home is on fire and about to crumble around you. That is why we should learn that home is where the heart is.

I don't even remember how we got naked and into bed. I don't remember wanting to screw, and I don't remember thinking he wanted to. I guess what we did had less to do with sex and more to do with need.

David dug his fingers hard into my waist as he entered me, and I saw his muscles and tendons tighten as he thrusted between my thighs. His face contracted with pleasure. I wanted to tell him he had constellations in his eyes and then beg him to hurt me, tell him I didn't care if all we got was two years. But I kept quiet. I kept quiet, either out of embarrassment or so I wouldn't miss a single detail of his face while he fucked me. While he made love to me. While he told me, quietly, slowly, that he wanted to stay with me always.

David dug his fingers into my ass as he lay on top of me and sped up his thrusting. I wish he left a cluster of purple fingerprints on my skin because, even if they changed color, they would remind me for a few more days of the painful sensation and the pleasure it provoked in me. I asked him not to stop, and he asked me not to forget him. I asked him to never stop touching me like that, and he asked me to never stop putting my hands on his skin.

David dug his fingers hard into my chest, into my neck, into my hips, into the pillow, the mattress, the handful of hair he grabbed at the end, when I came so hard it made me float and I needed him to hold me down to the ground and remind me that my skin was only mine and not his, even though that's how I felt now.

When he peeled off the used condom and went into the bathroom, I buried my face in the pillow and, when I heard him turn on the faucet, drowned out a scream with the feathers. I already loved him, and even though he didn't believe in us, I didn't know if it would be too late to save me from it without paying with too deep a scar.

~~~~

"Do you hate anything about Filippo?"

I rubbed my cheek against his chest, grazing the sparse hair between his pecs with my fingertips.

"Of course. And I'm sure he hates stuff about me too."

"But like what?"

"You mean what does he hate about me or me about him?" I clarified.

"I don't care about him. What do you hate?"

"Well…his need to plan everything, for one. He can't function on the fly. He doesn't know how to improvise. He's rigid to the point of exasperation. And I don't like that he's so proud, and he's the kind of guy who makes declarations when he talks. He's super emphatic." I looked at David to check his expression.

I couldn't deduce anything from his features.

"What else?" he pressed.

"Well…I don't think there's anything else."

"Nothing else?" He raised his eyebrows, surprised.

"I mean, that's not nothing."

"He doesn't chew with his mouth open or have stinky feet or leave his underwear on the floor all the time?"

"No." I smiled. "Do you?"

"Gorgeous, I smell like heaven," he announced smugly. "That's not it. It's just that I hate hundreds of things about Idoia."

"Like what?"

"I loathe one of her perfumes, the winter one… It makes me queasy and burns my stomach."

"That's silly." I laughed. "It's so easy to tell her. It's a perfume. Filippo hates my mother… That's more complicated. I can't just stop 'putting it on' and that's that."

"Well. I hate other stuff. I hate that fucking her is like acting in a porno where everything is preplanned and perfect."

"Ughh…perfect porn. Sounds awful," I teased.

"She's so condescending, it's a pain in the ass. And when she shows off her moral superiority, I wish I could tell her to go to hell. She doesn't like my friends, she never wants to make plans with them, and it makes me feel terrible because they could run a thousand circles around her posse of trendy pals. I hate that she takes drugs sometimes because, besides the obvious, she gets really violent and sometimes she goes crazy while we're fucking and…she really messes me up. It turns me off that she looks down on me and she constantly repeats that her ex was a big, strong, rough dude and I'm so 'little'…"

"You're not that little. That girl's mental ruler must be broken."

"She makes me feel tiny."

I sat up, grabbed his face, and kissed him violently. He smiled into the kiss.

"Does it turn you on that I hate all that stuff?"

"No. I just wanted to shut you up. What do you like about yourself, David?"

"What?"

"You heard me. What do you like about yourself?"

"Uh…" He blinked. "Well, I never thought about it. What about you? What do you like about yourself?"

"My perseverance. My patience. I'm empathetic and a good boss. And affectionate. And I haven't lost all the childish naivete that allows me to be genuinely surprised. I'm good at walking in high heels. I'm proud of not being like my mother, and I like how enthusiastic I am about taking on new projects. And I'm good with languages and…with people." David kissed me, and I took advantage of his closeness to insist, "Come on, your turn now."

He raised his eyebrows, and his doubtful expression transformed into a timid smile.

"I'm sensitive…and understanding. I can usually make people smile when they're with me."

"What else?"

"I'm good with flowers. And I have patience. Good with kids. I'm a confident person and a guy who doesn't need to dim anyone else's light to turn his on."

"Very good." I straddled him. "And?"

"You tell me." He smiled. "What else?"

"You're a pro at choosing songs for every moment. And you have a beautiful laugh. And you have these tiny dots in your eyes, little golden streaks, that make it feel like you're looking into a galaxy. You have a lot of hair, and it's really silky. And when you're about to come, you arch in this really sexy way…"

"And I have stamina."

"And you're very generous when it comes to pleasure. And smiles. And saying nice things."

"I'm a hedonist in love with beauty. What are we gonna do about it?" He smiled. "What about you? Tell me more things about you."

"I'm not a bad singer, and my niece and nephews adore me. I think I have good taste. And I smell good."

"You smell amazing. And you're very sexy, even though you don't know it." He sat up a little straighter, so his mouth reached mine. "When you're on top, you move in this incredible way… When you laugh really hard, it sounds like there are bells tinkling in your throat."

David smiled, and I returned the gesture.

"And I give good head."

"You give very good head." He nodded. "But not as good as your kissing. You kiss like they always kiss in the final shot of a black-and-white movie. And you make the people around you comfortable. So much that…I don't want to leave."

The smile faded from my mouth.

"It's a pity we can't love each other," I said. "Because we love each other really beautifully."

"Yeah. You and I would make poetry."

I snuggled into his chest and sighed. What a shame. What a shame magic doesn't exist if you don't believe in it…and that you need two people to believe in love.

"David…" I finally said. "Don't let anyone make you believe that what you're not is more important than what you are."

"Even better…don't go too far away. It'd be good to have you around to remind me every once in a while."

45

BACK TO REALITY

DAVID

The last few days in Mykonos were a honeymoon. I was pretty calm for that part. I told myself, many times, that at least I had been lucky enough to experience something so intense once in my life, even if it was brief. Back then, I thought that if the idea of love existed, it could only materialize, like a spell, for a short period of time before it broke down.

And despite that cowardly image of love, I have snapshots of Margot that I never took engraved in my memory. I remember her with her hair to one side, windswept on one of the island's most famous beaches. She wasn't looking at anything in particular, but she seemed to have everything under control. My little Margot would always survive and be stronger after every stumble.

We did it like crazy during those days. I even had to buy another box of condoms. I thought, greedily and gluttonously, that I needed to get sick of what I was about to give up to make the separation easier. But I didn't get sick of her. Not at all.

We made love, and we fucked. We fucked a lot and with a ferocity Idoia had never inspired even when she went nuts and demanded I fuck her in the bathroom of some dive bar we had met up in, against the tiles of the wall.

Margot demanded attention, dedication, and discipline, but at the same time she never really demanded anything. And when she moaned that she was dying of pleasure, pinned between my body and the table, the floor, the wall, the bench in the bathroom, or a door, I didn't feel even a hint of the shame that I felt when I manhandled Idoia like she was a doll…maybe because Margot didn't ask me to use her, lost in horniness, because of some drops that had dissolved on her tongue. I wasn't acting with Margot; I didn't have a role to learn and stick to. We improvised, and it was incredible.

We tried all the flavors we had left to try. And her kisses tasted like yogurt with honey. And mine only tasted of Margot. I don't remember ever being as happy as the moment when I let out the ghosts, the fears, and gave them their space so that they couldn't bother us anymore, even though they were still there.

We frolicked like kids on all the beaches we could visit. And sitting on the sand, watching the sunset with Margot nestled between my legs, her hair tickling my neck, I found more of myself than I even thought I had in me.

"Tell me a secret," I heard her say before she turned back to me with a timid smile.

"A secret?"

"Yes. Something no one else knows."

I looked at her, her cheeks reddened by the day in the sun and love. Yes, love. I already knew that Margot loved me. And I loved her. Her, as she looked at me with arched brows, twisting around so she could see my face. Curling myself around her, I grabbed her legs and spun her around in my lap before I kissed her.

"Don't try to distract me." Her index finger and thumb pulled my face away as she smiled. "I want a secret."

"Will you tell me one after?"

"Of course."

"Ah, well…"

Her gaze was on my eyes, mine on hers. Before we even realized, we were making out like teenagers.

"The secret…" she moaned, as I lay her gently down on the sand and tried to climb on top of her now that the beach was deserted.

"What if the secret is that I never want to stop kissing you?"

"Well, everyone already knows that," she teased. "A secret shouted from the rooftops isn't a secret."

I love you, I thought. My stomach and my heart flipped, and it scared me. No. I couldn't. I couldn't love her. And I couldn't let her love me. I barely knew anything about Margot's job or her family, but at this point, it was already very clear that I would never fit into her world. And I doubted she could ever be fully happy in mine. What did I have to offer her? A bouquet of flowers every once in a while?

"I'd like to quit my other jobs and dedicate myself fully to the florist," I said.

Margot raised her eyebrows, surprised. I was surprised too. I liked flowers, and people often told me I had a talent with them, but I had never considered something like that, at least not consciously.

"You should do it. Bring it up to Amparito and Asuncion."

"I don't think they can afford it."

"You have nothing to lose if you try."

"What about your secret?" I changed the subject.

She bit her lip. She seemed to be holding in something that was going through her head, and I fantasized that she had pushed away an *I love you*, just like I had.

"I'm terrified," she whispered. "I don't want to go back. I don't want to face everything I left in such a disaster."

"Me too," I confessed.

"Sometimes I feel like I dress up as another person every day before I leave the house."

"I feel like no one really sees me."

"And I have the urge to run away forever."

"Well, if you ever do, take me with you."

I guess that's how you know things, how you become sure of things: by chance, by playing. That's how I understood that Margot was the braver of the two of us and that, if I were a little braver, I would leave everything behind for her.

That day I posted a photo of our shadows intertwined on the sandy beach, and at the bottom all I wrote was an "Us" that I felt said more than I was willing to confess or understand.

~~~~~

But time ran out. That's how time is, ephemeral. Everything comes with an expiration date nowadays, and we were no exception. The honeymoon ran out as we played make-believe that it never would.

When I saw Margot gather up all her things and fold them into her suitcase with surgical precision, I felt like something was hopelessly wrong. I was afraid. I felt terrified. When we started this crazy relationship, I thought that by this point in the trip, I would have what I wanted, even if I wasn't exactly sure what it was I wanted so much. Sadness and anxiety about the looming goodbye, of course not. If we stuck to what we had agreed, in a few hours, the next day, we would say goodbye and not contact each other for at least a month. I would have to sit across from Idoia and fix things; mustering up the courage to tell her everything that would have to change to make us work wouldn't be nearly as hard as not having Margot by my side. Not even the dreaded conversation with Ivan and Domi about how I needed to move out of their apartment…dreaded in case they were too happy to see me go, I guess. The apartment hunt, quitting the bartending job, which made me bitter, maybe proposing adding some shifts to my schedule to Amparito and Asuncion or looking for another place where my experience with them would be worth something… None of those tasks weighed on me as much, either together or separately, as knowing I wouldn't be able to share it with Margot. But this was no time for negotiations.

We're always so sure in the beginning, but then human beings are specialists in not listening to a fucking word, I tried to convince myself.

We'll keep seeing each other.

We can do it.

What I feel is just a result of the trip.

She'll be my best friend.

How many lies are you capable of telling when you're the one you're telling them to?

"We should spend all day doing it like animals," I said to her, watching her get in bed and set the alarm on her phone.

"Man, if you put it like that…I just can't resist." She looked at me, leaving the telephone on the bedside table and stretching out dramatically on the bed. "Come on, take me! I'm ready!"

I smiled. "Fine, have it your way. I'm sure tomorrow you'll regret not having your way with this hot bod"—I pointed at myself—"when you could."

"Forgive me for saying that you don't seem that interested in spending the night screwing."

"You don't get any points for using the word *screwing*."

"Fucking, making love, screwing, copulating, having sex…call it whatever you want, but I'd say you're not in the mood."

"Of course I'm in the mood. I'm a guy."

She raised one eyebrow.

"I mean…that's bullshit, you're right. Guys aren't always in the mood," I conceded.

"And are you in the mood?" She let an equally sweet and condescending smile escape her lips.

"Yes."

"Really?"

"Really." I nodded.

"You're super horny."

"Super horny."

"Funny"—she gestured toward my crotch—"that looks pretty calm."

"It's the calm before the storm."

"Isn't the calm supposed to come after the storm?"

"Who cares?" I wrinkled my nose. "Let's screw until we break the bed," I proposed.

"That doesn't look like it's ready to party." She pointed at me again, teasing.

"You know that doesn't threaten my masculinity?"

"Dude, I would hope not. It's just an assessment of your current state. I didn't say that it's never given me a party or that it can't in the future. But, listen…if you say you're super horny…"

"Super," I said, unable to avoid a smile. "But like ready to come on your face and everything."

Margot covered her face with a pillow and burst out laughing.

"I'm serious!" I laughed too. "I'm going crazy over here! Come here. I'll show you a party."

I jumped out of bed, stripped off, and hurried over to her side, nice and close; I wasted no time finding her neck and kissing her and biting her there where I knew she liked it.

"David…"

I put my hand between her legs, but she stopped me.

"David…" she repeated.

I looked at her, confused. "You don't feel like it?"

"We don't have to do it."

"I know we don't have to do it. What are you trying to say?"

"Well, just that…we don't have to do it just because it's the last night."

"But…"

She grabbed my face with both hands and smiled the way women do when they've already understood something that we still haven't accepted.

"I'm scared too," she said, making it simple.

"What scares you?"

"Missing you, remembering all this too much, thinking about you when I sleep with Filippo."

I shuddered.

"Margot…" I sighed. "It's not that. It's just…"

"Yes, it is that. It's scary. And sex is easier."

"It's easier because I'm doing it with you," I clarified.

"Sex is easier than chewing over what you feel. When we're fucking, we don't think. All we feel is our hunger. Yesterday and tomorrow don't exist. Sex is sex and…"

"Are you going to miss me?" I heard myself ask her.

"Of course."

"I'm going to miss you a lot," I confessed.

"We'll just be apart for a little while so we won't have to be forever," she said to me, surely.

"What if…?"

"We can't worry about what we don't know will happen. We can't think about the worst part; we have to start from the basis that everything will go well. We'll separate, get back to our own lives, get what we wanted back, and when everything's fine, we'll see each other again. And everything will be like before."

"Like before…when?"

"Before this trip."

And for the first time I was completely sure I didn't want to go back to how it was before. Not just with her. With everything. With my life.

"Am I right?"

"About what? You said a lot of things. You always say a lot of things." I smiled.

"That you want to do it so we don't have to feel sad we're going back tomorrow."

"Maybe."

"I'm very wise."

I swallowed her laugh and gave her one back.

"You're right, sex is easier than talking. But let me just add that when we're doing it, there are things that we don't need to verbalize," I pointed out.

"Like what?"

"Like that I'll miss you, that I like the feeling of your skin under my fingertips, that I'll yearn for the smell of sex with you…"

And I shut up, trying to give us the opportunity to communicate again just with our skin; I didn't say that when I was with her, I finally felt like I could take off the mask of panic disguised as freedom; that when I talked to her, the future started to make sense; that in her mouth, I seemed like someone who was worthwhile and wanted to be for myself too… I didn't say that her breasts undulating under my hands were the most sensual thing I had ever seen and that I would go straight to a hundred when she moved her hips on top of me, even if I wasn't inside her.

"Maybe we could just cuddle and look at photos?" she said, her mouth shrinking, worried I would say something like "Don't get confused about what we are."

In answer, I reached over and grabbed her phone from the bedside table. We opened the photo app and went back to the first photo from the trip: both of us on the plane, smiling, excited.

"I was still convinced nothing was going to happen between us," I said with a teasing laugh. "But I was starting to think you were pretty cute."

"Jeez…I was already checking out your butt when we went shopping."

"My butt has always driven you crazy, queen. It's your kryptonite."

We scrolled through the next few photos, stopping to analyze and zoom in on our faces, to laugh if we were making weird faces (what she called a psychopath's smile) or our eyes were rolling back. All the memories buried under the sand were being dug up too: the jokes, the people we met in restaurants, whom we gossiped about the way two people wrapped up in each other can, thinking everyone else is weird, Martians, people who don't understand the truth. Our truth. And as we swiped through the photos one after another, Margot was snuggling, finding the perfect fit to my body, like no one had ever done. Her body was letting her be slowly rocked by fatigue, and her laughter was getting weaker.

"These are incredible photos," I mumbled, getting to the last one we had taken that day.

"Too bad you won't be able to appreciate them on your calculator."

"Ha. Ha. Ha. Are you asleep, funny girl?"

"No."

"Of course you're not…" I switched off the light, and she snuggled back into my chest, like a cat looking for the warmth of her litter.

"I'm not sleeping," she complained with a thick voice when I moved.

"Okay."

"I'll make you a photo album," she promised, drifting off a little more with each syllable.

"Sleep…" I whispered, kissing her hair.

Her throat made a little gurgle of pleasure when she found her position on her side. Her ass nestled right into the space between my legs. I stroked her arm and replayed the memories we'd had since we arrived. The people we were then, the people we were tonight. Who I thought Margot was, who she really seemed to be, who now I wouldn't know…

The sadness and anxiety about our looming farewell lashed my chest again. Yes, sex is much easier. But it becomes pretty damn difficult when you fall in love with the complicity and pure intimacy born from it. Would it ever happen to me again?

"If I had gotten hard," I whispered.

"I know," she responded.

"I'm actually a little hard now."

"I know, but your masculinity crisis isn't my problem."

And with a huge smile, we drifted. We slept.

46

~~~

"DO IT, AS IF YOU DON'T KNOW IT'S ENDING"

MARGOT

Maybe it wasn't the right song, but "Como Si Fueras a Morir Mañana" by Leiva started playing in my headphones as the plane took off for Madrid from the Athens airport. And I couldn't help starting to make some calculations that did not go well, by the way. I hadn't heard from my sisters for days because, honestly, I was over them; even though I knew I needed this time for myself and that distance had been a salve to my anxiety, I couldn't help but feel some regrets. We are brought up to take care of everyone else without taking care of ourselves, even though that's a contradiction in itself. Without an "I," an "us" is impossible.

Us. Like that photo David had posted on his profile. Our shadows projected on the sand of an already beautiful beach when the sun was starting to set and there was almost no one left there. "Us." As if that "us" were not a nice lie to tempt us, as addictions do, to believe that it wouldn't hurt us in the long run. That us existed, of course, but like ghosts or magic, if we didn't believe in it, it would eventually disappear.

No, that song was not the right one to scare away fear and

sadness. "Do it, as if you don't know it's ending." The lyrics in the song perfectly described our predicament.

Beside me, David was dozing with his headphones on, probably playing some song I would have no clue about, written and performed more than thirty years ago.

David and his songs from the eighties. David and his flowers. David and his black bathing suit. David and his way of arching when he was on the edge. David and his puffy eyes when he woke up. David and everything that would no longer be by my side and I couldn't even wish for.

I made a mental list of the things I had to face in the coming days, and when I realized how long it was, I was tempted to order a drink from the flight attendant:

- Figure out why the hell I was so terrified at my own wedding.
- Talk to Filippo.
- Fix (or do everything humanly possible to try to fix) things with the board.
- Get back to work.
- Talk Patricia down about this crazy idea that Alberto was cheating on her.
- Talk to Candela about my suspicion that she had made my apartment her base camp without any apparent intention of leaving.
- Do all of the above without David.

I buried my head in my hands when I realized that I had no idea what I would say to Filippo about our future. I didn't know what I wanted, where I saw myself in five, ten, twenty years. The board, full of those brave businessmen whom Mama respected so much, would never respect me or accept my position within the company. I would always be "the heiress" with no more merit than being born with a last name. Back in the office...would the gossiping have died down by now? I didn't blame them. I mean, your boss running out on their wedding day is juicy gossip. What the hell was really going on with Patricia? She always needed to be the center of attention, but...so much that she would just make something up? And Candela...how long had she been in Spain? Did she really have that much vacation time? Was all that really my problem? David.

"Hey..."

Fingers gently pulled the earbud out of my left ear, and when I looked at him, he gave me a sleepy smile.

"What's going on?"

"Nothing," I lied.

"Hey..." He brushed his thumb over my bottom lip. "You and I don't lie to each other."

"It's just that...I'm overwhelmed." I sighed.

"About what's waiting for you?"

"Yes."

"Can I give you some advice? I don't know if it'll be worth much coming from someone who lives on his best friend's couch, but..."

"Spit it out."

"Don't rush it. One step at a time. Figure out what you want to solve and what isn't worth the effort. Giving up isn't always for cowards; sometimes brave people know when to cut their losses. Nobody expects you to be efficient enough to solve all this in one fell swoop. Nobody expects you to be perfect."

"Yes, they do."

"Then they're idiots and egotists." He smiled.

"I don't know if I can fix everything at work based on your advice."

"We always have the option of running away without telling anyone."

"And they can search for us forever."

"One day someone will say they thought they saw us selling coconuts on the beach."

I wanted to kiss him, but I assumed our "us" had stayed behind in Athens, in the kiss we shared before we boarded. I just gave him a thank-you. And my hand. I held out my hand hoping he would take it. And he did. I wished he would never give it back.

~~~~~~

The Adolfo Suárez Madrid Barajas airport was still leading its fast-paced life, oblivious to the turn mine had taken. Over the loudspeaker, they announced that no announcements were made over the loudspeaker, in one of those unspeakably tender contradictions you sometimes find in the world. And while David and I waited for our bags, passengers from a flight from New York finished collecting theirs. Outside the terminal, a bunch of very swanky teenagers were standing by the check-in counters, ready for the study trip they had longed for. Some would come back in love. Others heartbroken. I wondered which group David and I belonged in as he cracked his neck and talked on the phone.

"Don't worry, I have keys. I was just asking in case you wanted me to pick up Ada from your mother's house." He turned back to look at me and winked. "Oh, okay, okay." A pause, where he raised his eyebrows and pressed his lips together in a face for my benefit. "No, no way, Domi. I'm exhausted. I'll just grab something for dinner on my way home and then go to bed. But don't tell your mother I don't want to go because I know you. In less than half an hour, she'll be pounding on the door with Tupperware in her hand, calling me a rascal."

I was filled with envy. What a warm world. I peeked at my phone discreetly. Nothing.

"I can't wait to see you all either. Kisses to all three of you. Margot says hi."

He hung up and slid the tiny phone into the pocket of his jeans.

"Were they already waiting for you with a plan?"

"Domi's mother's cooking is the bomb, and she says she loves seeing someone lick their plate clean like I do. But I don't feel like it today. I'm tired."

"We went to bed early last night," I said, knowing what he was going to answer.

"Oh, yeah. It would've been a long night of restful sleep if you hadn't woken me up at three in the morning with my cock in your mouth."

I smiled mischievously. I loved hearing him remember my feat out loud as much as I had liked waking him up in the middle of the night with a blow job. *The last blow job*, I told myself when I opened my eyes with a desperate sorrow in my chest. Do as I say, not as I do.

"If I'd known, I would've let you sleep," I retorted.

"You're the one who didn't wanna do it like animals when I suggested it, and now look…we were up the whole night. Every minute of it…" He side-eyed me and then directed his eyes back to the baggage conveyor belt that was finally creaking into action. "Doing all those things…"

"I don't remember a thing," I whispered. "And you say I was there?"

"Judging by the way you were grabbing my hair and moaning, it seemed like you were having a good time."

"Oh, wow…it must be that I only remember you growling behind the bathroom mirror."

"Were you left hungry?" He raised his eyebrows, looking at me.

"No. I ended up with my mouth pretty full."

David moved his tongue around inside his cheek while he laughed through his teeth and went over to our suitcases. Another perk of traveling business class…the luggage usually came out quickly.

"How are you getting home?" I asked.

"On the metro. You?"

"Someone's coming to pick me up."

The way his eyebrows shot up didn't get past me.

"I ordered a car," I clarified.

"Oh. I thought…"

"Hey…it would be no trouble for me to tell him to make two stops. Can we drop you at your house?"

His brow furrowed, and he shook his head.

"That'd be really out of your way. Shit…" He made a face. "I don't even know where you live."

"On Paseo de Castellana."

"Wow, look at the duchess," he teased.

"I'm not in any rush to get home."

"Me either."

We stood there frozen, not managing to leave the terminal. My phone beeped, and I glanced at it. It was a message from Sonia:

Filippo's assistant called me to check your schedule. I told her that you'll be back tomorrow and I can't disclose anything else without talking to you. I figured that you probably need time. If I did the wrong thing, let me know, and I'll call her back.

I typed quickly:

Thanks. You're the best.

"So what then?" I sighed, looking up at him.

"Filippo sends his assistant to talk to yours?"

"You know reading other people's messages is rude?"

"I couldn't help it. My eyes have a mind of their own."

"Well, yes. Our assistants talk a lot. It's easier that way. There are days when I don't even know what I have planned, and it's simpler if Sonia puts it on my schedule, and we make sure I don't take on too much."

"If you were with me, I would make sure you remembered to see me without needing a schedule."

In my head, an image appeared of a warm kitchen full of fruit bowls and utensils hanging on the walls, recipe books, opening onto a room full of paintings, with the walls painted a warm tan color and plants everywhere. David handing me a cup of coffee before wrapping his arms around my back and whispering in my ear, "I'll pick you up at half past six, my love."

I swallowed. He bit his lip.

"So am I giving you a ride?"

"Okay."

When Sonia sent one of the company cars to pick me up at the airport, she usually called Emilio. He was a kind, discreet, and sweet man who had two adult daughters (one of them was my age) and a lot of jokes; he always dropped a few, like it was as simple as "Good morning," when I looked worried during the journey. I was glad he was the one who picked us up. I didn't even think about how weird it would seem to him to take another boy with us…another boy who wasn't Filippo.

"Hi, Emilio. Do you mind if we drop my friend David off at his house? We just ran into each other when we got off the plane," I hurried to add, just in case the lie was worth anything.

"Of course not, Miss Ortega."

David shot me a look and raised one eyebrow.

"Leave the bags with me and go ahead and get in. I'll be right with you," Emilio said.

"Don't worry about it. I'll carry my own," David offered.

"Ah, no, no."

I left them arguing over who would load the bags and got in the car. David appeared a few seconds later.

"This isn't a Cabify," he whispered.

"No. The company has cars available for some of the executives."

"And you're one of those executives, right?"

"Yes." I nodded.

"What's your address, sir?"

David smiled.

"Sir…" He repeated mockingly. "Don't worry about it. Just drop me at Margot's house. I'll make my own way from there."

"Don't be silly. What do I care if get home in twenty minutes instead of half an hour?" I insisted.

"You don't want me to see where you live?" He raised one eyebrow again.

"That's not it."

"Well, then I'll get out at your house."

Shit. I'd have to explain a few things to him about my life that hadn't mattered over the last few weeks.

"Hey, where are you going to look for a new apartment?" I asked. "What neighborhood do you like?"

"Well…wherever I can afford. Maybe Oporto. I like Carabanchel. There's a brewery near there I have to take you to; they make their own beer and…"

Plans. Plans that I didn't know if we'd be able to carry out.

Emilio insisted on taking our bags out of the car, but David asked him to please leave it to him. When I said goodbye to the chauffeur with a wave and a smile, David said he was his father's age.

"I don't know about Emilio, but sometimes my dad's back kills him."

"You're…" I smiled.

"Normal," he quipped.

He leaned on the handle of his suitcase and fidgeted, toeing invisible pebbles with his black Converse. We had to say goodbye.

"Well…um…I'm not very good with words, but…thank you," he started to say without looking at me.

"For what?"

"For the trip." He glanced at the lobby. "You live here?"

"Yes. You don't believe me or what?" I smiled.

"Fuck, Margarita…" He whistled. "I don't know what the apartment's like, but the lobby looks like a museum."

"Don't exaggerate."

He raised his eyebrows in a clear attempt to say wordlessly that he wasn't exaggerating at all. No. He wasn't. The lobby looked like the mausoleum of a line of rich landowners or something.

"So thanks for the trip," he repeated. "Even in my wildest dreams I never thought I'd stay in those kinds of hotels or go to islands like that. You've been...really generous. I know this is all probably normal for you, but it was a luxury for me. Really. Thank you."

"Same to you."

"To me? For what exactly?"

"For the company."

"Ah..." He gave a crooked smile.

"And for recommending those songs. I'm not planning on thanking you for the sex."

"Wow. That was the part I put the most effort into."

"One doesn't give thanks for an orgasm." I smiled too, slyly. "But if you want I'll send you some chocolates."

"Very polite."

He licked his lips. He didn't want to leave. I wanted him to stay.

"Um...a goodbye hug?" He opened his arms wide.

I glanced around. One of my neighbors was on her way out, clutching her Birkin, with her perfect manicure, a bouffant hairstyle that rivaled the Petronas Towers, and a stare fixed on us.

"I'm going to sound like a snob and a half, but do you mind if we hug upstairs?"

"In your apartment?"

"A neighbor's on her way out."

"So?" His brow furrowed.

"The people who live in this building don't think of a hug as a simple show of affection. If we hug in front of this lady, it'll be in *¡Hola!* tomorrow."

"Should I pretend to be carrying your bags?" he asked.

"Are you stupid?"

I grabbed my suitcase and took my keys out of my purse. The neighbor came out and was still staring at me pretty impertinently. It's something I've never understood about this class that David says I belong to: so much finesse, so much primness…and yet still capable of displaying so much disdainful rudeness.

"Good morning, Madame Pitita."

"Good afternoon, you mean. Have you just arrived from a trip?"

"Yes."

"A honeymoon, I imagine. Very tan"—she looked me up and down—"but I see that relaxing has made you put on a few pounds. You young girls think once you're married you can let yourselves go. If you don't take care of yourself, he'll leave you in a few years. Is this the lucky gentleman?"

"Goodbye, Mrs. Pitita."

"Ah, he must be the bellhop," I heard her mutter to herself.

"Careful you don't slip, ma'am. It would be a shame if you broke your neck on that last step," David said.

My demonic neighbor didn't have time to answer. By the time she tried, we were already in the elevator, cracking up. Maybe I should have considered the possibility of finding Candela in the kitchen, making poor man's potatoes or something, but that completely slipped my mind because I was with David. I hadn't even told her exactly when I was coming back.

David's jaw dropped when he saw there was only one door on the landing, but he didn't say a word. I don't think he wanted to make me feel uncomfortable by pointing out the difference between the apartment he lived in and my situation. He put his suitcase to one side and waited until I turned around to open his arms. I snuggled up between them and felt…peace. A peace I didn't feel with anyone else.

"Thank you, really," he whispered.

"For the sex?"

"For the blow jobs, above all. You're incredible at them."

"I really am."

We settled into the hug, and he planted a kiss…on my cheek? No. It was my neck.

"Well then, so…I have to thank you for…" I started to say.

"For what?"

"Wait. I'm going to choose a specific moment that I appreciate even more than all the rest."

"I like that."

We squeezed each other a little tighter as we looked at each other, each looking for the other's mouth with our eyes.

"I think…thank you for that afternoon when you went down on me while I was sitting on the edge of the pool in our room in Mykonos."

"The day we fucked on the chair in the living room after?"

"Yes."

"The day you grabbed my neck and licked my mouth," he kept remembering.

I burrowed into his neck as I laughed.

"It sounds pretty outrageous out of context."

"Not more than when I pushed you down to swallow a little more of my cock…"

"And then you turned me around and fucked me on all fours."

"And I came on your stomach while you were fingering yourself and saying…"

"…that I wanted you to come on me…"

I felt his hips against me. At this point, I was panting surreptitiously.

"Do you want to come in?" I asked, without looking at him.

"Please…"

I fumbled with the keys and the lock until the door finally gave way and we both rushed into the hall. We threw aside our suitcases, and I dropped the keys on the round table that took up almost the whole space and whose only purpose was showing off a vase of flowers. Then I literally pounced on him.

He caught me, wrapping me around his hips and searching for my mouth like he was starving and I was offering him a piece of bread. His tongue almost tasted like yogurt and honey to me, like after every dinner over the last few days. David already tasted like something familiar that I knew I would have a hard time losing.

He put me down on the floor because he didn't know which way to go, and I tugged on his hand, leading him into my bedroom, passing by the living room, the office, the guest room, the bathroom and crossing over the living room, the open kitchen, and the dressing room. But I don't think David would have been able to answer if someone had asked him what color the walls were. He only had eyes for me. His mouth was only for me. His hands only wanted to touch me.

We collapsed onto the bed with him under me and his shirt half ripped off. We undressed as much as we could, clumsy but smiling, and then settled back with me on his lap. His mouth ran down my lips, neck, and breast as I slid my nails through his hair.

"One last time…" I proposed.

"Okay." As if he had to be convinced. "Do you have condoms? We finished the second box last night."

"In the bedside table."

"Are they his?" he asked, suddenly serious.

"They're mine."

And I'd never been kissed as passionately as I was then.

David lost his patience unrolling the latex over his cock when he was really horny. He threw his head back as he let out a groan from his young, juicy lips and then checked quickly that everything was in the right place. This time he seemed even more impatient than ever, and he must have been because once he had it on, he yanked my ankle to get me where he needed me. I opened my legs, writhing, but he turned me, got on top of me, and slid me to the edge of the bed. Then he moved so fast I didn't even realize I had changed positions.

His fingers dug into my butt as I began to move on top of him, pulling him in and out of my body. He liked to look for that place where we collided in a struggle to welcome and banish and kept switching his gaze between that, my breasts, and my mouth, but this time he was looking for my eyes.

"I like doing it with you so much…" he murmured.

"Are you going to miss my body?"

"And your scent," he moaned, when I squeezed him inside me. "And that thing you do…"

"Are you going to think about me?"

"All the time, fuck. All the time."

"I would do anything with you," I confessed.

"Let's go…" he moaned again. "Far away. To hell with everything. Let's go somewhere we can do this every day."

I grabbed his face between my thumb and my index finger.

"You want Idoia."

He didn't reply. He just let go of my ass and wrapped his arms tightly around me, pushing and pulling me the way he liked, like a crazy person.

"You want Idoia," I repeated.

"I want to fuck you until I die."

I put my thumb in his mouth, and he licked it while I watched.

"One last time," I said to him.

"Well, then it has to be amazing. Ready?"

He stood up, and then we fell back onto the mattress, with him on top. I saw us in the reflection of one of the mirrors in the room, sweaty, naked, sliding along each other like two enormous serpents fighting to devour each other.

"Make it so I never forget this," I begged him.

He twisted, still thrusting in and out of me, and grabbed my neck with his right hand while he held himself over me with his left.

"Fucking night you came into my club," he groaned. "Now I'm never going to be able to forget you."

We both moaned like a whimper. I saw him swallow. I saw his eyes. He was rabid.

"Don't look at me like that," he begged, planting his forearms on either side of my head. "Don't look at me like that. It makes me want to die."

"Look at you like what?"

"So rabidly."

Rabidly. We both looked at each other rabidly because love is precious, but it doesn't always come the way we want it or when it's the right time. And love, real love, the kind that's free, fun, warm, reassuring, serene, that doesn't flee, that is brave and selfless…that very love, when it doesn't find the right place, awakens rage that lives gagged in the depths of your stomach.

Look…this is the truth, beyond the farewell we promised not to succumb to: people fall in love and fuck every day, every minute, and if you're lucky, a love comes along that gives meaning to all the past ones, not because they weren't love or because a woman can't fall in love as many times as she wants. Only because it's the measure by which things that were previously impossible to calculate make sense. He or she arrives and they understand how you learned to love, what your successes were, your mistakes, how far your pleasure, your greed, your self-love went. And you discover yourself raining inside, splitting in two, drawing out dreams from the depths you didn't even know you harbored, just to be able to share them. And the light pours in. And you understand that the only perfect thing is that which doesn't aspire to be.

Amazing, he said, right? Not really. It wasn't amazing. *Amazing* is the end of a book that leaves you gasping or the song that gives you goose bumps. *Amazing* is the end of a meeting where confetti should be showering from the ceiling because you were incredible. *Amazing* is a kiss you have been craving for a long time or the sincere laugh in answer to someone who hates you too much to care about. For that, for that sex, they'll have to invent a new word. In the Olympics of fucking, of incredible sex, of love incarnate, of the hottest memories, the one that would get a ten in execution, difficulty, duration, strength, dialogue, and intensity. The most melodic piece of music in history performed by the best symphony orchestra in the world. Like the most delicious dessert ever created bitten by the most beautiful mouth.

When I noticed David arching in the way that meant he was ready, I let myself slip down into the abyss so we came at the same time in a shriek of pleasure that made the windowpanes and jars of creams on my dresser shake. And it still took us a couple of minutes to stop because it was like our hips had started a movement that, only through inertia, couldn't stop at our will. I noticed three aftershocks in him, tensing him from head to toe, two for me. I thought I'd have to scratch my skin viciously to stop the jolts of pleasure.

And when everything stopped, the world stopped spinning, and the two of us burst into laughter.

47

~~~

GOODBYE?

David was in his boxers struggling to turn on the stove in the kitchen, and I was watching him delightedly, wrapped in one of my silk robes. Outside, against all odds, it had started to rain, and a beautiful gray light was filtering in through the picture windows overlooking the Paseo de Castellana, one of the main avenues through the center of Madrid.

After the best (goodbye) sex of all time, we had fallen asleep in my bed, and when I woke up, I happened to blurt out that I missed hotel scrambled eggs…and David decided to make me a hotel breakfast at seven thirty in the evening.

"What's the square footage of this place?" he asked while he put the already cracked eggs to one side and figured out, all on his own, that they were gas burners. "Ah, cunt. These are back in fashion…"

"Three thousand," I said through a yawn.

David side-eyed me.

"Three thousand square feet?"

"Yes. It's one of those apartments that used to have rooms and a kitchen for the servants. The previous owners knocked everything down, and an English architect bought it and redesigned the whole thing. I bought it from him."

"Bought?" David's eyebrows were about to merge into his hairline.

"Yes." I nodded.

"Okay." He sucked his teeth, trying not to comment. "I'm not going to ask anything else."

"Ask whatever you want, David, but don't judge me for it."

"Ah no, of course not. If only you had warned me. Hey…don't you have the AC up pretty high?"

"I'm going to turn it off in a bit."

"Or bring me one of those robes like yours," he joked.

"Then you'd look so delicious I'd have to devour you."

"If you're going to devour me like you did not too long ago, please, bring me some kind of restorative tonic."

"That can't happen again. Remember that."

"Yeah, right. Turn off the air."

I went over to the console that controlled the air-conditioning in different areas and switched off all the ones that were on. Then I went to my closet and got another robe, which I slid across the bar to him, and then sat down behind it. He put it on, and I started laughing.

"Do I look handsome?"

"Very handsome."

He stirred the eggs in the pan and glanced over at me.

"I can see your nipples through that robe, and I think I'm getting a boner."

"Simmer down…"

"Can I sleep here?" he asked.

"What are your intentions?"

"To sleep." He smiled. "And eat you out. I didn't do that earlier, and now I'm regretting it. Goodbye, cunnilingus."

"That's goodbye sex, and we promised we wouldn't have it."

"Who cares?" He shrugged, taking a few more things out of the fridge and the pantry. "Hey, why do you have so much food in the fridge when you've been away for two weeks?"

I tensed up, and speak of the devil, a key suddenly scraped in the lock.

"Fuck my life!"

"Who is it?" He dropped the spatula, suddenly pale.

I didn't answer; I didn't have time to explain that the only two people who had keys and who came in without giving a couple of warning knocks were my sister Candela and Filippo. What if Filippo had decided to surprise me at home? What if…?

All I could think to do was shove David into my bedroom, my heart pounding, but…it was too late. The door swung open, and someone came in and saw me throwing him through the double bedroom door.

"Margot?"

"Hi." I smiled, my heart in my throat. "How's it going?"

Candela tossed her bag onto the couch and came straight toward me.

"Who did you just hustle into your bedroom?" she asked with raised eyebrows.

"No one."

"David…" she called out, commandingly. "Come out."

David poked his head out. He was still wearing my robe.

"Ay…" Candela laughed, covering her eyes.

"Want some breakfast?" he offered.

I hadn't noticed, but...he was still holding a frying pan full of scrambled eggs.

He got dressed and set the kitchen island with places for three people, but Candela wisely declined the invitation. She said that she had just come to change her clothes and pick up a few things. I knew that was a lie, so I followed her into the guest room to give her a chance to make fun of me, get mad at me, call me crazy or whatever she came up with in there, out of David's reach.

I leaned against the closed door while she changed her clothes; the sudden summer storm must have caught her in the middle of Castellana, where there aren't many places to take shelter.

"Where are you coming from?" I asked.

"You didn't tell me you were coming back today, ho." She made an excuse while she rummaged through a pile of clothes that looked like a donation pile, looking for pants. "I would've knocked before I came in."

"It doesn't matter."

"You didn't warn me you were coming back and David's here, so I get the impression I interrupted something."

"No way..." I bluffed.

"You forgot I was even staying here, right?"

"Totally." I shrugged.

"Sex takes up a lot of energy."

She put on a shirt that she found discarded on the floor and seemed to find the pants she was looking for in a corner of the room, where I discovered another stash of ugly wrinkled clothes.

"You're not going to say anything to me?"

"What do you want me to say?"

"I dunno. You're always giving me shit when it comes to David. Even though you're such a hippy about everything else"—I pointed at her—"you're still pretty conventional about certain stuff."

"Ah, no." She laughed. "Don't come at me with that shit. I believe in polyamory. I was giving you shit because you had just met him and he could've been a psychopath."

"What about when I told you I was sleeping with him?"

"I was worried about your emotional well-being. But I'm not going to judge you. I'm not Patricia. Or Mama."

"But…"

"But I am older than you and, you can probably understand, I do have doubts. What works for me won't work for you because I need two extra points of security. We don't hold ourselves to the same standards we have for our loved ones. You're my little sister. That's just how it is. But…well, I see you're back safe and sound, and you told me you had agreed that when you came back, it would be the end of this story, so I know how to read between the lines and leave you the house so you can say a proper goodbye."

"No, don't worry, we already…" I smiled like an idiot.

"Gross, Margot." She laughed. "You're a pervert. Poor little guy."

"Tomorrow you might have to help me get rid of the body."

We cracked up.

"What about Patricia?" I asked her.

"You don't need to worry about that right now."

"What about you? When are you coming back?"

"Let's talk tomorrow." She gave me a kiss on the cheek.

"Where are you going to sleep?"

"In the ballroom on the Titanic, obvs." She laughed when she saw my expression. "At Lady Meow's house."

"Stay here, Candela. It doesn't matter… Don't go to Mama's house. We'll be in my room quiet as mice. I promise you."

Candela smiled and pushed a lock of hair behind my ear.

"That's your problem, Margot. You always want to make everyone happy, and you know what? That's impossible. In the end, we all have our own shit, and you…you don't even know what's yours."

She elbowed me out of the doorway and went to stick her head into the kitchen, where David was staring out the window.

"Bye, David."

"You're not staying?"

"No way. My internal clock is not ready for breakfast right now."

"See you soon, then."

"Behave badly. And make a lot of noise." She winked.

"What's she talking about?" he asked me jokingly, pointing at her.

"Ignore her," I advised him.

Candela slipped through the door and disappeared, closing it stealthily behind her, as if she had never been there, interrupting a dinner that had little to do with the farewell we should have been undertaking. It was like when you leave your homework until the last minute. Like when you're afraid to rip off a Band-Aid so you leave it on even longer. Like when you realize your heart is breaking and you hold on a little while longer, dragging the whole ordeal out.

Some scrambled eggs, coffee, avocado toast, and cookies later, David and I were back in bed. And it was a good thing Candela had decided to leave.

～～～

Waking David up made me really sad. If you could see him sleeping, it would make you sad too. He was like a kid who still needed a lot of sleep to grow. It's not that he hadn't had his growth spurt yet; it's just that he seemed so innocent…

"David…" I kissed his neck, kneeling next to his side of the bed. "You have to get up."

"What time is it?" he murmured, his eyes still closed.

"Seven thirty."

"Margot…" he groaned, "it's not even light out yet."

"David…" I perched next to him and held out a very milky cup of coffee, just how he liked it. "You have to get up. Isabel will be here in half an hour, and I don't want her to see you here."

"Who's Isabel?"

"She takes care of the house. And she knows Filippo."

He sat up and blinked and then rubbed his eyes with his fist.

"Okay, okay. Um…is that for me?"

"Yes." I smiled, handing him the mug. "Sorry for the assault."

"What are you talking about?" He smiled. "It's your house. It's normal."

He took a sip of coffee, kissed me on the mouth, and stood up. We both froze.

"I have to stop doing stuff like that," he murmured.

"Um, yes. You really do."

"Do I have time to take a shower?" he asked, pointing at the bathroom.

"Of course. Hey…your phone was going off last night. Messages, I think."

"You're shitting me. I thought I turned the sound off."

He went over to the bedside table and checked his phone. He was right in front of me, still half asleep, super cute, and one part of his body more awake than the rest. He repositioned it with some discomfort and then discovered me looking at him.

"You can't want more. It's physically impossible." He smiled.

"I don't want more."

"Uh-huh. Right." He went back to his phone. "Wanna shower with me?"

"Yes." I nodded vehemently. "But I'm not going to."

He side-eyed me.

"We can shower without doing anything."

"Yeah, right," I teased.

He put his phone back on the bedside table and went into the bathroom. Man, that ass…

"Anything important?" I wanted to know.

I had spent half the night lying awake, wondering if it was Idoia texting him so insistently at three in the morning and resisting the urge to get up and find out. But I had to let go of jealousy. I had to let go of everything about David.

"No. Nothing. I'll tell you in a sec."

I took some sweet buns out of the freezer and heated them up in the oven. When David came out with his hair wet and fully dressed, he didn't waste two seconds shoving one in his mouth.

"What are you doing this weekend? Do you have plans?" he asked me.

"Is getting my act together a plan?"

"No, it's a bummer." He smiled. "What if I suggest one?"

"I probably shouldn't accept."

"As friends."

"I know your 'as friends,'" I spluttered.

"Come on, woman. This plan couldn't be more innocent." He

held up the palms of his hands. "It's one of my best friend's birthdays. I was so caught up in our trip I had completely forgotten about it. She's throwing a barbecue at her parents' house this weekend."

"It sounds so teenager-y, I think I'm going to have to pass."

"We'll spend the weekend in the village. It's less hot out there, her parents have a pool, and my friends are fun people."

"I won't know anyone, David."

"I'm sure they'll adore you, just like I do." He smiled. "Come on… let me show you a little more of my life. If we're going to be friends, you need to meet the rest of the gang."

"And you can just go around inviting randoms?"

"We're very open people. Come. Her parents' house has like two hundred rooms."

"But…will they be there?"

"No way! Cristina's parents have a bar, and they never leave Madrid until it closes in August. Come…it'll be fun."

"I don't know, David."

He pulled his phone out of his pocket and started to text.

"I just said I'm bringing a friend, so now you can't back out."

"David!" I yelped.

"Don't think about it."

"We agreed not to see each other for a month when we came back."

"Well, the month starts on Monday. Come on. I'm leaving." He came over with the half-eaten bun in his hand and looked at me. "I'm going to give you the final kiss, okay? So you can spend the day regretting not lathering up my back while I was in the shower."

"Don't even think about it." I smiled at him.

His lips were sweet, and they left a grain of sugar on mine that I rescued and let melt on my tongue.

"Bye."

"Aren't you working this weekend?"

"Well, no." He turned back to me while he slung his backpack over his shoulder and grabbed his suitcase. "Because I'm going to tell the club to go to hell."

"This trip really did a lot of damage to you. You're all bougie now."

"Go to hell, princess."

He winked. He left. I missed him before he even closed the door.

48

~~~~

FIXING THE DISASTER

Where to begin? Where to start correcting the chain of mistakes I had been making for years? Call Filippo? Call a board meeting to inform them I was back and that I was planning on rejoining the company immediately because I had thirty-seven percent of the shares of the company and I was over this shit? Sell the shares and move to my London apartment? Sell the London apartment too and spend the rest of my life with David on a beach?

I started with my suitcase. It was a cowardly way out, but it also demanded my attention. Isabel was stunned when she came in and saw me putting clothes into the washing machine. It's not like I was one of those girls who thought doing housework was beneath her; I just usually didn't have time (although I know there's time for everything if you're organized).

"But, Margot, leave that. I'll do it now."

"No, no, Isabel. Have a cup of coffee and I'll keep going. I need a task to keep me busy for a little while so I can think."

"But…"

"No buts."

Candela came in midmorning, horrified. Our mother was doing another fast, and she wanted her to do it with her because "you know how it is, we women always have to keep ourselves in better shape than the men so they don't leave us."

"Seriously…if we were in the Middle Ages, I would tell the Inquisition that I saw her invoke the devil. She's so toxic."

"She's an old-fashioned sexist and a fool, but let her be. Did she ask about me?"

"Well, she asked me if I thought Filippo could forgive you for how stupid you are, and she mentioned what a mistake it was to let you study so much."

I snorted. I suddenly had the urge to show up at her house with David and make out with him on her Louis XVI table, which was as hideous as the matching chairs.

"Have you talked to Filippo?" Candela wanted to know.

"I'm going to spend the weekend away," I said, changing the subject.

"Where?"

"In a little village."

Candela looked at me with one eyebrow raised.

"And where is this village?"

"No idea. I think it's in the Avila province."

"With David?"

I grimaced and begged her telepathically not to judge me.

"Okay. Get dressed, come on. We're going to see Patricia."

Okay. So the list of tasks was going to start there.

My sister Patricia lived in a huge chalet north of Madrid, the kind that looked like it was pulled straight from an American interior design show. It had an attic, where she and Alberto shared a beautiful office with wooden beams and skylights that in winter were coated with snow; a finished basement with a game room, laundry room, and gym; and two floors over which five bedrooms and six bathrooms were spaced out. And in those parts, she reigned like the princess in *Frozen*. The ice queen, affectionate, adorable, and beautiful, but never forget that she could freeze your insides with one flick of her hand.

A girl we didn't know answered the door. As a mom, Patricia changed staff constantly. Sometimes she became fixated on silly things, like that they were stealing fabric softener or Alberto was looking at them a lot. It was absurd, but Patricia had the misfortune of having inherited more genes from Mama's side of the family, and just as they had given her splendid beauty, they had also left foolishness in their wake.

We found her in the kitchen, drinking coffee, surrounded by papers with sketches for her jewelry collection and a computer with her website open on the screen.

"Look what the cat dragged in," Candela said.

"Oh, hello," she greeted me coldly, stirring her coffee with a spoon. "You're back."

"Girl, I'm in your kitchen and I don't have the power of teleportation yet, but give me a few more years to practice."

"Ha. Ha. Ha," she enunciated dryly, not looking up at me.

"Is something going on?"

"It's an honor you deigned to grace us with your presence."

"Hey girl, come on!" I complained.

"You know best."

Six months ago, the old Margot would have had two options: leave or kneel down so that Queen Patricia would forgive her with a touch of her scepter to her forehead. But I was aware that fleeing or hanging my head had never brought me good things.

"Patri, you're mad because I didn't return your call, I can see that. But I needed some time."

"And I needed my sister."

"You had Candela," I added, feigning calm and sitting down next to her. "If she'd had to leave, I would have found a way to make sure you weren't alone, but…I needed to get out of here. To breathe. To think."

She side-eyed me.

"I ran out on my wedding, Patricia," I reminded her. "And it probably wasn't fair to avoid you for two weeks but…"

She sighed and put her hand on mine.

"Does that mean you forgive me?" I smiled, looking at her perfect fingers on mine.

"No. It's just that the whole wedding thing makes me sad."

I looked at Candela out of the corner of my eye, and we both smiled.

"Look, Patricia, this is simpler than we think: you were dealing with your mess, and I was dealing with mine. Yours isn't more important, and mine doesn't deserve more attention. We just had to focus on our own shit."

"I have three kids," she groaned.

"I'm not going to get into a competition with you about whose life was more fucked," I warned her. "But if you want to tell me what's really going on…if you want to tell us both, we'll be by your side."

"There's nothing to tell." She stared at the fridge.

"You sure?"

"You dragged me all over Madrid following that detective," Candela pointed out.

"You followed the old man around too?" I said, not hiding my surprise.

"How do you know I switched detectives?"

"Candela kept me updated through messages," I fibbed a little. "Like a travel intermediary. She was Candela Reuters."

"So you answered her?" She shot me her iciest look. "Because you didn't even pick up my calls; you didn't even reply to a single message."

"She didn't answer me," Candela lied.

I took my phone out of my purse, opened our WhatsApp conversation, put it in front of her, and started reading out loud her last few messages.

"'Margot, call me, I'm not okay.' 'Margot, call me.' 'Margot, when are you coming back?' 'Margot, there's stuff going on here, you know?' 'Margot, you're such a narcissist.'"

Patricia shot me a look.

"When you read it like that, I sound like a cunt."

"You seem like a person obsessed with your own situation who hasn't realized that, sometimes, other people need space for their own stuff. To think. To breathe."

She leaned her chin on her fist, looking sullenly at both of us.

"I'm not a cunt."

"No," Candela said, stifling her laughter. "But you're doing some pretty crazy shit even for our family."

"Maybe," she conceded.

"Patricia, what's going on?"

She turned and stood up from the stool.

"Let's go out to the garden."

Patricia's chalet didn't have much land, but it had enough for a perfect, beautiful garden, which served as a gathering place on weekend evenings in the summer, and a small greenhouse, where Patricia pretended to take care of some plants that everyone knew survived thanks to the gardener. She led us straight into that little glass space. It smelled of damp earth, flowers, and summer. It reminded me of David.

Candela sat on some empty pots, and I leaned on a bench full of wilting orchids.

"Patri…these have one foot in the grave, eh?"

When I turned around to look at her, she was lighting a cigarette.

"What are you doing?" I yelled.

"Smoking," she announced.

"You hide tobacco in the greenhouse?" Candela pissed herself laughing.

"Yes. And I come out here to smoke to forget my life. Is that a sin?"

We both shook our heads and our hands when we saw how furious she was.

"So spill…" I decided to grab the bull by the horns. "Are you still paranoid about Alberto cheating on you?"

She shook her head, with her arms crossed, and let out a stream of smoke. Her eyes were glassy.

"If he hasn't seen anything by now, there's no way. The only thing you have to worry about, judging from the photos and the detective's report, is that he eats terribly. Seriously, Patri. Your husband must have mayonnaise running through his veins."

I couldn't help laughing. I thought Patricia was laughing too, but when I looked again, I realized she was stifling a sob.

"But Patricia!"

Patricia *never* cried.

"What's going on?" Candela got scared. "Girl, I've been with you for two weeks, and you wait until the defector comes back to cry?"

"Look who's jealous." I shot her a look. "Typical middle sister."

"Eat my cooter; that's a middle child too."

"Seriously, you're adopted."

I went over to Patricia and tried to hug her, but she pushed me away. We didn't hug much in our family. I surprised myself, wondering what David would do at a time like this. I dragged over an empty flowerpot, turned it upside down, and forced her to sit on it. Then I did the same with another, took her pack of cigarettes, and lit one. Gross. I coughed. She looked at me with her eyes wide open.

"What are you doing?"

"That's what I'm saying," Candela added, coming over.

"Creating an intimate environment. Come on. Tell us. If you know Alberto's not cheating on you…then what's going on?"

Patricia diverted her gaze, and a fat transparent tear slid down her face.

"Well, that's just it…" she said, her voice strangled. "He's not cheating on me."

Candela and I looked at each other confused. I remember what David said when I told him all about it.

"Patricia, do you love Alberto?"

She looked at us and took another drag.

"I love him, but…"

"But…?"

"If he were cheating on me, it would make everything so much easier."

"I'm so lost…" Candela spluttered.

"Shh. Shut up." I punched her in the leg. "Patricia...tell us. It's us. We're a safe space."

Patricia inhaled so hard I'm surprised she didn't suck all the oxygen out of the greenhouse.

"It hasn't been going well for years."

"These things happen."

"Mama told me that we had to go to couples therapy. She said she goes with Lord Mushroom."

"This is surreal," Candela hid her face to laugh.

"The thing is, we went. Poor Alberto would go wherever I said. He's crazy about me..."

Wow...she was all over the place.

"So then what's the problem?"

"The problem is that I realized I don't want this life. I used to want it, but...I don't anymore."

"So then split up."

"I have three kids."

"And I have three gray pubic hairs," Candela added.

"Cande, for the love of God!" I wailed. "Patri, you won't be the first or the last people to split up with three kids. Alberto is a good man, and he loves you enough to understand if you explain it to him."

"It's just that..." Patricia sobbed. "It's just that..."

"It's just that...what?"

She looked up at us, horrified.

"His name is Didier."

My eyebrows shot up.

"Didier..."

"Didier gives Santiago tennis lessons." Santiago is my eldest nephew. "He's from Marseilles. He's twenty-four, and...we're in love."

Candela let out a muffled laugh as I squeaked. It took Patricia about twenty minutes to get it all out. And she did so thoroughly. I never thought I'd hear my sister say things like, "He fucks me in the bathroom at the tennis club so hard it makes me cross-eyed." But hey, that's life. They had a connection. He made her laugh. He had brought back her mojo. She understood how wrong she was when it came to love. But listen, can you imagine the scandal?

Candela and I spent another twenty minutes explaining that scandals, like when you run off from your own wedding, perish in the mouths of people who have no lives of their own. She already said it when it came to my wedding. And anyway, a scandal is better than withering away in a relationship that doesn't make you happy.

So what if our mother was going to cry out to the heavens? So what if it was the talk of the club? All that mattered was that Patricia took accountability for things and didn't keep hurting her husband.

"Alberto's going to be the laughingstock, and...I love him. I respect him. But I just couldn't stop myself. I couldn't, I swear," she said, sobbing uncontrollably.

"Take your time," Candela advised her.

"Forgive yourself."

Candela went into the kitchen and grabbed a bottle of wine and a box of crackers that had Alberto written all over them who, almost certainly, had already sniffed out everything that was happening in his house and had been taking refuge in carbs.

We spent a couple of hours there, drinking, talking, playing it down, and laughing, convinced that maybe our mother was a punishment, but she had given us the greatest thing in life by giving us each other. And in the end, before I even realized, maybe because of the warmth of the red wine on my tongue, I heard myself telling Patricia a story I knew by heart:

"His name is David, he's twenty-seven, and he helped me discover that life is beautiful."

I never felt more supported…except when I was with him.

49

FIXING THE DISASTER (II)

"That's why she was so obsessed with finding out if Alberto was cheating on her. She needed someone else to blame." I sighed. "We've had such shitty values ingrained in us. It's impossible to be free like this."

"Poor thing…" I heard David say on the other end of the phone line. "Minds can be so fucked."

"What?"

"Our heads can beat us up pretty bad," he explained. "Sometimes understanding that we're our own worst enemies can take a whole lifetime. I hope this encourages her to take the first step. Do you think Didier will really want a relationship with her if she leaves everything else?"

"I mean, of course she thinks so, but…he's twenty-four years old. I don't know if all this is gonna be too much for him."

"And is she going to talk to both of them? Her husband and her lover, I mean."

"That's what she says, but she has to get her thoughts organized first."

"I bet the husband already suspects."

"Poor Alberto," I muttered sadly.

The doorbell rang, and I jumped up.

"Are you expecting a visitor?" David asked.

"Not at all. It's not you, is it?" I smiled reflexively.

"I wish. I'm at work." And from the way he said it, I could hear the smile in his voice too.

I glanced through the peephole and was surprised to see a messenger. I couldn't make out what he was holding.

I opened the door.

"Margarita Ortega?"

"Yes."

"Sign here."

A bouquet. A huge beautiful, stunning bouquet with pale-pink roses mixed in with white and green. My heart was racing.

I thanked the messenger and stood there with the bouquet in my arms and the phone pressed to my ear. I was afraid to ask David if it was from him because if it wasn't I would make a fool of myself. I was afraid to not say anything in case it was from him. I was afraid it was from Filippo.

"What'd you get?"

"A bouquet," I answered, closing the door.

"A bouquet?" He sounded surprised. "Is there a note?"

I plucked it out of the flowers, put the bouquet down on the table in the vestibule, and tore the envelope open with clumsy fingers. Yes, there was a note written in English, but nobody had signed it.

Through the storm, we reach the shore.

"Through the storm, we reach the shore," I translated out loud.

"And nothing else?"

"No."

We both fell silent. I swallowed.

"I'll let you go, okay?" David said in a strange tone. "I need both hands to tie a few bouquets."

"Okay."

"I'll see you tomorrow. I'll send you a message when I know what time we're coming to pick you up."

"Fine."

"Great."

We both fell silent again.

"Bye," I said, looking at the bouquet and the note still in my hand.

"Bye."

The doorbell rang again. I mean...

I opened it without looking through the peephole. I don't know why, I was still harboring the stupid hope that it would be David and that when I opened the door, he would say one of his nonsense things, something terribly sensitive disguised as a stupid comment. But no. It wasn't him.

Filippo was standing there. White button-up with the sleeves rolled up. Tan. The top button undone and the light hair on his chest peeking out, like a promise. His endless legs sheathed in navy-blue chinos. His blond hair combed, neat. His eyes bluer than ever.

"Hi," he mumbled. "Did you just get back? My secretary told me that Sonia said you were coming back today."

"Uh...no." I blinked. "I got back this morning." I didn't want to be more specific.

"Can I come in?"

"Of course."

He was staring at the bouquet, and for a moment, I expected to hear him say, "Do you like it?" But he didn't.

"What's with the flowers?" he interrogated me.

"I don't know. They just showed up."

"Who sent them?"

I was waiting to see a glimmer in his eyes that confirmed they were from him, but he seemed genuinely surprised. The bouquet wasn't from him. Which meant…

"Isabel must have ordered them to replace these ones, which are starting to wilt." I shoved the card into my pocket. "Would you like something to drink?"

"Maybe some wine?" he asked with a timid smile.

"Wine, perfect." I returned his smile. "Make yourself at home. It is your home after all."

"It's really always been only yours."

So…this was how we were starting off.

"I thought you liked that about me. That I wanted to maintain some independence. That I didn't feel the need to share everything with you."

"It's not about whether I liked it or not. It's just that I understood it. You're the heiress to a hotel empire. I understood that our marriage wouldn't have… How do you say it…?"

"Marital property." I rounded the island and reached for a bottle of wine from the wine rack, and when I pulled the opener from a drawer, I remembered David nervously opening that bottle in Santorini before he kissed me for the first time.

I was kind of dazed and forgot to ask Filippo (for the millionth time) not to refer to me in those terms, mainly because Patricia still owned seventeen percent of the company and, on top of that, it made me feel like a social parasite who hadn't earned her position. But I was too busy struggling to erase the scene of broken glass and French kisses that was playing in my head, straight from memory.

"How've you been?" I managed to ask.

"Very lonely without you."

I looked up. The force of Filippo's beauty smacked me in the face. It was solid, like a sturdy effigy sculpted a thousand years ago. Handsome, huge, and imposing. The Iron Man of fiancés, David had said. To be honest, next to him, David would seem like the protagonist of a movie about prom kings. Handsome…but young. Too young?

"You look great," I said, looking away.

"I relaxed. I sunbathed. I didn't do much besides swim, think about you, and sleep."

"You must have done something else." I smiled sadly.

"I got drunk a few times, to be fair. But do you really want to hear about all that, even the embarrassing parts?"

I grabbed two glasses from the cupboard and slid them over the bar. I suddenly felt so sad…

I poured the wine and sat on one of the stools, opposite him.

"Should we toast?" I asked.

"To the truth."

Jeez. Great, exactly the opposite of what I felt like toasting. I gently clinked my glass against his.

"How was your trip?"

"I don't know what to tell you," I confessed.

"Wasn't it illuminating?"

"Sometimes. Others… I think instead of finding myself more, I went in the other direction."

"They say that the more we know ourselves, the emptier we feel."

"Well, they must be right."

Filippo held out his hand, reaching for mine. I looked at his long tan fingers. He had very manicured hands, elegant, soft…like those of a man who has never done any more manual labor than sailing for a summer.

"Why?" he said quietly.

"Filippo…"

"I need to know."

"I know how much it must have cost you to swallow your pride and come here to ask me that, but…"

"It's not a question of pride."

"I jilted you at the altar in front of five hundred people. If it weren't a question of pride, I'd be worried."

"Seriously, why?" And his soft, familiar accent made me ask myself the same thing for the umpteenth time.

"Maybe there wasn't a reason. Maybe it just… Everything became too much for me."

"What is 'everything'?"

"Well…" I lifted my glass by the stem. "That huge, perfect wedding, the demands on me that I was obsessed with, and my idea that…well, that I'm not enough for a guy like you."

"That's just in your head."

"Maybe, but it is in my head. Accepting that is the first step." I took a sip. It was hard to look him in the eye. I was mortified. Less than twenty-four hours, before I had been making love to another guy in our bed. Although was it ours? It was mine. That much I was sure of at least. "Tell me something, Filippo…were you happy with me?"

"Of course I was happy with you. If I hadn't been, why would I have asked you to marry me?"

"You wouldn't change anything about what we had?"

"What we had? Margot..." He sounded so insecure he didn't even seem like himself.

"I mean it. You wouldn't change anything about the way it was?"

"Your mother?"

We both smiled. I heard my phone vibrate on the table in the entrance hall, and I wondered if it was Patricia with news.

"You're obviously asking me that because you've reached the conclusion that you weren't," he countered.

"No. I was happy with you, Filippo." I finally looked up at him. "But I wasn't with myself, I don't think. I felt very small next to you. I think I still feel that way."

"What do we need to change, Margot? Tell me. Because I spent almost a month without you, and honestly, I don't even want to picture what doing that for the rest of my life would be like. And I know I was hard on you and about us, and I'm aware that I said things to hurt you...like that you were my ex even though, as hard as I tried, I never stopped thinking about how much I loved you..."

Seriously...conversations about relationships with an Italian are totally complicated.

"Filippo...what if I'm not like that?"

"Like what?"

"Like I was. Dying of fear like this, always worried about everyone else's opinion."

"Yes, you are like that." He smiled. "It's one thing if you want to leave me because I don't make you happy. But that's what I'm here for, right? To complete those pieces of you that try to stop you from being happy. That's what you're there for too, right? To make me better. That's what couples do. A puzzle that complements each other."

I looked at him, not knowing what to say.

"Tell me…what did you do in Greece?"

Made love. Felt free. Walked on the beach half naked. Cracked up.

"The usual," I answered.

"You took a really important step going alone."

My inner villain rolled her eyes and laughed silently. The normal Margot blushed all the way to her ears.

"Well. Um…what about you?"

"You already asked me that." He smiled. "You're nervous. Calm down, Margot…it's me. Just tell me…what do you want? How do you want to fix this?"

Filippo was a good man; I knew that from practically the first moment I met him. He was caring, attentive, understanding. But I never would have imagined him coming back and asking me that after I left him at the altar. He was proud, a little haughty…traditional to the core in family matters. Maybe…maybe the plan that David had outlined for me to get Filippo back had actually been one to turn me into a freer person; maybe that had scared Filippo enough that he believed I could take steps without needing him at all. But…is love about necessity at the end of the day? Or something much bigger?

For years I had resigned myself to the idea that, for him, my job was an obstacle to creating the family he wanted. Filippo wanted three or four children, to summer in Italy, and to retire as young as possible in Tuscany. Or in Málaga, he sometimes said. But he fell in love with me and accepted that might never happen because I wouldn't quit my job or reduce my hours and, after the way I grew up, I wouldn't let someone else raise my children for me. He settled for the lite version of his dream: a couple of kids at most and short trips to see his family, where I would lug along my laptop and my work phone.

Maybe, when I thought that Filippo was too proud to overcome this, I hadn't stopped to think about how he had already left behind some dreams for me and that he would make more concessions if it meant not losing me.

They were all maybes. No certainties. And what about me? What did I want?

"What if I don't want to have kids?" I asked.

"You don't want to?"

"I don't know." I shrugged. "Not right now."

"Okay." He nodded. "We'll talk about it. We can freeze eggs and think about it later. It doesn't matter."

"Actually, I'd be the one freezing them," I replied smoothly. "The royal *we* doesn't work for everything."

"Okay." He spread his two big hands out on the marble counter. "We're getting into a stalemate. Maybe...maybe we're taking this all too fast. Maybe we need to mentally settle back in before we do this."

I took another sip.

"Why don't we see each other on Monday?" he proposed. "We can have dinner at that restaurant you like so much, the one in Velazquez...and we'll talk. Spend that time thinking about how you want your life to be, where you see us in a few years. We'll find a way."

"To tell the truth..." I started to say, "I never thought you'd be this open to reconciliation after what I did."

"That's because you never believed I was crazy in love with you." He stood up. "I'm going. Will you walk me out?"

"Of course."

We looked like the dot and the *I*, as Candela always called us. He was six foot five, and I was barely five foot seven. It made me laugh to think about how we looked from the outside, and I smiled.

"You're different," he said when we reached the door. "It's hard to believe it's only been a month. You seem like you've been on a retreat in India for a year."

"Now you're making fun of me." I smiled.

"No. It's true. You're different. Like you've, I don't know, grown up."

"I'm still stumpy next to you."

"But that was never a problem."

I hardly had time to think about it; in the blink of an eye, Filippo was kissing me. And I'm not going to lie; his kiss tasted like home, love, dreams, a life I still wanted to have, halfway between my aspirations and his longings. I couldn't throw it all away.

When the kiss ended, I felt a warmth in my chest that reminded me of so many things...our first kiss, that trip we took to Paris, Sunday mornings, the first time he introduced me to his family, the house of our dreams, the excitement we felt planning our honeymoon, his hands on my hips when we made love, the Vietnamese food on Thursdays...

"I'll make a reservation for Monday, okay?" He smiled. So handsome. So perfect...

"Yes."

"See you Monday."

I waited until I saw him disappear into the elevator to close the door, and when I did, I instinctively clutched my chest and smiled. Filippo made me feel safe, calm, at home, without fear. He was a protector. Everything was peaceful.

I picked up my phone on the way to the kitchen and checked it. I stopped dead before I got to the countertop, where we had left our half-drunk glasses of wine, reading the message I had gotten while I was talking to Filippo.

It was from David.

The values they ingrained in you aren't chains. You're free, Margot. I've seen you be. You wear armor made of prejudice against yourself, but you don't let it touch your skin. But it's only a matter of time before it weighs you down too much and you decide to take it off. Remember, you don't need anything or anyone to complete you. You are a whole universe yourself. The bouquet has field lilies, mastic, eucalyptus, roses, sea lavender and bouvardia. The line on the card is from a U2 song, "With or Without You." My English is bad, but Google is always right.

The warmth Filippo had left in my chest exploded into a ball of fire.

50

~~~

THE WEEKEND.
THE PASSION.

"I don't know if I should go."

David didn't say anything, and the silence on the line was deafening.

"I don't know if I should, David," I repeated to try to get an answer out of him; I don't know if I wanted him to accept that it wasn't a good idea or to desperately insist that I come with him to the village that weekend.

"I thought you had already decided. What's the problem?"

"Everyone's going to think I'm your girlfriend."

"I couldn't care less what they think."

"They're your friends. Of course you care what they think. Plus, I don't think we know how to act like colleagues."

"Yes, we do know how," he responded in a much less certain tone.

I climbed back into bed, curled up, and clutched the phone. By the door, my closed travel bag reminded me that not too long ago I had thought the opposite. I was a mess. The bouquet, the note, the farewell, Filippo, the smell of David permeating my pillow.

"What's going on? Come on…tell me," David cut to the chase.

"You already know." I reminded him. "We should stop making plans. We're delaying the inevitable."

"Well, we already agreed we'd start our detox on Monday, right?"

"When you say it like that, I feel awful," I grumbled.

"Is this because of my friends? You don't want to meet them?"

The unspoken plea behind his question broke my heart. I remembered him complaining that Idoia never wanted to hang out with them and how insecure that made him feel.

"That's not why." I promised him. "It's just…"

"Everyone'll think you're my girl, okay, but…so what?"

"We'll be sleeping in the same bed and…"

"We're not animals, Margot." He teased. "There are tons of bedrooms in Cristina's parents' house. You can sleep alone if that's what's bothering you."

How could I explain all the things that were really worrying me in a way he would understand? When I wasn't even capable of compiling, organizing, and facing them myself?

"Please…" he said quietly. "Please, Margot. I want this weekend."

Yes. I wanted it too, but…we shouldn't have.

~~~~~

They picked me up at six thirty in the evening in a bright-yellow three-door Ford Fiesta from the Middle Ages. When he rolled down the window and smiled, I realized that David could make a girl used to luxuries forget everything except the company. I walked over and smiled.

"Please tell me this thing has AC."

"Who do you think we are? There's no princess without her carriage."

David and I stared moony-eyed at each other until the guy driving cleared his throat, which snapped David out of it.

"Margot, this is Felix. We've been friends since preschool."

"Hi, Felix! How's it going?"

"Nice to meet you, Margot. David's told us all about you."

"Oh, yeah?" I smiled.

"Yes! He wouldn't stop sending photos of your trip. It pretty much felt like we were there with you guys."

David grabbed my stuff a little awkwardly and went to load it into the car.

"Hop in. It's gonna take us a while to get there."

~~~~~

When we pulled up, everyone was already there. Cristina, the birthday girl, greeted us with two kisses and cold beer. As I introduced myself and apologized for showing up so last-minute, a pack of very funny girls jumped all over each other and recited their names quickly (Rocio, Marta, Laura, Esther, Maria). It didn't take me long to realize I had somehow become something of a spectacle. Who was this girl David had gone to Greece with who was now showing up at Cristina's birthday? Where did she come from? And, most importantly, was she going to become part of the gang?

David was clearly an essential part of the group, which all his friends made obvious by pouncing on him, hurling him onto the grass, and showering him with kisses, tickles, and screams. I looked on, not sure what to do, feeling a little out of place and trying to soothe the jealousy burning in my gut. Those girls didn't have to distance themselves from him like I did. Those girls would have him their whole lives. It was hard not to wonder what I would have left of him in a couple of years…maybe nothing more than a nice memory.

The rooms on the first floor were already taken, so we had to leave our stuff in the attic, where something told me it would be hotter than the rest of the house. I almost wished they did think we were a couple and needed the privacy of our own room because…there were three beds crammed into the space, and Felix didn't hesitate to dump his bag on one of them before he disappeared downstairs in search of the rest of the gang and something to eat.

"Everything okay?" David wanted to know, as he opened his bag and took out his bathing suit.

"Yeah. I mean…it's all a little weird, but they seem nice."

"We'll have a good time, you'll see."

Before I could add anything, he unbuttoned and unzipped his jeans. I raised my eyebrows.

"You weren't going to change here, right in front of me?"

"It's my room, and I want to go for a swim." He smiled mockingly. "Plus it's nothing you haven't seen before."

I raised my eyebrows while he pulled off his shirt. In a few minutes, the bed could be covered in clothes and all the control we were making such a show of could be out the window. I could go over, kiss his neck, stroke his chest, and pull my dress up in a silent invitation that he would take advantage of by letting his hand run…

"I better go and let you have some privacy." I interrupted my own reverie. "There are things that, as a friend, I'd prefer not to see."

~~~~~

I couldn't complain. They treated me like the guest of honor. They were friendly, attentive, and familiar. They made me feel, very quickly, like part of what had united them for so many years. They were like him—warm and funny—and they didn't seem to care that I had just appeared in their lives. My visit wasn't an intrusion but something natural. David laughed with his mouth open and patted his friends as he made sure I was part of every conversation. He didn't leave me alone for a second, although after a couple of beers I stopped feeling out of place when I wasn't glued to his side. It was one of those nights when everything seems magical, even when you're eating highly processed tortilla and potato chips. I was having fun in a way I hadn't in a huge group of people in a long time. So... this was what having friends was like, huh?

Of course, everyone wanted to share something about David that "he definitely hadn't told me." In a little while, all his dirty laundry was being waved around in both hands, like how he used to have very long hair or that his brother-in-law once slapped his ass in front of everyone because he confused him for his sister.

"People drink a lot in the villages," he made excuses with an embarrassed face. "As you're about to find out."

~~~~~

After eating a little and toasting a lot, at one thirty in the morning, everyone decided it was time to go down to the plaza, which I soon discovered was a small space where five streets converged and where what seemed to be the busiest bar in town was located. They were celebrating the week of patron saint festivities and had set up a bar outside to serve the clientele clamoring for drinks. A stage for an orchestra took up at least thirty percent of the plaza, and everyone was crowding around a man who was selling something.

"What's going on?" I asked David.

"Bingo," he smiled. "Welcome to the independent republic of my village. Before the dance, they raffle off a ham. But don't bother buying a ticket, Esther wins every year."

All David's friends went to buy a few tickets. Apparently it was tradition to buy the tickets behind Esther's back and tell her over and over that this year didn't seem like her year. Before we could find out whether it was, David seemed to recognize someone in the crowd.

"Give me a second?" he whispered in my ear. "I'll be back in two minutes."

"Where are you going?"

But he didn't answer. He blew me a kiss with a mischievous grin. He was disheveled, his clothes rumpled, and his eyes red…a little drunk after all the toasts. How could he be so handsome? How could someone I just met seem so trustworthy? How could I long so much to hold his hand and tell the rest of the world to go to hell?

"What you're trying to do is impossible." I said out loud to myself.

Pretending we were just friends was impossible. It was obvious even to me that every time I blinked, handfuls of hope poured from my eyes, like glitter.

I looked over to where David had gone and saw him go up to a woman who smiled derisively at him and then gave him a big hug and the universal gesture of "You're gonna get it." Who was this beautiful woman? Brown hair pulled back in a ponytail, huge eyes with very little makeup, and a small thin body. There was a certain resemblance between them and something in the way they embraced that made me feel at home.

"Want a drink, Margot?" one of his friends egged me on.

"Of course."

The open-air dance started with *paso dobles* and stuff like that. Everyone was lively, old and young, in the typical festive and homely atmosphere of small towns where everybody knows your name. Esther was really busting a move…with her ham, and when David came back to us we became part of the dancing body, clinging to each other, laughing, clumsy and mocking. And the group of neighbors must have liked how we danced because as we passed by they would throw out an "Olé" and a smattering of applause.

As the clock ticked down, the older ones retired, and the younger crowd demanded a different kind of music. Some salsa song, halfway between the present and the past, was playing when David waved goodbye to the woman he had greeted when he arrived.

"Is that your sister?" I asked him.

"It's my darling mother." He smiled. "But she'll be thrilled you thought she was my sister. Next year'll be her fiftieth birthday."

"She had you when she was twenty-two?"

"And my sister at sixteen. Scandalized?"

I raised an eyebrow.

"Please, David. You'd need a little more than that to scandalize me."

"Not much more. If I told you I'd be licking you for hours, that'd do the trick."

And it did. He did.

David was even more fun when he was with his friends. He soon forgot that he didn't like reggaeton and started twerking with all his friends until they yelled at him that he was scaring away all the suitors. And he laughed like I had never seen him laugh. Relaxed. Happy. Gamboling around. Holding my arm and spinning me around. Watching David singing and dancing to "There Goes the Fireman" was traumatic but also a lot of fun. Apparently…another tradition because he had very drunkenly danced to it with Jose's aunt a few years ago.

It only took two more drinks before I was twerking to songs I had never heard before, and it soon became obvious that David and I weren't ready to control what we felt.

When the orchestra finished, a DJ took over the decks to play more music until five thirty in the morning, and people seemed to keep coming out of the woodwork. It was then, amid all the chaos, that I felt David's hand on my belly, pulling me into him. I knew he was smiling without having to look back. His hips pressed against me, and he led me to the beat of the music, grinding too close to just be friends. I didn't complain, in case anyone was wondering.

"You look beautiful," he whispered in my ear.

"I'm disgusting." I looked down at myself, speckled with Cuba Libres, which kept splashing onto me as people bumped into each other, on my simple black shirt and one of the skirts I bought with him, floral with slits up the side.

"Well then, let's go home and you can change. I'll go with you."

"Are you an idiot?" I turned back to look at him.

"I can be whatever you want if it means seeing you without clothes." He waggled his eyebrows.

"You're drunk."

"The last time I was drunk I told you I wanted to eat you out for hours."

I turned, smiling, and covered his mouth. He licked my hand, and I let go.

"Shut up!"

"I'm just reminiscing. You and me are just friends. Friends who sleep in separate beds."

"Yes." I nodded, looking at his mouth while I threw my arms around his neck.

"Don't look at me like that." He laughed, showing his perfect white teeth.

"I'll look at you however I can."

"However you want. You could look at me a little closer."

"I couldn't. We can't."

"No," he said, and he pouted as he danced. "We can't hold hands, run down that street back there behind the stage, and make out against the wall of the old bakery. That would be...well...crazy!"

"Of course it would." I pressed myself into him and stroked his face until my thumb was under his lips and we were dancing so close not even light could fit between us. "Because our fling is over."

"Right. The last time was pretty good, eh?"

"And the one before."

"Fuck..." He was staring at my mouth, and his hands were on my hips until they suddenly slipped down and grabbed my ass. "Fuck, I like you so much."

"David..."

"You know what kills me?" he asked, leaning down to my ear. "I don't just want to fuck you in the middle of the street. I want to hold you after. And that, dear Margot, is a drag."

I took a step back with a knot in my stomach, but he didn't let go. "What?"

"Nothing." I shook my head, trying to make him let go.

"Like I believe that..." His mouth twisted into an understanding smile. "Should we think about this all tomorrow?"

"No. You said it yourself. It's a bummer."

"So what are we gonna do? It can't happen."

David bit his lip and raised his eyebrows while he reached for my hand and tugged on it a little, trying to lead me out of the crowd of people dancing and drinking.

Let's go, I read his lips.

I intertwined my fingers through his, and we ducked down so we wouldn't be seen as we circled the crowd and snuck into the alley behind the plaza. We didn't drop each other's hands until we turned the corner and the darkness of the alley enveloped us, and when we did, it was just so we could entangle them elsewhere. Mine went straight to the back of his neck and his lower back. His to my waist and my right butt cheek, under my skirt through one of the slits in the fabric.

I didn't close my eyes when he kissed me. He didn't either. We didn't want to miss anything. The outdoor disco had changed to rock, and the song drifted over to us, muffled by the walls and the streets: "Use Somebody" by Kings of Leon.

"We said we should stop this," I let out between the fourth and fifth kiss.

"What if I can't?"

"You can, but you don't want to. You said…"

"I said, I said, I said."

Yes. He said if we didn't stop, we'd end up falling in love, and it would be a disaster. He said he didn't want to find out if our relationship could make it past two years. He said.

He grabbed my thighs and lifted me up to push my back against the wall while biting my neck; I realized he was trying to pull down my underwear and saw that just a few feet to the right of us, there was the door to a house.

"David, what if the neighbors come out?"

"They're not going to come out."

"David…what if they come back from the festival and find us here?"

He looked at me and smiled.

"It's my house. They're all asleep."

My panties went down a little farther, and I hurried to unbutton his pants. With that explanation, all my walls of resistance had crumbled. I went crazy. I had never done anything like that on the street and…fuck, I wanted to do it as much as I wanted to dismiss those boundaries that at this hour seemed so silly to me. So what if we fell in love, so what? Weren't we already?

I touched his cock under his boxers and pulled it out. As I stroked him, I provoked him with the most lascivious expression I could muster. I saw my panties dangling from one of my ankles, caught on my sandal. I didn't even know how they had gotten there, although the skin they had chafed as they were slowly pulled down was starting to sting.

"Wait, wait…" I said, when he was about to enter me. "Condom."

"I don't have any on me," he moaned.

"Not even in your wallet?"

I grabbed my panties before he put me down on the ground. He shook his arms to soothe them from the effort of holding me up. I don't blame him; holding someone up must be hard. He reached for his wallet in the back pocket of his jeans and tore it open. He had the courtesy to put his cock back in his clothes first, and that made me laugh.

"What's so funny?" He laughed with me, looking up at me, as his fingers fumbled inside his worn leather wallet.

"Nothing. I pictured you doing that with your dick hanging out."

"My dick hanging out?" He raised his eyebrows and let out a laugh. "Well, look what I told you." He pulled out a condom with a flourish. "Always prepared," he murmured, searching for my mouth.

"You're not going to be able to hold me up against the wall the whole time."

"I know." He licked his lips. "The only thing we can do here is fuck like animals. If you don't want to, we ca—"

He didn't finish the word. I smashed my lips into his and stuck my tongue in his mouth. David pulled me into the opposite corner, where we leaned against a car.

"Half the village is gonna see us," I complained.

"Hope they enjoy the show."

He ripped open the condom, and as always when he couldn't handle his impatience anymore, he threw his head back and muttered a couple of profanities as he unrolled it. Then I climbed up to the edge, hooked my legs around his waist, and let him do the rest. Let him push, growl, hold us both, with one hand under my skirt and the other against the body of the car. My core burned from the effort of keeping my balance in that position, but it was worth it every time David thrust hard between my thighs and his jeans drooped a few more inches down his legs.

"For the love of God, please don't let the alarm go off," he begged. "This is my grandfather's car."

I got the giggles. He did too. Even fucking like animals was happy. It was…straight out of a fairy tale.

He had to really struggle not to finish quickly. In his defense, his hips were rocking wildly. Still, we didn't go too fast until I got into a position where I could touch myself until I came. We, came at the same time, keeping time with my fingers, our mouths hanging open, staring at each other, somewhere between surprised and happy at not being able to keep our promises.

51

~~~

THE WEEKEND.
THE TENDERNESS.

DAVID

My headache wasn't as bad as I deserved it to be. That was the first thing I thought when I woke up in my boxers, sweaty and dry-mouthed. In the next bed over, Felix was snoring softly even as the midday sun poured in through the slats in the blind, making slashes of light across the bed.

When I opened my eyes, I perfectly remembered fucking Margot on the hood of my grandfather's car, parked right in front of his house. But that was fucking crazy. And if she hadn't stopped us, I would have done it without a condom.

And without telling her that I had seen Idoia and we had talked.

It's not that I wanted to lie to her, it's just that…in the little time we had left, why waste it talking about another girl?

Jesus! I clutched my head when I remembered that when I got home, when Felix's breathing slowed and I could tell he was fast asleep, I slid under her covers. I needed to kiss her more, caress her, feel her hands on my skin. Margot arched as she asked me to go back to my bed, to make it a little easier, and I…I acted like a teenager in love. In love and out of control.

And now there was no trace of her in the room.

I snuck out of the room, thinking my friends would still be sleeping like logs and that the house would still be quiet. But as I went downstairs I realized there was already a commotion in the kitchen, the nerve center of any party worth its salt.

I found them all fighting to get their hand into a bag of churros. A bunch of sharks on a wounded seal would make less of a racket.

"This is a novelty," I said with a gravelly voice. "You guys went and bought breakfast?"

"No, she did."

The group parted to reveal Margot in the middle, smiling and diverting her gaze to the floor. Another thing that reminded me of the night before and I didn't feel exactly comfortable with the memory.

"So sweet." I couldn't think of anything more natural to say, and they all looked at me, confused. It had been a shitty answer. I cleared my throat. "Don't spoil them. They'll get used to it."

Margot smiled politely and looked down at her feet. I did the same and discovered that I hadn't even put on a shirt. I was wearing cotton shorts with nothing underneath. I wasn't even wearing flip-flops.

"Why the hell did I come down so naked?" I said out loud.

"We can see your foreskin," Laura pointed out with a smile.

"Don't worry, Margot, we look but we don't touch," Rocio added.

"Ah, they're blushing," Esther and Cristina chorused in a stage whisper.

"Suck my balls," I offered, shoving a churro into my mouth. "I'm gonna take a shower."

Margot and I exchanged a sly look. My friends were looking at us with stupid little smirks on their faces. We thought we had been as silent and discreet as ninjas, but maybe all of them (and with them, the entire village) had seen us fucking against a red Seat Ibiza from the year 2000. Or maybe they were just witnesses to how flustered and red we got after a few words.

It would be better to tackle the problems head-on.

"Queen, will you come with me for a second?" I asked her, once I had chewed the rest of the fried pastry.

"To the shower?" Esther exclaimed, surprised. "OMG, David, you wake up raring to go."

"Upstairs. To talk." I exaggerated the word *talk* with an irritated tone. "You coming, Margot?"

"Um…yes, yes. Of course," she replied, grabbing a churro and wrapping it in a paper napkin to soak up the grease.

I stole Marta's glass of juice from her hand and, with a pretty ironic thank-you, went back upstairs, followed by Margot brandishing her churro.

I went into one of the bedrooms "the girls" had left empty and closed the door. Margot had kind of a shocked look on her face. Something like "You're not going to ask me to do it here, are you?"

"I'm not going there," I warned her.

"So this is about last night."

"I'm really sorry." I put the glass down on the chest of drawers and expelled all the air from my lungs. "I lost my mind."

"We both lost our minds."

"It's not that it wasn't good," I hurried to clarify. "It was really good, to tell the truth. But the thing is…this isn't going how we planned."

"It's okay. Breaking up isn't an exact science."

As soon as I heard "breaking up," I'm not gonna lie: I got a little freaked out. *Breaking up* implied something solid before. Something that could be broken had to exist by necessity. And "we" had existed, there was no doubt about that, but it scared me. It really scared me. I could still hear myself saying that if we didn't stop, we'd end up falling in love. And it was happening. In some way, either cowardly or childish, it was happening.

"Right." I couldn't say anything else.

"It doesn't always go as planned." Margot sat down on the edge of the bed, unsure what to do with her churro. She looked at it and laughed.

I laughed too. It was always easy with her, even when it scared me.

"What do you think?" I asked.

"About last night?"

"Yes."

"Well, I think…" She took a deep breath and swept the room with her gaze. She looked beautiful, with her hair tousled, a little wavy, wearing that black shirtdress she had worn in Santorini. I forced myself to focus. "I liked it. And by I liked it, I don't just mean the obvious…" Her tone became a little lighter. "Obvious because I don't think I was that silent when I came." She breathed in and took up her old tone again. "I mean, I liked doing it again. And the one in the bed. I liked the one in the bed too."

"But…we have to stop doing it."

"Is that a statement or a question?"

"I have no idea."

I bit my cheek and sat down next to her. We both smiled.

"I liked doing it again too," I said, unable to stop myself from locking my eyes on her mouth.

"Well now, I'm the one saying, and it is a statement, that we have to stop doing it."

"Okay. You're the boss."

"No." She smiled sadly. "The boss is the things you said in Mykonos."

Stopping it. Not letting it go any further. Turning our backs on the possibility of falling in love. What if it was too late for that? But since I didn't say a word of what I was thinking, Margot kept talking with a sadder and sadder smile.

"Plus we should concentrate on sealing the deal on winning them back and reap what we've sowed."

"You're right," I admitted, but I still hadn't found the courage to tell her that Idoia had come to surprise me at the florist a few days back. The same day I sent the flowers.

We looked at each other again without moving, like we both wanted to add something but neither of us dared. I wanted to kiss her, but I didn't.

"Well, then it seems like everything ended up how we wanted… right?" I looked at her, in case I saw even the slightest doubt and, surprise, not the slightest; her whole face was a question mark with eyes.

Maybe it was time to tell her that I hadn't liked being away from her these last few days. Maybe it was time to announce that I was more than a little lovesick. Maybe she felt the same, although she was definitely still waiting for the Iron Man of fiancés.

"Yes," I responded, despite the doubts I thought I could read on her face. "A happy ending."

We looked away. We searched for something to say. We were suddenly very awkward.

"I'm going to see my parents." I stood up. "Wanna come?"

She raised an eyebrow.

"No." And a very warm smile spread across her face. "Because bringing me to meet your parents, fully aware that your mother forbid you from bringing anyone through that door unless they were the final one, doesn't seem very…um…coherent."

A flash of a life together dazzled me. A bright room where old vinyl would be playing, where it would smell like plants and flowers, where it wouldn't matter if I came home with dirt under my nails and if she got home when dinner was already cold. The life that could be slapped me in the face, and I had to blink.

"You're right. I'm going to take a shower. My grandmother can sniff out a hangover from a mile off, and I want to throw her off the trail."

I'd say Margot seemed disappointed, but I don't know. What I do know is that I had hoped she would say something else.

~~~~~

My mother was wrapping soaps in floral-printed wax paper. Now she had decided to make her own soap because she said commercial soap was made from pork. The whole house smelled like those scented glycerin pills, even though my grandmother was in front of the stove, trying to compete by cooking something I thought was rice with rabbit.

"Hello!" I called, stopping in the open doorway to let my eyes adjust to the dim house.

"Well, well!" my grandmother said. "The skinny one."

"I'm not that skinny!" I defended myself, going inside and flexing. "I'm built like a bull."

My grandmother looked at me with a pretty derisive disappointment. "Look at you. You're so scruffy."

I gave her a kiss and sat down next to my mother.

"Mother." I winked at her. "As you can see, I'm a very good son, and as I promised, I dropped by to say hello."

"If I hadn't seen you at the festival…" She rolled her eyes.

"Do you want a glass of gazpacho?" my grandmother offered.

"A beer."

"A hair-of-the-dog beer because I can smell your hangover from here."

My mother and I laughed.

"I didn't even get that wasted," I declared.

"Right. When I went to get bread this morning, everyone was talking about your infamous fireman dance," my mother pointed out.

"That was just a silly joke."

"What's going on with you?"

"With me? Nothing."

My grandmother put a glass of gazpacho in front of me and gave me a few tweaks on the ear, letting me know that I wasn't leaving there without finishing every last drop.

"Granny, did you want to add some gazpacho to this garlic?"

"Garlic is really good for your heart."

"If I drink this, I'll never be able to kiss anyone again."

"You don't need to."

When she'd disappeared back into the kitchen, I took up the conversation with my mother again, who was chuckling at my grandmother's zeal.

"Where's Papa?"

"At work." She smiled. "He works on Saturdays now too."

"Wow. Um…" I looked around. "Ernesto and Clara didn't come home for the festival this year?"

"You're a disaster, David," she said, her eyes back on her work. "They're your siblings. A call every once in a while wouldn't hurt."

"I do call them… It's just that lately I've been a little…distracted."

"Does that have anything to do with the girl from last night?"

"No," I lied.

"Who is she? Are you two dating?"

"No," I lied again. "I'm dating another girl called Idoia."

"And knowing you, I'm sure she's one of those girls who drag you down a path of bitterness, who says she loves you one day and then doesn't return your calls the next. You don't know how to love someone who loves you. And there's something there that doesn't work, David. Something you have to fix so you love yourself a little more because you don't deserve that kind of love."

"That's me." I raised my eyebrows, resigned while I settled into another chair, this time opposite her.

"That one from last night looked like a nice girl."

"And she is."

"And that's why you don't like her, I imagine."

For God's sake. It doesn't matter how young your mother is. She never stops being your mother and doing motherly things.

"I do like her, Mama, but things aren't as easy as you…"

"Oh no?" She side-eyed me. "Tell me, tell me. Maybe I'll learn something."

"You're teasing me, and that's why it's no fun talking to you," I sulked.

"Are you going out with either of them? And if you say both,

I'll make you swallow so much soap you'll have bubbles coming out of your butt until you die. I didn't raise you to treat women like cattle."

I gave up. I rested my forehead on the table.

"Do you see why I didn't feel like coming to say hi? You're giving me a headache!" I complained. "I'm not going out with both. Actually, I don't think I'm going out with either."

"What a shame. Considering how handsome my skinny little boy is." My grandmother appeared out of nowhere to kiss my temple.

"Granny, please! Make noise when you walk or something. You're going to be the death of me."

"This village is going to be the death of me! Can you believe that last night someone…fornicated…" she said, lowering her voice, "on top of your grandfather's car?"

I opened my eyes as wide as plates.

"How would you know that?"

"I woke up and heard heavy breathing, and this morning…guess what I found: a butt print on the hood!"

I barely said hello to my grandfather. Suddenly it felt like the house was on fire and I had to cut and run. It was very obvious, from the look my mother shot me before I left, that at least she was aware of the source of the "fornication" on the car. But still…I had to down the gazpacho. I had to brush my teeth twice and chew five pieces of gum to get rid of the aftertaste of garlic.

～～～

In a naive corner of my chest, I had hoped the visit to the house I grew up in would clear some doubts, the mental fog of priorities, but the truth is that the house was still chaos (fun chaos, but chaos after all) since I became independent. So if I was looking for answers, they weren't there.

When I got back to Cristina's house, I found Margot swimming with the others. They were talking about which swimsuits were flattering on them and which looked awful. And I thought, somewhat bewildered, that it was a gift. I pictured Idoia there. She would be sulking at having to hang out with people as un-glam as my friends, with their ridiculous sunglasses, like Miss Rottenmeier, tanning in hostile silence far away from everyone else. Seriously, did I really want to get back together with her? Since I had gotten back from the trip, I'd been having a hard time finding the pros in our relationship. Idoia wasn't like Margot; she didn't have any warm corners to take shelter in. There was no life in her laughter. She wasn't supportive and kind. I reflected: How much did I actually like being hit during sex? I was starting to think I might be a masochist and not know it.

I snorted.

"What are you doing?" Laura asked, sitting down next to me.

"Thinking about my ex."

"Why would you do that?" She threw me a baffled look.

I turned to look at her again, with my arms crossed over my chest and a feeling of pressure in my stomach.

"Laura…what do you think makes a relationship work?"

"Jeez, David…that's quite a question. Well…I guess respect, skin, and desire, to boil it down."

"What about without boiling it down?" I wanted to know.

"Respect means giving admiration, empathy, affection, warmth, understanding, reciprocity…"

"What about skin?"

"Sex and intimacy. Laughter too. Skin is what makes it fun. The respect, stability. The desire, long-lasting."

I stared right through her. Of all those things, Idoia only fulfilled sex because she was a fucking machine, not because she left a rainbow of intimacy in her wake. She didn't admire me in any of the ways it's possible to admire someone, she didn't feel the slightest empathy for me, she wasn't affectionate, she didn't give me warmth when everything around me seemed cold, and she would never understand the way I saw the world or relationships. She didn't make me laugh or laugh with me. It was never really fun with her, though it was very intense.

"What about intense?" I asked. "What do you think about intense?"

"Intense or toxic?"

She smiled. She smiled with her teeth, and I did the same out of habit even though I didn't feel like smiling at all. We must've looked like two loons.

Margot climbed out of the pool, and I locked my eyes on her. What a sight. The curves at her waist would kill you if you tried to drive too fast. She turned around. That ass. I thought I could see some round marks, and my stomach flipped at the thought that it could be a reminder of my fingers digging in there.

Laura pinched my arm to bring me crashing back to reality.

"Sorry."

"David, you need to clear out the old broken stuff if you want to fill yourself up again. I don't know if you get me."

I didn't get her. Not then, at least, even though I couldn't stop thinking about it. I couldn't stop going in circles in my head about whether turning my relationship with Idoia into something healthy was mission impossible, if what I felt about Margot was really valuable, and this whole thing about clearing out the broken to make room for the new.

And even with all the mental mess I was carrying, after we finished eating, when everyone else was playing cards in the living room and Margot was dozing off on the couch, I felt an irresistible temptation to snuggle in next to her.

"Hey…" I whispered to her. "Won't you be more comfortable in bed?"

"I'm fine here," she murmured drowsily.

"But I don't fit here."

She opened her eyes and smiled. And when she did, I was even more scared.

I didn't love Idoia, damn it. I loved Margot. And it was really fucking messy.

So we went upstairs. I didn't fall asleep. I spent the whole time stroking her. Her arms. Her shoulders. Her back. Her hip. Her hair. And when she woke up, wordlessly, I reached into her panties with the intention of slowly fingering her until she came. I needed to have her in my fingers one more time, but she stopped me.

"We said we weren't going to do goodbye sex, and I've lost count of how many times we've said goodbye by doing it."

And she was right, but when I leaned in to kiss her again, she forgot all about it.

We ended up having sex silently, with me on top, in the bed in the attic, which squeaked more than we would've liked. This time she was the one who took a condom out of her wallet.

"I grabbed it at the last minute. Just in case."

"And it didn't occur to you to whip it out last night?" I asked her.

"I left my bag here."

We made love like a sweet summer siesta, rocking ourselves. And in the end, I mentally told her the reason goodbye sex didn't make any sense. If it was bad, which wasn't the case, it left a bad taste in your mouth and spoiled the memory. And if it was good, you'd always want more.

As always, Jose was behind the grill…until he threw a tantrum because he couldn't get the fire to light and he left it to us. So I took over and yelled for my friends to help me, at least by carrying things over. Margot was the only one who volunteered.

It was hot next to the barbecue, and I ended up in nothing but shorts, fanning myself with a cardboard plate.

"Holy shit, it's so hot," I moaned when Jose brought me another beer.

"Hey, kid, I like the view," Esther teased. "With your torso all sweaty, you look like a male stripper who came to save the night."

"I'll give you a private dance later." I winked.

Margot came over to offer me a damp cloth, which she had wet in the cold water from the cooler, and smiled, looking back and forth between Esther and me. I thanked her and stopped on my way to give her a kiss when I realized everyone was looking at us and that I was about to break the promise not to kiss her again for the umpteenth time.

"Don't hold back, dude," they teased. "After the squeaking from the siesta…"

"Please, so mortifying."

Margot leaned on my shoulder, hiding herself and making the whole group burst into laughter. I put my arm around her and kissed her temple.

"You're all so rude!" Marta chided them. "Poor thing, she just joined the group. And she's so nice. Good thing you dumped that grouchy girl who sounded like a drone, David."

"Don't you mean a cyborg?" I answered, confused.

"Yeah, that's it, the ones who seem like humans but they're robots. Are they called cyborgs?"

"Drones are the things that fly," Laura pointed out, filching a potato from the plate next to her.

"Well, I didn't like the cyborg at all. She was such a jerk."

"Marta…" I started to say.

"Sorry, Margot, I know it's not tasteful to talk about the ex, but it's just that…I only met her once, and that was plenty."

"Marta…" I tried again.

"She was stuck-up, grumpy, a snob and a half…a 'trendy' woman who bought cheugy, expensive clothes and thought the whole world had to kiss her ass. And I mean, not gonna happen. My David is so David. He needed a girl like you: elegant, discreet, funny, sweet, beautiful…"

Margot quickly glanced over at me, putting the ball in my court.

"Marta, Margot and I aren't together."

They all grimaced at each other. It was clear they had just assumed, and I didn't blame them. There was something between us that I'm sure was as beautiful from the outside as it felt from the inside.

"Ah…seriously?"

"Seriously." Margot smiled sadly.

I glanced at her and turned back to the barbecue, clacking the tongs in my hand, to turn over the two kilos of pancetta the gang of nutjobs had bought. I pulled a piece of meat off the grill, waved it around to cool it down, and gave it to her to taste.

"It needs another minute," Margot responded.

"Seriously, you guys make a really cute couple," Marta insisted.

"Hey, Margot, what *do* you do?"

"Yeah, Margot, what do you do?" I said as a little dig.

"I work in the family business." She leaned into my side and was unconsciously stroking my back. Everything felt so natural with us... "My grandfather founded a hotel chain. He built a hotel in Galicia, and little by little it grew until it became a giant."

"Which hotels are they?"

"The Ortega Group." I could feel her looking at me sidelong.

The Ortega Group. Everyone knew the Ortega Group. It was iconic. Everyone fell silent. Except Esther.

"So what do you do at your job?"

"I'm the vice president of the company and the associate in charge of customer relations and brand image."

Margot looked at me anxiously, and I understood that she hadn't told me before because she didn't want that (her money, her hotels, her family of origin) to get in the middle of our relationship. With me, she just wanted to be Margot and...fuck, that's how I had fallen in love with her. With nothing in the middle of us, just skin, desire, and respect.

She kissed me on the shoulder while stroking my back. I wanted her to be able to do that all the time. I wanted us to be like that, two people who love each other beautifully, sweetly, slowly, without anything else mattering. Not stocks or my three shitty jobs.

I turned back to the barbecue and pretended to be very focused on my task; I heard them resume the conversation, but I drifted very far away. I went to Neverland, where relationships between people like us worked. I went to Wonderland, where no one would look at me like a fucking parasite if I risked working through my fears and starting something with Margot now that I knew who she was. I went far away, into space, where all the lives we could've had were exploding from pressure and lack of oxygen. When I landed, I found refuge in the knowledge that suffering now so we would suffer less in the future was the most elegant option. My pockets were empty, and my head was hollow, dreamless. I don't know when I let life engulf me and throw me in so deep that even if I stretched my arms so hard I dislocated them, I could never reach a love like the one Margot offered.

52

~~~~~~

BECAUSE I LOVE YOU

MARGOT

I'd be lying if I said I expected the weekend to go well, and by well, I meant a leap into accepting that our old lives, the ones we were leading before we met, no longer existed. I knew that we were both tempted to flee toward the familiar. But a part of me, a kind of kamikaze part, wanted to put aside all the information I had kept quiet until the moment it all became clear, just in case I wasn't such a coward after all. Some might think that in that exact moment, I revealed my origins, my last name, my position, to try to tempt David to see another reason to stay with me, but it wasn't like that. I knew him well enough to know he'd die of shame at the mere possibility that someone would point the finger at him and accuse him of trying to take advantage. Of only loving me for my money. And my houses. And maybe a job in the company. No long hours, but well paid. It's what people expect a couple with such different backgrounds to do. Let the wealthy one elevate the other until he is lifted out of the world he once belonged to and disguises himself as a native in hers. But that wasn't me. And it wasn't even part of the equation for David.

The barbecue was fun, even though David seemed to be somewhere else. Ever since I had revealed that I was the last Ortega standing in the Ortega Group, the heiress who had preferred to stay in the shadows rather than participate in photo calls or syrupy articles in the press licking my ass, David had been avoiding me.

We had made a hell of a mess, not to mention that my heart had turned into a knotted skein of wool. Plus, any moment seemed like the right time to begin the distancing maneuver. This was the last weekend we had, and we both knew it. That certainty was one more guest at the table.

The group suggested going back to the plaza to see what the patron saint festivities had to offer that night, but we weren't very hyped. We were mentally immersed in our farewell. If either of us had hoped the hard part was over, we had been deluded.

"I have a headache. I think I'm going to go lie down," I said, at the first opportunity. "I'm not used to letting my hair down this much, and…girls, I'm getting too old."

Even though I was on the edge of a breakdown, I wanted to be nice, friendly. I wanted to be what Idoia hadn't been and to beat her at that at least, since she was going to get the boy and the simple and beautiful life.

They insisted a lot. They tossed out all kinds of reasons, like that it was very early, that the night was just getting started, or that they didn't want to leave me home alone. David solved it by saying he was going to sleep too.

"Fine, that'll give us something to gossip about." They smiled at him.

And the smile he returned was as sad as the one he had behind the bar the night I met him. He wasn't fooling anyone.

We climbed the stairs quietly, and without a word, David closed the door and then leaned against it with his arms crossed.

"You seem weird."

"Well…"

"This is about my job, right?" I asked him.

"I don't know why you hid it from me, seriously."

"I didn't hide it for any reason in particular. I just…wanted to forget about it for a while, to have it not matter in my life."

"It wouldn't have mattered to me. Not in a good way or a bad way."

"But I didn't know that back then. And you made me feel…like myself."

He nodded understandingly.

"Actually…I don't want to throw anything in your face. I have to tell you something," he said.

"Me too."

"Who goes first?"

"You."

He looked at the ceiling, looking for strength or maybe a blessing from the Virgin Mary the owners had hung on the wall, who knows why. He rubbed his hand over his cheeks, mouth, and chin. Here we go.

"I saw Idoia the other day," he started. "We made a plan to meet up on Monday and decide what we were going to do about us."

He watched me bite my cheek in a gesture that I had probably picked up from him, mimicking his habit of doing that when he didn't know what to say.

"I saw Filippo. We made a plan to have dinner on Monday and… talk."

He seemed kind of relieved, I don't know why. And that relief made him seem a little cowardly.

"What are you going to say to her?" I asked in a small voice.

He made a face, shrugged, and paced a little. But since he didn't start, I decided to keep talking.

"Do you regret what happened last night? And when I say 'last night,' I mean what happened today and this whole trip. I guess it's just a different way of asking, 'What are you going to do?'"

"I don't regret it. But…"

I swallowed and stood up from the bed where I had sat down. I recomposed my expression as convincingly as I could and smiled.

"That 'but' says it all. That's it. You know what to tell her."

"We're not talking about Idoia, Margot, and I don't want to leave you with that 'but.'"

He leaned against the chest of drawers. He seemed sad. I was too.

"What then? Because this morning you seemed pretty convinced you wanted to get back together with her…"

"This morning you seemed very happy to have another chance with Filippo."

He slumped, looking resigned.

"We fucked it all up, right?" I let it hang in the air.

David was staring at me; I think in that moment he was wishing he could send me all the information through Bluetooth waves, but it wasn't possible.

"Maybe it got out of hand."

"What did?"

"This…" He sighed. "Us. It got out of my hands, and…I feel something beautiful and warm for you…" He put his hands on his stomach, like that was where he harbored these feelings toward me.

"Something healthy. That's why I don't regret it at all. I don't regret it, and I won't regret it, but…"

"But. Here comes the *but*." I tried to smile, but I don't know if I managed it.

"It'll end badly." And he almost moaned with pain saying it. "It'll end terribly. And you'll end up…"

"Yeah, I'll end up hating you for never becoming what I wanted. I get it. I've heard it all before…"

"But it's true. We'll hurt each other."

"You know what would be nice, David? If you leave me to pick my own battles."

My heart started racing. Had I just told him I would fight for us?

Yes, I had just said I would fight for us.

"You're free to…"

"No." I smiled cynically. "You don't give me the chance to be free to do anything like that."

"The thing is there are two of us in this, and I don't want to go any further. I'm going to end up hurting you." He looked at me and sighed. "I met you less than two months ago and look at us. What do you think will happen as time passes? Do you think it'll get easier? Love isn't like that."

"I stopped believing you have to suffer for love a long time ago, David. So if you're telling me that we shouldn't even try because it'll end badly and we'll have to deal with the consequences, then what I'm really hearing is that…you don't love me."

"And you do love me?" His eyebrows shot up.

I didn't answer. He hurt me. Asking me that hurt me because I felt it somehow underestimated how I felt about him. Or what David himself felt about me. Maybe it questioned everything, like we were dying of thirst and in the distance we could see an oasis. Who knows. Any answer that wasn't "I love you" would've hurt me.

"I'm sorry," he whispered.

"Why are you saying sorry exactly?"

"For avoiding having an adult conversation about how we feel. For trying to get out of here without saying all the things that could go well because I don't want to hear them."

"What are you going to say to Idoia?" I said again.

"The truth. That I fell in love with you, but it won't work."

I shot him an incredulous look. I don't think he blamed me; he didn't seem to believe what had just come out of his mouth either, judging by how quickly he bowed his head. I felt the five-year age difference between us crushing me, like he was little and I was old.

That I fell in love with you, but it won't work. No one wants to hear those words, and I was no exception, especially when I felt like I was about to throw myself into exchanging my life for whatever would mean I had a chance with him.

"Look, Margot..."

"Do you realize you've never even asked what I want?" I cut him off, trying to keep my tone friendly, sweet.

He raised his eyes to mine, and I kept talking.

"You decided for both of us. You do, you say, and you move ahead without my opinion even mattering. And I know you, it's not because you're egotistical, it's because there's something you don't want to hear me say. Does it scare you to hear me say that?"

"At this point, it's obvious I don't want to hear you say you don't feel the same way, but hearing the opposite terrifies me too."

"But why the fear?"

"Because I'm not ready for you."

"So?"

"I don't know. Why don't you tell me?" he retorted.

"Because I can't give you the answers, David, if I don't even know the questions." I filled my lungs, hoping the air would relieve the feeling of drowning. "I need you to summarize the situation for me."

"How can I summarize the situation for you?" He pushed a lock of hair off my forehead so he could study my expression.

"Come on. Give me the headlines of where we are now and where you're thinking of going."

"Bah," he snorted.

"It's not that hard. Say it."

"It's just that everything would change."

"Everything already has changed!"

He shrugged.

"You haven't even given me the chance to say it to myself and believe it. Or accept it. I don't know what the right word is." He didn't look at me as he spoke. "All I know is that if I insist, if I tell you I love you, that I've fallen in love with you, that I feel something stronger than the connection between two friends...everything will change. Because how does it make sense to not even want to try if all that is true? It doesn't make any."

"I don't care if things make sense. I care about what's done and what isn't."

"I don't know if I'm going to know how to handle everything you deserve. I know I was the one who forced things the last few days so we didn't have to say goodbye so soon, but...fuck, Margot, I don't want to be the one who ruins everything. I don't want to be an obstacle. I don't want to be the poor little boy who makes the poor little rich girl unhappy. And it's not that Idoia is worth the effort and you're not. It's just that I'm not that worried about disappointing her because I already have."

I sat down next to him, and we stared at each other.

"You don't have to say these things," I said in a small voice. "We laid this all out from the beginning: we'd have a fling and then we'd go back to our lives. If that's what you want, all you have to do is say yes to Idoia or that you don't like me enough. You don't have to justify it."

"I'm not trying to justify it." He raised his eyebrows. "Exactly the opposite."

"Well then, I don't think I get it."

"I feel like I'd have to tiptoe around." He smiled sadly. "And make you think that everything's fine, that none of this bothers me…but that's not true. Because I've discovered that I don't like being without you and that scares me."

"So what's the problem?"

"I don't know how to make you happy. I'm nothing, I haven't found myself, I don't have a life or plans or dreams. The problem, Margot, is that love can't fix everything that's broken. I don't want to need you to be okay, to be someone, to make plans. I want to have something to offer you. And right now I have nothing."

I went over and gave him a kiss that threw him for a loop. I don't think he was expecting it. He was expecting an outburst of reproaches and tears that wasn't about to appear. At least not from me. Because he had already decided. And I had too.

"If that's the situation, we shouldn't see each other anymore," I said.

"I'll wait a month like we agreed and…"

"No, David," I shook my head vehemently. "It's not about a

month. I don't think I can be your friend. If this is a yes but no, I'm going to have to ask you to go away, really."

He furrowed his brow, and I found myself obligated to explain:

"A month is nothing. In a month, no matter what we think now, it'll just give us time for the memories to become more beautiful, to miss each other. And when we see each other again…a few beers at some place in Carabanchel, that concert you wanted to take me to, whatever, it'll be like a spark that will set fire to all the tinder we've piled up. But you still won't be clear about it because a month is nothing."

"And you'll be clear?"

"As clear as I am now." I made a face. "It's clear to me that you and I would be amazing together, but I don't know how."

"So then…forever? That's the choice you're giving me?"

I swallowed the lump in my throat. "If this isn't enough for you, it isn't. I don't want to keep forcing things in my life. I've already proved that doesn't end well."

"And asking you to wait for me doesn't make sense." And I knew that this was a question, even though there was no question mark in his mouth.

"No, I guess not. Because I would wait."

David sniffed. "It's not that I don't want you in my life. It doesn't make sense."

"I don't want you to go either, but it makes all the sense in the world. I don't want to suffer, and you're too indecisive."

"Are we playing all or nothing?" he asked.

"We're not playing, David. This is real life, and blows hurt here and break your heart."

"What are you going to say to Filippo?" He raised his eyebrows.

"I don't know." I shook my head. "I don't know yet."

"Nobody should matter more than you when you make the decision."

"You give shitty advice. You sound like a fortune cookie." I smiled.

"Margot…" he said in a thin, pleading voice. "You are, even if you don't know it when you look in the mirror. You are, you don't just exist. You're everything that's good."

I stood up.

"Right…yeah." I swallowed a sob.

"I never really had you." He smiled sadly. "I have nothing to give you in exchange. And I have to leave you behind. Because it's the only way I know how to love you well."

Looking back now, I don't think I meant it when I told him to go. I think that I was possessed by a kind of recently recuperated dignity, independence, or self-love, and I said something I knew was good for me without really thinking it through. Maybe, in the deepest down part of me, I was hoping it would work as a spur and make David stop seeing what we felt as a problem. It's possible I just wanted to scare him, but I admit the result was not what I was hoping.

A lot of time had to pass to understand everything we said to each other, word for word. Time had to come and knock me down, like a wave you weren't expecting from a sea you didn't think was that rough, for me to admit that he was right: of all the beautiful things David and I could be, we never would have survived more than a few years.

53

~~~

BECAUSE IT WAS
NEVER OUR TIME

In my memories of all the sad nights of my life, that's the one that hurts the most. I knew sometimes you have to break up with someone when you still love them, but I wasn't prepared to mutually decide that love wouldn't be enough after feeling it so deeply. We were robbed of the chance. It was weird, but...when someone tells you they love you enough to let you go, it's because they can't give you what you need.

We arranged our life like it was a bulletin board, and we drew the lines so we wouldn't hurt ourselves. We accepted that it's not always enough to feel butterflies, and I realized, behind closed doors, what I already suspected in Greece: magic doesn't exist if nobody believes in it.

We wouldn't look for each other. We wouldn't message each other. We couldn't be friends. We couldn't pretend it hadn't happened. "We" no longer existed.

And although my disappointment weighed heavily and I didn't have enough hands to take on his too, I have to be fair and admit that when we said goodbye, he was more broken than me. What once united us, a mutual recognition of the two saddest eyes in a bar, now became almost like the last wink of our farewell because… among all the people saying goodbye on that sidewalk in front of Atocha station, we were the saddest. We were never going to see each other again.

Sorry if I'm telling it wrong. But we're often unable to tell the stories of what we love most the way they deserve. Let me try again.

~~~~~

He says he loves me but he can't make me happy; ergo he already made a decision.

When I realized all the possible lives he was saying no to, I was crushed. It was so curious; they were all a disaster in some way, but I wanted them. I wanted them all. It's surprising that, in the midst of his postadolescent drama, David had made a relatively mature decision, even if it was for the wrong reasons: we weren't ready for a relationship. We hadn't even taken the first step of getting over our last ones.

We spent the night together, though nothing happened the way it had been happening since he first kissed me. We lay facing each other and promised not to hurt each other. Then, we remembered. We recited all the beautiful things that we would keep like a gift between us and treasure until the end.

There's nothing more beautiful than the time you can no longer reach.

When I woke up the next day, he wasn't there. When I went down to the kitchen, one of his friends smiled and told me David had already announced that something had come up and we had to leave early.

"No worries. As soon as Jose wakes up, you can go with him."

"Let me help you clean up," was the only thing I managed to say.

David was at his parents' house, they told me as we mopped. It was crystal clear that he wanted it to be swift, to create some distance so we wouldn't have the chance to regret it, and…I thought that was fine.

We cleaned. We said goodbye. I listened to all the plans his friends were counting me in for and nodded along, knowing I would never see them again. They were trying to be sweet and attentive, but they just made the whole scene even bleaker, and unfortunately, it didn't dissipate when I got into the car.

David and I made the journey back in silence. David was in the passenger seat, resting his forehead against the glass, and I was in the seat behind the driver, pretending to sleep.

"Where should I drop you guys?" Jose asked halfway through the trip.

David glanced back to check that I was "still sleeping."

"At Atocha if that works for you. We can figure it out from there."

I opened my eyes twenty minutes before we arrived, but I didn't talk until the car stopped. We got out at Atocha as planned. I remembered, just like he remembered, that we had agreed to do this on neutral territory, in a place that wouldn't remind us of each other and we wouldn't need to go to that often. Atocha train station. I could've told him that I take trains all the time, but we had already broken every promise we had made, what did one more matter?

When Jose's car disappeared, David swung his bag onto his shoulder and smiled at me.

"Don't even think about it," I said. "Don't smile. You know your eyes are too loud."

"Fuck, Margot," he mumbled. "Even at first sight, you already knew me better than everyone else." He ran his fingers through his hair. "Maybe we don't need to be so harsh? What if we let some time pass and...? We could be friends."

I think I was about to falter until he said that last part. I couldn't be his friend, for fuck's sake. I had fallen in love with him, and being friends would never cancel that out.

"Goodbye," I said, stuffing down my tears, and a ridiculous little voice eked out of me, halfway between a sob and a plea.

"Don't cry, please."

"I just don't want to miss you."

"Me either. Listen, Margot, let's let it be, let it all pass a little," he insisted. "Let's take a breather for a few days and I'll call you in a month. A month and a half if you need."

"If we don't do this right, it'll be a disaster."

"It can't be forever," he said, very seriously.

"It wouldn't work."

"I know." He pressed his lips together and swallowed. "We wouldn't work."

"So?"

"We can be friends."

"No. We can't. If you stay my friend, you'll really hurt me."

"Fuck."

"We wouldn't work, and I can't be your friend. Getting some distance is the only solution I can think of."

"Well, I'm not going to ask you to wait for me. Your wings are yours, sad eyes. Only yours."

I wiped away a tear before I turned and nodded.

"What are you going to do?"

"I don't know," he shook his head nervously. His eyes were welling up, but he was hiding it well. "Get my shit together. Find out why the hell I've done so many stupid things that I ended up living on a couch is a good place to start."

"You're going to leave Madrid."

He didn't answer. He kicked the ground with the toe of the Converse I gave him.

"Thank you, Margot."

"I don't need to be thanked for sex." I smiled, trying to be funny.

"No. Not for the sex." He pressed his lips together. "Thank you for the trip of a lifetime."

"You'll travel more and go to more beautiful places."

"But not with you."

I hung my head and silently dried my tears.

"Another promise goes to hell," he said. "You see, Margot? I don't know how to do it better. But thank you, really, for bringing me back to the real world. It's not always beautiful, but it has its own appeal." Finally, his lips curved into a smile. "I've been really happy with you. Ours might be the shortest love story never told, but I think it's also the most beautiful. Beautiful in the way the tiniest things can be beautiful."

I wanted to tell him it made me furious thinking about him falling in love again and forgetting this tiny love story, but I couldn't because he didn't deserve it.

"What about you? What are you gonna do?" he asked.

"Well…" I took a deep breath. "Go back to work. Break up with Filippo. Stop giving explanations and trying to prove things to the rest of the world. Maybe sell my house."

"It was never our time," he muttered. "I feel like a little kid. I wish we had met a few years from now."

"In a few years, I'll run into you strolling along holding hands with the good girl you wanted to meet."

"Or someone will say they saw us selling coconuts on a beach, very far away."

"If I flee, should I look you up?"

"You'll never flee, Margarita Ortega." He smiled and pushed a lock of hair behind my ear. "We'll find each other again."

We'll find each other again. Another lie.

"Tell me one thing…I scare you, right? My last name, my job…"

"No. What scares me is not having anything to match your love. Loving you a lot and badly is the thing that really scares me."

We looked around us.

"We were so lucky to meet each other out of all these people," he murmured, coming closer. "It didn't last long, but it was real. We can hold on to that."

I grabbed his waist. He grabbed mine. We pressed our foreheads together.

"Goodbye, Margot," I heard him say. "I hope life smiles on you."

"That's it?"

"I hope someone loves you the way I didn't know how. That the whole world's yours. That you never remember me again. But keep the songs, okay? And if you can…forgive me because this love was too big for me."

"Goodbye."

"I don't want to leave," he confessed, his voice hoarse, and his nose brushed mine. "But I'm going, okay?"

"Okay."

We stared at each other for a few more seconds before we melted into a hug. It was just a hug, but we locked away the life we would never have in it so that each of us could carry part of it away.

"Fuck…" I heard him say. "How is it possible that someone invented electricity and I can't even figure out how to do this differently?"

"If only love were science."

"Don't change your number, sad eyes. In a few years, I might have to tell you that I never forgot you."

David took a step back. I did too. We took a few more. A few people cut through the space we had left between us, and we turned back to walk in different directions. "We" were over; at least we followed one of the rules we had set in Santorini. At least we knew how to respect the most important one.

We turned back to find each other through the crowd at least five more times, but that gesture, far from meaning anything, was just the precursor to the final goodbye. Until we disappeared.

We disappeared.

Us.

54. A

~~~

FLIGHT

The restaurant where Filippo was waiting for me was one of my favorite places in Madrid. A French bistro with a garden courtyard full of pergolas and small private booths glowing in soft candlelight. Plus, the foie gras was insane. As I followed the maître d' between the tables, I thought what a bummer it was to break up in a place I liked so much. Now I would think about it every time I came back. Then I realized my mind was so made up, maybe it wouldn't even hurt.

"I'm going to do it," I had written that afternoon in a message to David that I didn't send.

Filippo was dressed in a nice light-blue button-up that fit him like a glove. On the table, I spotted a box from the jewelers who had made our wedding rings for our dream wedding. I was sure he wanted to perform some kind of private ceremony, a romantic grand gesture to illustrate that he forgave me. But as much as I wished otherwise, those rings already meant very little to me.

I sat down without kissing him, but I offered him a smile instead, which he reluctantly accepted.

"You look beautiful."

I was wearing one of the dresses I had bought with David, but I pushed the thought away.

"You look nice too."

"How's it going?"

"Good." I nodded timidly.

"You're very tan." He flashed me his Prince Charming teeth. "It suits you."

"Thank you."

"What did you do this weekend?"

"Uh…" I fidgeted with the silverware. "I went to a friend's village."

"Yeah? Whose?"

"You don't know her." I pressed my lips together.

"Did you…change your hair?" He pointed at my hair, which I had let air-dry with my natural waves, a little messy and parted on the side.

"What?" I had trouble understanding. He had been with me for three years, was he seriously asking…? "No, Filippo. This is my natural hair. I always wear it straight, but…I got tired of flat-ironing it. This is me."

Filippo stared at me, the way he always did when he was waiting for me to rethink something I had just said, but I didn't open my mouth.

"Are you angry?"

"Did I sound hostile?"

"Kind of."

David would've said, in a poor imitation of the Andalusian accent, holding up his hand with a little space between his thumb and his index finger: "Just a touch, my little bombshell." And I would have laughed.

"What's going on?" he cut to the chase.

"Nothing. I have a lot going on in my head."

"Did you start back at work?"

"No. Not yet. The board thinks I need to take a long vacation."

"How considerate." He raised his eyebrows.

"No, not really. They just wanted to get rid of me for a few months."

"You work too much."

I sighed loudly. A waiter came over, and I ordered a glass of cold white wine. He asked if we knew what we wanted to order for dinner, and before Filippo could talk, I answered with a firm but polite *no*.

"You don't want foie gras? Or that carabinero shrimp dish you like so much?"

David would've asked if that was seafood or a naked Italian *carabinieri* officer swimming in noodles.

Get out. David. Out.

"I don't want to eat dinner," I said.

"Do you want us to leave?"

"Filippo…" I stretched my hand across the table, reaching for his. When he squeezed my fingers, I felt a warm, familiar, cozy current that connected straight to my pain. "I'm sorry. I'm sorry I didn't know how to tell you that everything got too big for me."

"I'm sorry too. I thought you wanted a huge wedding. I thought that would make you happy."

"No." I shook my head. "But I didn't even know that myself. I'm sorry it had to go that far for me to realize."

"We'll get over it." He smiled.

"I don't think so, Filippo. These things always linger internally, and that's fair because I never meant to break your heart, but that's exactly what I ended up doing. And you don't deserve that."

"Margot." He squeezed my hand. "It's just a stupid thing we'll forget. No, even better…a stupid thing we can laugh about with our grandchildren. We're going to be happy."

I bit my lip and pulled back my hand.

"Filippo…"

"No, Margot. I'm not going to let you do this. Are you unwell? You're feeling a little a lost? It doesn't matter. We'll find a way to make you feel better. But don't throw three years of a beautiful relationship overboard. You and I love each other."

"You and I need each other. We fit together exactly where the other's puzzle pieces are missing, in the empty spaces. But that's not love. That's fulfilling expectations. Love is something else."

"Ours is a fairy tale, Margot."

"Yes, but I never wanted to be a princess."

Filippo propped his elbow on the table and massaged his forehead with three fingers.

"You're breaking up with me."

"It was already broken. I'm just giving us the opportunity to say goodbye well. You deserve someone who loves you the way I didn't know how." I struggled to swallow when I realized this was the same thing David wanted for me. "You deserve to find someone who wants four kids and a peaceful life too, who knows how to find a balance with all the things she wants. Who's not just what's expected of her."

"But I love you."

I grabbed my purse and tried to stand up, but he seized my wrist.

"I deserve more of an explanation than that, Margot."

"The thing is, you're not listening to me."

"All I'm hearing are vague platitudes about how the wedding got too big for you and you discovered that love isn't what we have. What's going on? Did you meet someone else? Did you have a wild summer and now you think that's what life is? It's not, Margot. Don't send everything to hell for a summer fling that wouldn't last the fucking winter."

"My sister Patricia is getting divorced," I suddenly burst out. "She fell in love with someone else. She's going to leave it all to try it out with someone thirteen years younger than her. And you know what? She doesn't seem crazy or fickle to me. She seems like a brave person who doesn't want to stay with what she has just in case it's colder outside the house. And I want to be brave."

"What does that mean? You want to try your luck with someone else?"

"No. I want to try my luck with myself, to see if I finally fall in love with myself, without needing someone else to tell me what I am and what I'm not. I'm thirty-two, and I don't even know myself. I don't even know what I like. How could I possibly know if I want to grow old with you?"

"If you're doubting it, that means you don't."

"Or that I have the balls to ask myself questions, Filippo. We never questioned anything. We followed the plan, we did things how they were supposed to be done, but we never asked ourselves if that's what we wanted."

Filippo picked up the box holding our wedding rings and toyed with it in his enormous hands.

"And that's what you want, Margot?" he tossed out, not looking up at me. "You want to be there, in no-man's-land, looking for something you might never find? Or do you want to build something real? A family, Margot. A family where you can prove to yourself that you're not like your mother, which is the only thing I think you're really obsessed with."

"I don't want to have to prove anything to anyone, and that's the problem. That's all I've ever done in my life."

"So do whatever you want by my side. And I'll always support you." His eyes were shining. "Always. And in me, you'll have a companion, a husband, a brother, a father, a…"

I lost the thread of what he was saying when I imagined how these comments would seem to David. He would make a scared face and exclaim, "A brother! Please! That's incest!" I smiled. Sadly, but I smiled.

"Filippo…" I stopped him. "I'm going to do you the biggest favor anyone's ever done you: I'm asking you to let me go. And do you know why I'm doing you a favor? Because if you try to satisfy me, you'll make yourself unhappy. And you don't deserve that. You're good, reliable, intelligent, thoughtful, polite. You're handsome and sexy and…"

"Apparently that's not enough for you."

"Of course it's enough. The thing is…it's not for me," I shook my head. "It's for someone else, and I know I'm stealing it. I'm stealing your fairy tale, Filippo, because I'm not your princess. I'm sorry."

I stood up and picked up my bag, but I couldn't move. Filippo was staring at the rings in their box.

"You can hate me," I whispered. "You have every right, and it'll help you get over it."

"You don't deserve for me to hate you."

"Maybe I do. We're all the villain in someone's story."

He sighed. I put my hand on his shoulder, and he squeezed it for a second. When he let his arm fall onto the table, I knew. I could go.

~~~

I cried as I wandered down Velazquez Street. I cried in the taxi I hailed on Goya. I cried in my lobby. I cried leaning on the table in my entrance hall. I cried in the kitchen, in the bathroom, in the closet, in bed, and finally in my dreams. I cried for not being capable of being a princess, I cried for having turned my back on the sweetest memories, I cried because, in a convoluted way, I had made my mother right because I was so ordinary that I couldn't even figure out how to enjoy a fairy tale when it was served up on a silver platter. But, apart from the tears of sorrow I cried over letting him go, I cried tears that were more bitter, hotter, fresher…and those tears were because, whenever I had imagined doing something like this over the last few weeks, David was always there hugging me and telling me he would wait however long I needed to do us right; that he would wait for me because I was worth it. Always. And in his arms, all the words I said to Filippo would have made sense. Or they would have gotten lost. I don't know.

I cried when I texted in our WhatsApp chat: I broke up with Filippo and I miss you being here. Why did we decide to keep our distance, David?

I cried when I deleted it and closed the app.

The next day, however, I felt like a bird that is terrified of heights but gets tired of plucking out its own feathers and is now going to test what it feels like to fly.

~~~

The last post on David's social media, the only way I had to keep track of him without breaking our agreement, was that photo of our shadows tangled up on the beach in Mykonos, and the caption below it, even though I had read it so many times, still hurt. A lot. I think every time I saw those two letters it hurt even more. "Us." It encapsulated everything that was, everything that could have been, everything that would never be. It held all the memories that, damn, we hadn't even seen be born. It was worse being left with the feeling that it could have been better than it seemed. Or maybe that's what the losers always say to themselves when they see the prize drifting away.

The flowers he gave me were wilting more every day. I poured in a water-soluble aspirin when I changed the water and carefully cut the stems diagonally hoping they would dry beautifully. I often found myself caught off guard when I realized that those flowers would be the only thing I'd have left of a love story that didn't turn into love.

I don't know what the hell I'm trying to say. All I know is I became obsessed. With him, with the memories, with the smells, with the hope. And on the second day of singleness, after forcing myself to pack everything Filippo had left in the house into boxes, after writing and deleting five messages to David, I decided that there were things that couldn't wait. And I went to the office.

———

Sonia's eyes almost popped out of her head when she saw me come in, and I don't think it was just because I hadn't warned her about my "visit." I had "played" with my wardrobe, which that rebellious soul (innocently rebellious, to be fair) awakened in me, to pair a hound-stooth pencil skirt, which I normally wore with a white blouse, with a pastel-yellow T-shirt and black heels. I was carrying a purse, my hair wavy and parted to the side, and I had only put on mascara.

"What are you doing here?"

"Working." I smiled at her. "Come in and get me up-to-date."

I tilted my head toward my office and poked my head into the meeting room. Nobody was there yet.

"You can tell the boss isn't here." I laughed.

When Sonia finished reviewing everything, I felt strange. Nothing big had happened in my absence. After all the movies I had played in my head when the board "invited" me to take a long vacation, it actually hadn't mattered at all. Nobody had tried to meddle in my accounts or bossed my team around or tried any sneaky tricks to embezzle control. They weren't trying to drive me out and get me to leave, or drive me crazy so they could make themselves comfortable without me. Nothing. Everything was still exactly the same as I left it.

That should have encouraged me to settle down between these four walls, but actually I learned a different lesson: our own worst enemy is always staring back at us in the mirror.

The gentlemen on the board didn't appreciate having me there and especially in a position of power. That was a fact. But it was also a fact that I had been obsessed with being locked in a power struggle with them. And it wasn't worth it because in recent years, I had struggled a lot and lived very little. That's why I always felt more at home in that office than I did in my own apartment—because I never fought to make my life a place to feel comfortable, the way I did there.

The feeling I was filled with when I realized this was mostly tired. Tired of the carpet, the walls, the paintings, the views, my mammoth office, the rigidity of the business, corporate culture, the partners, the reports, the teams, approving and interrogating lines of business… Okay. I had already proven I could do it.

So now what?

I stared at Sonia for a while, looking straight through her, until she got uncomfortable.

"Are you frozen, are you planning a murder, or are you going to tell me you have postvacation depression?"

I smiled, and she smiled back.

"What if I just leave it all?"

Sonia's smile faded.

"What?"

"What if I leave it all? What if I keep my shares and draw the dividends, but I just dip out and go somewhere else? Or I build something of my own? I could open a bookstore. Write a book about business strategy. Or travel to improve my German or to learn Chinese."

"I'm not following."

"What am I doing here?"

"Uh…that's a rhetorical question, right?"

"Listen…over the last few years, my whole life has consisted of proving to a bunch of misogynist old fogies that I deserve this position beyond just my last name. I've spent months packing and unpacking suitcases. I traveled to London so much that I ended up buying an apartment there to create the false impression of being at home there."

"Well, you met Filippo too and…"

"Filippo and I broke up," I announced. "I'm not talking about love. I'm talking about myself. I've been obsessed with proving stuff to everyone else, but…what do I want? What makes me happy?"

"Uh…" Sonia had a look of terror on her face.

I stood up and looked around me.

"I've always wanted to take a class," I said.

"Margot…" Sonia murmured.

"And the book thing sounds good. A leave of absence? Maybe I could try a startup."

"Margot."

"What if I invent an app that cross-checks the data of the places you mention on WhatsApp…?"

"Margot!" Sonia put herself in my path and waved her arms, stunned. "Stop the brainstorm! Calm down for a second. It's not even nine a.m. and you've already thought of, what, ten new businesses? The weird part is you haven't even mentioned becoming a meditation teacher."

"That too…"

"Margot…you can't do everything at once. It's like going on a diet or quitting smoking. Some brave people do it cold turkey, fine, but, what if you don't rush into anything? What if you feel and think it all through calmly?"

I glared at her. I was more comfortable in my own mental spiral, in that bacchanalian verbal diarrhea where suddenly I could be whomever I wanted… My wings were eager to test themselves, but they probably still only had a couple of feathers on them.

"This is your home. If you don't like it, that's fine," she said, understandingly, "but don't give away the keys so you can go sleep in the street. Maybe consider moving instead."

I rounded the desk and let myself collapse into the chair. I thought. I thought about David, of course, like I always did when I let myself glimpse beyond what I had in front of me. I thought about how making any decision right now would just be part of a tantrum and/or the quest for his return.

Sonia perched on the desk, throwing all protocol out the window, and put her hand on my shoulder.

"Whatever happened on that trip, Margot, use it as a catalyst. You left Filippo. That's huge. That's a huge decision. Give yourself time to get comfortable with each step. If you run, the pain and grief won't be left behind; they'll just be hiding, waiting to pounce on you when you least expect it."

I tutted. "Since when did you get so wise?"

"I had a revelation after trying to turn my life into a rom-com. If you bump into a guy with a coffee in your hand, he doesn't fall in love with you; he just makes you pay for the dry-cleaning."

I sighed. "Notify everyone on the team who's not on vacation and call them in for a meeting in my office. Nothing formal. Just to bring us up-to-date and tell them that I'm here."

"And that you're not planning on running off and opening a florist."

A stabbing pain lashed me, in my lungs. I don't know if I managed to smile.

"Can you order breakfast for however many of us will be there? And count yourself too. Maybe the time has come to start giving you more responsibility, if you want it."

She nodded, grinning, and walked toward the door. When she got there, she turned back; I was holding my phone in my hand.

"Should I close this?"

"Yes."

I typed: Today I tried to fly too high and I almost fell. You should have taught me a little more about being free. It's scary. Like being without you.

I deleted it.

At midday, I got a vase of white roses, but when I opened the card, I didn't find lyrics from the eighties or an *I miss you*. Just a *Welcome Home*, signed by my godfather.

55. A

~~~~

FAIRY TALES DON'T EXIST

Patricia was destroyed. Candela and I had tried everything. The kids were at their paternal grandmother's, who everyone knew wouldn't drown them in a bathtub, which is more than you could say about our mother, and Alberto had left the house with a suitcase. He was going to stay at a hotel for a few days. Then they would see. They would see because they'd probably have to sell the chalet and organize their lives in a very different way. I saw many things in Patricia's inconsolable crying: I saw sorrow for what was; I saw the mourning of a happy relationship; I saw doubt about her future and a somewhat naive anger brought on by everything that would change with the divorce. Life would not follow its old rhythm; a different song would have to be sung. And she wanted to figure out a way to keep dancing exactly the same way except with a new partner.

We didn't manage to drag a single smile out of her, and she wouldn't stop crying even when we popped a bottle of her favorite champagne and opened the box of chocolate-covered strawberries we got from a bakery in the town center, which cost their weight in gold. Nothing. We were resigned when she told us she needed to be alone because we both knew that in her situation, we'd want to stay in the dark, drinking straight from a two-hundred-euro bottle and drowning our pain in sugar too.

But...surprise: as we were leaving her house, we ran into Didier. Suddenly we understood why we'd been rushed out of the house. The poor thing didn't think we would run into him at the garden gate, that tall, thin, elegant dude carrying a bouquet of flowers.

"What if they really love each other?" I asked Candela.

Two weeks without David. That same morning I had written in our chat: I can't take it anymore. Come back. I deleted it, of course.

I wanted to call him then, to tell him everything about Patricia and for him to tell me, while he put together bouquets like the one this boy was holding, that I shouldn't worry about my sister, that life would always find a riverbed to run down, like water.

"The point isn't whether they love each other," my sister responded, bringing me crashing back to reality in the car.

I had borrowed a car from the company's fleet but with no driver. A few days before I had wanted to be the one to brake, change lanes, slow down, and complain that traffic in Madrid is hell.

Candela and I had talked a lot about Patricia's situation. We didn't want to judge her, of course. But throwing it all away for a twenty-four-year-old? It seemed brave to me that she'd taken the step of breaking up her marriage if she no longer loved Alberto, but I doubted this new relationship would end well. We both doubted it, in fact, because we both seemed to be on the same page.

"If them loving each other isn't the point, then what is?" I looked at Candela.

"The point is whether they're in the same life stage. Whether he'll miss, I don't know, the freedom of being in his twenties and if he won't get sick of needing to organize everything around his girlfriend's three kids. And the same with everything else: they'll have to agree on where and how to live, whether love means the same thing to both of them, if they've both healed from previous wounds…"

I glanced at her, leaving the car in park.

"Are you still talking about them, or have you moved on to me and David?"

She sucked her teeth and stroked my hair. "It will pass, I promise."

"What if I don't want it to pass?"

"Well then, you're going to have to do something else."

"But he's so sure it won't work that… How would it work?"

"You're not in the same place, Margot. If you had been, you would've worked harder to find a middle ground."

"Right."

I looked ahead, clutching the wheel.

"When are you going home?" I let the question drop, looking through the windshield.

Candela bit her upper lip and avoided the question.

"Hey!" I complained. "You've been stalling for a month! What's going on?"

"I quit my job a month and a half ago."

I turned toward her in shock. "What are you talking about?"

"You heard me. I was sick of the cold and so few hours of sunlight."

"But…what are you going to do? It was your dream job! Far away from Mama! You're nuts. What the fuck is going through your head?"

She looked at me with a Mona Lisa smile and gave me a few pats on the back.

"Sweetie, get a grip."

"But…"

"I got a position at Doctors without Borders, and I'm going to work on a boat assisting rescues in the Mediterranean."

I slowly let out the breath I had been holding the whole time Candela had been talking, gripped the wheel, and to my complete surprise…I burst into tears.

"But, Margot…why are you crying? I'm not going to be in a war zone or risking my life, I promise."

I sobbed.

"Idiot," she said in a hoarse voice. She was getting emotional. "It's not dangerous, seriously."

"That's not why I'm crying."

"So then why?"

"Because I'm really proud of you."

"I'm proud of you too."

Candela and I hugged awkwardly across the gear stick, crying. I leaned on her shoulder, like I had so many times when I was lonely at boarding school. I thought it might be harder to see her now because it wouldn't be possible to travel to where she was, like when she was in Switzerland. We wouldn't spend sister weekends drinking wine and strolling through the city. It made me sad, but it made me happy too. Someone strong, intelligent, good was going to dedicate herself to making the world a slightly better place. Or at least trying.

"Does Patricia know?"

"Yes."

"How did she not tell me?"

"Because right now all she can think about is how chafed her *chocha* is from doing it so much with a twenty-four-year-old."

We both burst out laughing.

"Bah…you didn't need to be thinking about that. I almost told you a few times before the wedding, but"—she raised her eyebrows—"then you kicked off the whole mess."

"I know, I know…"

"But all this has a silver lining: your guest room will stop being occupied territory very soon."

"It doesn't matter. I hate that house. It's like living in a hotel."

"That makes sense, considering what you do for a living." We pulled apart and looked at each other.

A smaller apartment, warmer, full of plants and flowers in every corner, where the smell of home-cooked food would waft and the paint on the walls would sometimes be chipped. An imperfect home where I could be happy without trying to seem like someone else.

"Are you listening to me?"

"What?" I landed in the car again.

"I was saying I can leave calmer knowing that you're capable of leaving work early every once in a while." She pointed to the clock. It was barely seven in the evening.

David, did I ever tell you I have a flat in London? You won't believe it, but that apartment is so warm and homey…

"Do you mind if we leave the car in the office parking lot and walk home?"

"Not at all."

My sister was describing how her life was going to be when she started her new job at the end of the month, and I was doing a stellar job of pretending to have all five senses on what I was doing, asking questions and laughing at her jokes while concentrating on not wasting a minute. Candela had no way of knowing, since I seemed so unbothered, that my steps were directing us toward the florist. What was I hoping for? A chance encounter? One last desperate attempt? I had no idea. I was just responding to a need. I wanted to get there before they closed.

"Hey, aren't we going the wrong way?" Candela asked me, peering up at the name of the street we were on.

"A little. But I thought we could grab a beer on some terrace in Malasaña."

"Oh, okay. Sounds cool."

"I know a place where they make really good hot dogs," I said sadly.

"If they're really good, why do you sound so sad?"

"Because David showed it to me."

"Right." She elbowed me gently. "And…where are we really going?"

"To walk by the florist," I confessed.

"That's stalking."

"I'm not gonna go in."

"Even worse. That's so creepy."

"Too much?" I looked at her, worried. "I'm probably losing my mind."

"What if he sees you?"

"Well, probably…"

"He'll probably come out and kiss you, and then the Disney magic will transform all of Malasaña into an enchanted place full of chubby birds who know how to sew."

"Don't make fun of me."

"If you regret leaving him so much, why don't you call him?"

"Because some things can't be said on the phone. And because he was the one who was so sure he wouldn't be able to love me."

We walked a few more blocks in silence, until I stopped dead on a corner diagonally across from the florist.

"That's it over there."

"That one? It's so cute."

"Two super sweet ladies run it." I smiled without looking at Candela, with my eyes glued on the exterior filled with flowerpot stands.

"Right…what do you wanna do?"

"Turn around and go home," I answered.

"Why don't you go in?"

"Because he won't want to see me."

"Why won't he want to see you?"

"Because…he doesn't think we could work."

"Margot…" She pulled a fed-up face. "Should I buy you a copy of *SuperPop*? You're not sixteen."

"What would I say to him?"

"How about, 'I miss you'?"

I stared at her, hesitating. She nodded encouragingly.

"I'll wait here for you. If it all goes well, send me a thumbs-up emoji on WhatsApp and I'll go home without you."

"What if it goes badly?"

"Come on…" She pushed me gently. "Go. I'm not gonna say it again."

They were the most difficult steps I've ever walked in my life. Not even my race in the opposite direction from my wedding had been so hard. Once I was at the door, I made three attempts to go in and ended up scurrying away all three. Candela whistled and waved her hand at me. For fuck's sake.

"Chicken!" she yelled.

"Shut up," I begged her, without raising my voice, trying to make her read my lips.

"You're the biggest wuss of all the Ortega sisters."

I sighed. I grabbed the door handle and pulled it open. Amparito had her glasses on and was leaning on the counter over something that looked like an invoice. She looked up at me and smiled, taking off her glasses and letting them fall onto her chest, swinging from a colorful beaded chain.

"Hello! How are you, beautiful?"

"Very good." I took a few steps into the room. Everything smelled of flowers. Everything smelled of damp earth. And I must have been giving off a terrible stench of fear. "How's it going?"

"Well, it's going. We've having kind of a hard time."

I furrowed my brow.

"Asuncion!" she yelled. "David's girl is here." She squinted at me. "I'm sorry, sweetie, I seem to have forgotten your name."

"Margarita," I said.

"How appropriate. David loves daisies."

Asuncion poked her head out through the beaded curtain from the back, smiled, and then made a kind of pout. "But, beautiful… how are you?"

"Fine."

"Not fine. If we're sad…imagine how you must feel."

"Uh…" I looked around nervously. I took a few deep breaths. I was starting to get an inkling of what was going on. "He's not here, is he?"

They looked at each other.

"No, he's not here. He…he didn't tell you?"

"About what?"

Another look passed between them. Amparito pushed a stool out from behind the counter and told me to sit. I obeyed without knowing why.

"I don't know if you should tell her," I heard Asuncion say.

"How could I not? Can't you see the poor girl's face?"

"The more you stir shit up, the worse it smells."

"Margarita," Amparito said to me, trying to crouch down to my height and look into my eyes. "He's gone."

"Very subtle," her sister said exasperatedly. "Leave it to me."

"What do you mean he's gone? Did he go to another florist?"

Asuncion appeared in front of me, elbowing her sister aside.

"He came here on Monday. It seemed strange because he only worked Tuesday to Thursday, but the thing is…he was upset."

"Upset?"

"Yes. He told us he had to quit; he was leaving. He had gotten a full-time job, that he had to save up and I don't know what else. He was very unhappy."

"Another job? Doing what?"

"As a waiter, I think? In a restaurant. Isn't that what he said?"

"I don't know," Amparito replied.

"He left us phone numbers of a few friends who could help us move boxes, flowerpots, and all that stuff. That's how he started out, but we saw he had a knack for flowers…and, anyway, it doesn't matter. He came to say goodbye and sorry, to let us know. He worked that week and on Thursday…he packed everything up and left."

I stood up from the stool and took a few steps toward the door, half groggy.

"Sweetie, are you okay?"

"Thank you. Thank you both so much. Have a good day."

I slammed out of the store, pushing the door harder than I needed to because I needed air. I was suffocating. The smell of the flowers, the wet earth, David's absence...they were taking over my lungs, pushing all the oxygen out of my body.

Candela rushed over to my side.

"He's gone," I said.

"Ay, Margot...I'm so sorry."

"He's gone, Candela."

"Margot..."

"What day is it?" I asked, dazed.

"Wednesday."

I lifted my hand up like a robot, hailing the first cab that passed and throwing myself inside.

"Wait, where are you going?" my sister asked.

"Hang on, hang on..." I said, scrolling through my WhatsApp chat with David. "Here!"

I gave the driver the address and turned back to look at Candela through the open door.

"Are you coming or not?"

The street where David lived with Ivan and Dominique was just as tree-lined as the first time I visited, but in the light of day, everything looked a little shabbier. The walls of the buildings had the faded color of paint jobs that hadn't been refreshed in years, graffiti, and smoke stains I hadn't noticed the last time. Or maybe it was just that everything lost its shine without David.

Candela didn't say anything, and I didn't either. It wasn't the neighborhood that shut us up. It was the anxiety breathing at my side.

I rang the buzzer rudely, again and again. But they didn't take long to answer. It was Dominique's delicate, melodious voice that answered with a soft "Who is it?"

"Is David here?"

"Who is it?"

"It's Margot, Dominique. Is David there?"

I don't think the desperation in my voice went unnoticed because she buzzed me in without a word.

Candela didn't ask if she should come up with me or wait downstairs. She just followed me into the elevator and studied my expression as I pushed the button for the third floor. I remembered being in there with David, how he came closer just for the fun of seeing how nervous it made me.

"Don't cry, Margot."

I hadn't even noticed I was.

I didn't have time to pull myself together in front of the door, just to swipe away the tears with my forearm. Dominique was waiting, with Ada in her arms and a sad expression.

"He's not here, is he?" I said.

"Come in. I'll make coffee."

The apartment was cozy and smelled exactly like the last time I had been here: a mixture of homemade food, baby smells, and cleanliness. It was like going into your much-loved grandmother's house.

Domi asked if I could hold her baby, and my sister took her in her arms when she saw I hadn't even heard the request. In my head, I was spinning through all the possible explanations for why David wasn't here. Or in the florist. Or in my life.

We sat on the couch in silence. Candela was playing easily with Ada; she had always been good with kids. She laughed, and the walls happily embraced the sound as part of the happy life inside it.

Dominique came out quickly with a tray covered in drawings of coffee beans, containing three mugs, a pot of coffee, a sugar bowl, and a small jug of milk. She left it on the table and sat on a footstool very close by. I wasn't used to physical contact and the affection of friendships, but I still let her take my hands in hers.

"He's gone," I put forth. "Isn't he?"

"Yes. A friend of his called him about a waiter job on a cruise ship. They said it paid well and you could get a pretty good bonus in tips."

I raised my eyebrows. A waiter on a cruise ship? That didn't seem like him at all.

"But…"

"Okay, girl, do you want the truth, or do you want it to be easy?" she asked me.

"Easy," Candela blurted.

"The truth," I corrected.

She looked at both of us with a tender smile. "You're sisters, aren't you?"

"But we're like night and day!" Candela said, surprised.

"You have the same eyebrows."

I would've laughed if I hadn't been so sad, dazed, angry, disappointed, and embarrassed.

"Is he ever coming back?"

"Girl, I don't think he's going to be stuck sailing the Adriatic Sea forever. But he told us he wasn't coming back to live here." She straightened up, picked up a mug, and handed it to me. "He was pretty torn up when he got back. We had never seen him like that."

"When he came back when?"

"The Sunday you guys said goodbye. He wouldn't stop repeating that he had thrown his life away, that he had aways made the worst decisions, that he had missed the boat. Ivan tried to cheer him up, but there was no way. It was hard, but…he talked. He talked clearly, I mean. You know how David is…he never shuts up even underwater."

I smiled.

"He was destroyed. I had never seen him cry. He was overwhelmed because he had nothing to offer you and he had spent so much time bumming off you. He kept repeating that he couldn't have fallen in love in a month, that it was all a personal crisis and he had to get his life together."

He couldn't have fallen in love in a month.

"I mean…" I said.

"The next day, he went back to walking dogs, saying that he needed time to understand, and…that very afternoon his friend called him to tell him about the cruise. He saw his shot. Three months on a boat, well paid, with no immediate need to find an apartment but still getting out of the house right away. It seemed perfect to him."

"He gets seasick on boats," I whispered.

She patted me on the leg. "You must feel terrible. I guess in a way he escaped; everything got him tied up in knots and…"

"No," I said, not looking at her. "I know that feeling. I guess it's the same thing that made me run out of my wedding."

"No, my girl. You didn't want to marry that man. David…David sometimes feels too much. If you want my opinion, I'd say that I think you're still the only priority in his decisions. He's a great guy, but in some ways, he's still a…little boy. I guess he left thinking he could come back in style, you know? With a plan, with a future…I don't know. He's a romantic. And look, I thought he was crazy when he told me that if you showed up, I should tell you…"

"Tell me what?"

"Wait. I wrote it down in my phone so I wouldn't forget."

Dominique stood up. Ada was still trying to pull on Candela's nose, which was apparently hilarious to both of them. When she came back, I had put my mug down on the tray untouched.

"Let me see… Here it is: 'Life will decide whether or not we are *us*. Tell her to fly. And to not change her number because, even if we never dare to knock on that door, we need to feel like it's open.'"

She took her eyes off the screen and looked at me.

"Does any of that mean anything to you? I probably typed it wrong. I don't know. Now that I'm reading it out loud, it sounds all weird. He said it quickly, and I typed it after he left, so I don't know if…"

I stood up. Candela looked at me from the couch with the baby in her arms, surprised by my reaction.

"I have to go," I said to Dominique. "But thank you so much."

"You're welcome, Margot. Come back whenever you want. We're making *chicharrones* on Sunday if you want to join."

I swallowed and thanked her, knowing I would probably never see her again. I gave her a hug, and Candela handed back her child when we drew apart.

As we were saying goodbye at the door, Dominique said to me, "It's too bad David was so scared of being loved right, Margot, because he was crazy about you."

The roof of our house, imperfect but warm, had collapsed under the weight of our doubts and crumbled in over the furniture and plants, smashing everything and leaving the four walls coated in dust, warped, tearing photos we never took of trips we would never go on.

The couple we could have been, passionate but ready to learn it all, stopped speaking the same language and, as much as we wanted to say *I love you*, we didn't understand a word and had to let each other go.

The woman who could have been at his side. The man I imagined he was harboring inside. The kids who would've grown up knowing that being free doesn't mean not being tied to anyone but instead knowing that the truth is what matters, were never born.

I never crossed the threshold of his parents' house.

I never defied my mother, introducing him at Christmas lunch.

We never bought furniture together.

We never argued again about a stupid misunderstanding.

We never made love in any bed, car, or pool again.

Because the absence, the empty "forever," crashed onto me all at once, like a conviction I couldn't possibly swallow in one bite.

Like Cassandra…I suddenly knew what the future held, that I would wait without him, but nobody, not even me, was ready to believe me.

No, fairy tales don't exist. And if they did exist, it's possible that Hansel and Gretel never would have gotten out of the candy house alive.

56. A

~~~

ACCEPTING LIFE

It took me two years to accept that I had been abandoned. Plain and simple. I'm not going to sugarcoat it. I took two fucking years to accept that David wasn't coming back. And that I didn't want to go looking for him.

The first three months were the longest, I think, because back then I was still living in the fantasy that, after his adventure on the cruise ship, he would come back. He would show up at my door, tan, smiling, regretful…and he would say something stupid but very meaningful, something like, "Has it been 'forever' yet? I'm tired of waiting."

As you can imagine, that didn't happen, and the three following months turned into overtime where every thought was followed by *He'll probably come back.*

I heard from him nine months after the last time I saw him at Atocha station. Sometimes, in the middle of a crowd bustling down Gran Vía or crossing Castellana, my heart would stop because I thought I had seen him. I would normally freeze, barely even blinking, waiting to find out if it was him, but it never was. Until it was, because Madrid isn't very big. I was talking to my sister Candela on the phone, with the windows of the company car rolled down, while I checked a few things on my iPad. Multitasking, as they say in America. I was overwhelmed because the next day, I had an important meeting, and I rolled the window down so I could feel the still-brisk spring air on my face. And I saw him.

He didn't have anything with him except his hands shoved in the pockets of a leather jacket that looked good on him. His hair had grown, and he wore it combed to one side, in a kind of grunge but tidy look. I didn't know where he was coming from or where he was going. I just knew that I didn't want to stop to find out.

He saw me. Yes, he saw me too. He saw me looking at him, letting my hand holding my phone fall into my lap and tracing his name with my lips, barely moving them. He saw me choosing to abandon the possibility of asking him for explanations, of demanding he come back. He saw me pull away, in my car, in my life.

He texted me that night. I knew he would, and even though I was prepared, I still cried a lot.

I never thought it would be like that if we ever saw each other again. I'm sorry for taking off the way I did. I'm sorry I didn't face what we felt. I'm sorry I made myself small when it was time to be big. I'm sorry, Margot, because by trying not to suffer, I hurt us. If you get this message, it means you haven't changed your number, so thank you for giving me the chance to tell you that I've never forgotten you.

I cried for almost an hour without stopping, and when I was

finally able to calm down, I threw the flowers I had worked so hard to dry down the trash chute because they didn't mean anything anymore.

Another lesson: love doesn't expire, but you have to conjugate it in time; otherwise it will stop meaning anything.

Because I had been waiting nine months and he was there. Because neither of us texted each other. Because we both hid in the romantic and childish fantasy of star-crossed lovers so we didn't have to accept that we didn't have the guts to make it work.

I tossed the flowers, and then I hated myself for it, but the next day, there was no turning back. I had fully entered the second phase of grief. Anger.

I hated him for five more months, but it wouldn't serve for anything until I stopped monitoring his social media, in case one day he posted a photo that would cause me enough pain to burn even the memories I held in my chest. But no. The last photo was still "Us," like someone who likes seeing the bow of the ship she was shipwrecked in floating adrift.

After the next summer, it was easier. They say the earth has to spin all the way around before anniversaries will stop hurting so much. By that I mean that when we've already completed a year of all those first times (the first anniversary of the first kiss, the anniversary of the first time we had sex, a year since he told me that thing, a year since we experienced this other thing…), only two options unfold in front of us: one is to cling to stuff that no longer exists; another is to keep walking alone in search of something new.

I chose to keep walking, even if it still took me a few more months.

I say it took two years because that's how long I put off concluding that if I kept living in the same place, it was just so he could find me if he looked for me. I took two years to put the apartment on the market, and it sold in two months to a Chinese magnate. Furnished and everything. I didn't even want to pack up memories from that house. It was a symbol of having let everyone else tell me who I should be. It was a kind of mausoleum where the Margot who never felt good enough would lie in rest forever.

I sold it, pocketed the money, and moved to my flat in London. Candela was sailing the Mediterranean from top to bottom, and Patricia was too busy trying to make the pieces of her life fit together…as usual. If I was going to be lonely in Madrid anyway, I'd rather do that in London. And I learned there that everything was much easier than we insist on believing.

The office in London was smaller than the one in Madrid, but it ran like a Swiss watch. In two weeks, I was more settled in there than I had ever been in Madrid. Sonia didn't mind the change either. She was happy. She said that now her life could turn into a Marian Keyes novel. I guess romantics never learn.

It was hard, but I started to be happy. No longer waiting for anyone. With my loneliness. Learning about my own shit. Congratulating myself for my successes. Toasting myself, with a glass of good wine and a book, on the good days. Going out to drink a pint with Sonia and other people from the team when we had a bad day. I guess that was my rule: everything goes better with a glass of wine, but never drink alone if you're swallowing something bitter.

If someone asked me if I had forgotten David, I would say no. Not for a second. But I stopped hating him because I had distanced myself. I stopped thinking about it as an abandonment. I learned that we were two different people who didn't need the same thing. He still needed to grow, to learn, to accept. And, listen, when my rage disappeared, so did the certainty that I would never love again the way we loved each other that summer.

I met someone. Life, like water, always finds a place to flow. And it turns out sometimes it flows back to places you thought were all dried up. I met him in a park. Sometimes, when the weather was nice (and in London that meant, "If it's not raining, that's good enough"), I went there to read on a bench and get some fresh air. One of those days, his dog pounced on me, barking like crazy because he wanted to eat the squirrel I was feeding a nut to. It scared me to death because, even though he's a good, playful dog, he's still a hunk of muscle full of teeth. His owner insisted on buying me a coffee to make up for it.

We talked. He asked for my number, and since I didn't want to give it to him, in a cloud of embarrassed giggles, he gave me his. Then I went home and cried because David did the same thing. He gave me his number so we could talk, but it couldn't work because neither of us was brave or irresponsible enough to throw ourselves fully into loving each other. And I didn't feel like being a coward anymore.

I met up with Barin a few times (I know, what a weird name) before it became clear that this wouldn't work if I didn't do something about my past.

So after we went on a date where he finally kissed me, I bought a return ticket to Madrid, and not exactly to see my mother, who, by the way, had told me in a very formal email that she had taken half a kilo of fat from her ass and injected it into her face. Or something like that. We were living for it in our sister group chat. She wasn't Lady Meow anymore. Now she was Mrs. Butt Face.

~~~~

The truth is it wasn't hard to find him. Not hard at all. If I hadn't gone to see him before, I guess it was because I needed to get over him first.

When I went into his spot, I felt a shiver of pleasure. The inside of the store was a perfect temperature. It smelled like flowers, like damp earth, like David.

I went up to the counter, and a masculine voice announced he would be right there. I combed my hair with my fingers, a little nervous, and…he came out.

He was wearing jeans and a wool sweater, the chunky kind, the kind that look so good on cute boys…even though he was no longer a cute boy. He was an incredibly handsome man. He had turned thirty now, but he still had the face of a sad boy. I think it grew sadder when he saw me.

"Fuck." He leaned on the counter, and then, as he straightened up, he took the chance to push his hair out of his face. It was still tangled.

"The weird thing is…I knew that's exactly what you'd say," I said with a smile.

We didn't move. We stood there frozen for a few seconds, studying each other, looking for the differences between the person we had in front of us and what we remembered from that brief love.

"Come back here," he said finally.

"If you have to work, I can come back later."

"Don't be silly. Come back."

He came out from behind the counter and pointed me to the back room and locked the shop from the inside, turning around a super vintage sign that said, "Open," and "Closed."

"Do you want a coffee?" he offered.

"Thank you. It's freezing out there."

"Do you still take it plain?"

"And you still drown yours in a liter of milk?"

"I never liked coffee. It's time to admit it. I was young, and I wanted to impress you." He grimaced.

"A latte is so impressive." I smiled. "You're still young."

"Yeah?"

"Only three years have passed."

"Well, I feel like I've aged at least fifteen." He bit his lip and shoved his hands in his pockets.

"It's probably because years without me are like cat years."

"You were always a little like a cat, that's true. Come in and sit down, please."

The back room had its own back room, and judging by the way it was set up, I'd say David spent more time here than at home…if he had one. There was a couch, clearly secondhand, dark-green velvet, beautiful but sagging from the years. There was a neatly folded soft blanket on the backrest.

A table, made of a rough wooden board and black metal bars, held what were clearly the leftovers of a meal: a plate coated in crumbs and a crumpled napkin. An almost-empty glass water bottle. A very old book with yellowed pages.

I was surprised to see a fireplace in one corner…or what was left of it because it was clearly decorative. There was a basket of dried flowers in it. On the mantelpiece, there were small glass vases filled with more flowers and a few pots around it filled with tall, lush plants. Curtains, which seemed heavy and dusty, covered two windows, and when I looked out them, I discovered they overlooked a cute little patio shared with a small community of neighbors. Where David was making coffee in a Nespresso machine, there was also a mini-fridge where I could see a couple bottles of wine.

I noticed two glasses sitting there, with the dregs of red wine, next to him on the counter where he kept the coffee maker. One of them had a smudge of red lipstick. I wondered if he was still attracted to beautiful women who would never love him or if, instead, he had found someone else like me, yearning to love him.

"It's not what it looks like."

"Which part?"

I went over to the couch and sat down.

"Well…" He took a deep breath and handed me the cup, an antique one, floral with gilded edges. "I don't live here, even though I know it seems like I'm pretty settled in. I have an apartment a few blocks from here. I walk to work every day."

"You seem happy."

"Well, as I said, it's not what it looks like."

"You're not happy?"

"The glass." He didn't turn to look at it; he just pointed fleetingly behind him. "That's not what it looks like either."

"It's been three years, David. You don't owe me any explanations."

"So what are you doing here?"

I swirled my coffee and took a sip. He sat opposite me, first moving some of the detritus off the table and sitting down on it.

"You met someone," he said.

"Yes. How about you?"

"No one who made me feel the need to buy a ticket to come find you in London."

"How'd you know…?"

"How did you know where to find me?"

I fell silent and put the cup aside. I needed to be closer for this. He still smelled exactly the same. In three years, he hadn't changed cologne…the one he had swapped out baby powder for because in my absolute stupidity, I had told him that would help Idoia fall in love with him.

"I came to tell you that I don't hate you anymore," I said to him. "Because I guess you know that I hated you a lot."

"I can imagine." He looked away and bit the inside of his cheek. "And you had every reason to."

"No. I don't think so. I think I was angrier at the time because it didn't bring us together than I was angry at you. That's why I don't hate you anymore. Because I understood it."

"It was an excuse." He shrugged. "I was terrified. I was scared it would end badly, and I was scared it would end well. I think I thought I wasn't ready for a 'forever,' and I ended up swallowing something else…an even more bitter pill."

"We wouldn't have lasted forever. I've had time to think it through, you know? And in the two hundred lives I've imagined with you, in all of them, there was some insurmountable problem. Kids, routine, work, my obsession with control, your untidiness, another girl…"

"I never would've cheated on you."

"Or maybe you would have." I smiled. "We don't know."

"That's why I can't forgive myself, because we'll never know."

"I could've looked for you too."

"And you did." He looked down at the floor and took a very deep breath.

"Yes. That's true."

"Did I break your heart?"

"Into tiny pieces. Not because you left, for the record. You broke my heart with your doubts about whether what we felt was real. You broke my heart by not coming back."

"I realized when you didn't answer that message I sent you. I realized it was too late, I mean. I went from one cruise to another, and when I got back, I wanted to show up on your doorstep, but I was embarrassed that I didn't know what to say. *I love you*? An *I love you* isn't enough, Margot. We both know that."

"It doesn't matter." I reached out and clasped his bare forearm. The sleeves of his sweater were rolled up. He was so handsome. "It wouldn't've worked."

"Or maybe it would have. But we'll never know. And even if it hadn't worked, we would've experienced something beautiful. Maybe we even denied ourselves the possibility of discovering that we were dreaming of other things. Look at me. If it hadn't been for you, I don't think I ever would've known that this is what I wanted."

"Are you happy?" I asked again.

"I'm as happy as I think anyone can be. I'm finally at peace with the decisions I made. I'm alone, but…"

"Why? I'm sure there are dozens of girls who'd want to spend their nights wrapped in this blanket, tossing and turning on this couch with you."

"Only you wanted to do that," he teased. "Because you're crazy. Even if you try to hide it with your high heels, your fancy haircut… you're just as crazy as me. And you would leave everything behind for love."

I hung my head. He gently lifted my chin.

"I'm not saying that because…"

"Don't judge, David. I already know that. It's just that…well, the crazy part of me wants to stay on this couch."

"So stay. And leave everything for love."

I laughed reluctantly.

"Yeah, yeah, I know. That's crazy. You can't," he admonished himself.

"I came here to tell you I don't hate you anymore and so you can tell me that you don't love me anymore."

This time it was his turn to laugh, but he did it even more reluctantly. "Do you need me to tell you that to move on with your life?"

"I have moved on with my life, but I need to hear it. Even though you never actually said, 'I love you,' properly."

"I didn't even have enough to give you that *I love you*." He made a face. "I was a kid. But I loved you. Fuck, I really loved you. And…I'm really sorry, Margot, because I can't tell you I've stopped. I don't wake up in the middle of the night anymore, hating myself for leaving, but I still think about you, about what we could have been. And…"

I put both hands on his knees; he put his hands over mine. He understood that I just did it to stop him. I didn't want to hear anymore, at least not if that's where he was heading.

"Well. At least," he whispered with a shaky voice, "we'll have a grown-up goodbye. And now I have no excuse not to forget you."

He stood up and turned around, and I thought I saw him sweep his forearm over his eyes.

"Forget the coffee. Do you want a drink?" he offered me.

"I can't stay."

"Just one. Come on. To the past."

I stood up. I picked up my bag and headed to the door. I stopped next to him. His eyes were glassy, and I put my index finger on his nose.

"Don't even think about crying."

"I'm not going to," he assured me, trying not to blink.

"If you can't tell me you don't love me, I guess we can leave it all with a thank-you."

"Sex shouldn't be thanked, even if it's the best sex you've ever had."

"Not for the sex, but for giving me the chance to realize that love really exists, just like they tell it in books. That can be thanked," I clarified.

"It was so short that some would say it didn't even happen."

"What others think doesn't matter to me."

"That's my girl." He smiled.

"I'm leaving."

I went over and kissed him on the cheek. He grabbed my waist, and we stayed there, not moving, with my nose in his stubbly beard and his hands around me. How is it possible to love someone so much that you don't love anymore?

I pulled away.

"I brought you a gift."

"What?" He looked away. "A gift?"

"A song. Look it up and listen to it after I leave. It's called 'Ojos Noche' by Elsa y Elmar. It's not from the eighties, but you'll like it."

"Take some flowers," he said. "I'll put together a bouquet for you in two minutes."

"Oh, no. I don't want to keep a little of something I can't have." I stroked his cheek, and he nodded.

I turned and crossed the back room that functioned as a storeroom. I pictured him working there, and I was jealous for a few seconds of whoever would pass through here every day to tell him it was late, and it was time to come home.

"Be happy." I let it hang in the air.

"That's it?"

"I hope someone loves you the way I didn't know how. That the whole world's yours. That you never remember me again. But keep the songs, okay?"

"Motherfucker," slipped out of his lips through a huge smile.

"Let someone love you the way I wanted to love you."

"And you let someone see what you showed me."

"Goodbye."

"Goodbye, Margot. I love you."

When I left the store, I knew I would never see him again; I couldn't even turn back and get one last look, or I would stay and we would do everything badly.

I'd have to engrave in my memory the name that was everywhere, on all the shop's awnings, so I wouldn't forget, at least, that he named his florist Come Back, Daisy.

54. B

~~~~

THE OTHER PATH

DAVID

When I turned my back on Atocha station, I promised myself something. Some nonsense, like when you're a kid and you tell yourself that if you don't step on any cracks on the way home from school, you'll be given the gift of magic. Something like that. I said: *David, turn around. If she does the same, she's the one...and everything else can fuck off.* I think it was fear that made me look for an excuse, however absurd it was, to not leave.

I turned. She stopped and turned back toward me. My heart was going to jump out of my chest. She smiled sadly. I saw her crying and turned to keep leaving. I checked that she was too.

If she turns twice...then there's definitely no doubt, David. Have some balls.

I turned. She stopped and turned toward me. Fuck. Fuck. Twice. I wanted to drop-kick the gang of teenagers who crossed between us right then and made her turn her back again and move farther away in the opposite direction.

Third time's the charm.

I turned. She stopped and turned back to me.

So messy. So messy, man. She's five years older than you, she wants a man and you're just a kid, you're full of doubts, and you have nothing of value you can give her; if you say yes, you won't have the balls to destroy everything; you'll marry her, you'll have kids, and you'll end up in Bermuda shorts playing golf, which is the opposite of flying…

To hell with it.

I rammed through everything in my way, and when I got to her, I clasped her elbow gently. Margot was startled and gave one of those little jumps I liked so much.

"What…?"

"To hell with it," I said out loud. "To hell with everything, Margot."

She furrowed her brow, and I let go of her arm.

"What are we doing?" I asked her.

"Making an adult decision because…"

"Why?"

"For a lot of reasons." And she shifted her weight from one leg to the other.

"I want to go into that bar and you can explain them all to me," I begged.

She tilted her head to one side, looked at the bar I was referring to, and started to laugh.

"That one? No way. I don't feel like catching dengue fever."

"Margot…"

"David!" she complained. "It was you, for fuck's sake. You were the one who said it would be a disaster."

"Well, it doesn't seem that clear to me anymore."

"Go to hell!"

But right after she told me to go to hell…she smiled.

Next to the Reina Sofia Museum, there's a terrace. A wonderful terrace, the kind that charges you twelve wonderful euros for a gin and tonic but is blanketed with plants, flowers, an air-conditioning system outside that even has a cool mist spraying gently over everything…that was much appreciated that almost August afternoon.

We sat in a corner shielded from stares, and I dropped my bag on the floor. She sucked her teeth, stood up, and put it on a chair with hers.

"That thing's a piece of shit!"

"It'll be more of a piece of shit if you keep treating it like that," she chided me.

We both smiled immediately. At how stupid we had acted in the car. At the stupid stuff I had said the night before.

"What's going on?" she asked me. "Because honestly, this seems like a yes or no."

"No, no. It's a…whatchamacallit? An amendment."

"An amendment, eh? And what does the amendment propose?"

"What if I was wrong?"

"About what exactly?"

"About everything. What if I keep making the wrong decisions? Like when I left university just in case I didn't find a job I liked. Like when I didn't look for an apartment just in case… Well, the apartment was another stupid thing. And what if I can?"

"What if you can what?"

"Love you the way you deserve."

Margot blinked and rubbed her lips together.

"What if I can give you what you deserve, love you well, prepare myself for what comes, whatever that may be? What if we can? What if it doesn't have to end badly?"

"It'll end badly." This time she was the one who called it. "Whether I like it or not."

"Why?"

"Because you're young."

"I'm five years younger than you. That's not an insurmountable age difference. I'll mature."

"You feel hopelessly attracted to women who will never love you."

"No: I feel hopelessly attracted to you."

She sighed. She waved over the waiter.

"Two white wines, please."

"That thing where you order for me," I said as soon as he was gone, "we can fix."

"Your life"—she gestured—"your life is a disaster."

"I know."

"What are we going to do about that? Where would a healthy relationship fit into your life?"

"Okay. I know my life is a disaster, but there's nothing that can't be undone. I'll find an apartment. I have enough money saved to rent a room in an apartment with roommates."

"You have three jobs," she pointed out. "And one of them you hate."

"I'll quit."

"And what are you going to live on?"

"I'll offer to work more hours at the florist, and if they can't give me more shifts, I'll find another one that's hiring."

"And…?"

"Margot, I don't want you to take this as an attack, okay? But you have stuff to figure out too, and that doesn't make me doubt that we can find a way with what we're feeling. Because we are feeling it."

"Yes," she confirmed. "But…are you aware a lot of people will think you're with me for my money?"

"You'll never give me a cent, and we'll put a price cap on gifts."

"What if I feel like going to a restaurant that's two hundred euros a cover?"

"You can bring your sister Patricia. Now that she's getting divorced, she'll want to go out even more."

"You're a dick!" she groaned with a smile.

"I'm a million things, Margot. I'm a disaster, I'm chaotic, and sometimes I don't have balls. I hate waking up early, I don't like coffee, I don't have a cent in my pocket, and I don't know how to speak English. I'm nostalgic, and I like music from when my parents were too young to go to bars. One day, I wake up thinking the meaning of my life is to be a father, and the next day, I think I hate all little snots under eighteen…and sometimes twenty-five. Sometimes I come really fast, I like doing it in public places, and sometimes I fantasize about two chicks going down on me."

"Jesus…" Margot covered her face when the girls at the next table turned to look at me, appalled, when they heard me say those last things.

"Listen to me…" I pried her hand off her face and held it in mine. "I'm all those horrible things, but last night, when you were talking to my friends and you kissed my shoulder…I thought that was exactly how I wanted my life to be until I died. I want you to help me with the barbecue every year at Cris's birthday; I want to save every cent I have to go on trips with you, even if I have to go in coach; I want you to look at me one day and say, 'I'm so proud of you.' I have all the certificates that say I'll never accomplish that, but…this time I want to try. If you let me, I want to try."

"David…it's not that I don't want to; it's just that last night I felt like you were so sure…"

"A shitty kind of sure. I was just scared."

"Is it possible to feel so much in just one month? What if we're just throwing ourselves into each other's arms to avoid the pain of what didn't work with our last partners?"

"There are people who spend their whole lives in love with someone they crossed paths with one night. How can this not be true, Margot? Who decides what is and what isn't? And about the other thing…we'll take time."

"A month?" she said sarcastically.

"However long we need. We'll go slow. We'll do it right."

I saw her hesitating and decided to play my final card.

"I've seen what was going to happen to us. I saw it, Margot. In the car, I started thinking, and…do you know what'll end up happening? I'll leave. To some city, to some shitty job. Just to get away from Madrid and the feeling that I lost the love of my life. And you'll hate me even more than if this turns out badly. In the end, you'll forgive me because you're a good person, but we'll always have a wound called 'Us,' and we'll never be able to love the same way again."

"I want to fall in love with myself before I fall more in love with you."

"And I'll encourage you to do that."

"So now what?"

"Now tell me you love me and I'll give you all the time in the world."

She shook her head. Then she sighed. She rubbed her forehead. She ruffled her hair and then smoothed it down again. She looked at the girls at the table next to us and their shoes.

"Sad eyes…" I murmured. "Please, do what you really want to do."

Margot looked at me, pressing her lips together, and…she smiled. She smiled! And I did too. Because when someone gives street dogs love, they feel rich.

55. B

~~~

YES

Idoia was beautiful, I have to admit it. She had put a lot of effort into it. She wanted the David who drooled at her feet, the lapdog, the one who had learned that even being beaten with a stick is better than being alone. I was wrong about that.

But I didn't really care much about looks. She was wearing booty shorts and a white blouse knotted at the waist and hanging half open with a black bra peeking out. I was wearing a pair of super-torn jeans and a gray T-shirt with a huge hole where the label used to be.

Two months earlier, I would have crawled for her; now I just thought, as she kissed me on both cheeks (thinking she was so cool for not giving me one on the mouth), that I should take advantage of the sales to get a few clothes with no holes.

"Hey," I greeted her. "How's it going? Listen, I'm in a hurry. Do you mind if we just grab something right here?"

I pointed to a tapas place with a bar full of faithful regulars, all total characters.

"Here?"

"It's just that I'm in a hurry," I repeated.

I went inside for two bottles of beer while she waited for me, leaning against a wall, smoking a cigarette, and looking mortified. The waiter told me we couldn't take the beers farther than the high table next to the door for smokers.

"Thanks, chief. I'm not planning on going very far," I replied.

"Well, I'd go to the end of the world with that girl," a dude at the bar let slip.

"You need to get to know people from the inside, sir, but I guess hoping not to judge a woman like that for her looks would be very hard work, so we'll leave it there. Have a good one."

Being polite doesn't cost a thing.

"So," Idoia said flirtatiously when I handed her the beer.

I took a sip of mine. I realized I wasn't in the mood for it, and I left it on the high table, where she was leaning.

"How do you want to do this?" I asked her. "The easy way or the truth?"

"Can't it be easy and the truth?"

"No, sorry."

"Well…the truth." She sighed slightly condescendingly, like I was a kid who wanted to show her a magic trick I had learned but that she was completely sure wouldn't work.

"Okay. Well…" I leaned on the table, swallowed, looked her in the eyes, and smiled. "I don't want to get back together with you. Our relationship was awful. Total garbage."

She straightened up, surprised.

"I swear even on Friday I still had doubts; that's why I said yes when you suggested meeting today. I thought I was probably wrong, that I should fight for this since up until recently it had been so important for me to get you back. I never meant to play you."

"You couldn't have even if you wanted to."

I looked to the side and snorted. "I wanted to do this nicely."

"That's your problem, David, you have no balls. You always beat around the bush and…"

"Okay, cool. Look, I wanted you to love me. I was dying to get you to love me, since I love myself little and badly. I thought someone like you giving me your love would make up for it, but…to hell with it, Idoia. I don't need you to give and take away your attention all the time to feel alive or important because I realized that you're a girl with little to offer, not because you don't have it, but because you don't feel like sharing it.

"I fell in love with Margot, and I understand that I have to get my shit together to be able to enjoy that love. And I have to thank you for having been a true bitch to me because, in one of life's lucky coincidences, you pushed me into her arms."

"I don't know where all this resentment is coming from," she declared, taking another sip of her beer. "It wasn't even that serious. A few months and…"

"It's not resentment. I'm over that too. But you know how happy it makes me to see her laugh? It's a whole other thing, like it's from another planet. And I'm only telling you this because I think you're throwing a huge amount of time and intense energy down the drain. I'm not one to give advice, but, my girl…what we had, for me it was serious; stop acting like you have to impress someone all the time. Embrace yourself. I'm sure you're so much cooler than all this bullshit about being a cold heartbreaker girl. Tomorrow some wire might get crossed, a nuclear missile could be launched, and we'll all be toast… Make your time worth your while. I'm going to."

"Wow, that'll be a change," she said maliciously.

"Whatever you say. I'm out. I have an appointment to see a few apartments, and I don't want to be late. Be happy."

I smiled, did a kind of military salute, and turned away. I hadn't taken more than ten steps away when she yelled, "Be happy? That's it?"

I turned and laughed. I had spoken from my heart. I nodded.

"Yes. That's it."

56. B

~~~

OUR OWN FAIRY TALE

She took her time. Boy, she really did take her time. A disaster like me is not reformed with a click of the fingers. And she had her own stuff to figure out too.

My messiness. Her obsession with control. My tendency for drama. Her exaggerated pragmatism. My underachieving. Her paranoia about work.

I never would have imagined that breaking up with and forgetting her Iron Man of a fiancé would be the least of our problems as a couple. Even though, well, in the name of full disclosure, it still took us a while longer to become a couple.

Until December, we kept a comfortable distance, but still distance in the end, during which we, well, we saw each other, we talked, we made plans, but…zero sex. Because, according to my dear Margot, when we fucked, she forgot to think for a few days, and she didn't make premeditated decisions.

I don't know if I meditated on the decision or not, but, by the way, I quit the club job a month later, and I said I wouldn't embark, no matter how good the pay or the tips were, as a waiter on a cruise ship.

I moved near the Oporto metro stop, to a place pretty far from the idea of a shared apartment I had when I started university. My roommate was a physicist who worked for a company that did things I didn't understand and meditated every night, letting off an "ohmmm" that leaked into my bedroom like a giant bumblebee buzzing. But he was calm. And clean. And it was almost like living alone except splitting expenses.

The first day Margot came to sleep here with me, I felt kind of like a schoolboy, even though the little minx, after kissing me, making out with me, and purring and rubbing against me like a cat, told me it was better to leave it there. I had even cleaned out the dust bunnies under the bed in case we got creative with the first fuck in months... so I started laughing.

"Give me a hand job at least," I said jokingly.

"I'd probably eviscerate you and, hey, problem solved."

I asked if I could change her mind with polite insistence. When she smiled and said no and threatened to take her stuff and go home if I didn't stop thinking with my dick, I realized I had jumped the gun by buying the jumbo pack of condoms.

But I'm not complaining. Two days later we went to see the latest Woody Allen movie, and while it was raining on the screen, Margot said she couldn't take it anymore, pulled her hair into a ponytail, and gave me a blow job.

It wasn't too long before our relationship was official. In February, Margot was already introducing me as her boyfriend to her colleagues at work drinks. She was wearing a black dress with a slit that exposed one of her legs. She looked incredible, and I felt like the luckiest dude on the face of the earth. I was stunned when I saw the boss and shareholder side of Margot, and I understood why she was so burned out; she had to be hard, and my small, tiny, huge Margot wasn't hard, and she had to wear a shield that weighed her down.

"What are you afraid of?" I asked her that night in her house, as I was taking off the suit she had forced me to buy.

"Them seeing my weaknesses. They're like misogynist vultures."

"I have no doubt those dudes are total pigs, but...why do you care? You hold thirty-seven percent of the shares, my boss bitch. If you wanted to, you could go around barking."

I watched her roll her eyes and launch into a monologue about how wrong I was. Sitting there, pulling shiny bobby pins out of her hair, tousling her locks between her fingers, unzipping her party dress, leaving on nothing but a delicate little black slip, unbuttoning the strap of her heels.

"Come here. This dog does want to bark at you," I said.

Thank the universe, our relationship was now allowed to cause bad decisions through sex. I lifted her up, carried her to the bed, and called her Khaleesi, mother of hotels and every sweet nothing I could think of until, very seriously, straddling me, she said, "The problem is I'm scared of them, David, because I was brought up being told that they know what they're doing and I don't."

"So what can we do to change that?"

"I could open a haberdashery and spend my life selling stockings?"

I grabbed her firmly by the hips and shook her a little.

"Margot, babe...you can do whatever you want. You're the boss, and you have wings. What more do you need? But don't waste your talent fleeing to a job that won't turn you on as much as yours does."

The second I said that…even though the sex that came after was incredible, like the kind we had during the days we thought were our goodbye.

She took two more months chewing over an idea so that when she brought it up to me she was more than sure. And I have to admit she did a good job. She sold the movie well.

"David…you know I have a flat in London?"

"Seriously?" I don't know why I was surprised.

"Yes."

We were in her office. I had surprised her by bringing hot chocolate when I left the florist. I knew that my little work addict would still be there, and…I hit the nail on the head.

I flopped into one of the chairs opposite her desk.

"I've been postponing my trips to London since I've been with you because"—she turned red and started to fidget with the stuff on her desk—"because I didn't want to go too far away."

"Dummy." I winked.

"The thing is, I have to go to London for a few days because I have meetings with partners, clients, and…well, I thought maybe we could take the chance to spend a few days there, both of us. I think you'll like my flat."

"I can't take any more days off," I said, pouting.

"From Friday to Monday. You'll be back in time to get to the florist. I'll make sure of it."

In a very serious conversation (as serious as it could be, you understand) with Amparito and Asuncion, I had managed to get them to add a day and a few hours to my schedule, and that almost got me up to a half-decent salary, but that meant from Monday to Thursday I was all theirs. And those ladies were very possessive.

"Fine. If I don't have to miss work." I shrugged. "But I'm buying the tickets."

"They're crazy expensive," she said with that business air she pulled out of her sleeve every once in a while. "I already took the liberty of buying them. They're for the day after tomorrow."

"Some things never change. You're pretty ballsy."

The complaint served for nothing. We went to London.

While Margot was at her meetings and eating in those two-hundred-euro-a-plate restaurants, she left me in her apartment. She had sent someone to clean it and fill the refrigerator a little, and I had brought my book, so it wasn't exactly torture being there. I had keys too in case I wanted to go out and take a walk, but…with my terrible English, I didn't want to risk needing to communicate with someone and not being able to.

I sat on the couch. It was very pretty, classic, very comfortable. I opened my book, but I sat there with it in my lap staring, smitten by the beautiful, Victorian-era fireplace in the living room. Did it work? My eyes swept over every detail in the room, and I was surprised by the amount of flowers and plants she had here. Who the hell watered them?

I stood up and paced the living room. It was warm, cozy, light-filled, despite being in a city that, you have to admit, wasn't exactly what I would call full of light. The apartment had two bedrooms: one big one with a wardrobe, a double bed, and an en suite bathroom, and a smaller one, next to the bathroom in the hallway, which Margot was using as an office for now. I loved the kitchen, with its green cabinets, an island, and a long wooden table for throwing dinner parties and…

Suddenly it dawned on me what was happening here. When

she came home and asked me if I liked it, if I had looked around the neighborhood, if I noticed the tiny Lebanese restaurant on the corner…I cut to the chase.

"Do you want to move to London?"

She made a face and flopped onto the couch.

"Not if you don't want to."

"I don't speak English, babe," I answered anxiously.

"With a private tutor, doing an intensive…"

"I'm scared," I confessed.

"If you don't want to, it's fine. It just…it occurred to me it could be a good place for us. It's a big city, so free… I can work here without having to deal with that gang of pigs every day. And anyway, with Candela here and there and Patricia so busy piecing everything together with Didier and the kids…why not start fresh here?"

I promised her I would think about it. It meant a lot of things that scared me, like ending up becoming a boy toy, stuck in the house every day, a lazy bum.

But still, when I found myself in my village, asking my mother what she thought about it, I knew I had already done more than think about it. I had pretty much made up my mind.

"Hey, skinny." She smiled at me tenderly. "Live adventures."

"But, Mama…London?"

"If it scares you, do it scared."

My birthday present for Margot that year was English lessons for me, which I started two months before she turned thirty-three. That day, at dinner, I told her in pretty embarrassing English that I had spent a week practicing with my professor: "I want to go with you because I realized that home is wherever I'm with you."

We left four months later. The good thing about Margot's

obsession with control is that she's really meticulous when it comes to organizing things. I don't know how that trip to Greece even happened, to tell the truth. I guess it was a destiny thing.

We settled into her flat in Notting Hill, which cost God knows how much, and I kept taking classes until I felt like I could face a job interview. I'm not going to deny it, Margot helped me by recommending me to a contact who usually did the floral arrangements for her hotels there.

And I started working. And I liked it.

Margot promised me that if I didn't adapt to the city, we would go back, but the truth is I got the hang of it. Not just London, but the idea of starting over far from home. I understood, at twenty-eight years old, that it's never too late to decide who you want to be.

Margot secretly invited all my friends to London for my birthday. Behind my back, the nutjob chartered a private jet with the whole gang of maniacs from the village, Ivan, Domi, Ada, my siblings, my parents, and even my grandmother. She rented out a pub, decorated it with our favorite flowers and candles, and hired a catering company that served nothing but hot dogs and beer. The thing about not going over a certain budget for gifts must have slipped her mind.

The truth is, I wasn't in the mood that day. Having a birthday far from home and all your people can be a bummer, even if you're with the person you love…because life can't be sustained just on romantic love. So when she told me she had reserved a table for dinner that night, I scowled.

"I don't feel like it. Can't we stay home?"

"Come on, let's go…" she begged me, very sweetly. "I really want to show you this place. I'll wear a hair tie on my wrist to make up for it."

She always knows how to cheer me up.

When I went into the pub and everyone yelled, "Surprise," the only thing I could do was turn to look at her. And there, leaning against the wall, she looked at me with a generous smile and a guilty air. She had spent an obscene amount of money, but I couldn't be mad at her. If I had it, I would have blown it all on her.

The next day, while Margot worked, I picked up my mother and my grandmother from the Ortega Group hotel they were staying in, and while the rest of the family went sightseeing, I took them to a vintage store to help me pick out a ring. It was secondhand, I didn't spend too much money, and I spent the whole first month convinced that they had swindled me, it was terrible, and it would turn her finger green, but she said yes. And I realized that most of the time when you're happy, you don't even realize.

The questions cease, clocks stop, everything spins, and I danced with the girl with the sad eyes until I lost my feet and grew wings. Before we realized, the clock had started ticking again and three years had passed. And I turned thirty.

The decision to go back to Madrid was mutual, but it was Margot's job that expedited it. After a shake-up in the way the business was organized, she had to go back to take over a position with more responsibility.

By then, Margot had already managed to sell her apartment on Paseo de Castellana to a Chinese magnate, so we had to start from zero there, buying one for the two of us together. That caused many headaches and many arguments and made obvious how different we were. Princess stories always end with the happily ever after, but our path was littered with poison apples. Where to live, how to live, our schedules, my chaos, the systematic postponement of the decision about being parents, the age difference, some temper tantrum of mine, her habit of getting her way...Life, in all its magnificence, is a scale weighing good and bad so that once the little rough patches were worked out, we could feel as happy as we did. That's life; you get washing-machined by waves taller than you, and it's sink or swim until you learn to ride them. The first big wave in my life was called Margot, and thanks to her, I conquered my fear of the sea.

Life isn't a fairy tale, but if it is, I guess there will never be a perfect one.

We're still writing our own story, every day, ours, but if one day you pass by my florist, come in and say hi. You can't miss it. It's on the corner, it has a maroon awning, and painted onto the window in gold letters, it reads: "Fly, Daisy."

Epilogue

~~~

LIKE LIFE

This might be the shortest epilogue ever written, but I think I need to explain to you, at this point, why you read two endings to the same story. And it's because everything depends, every single thing, on the way you look at the world.

This story could have gone one way, and it could have gone the other. Each would have polar opposite results based on just one different decision. Fighting, dragging each other through the mud, being thoughtless, trusting too much, trusting at all. Everyone can call it whatever they want.

But here is the end of a story that doesn't have one ending written, just like life. It all depends on what you decide to save through all the noise.

So what would you save?

AUTHOR'S NOTE

Can we make a pact? A pact between you and me. From *coqueta* to *coqueta*. Promise me you'll help keep the secret of the endings in this book because I want, with all my heart, for everyone to live the experience of choosing their own ending without knowing what they'll find on the next page.

Promise?

Thank you, *coqueta*.

Thank you.

LOOKING FOR MORE FROM
ELÍSABET BENAVENT?
READ ON FOR A TASTE OF

Everything I'll Say to You Tomorrow

1

I FINALLY UNDERSTAND ALL THOSE SAD SONGS

The sky is leaden. It's one of those chilly spring afternoons, but you could tell everyone picked out clothes this morning based on the weather they wanted, not on the weather they got. Girls are wearing ballet flats with no socks (as it should always be, if my opinion matters to anyone) and you can see tons of jean jackets and very few trench coats. *Trench coats are made for weather like this,* I think. But I'm also thinking about how pretty people fall in love more. I'm talking about quantity not quality. They fall in love more. They probably even get their hearts broken less.

Thoughts are piling up in my head, it's chaos.

I don't consider myself ugly, or pretty, to tell the truth. I have a lot of things going for me, but stunning and obvious beauty is not one of them. I guess you could say I'm attractive. Once, in a work meeting, they described me as a girl with a unique look, full of character. It's true there's something about my face people remember. They usually remember me, but that could also be because of the fact that I've always been one of those honest people; I don't even come close to rude, but I do usually tell the truth when I'm asked. Telling the truth politely when asked is revolutionary these days.

He *is* handsome. It hurts to think about and pops up in my head like a red thread tied to the previous thought: pretty people fall in love more. Maybe that's why the man I share my life with is dumping me.

Because he doesn't love me anymore.

Because our time is up.

Because he's really hot and, dammit, hot people have to share their love around with loads of girls and I'm trying to hog it.

My reptilian brain, the most primitive part, the one that I think will have to take responsibility right now for throwing my survival instinct into turbo-drive, wavers. Tristan is attractive. The typical guy who wouldn't turn your head on the street, but who you'd keep looking at on the metro because…what is it about him? At first you don't know how to put it into words. It's that very Parisian *je ne sais quoi*, even though he's only ever been a tourist in Paris. Then you realize that he's too much. Tristan is a delicious *mille-feuille* in many ways, he's got layers. There are lights and shadows that give volume and texture to his attractiveness. His bad sides are what give meaning to his good sides and make them better. Tristan…with his thick, black hair combed to one side, with no prissy part, his nervous smile and his seductive smile which, paradoxically, are very similar. His long-fingered hands. His full lips…God, they're so full. The leaden sky of the Madrid afternoon in his eyes.

"I'm sorry," he says.

I'm vaguely aware that it isn't the first time I'm hearing that phrase, but I don't think it was really getting through until that moment. Ever since he blurted out: "We need to talk," everything that has come out of his mouth has sounded like Esperanto. And I don't speak it. Esperanto is a dead language, for fuck's sake, no one uses it.

"Miranda…really…I'm sorry."

I'm vaguely aware (or starting to be) that my name doesn't sound the same on his lips anymore. My name, that has always taken so many forms in his mouth: Mir, Miri, Miranda, baby. And sometimes "Miss" which he always made sound so cheeky. My name doesn't sound like it belongs to him anymore. Whatever it was that bonded us has broken for him.

"I need you to say something, Miranda." He closes his eyes and presses his knuckle to the hollow formed by the perfect arch between his eyebrow and the corner of his eye.

If I didn't know him so well I would think he was fighting back tears, but this is Tristan. He doesn't cry in public. He's Tristan, the reserved. He's Tristan, who handles most feelings with his head. I've envied that relationship between his brain and his heart so many times. He is definitely the most balanced partner I've ever had.

"I'm begging you," he insists.

"I don't know what you want me to say. You're dumping me. I feel like this is completely out of the blue."

"That's not fair. We've been fighting for a while."

"Fighting to fix it," I retort.

"Fighting, one way or another," he insists.

Our eyes meet for a second, before mine dart back to the cup of tea I didn't realize I was clenching.

"You don't love me anymore?" I ask him.

He huffs. He huffs and looks up at the sky, watching the heavy, gray clouds skitter across.

"Of course I love you. That's why we need to end it here…"

"You're leaving me because you love me? What's next? You're dying to live?"

Tristan's expression changes. It would be imperceptible to anyone else, but not to me. He's getting tired of this, with each passing minute he's losing patience and faith.

"Look, Miri…this isn't one of those 'it's not you, it's me' things, it's a 'let's be mature and stop hurting ourselves' thing. We can't sustain something that has one good week, two average, and one really bad. I love you and you love me, but choosing each other over all that means we'll be unhappy and you have to be able to see that. We don't deserve that."

"Is this about the kid thing?"

He pinches the bridge of his nose. I know perfectly well that's only part of the problem, but in that instant the only thing I can think to do is wield that weapon. I don't know why, maybe I feel like it will buy me time.

"We've already talked the kid thing to death." He sighs.

"Maybe next year, Tristan. Maybe next year I…I could consider it. I'm at a point in my career where I want to enjoy my freedom a little more and not have any burdens."

"Children aren't a burden," he objects, putting both elbows on the table. "I think you get more and more confused about that subject the more we talk about it."

"That's not true. It's just that…"

"I'm not going to pressure you about that." He looks away. He's thrown in the towel.

"You're leaving me because I haven't found the time to be a mother?" And I'm trying to cause him maximum pain with that question, even though I know he won't feel as bad as I do.

"I don't know how to do it anymore. I feel like everything I do and everything I am makes you deeply unhappy. I'm sick of your job. The truth is your job at the magazine is worse than having a colicky baby, Miranda. It always needs attention. Because of it, we've postponed decisions, vacations…I can't stand this city anymore. I came for one year…or two. I've been here five! For you! I can't do it anymore. And I can't blame you for not feeling at home, because you don't deserve that. We're both tired, grumpy, angry…We don't even have sex anymore. At most every two or three weeks, and it feels suspiciously like we're just ticking a box because we have to. You're always too tired to tell me anything about your stuff, and I'm not enough of a zombie or alienated enough not to care."

"I'll quit my job," I blurt out without thinking.

And even as I say it, I know I'm lying. I would never quit. The magazine is part of my life. It's my passion. I adore my job as deputy editor. Tristan, who knows that, sucks his teeth. I'm starting to get the feeling that I'm making a fool of myself.

"Miri…you know I would never let you quit your job for me. You love it. And you know what? Even though I've had it up to here with everything it involves, I'm envious of it. I feel jealous. I want to feel like that too when my alarm goes off and I have to go to work. I'd like to love more things, more than you. I…you're the only thing I love anymore." Tristan's voice quavers on the end of the sentence, but he recovers by clearing his throat, which, much to his regret, doesn't camouflage the whimper of pain behind it.

He looks away and taps the table rhythmically with his thumb as he bites his top lip, waiting for the lump in his throat to dissolve. This never happens in movies and it's difficult to describe in books. When a couple is fighting, there's a lot of silence. Long pauses where no one says anything while they're screaming inside. There are minutes and minutes, all of them violent and uncomfortable, where they both understand that actually, there's nothing they could say that would act as a lifesaver.

"It's not healthy," he tosses out finally.

"You don't think our relationship is healthy? Since when?"

And suddenly I feel like a bag of ultra-processed food while he's an organic vegetable garden.

"For a while now."

"Why?"

"Because we argue too much, we don't talk enough and we don't understand each other at all. We don't love each other the same way anymore. I don't understand why one of us always has to end up hurt."

I open my mouth to argue, but I hit the brakes because I know it's ridiculous. Yesterday we got pissed off about something so trivial: one of us had bought chicken strips instead of whole chicken breasts. The truth is neither of us had the nerve to bring up the topic of vacations. He had been asking me for a year to take a month of vacation days so we could go on a long trip. I didn't want to and I couldn't leave the magazine for that long and I was frustrated that he didn't get that.

"I feel alone," he confesses, "hemmed in, ignored and anxious. I know you're not trying to make me feel like that on purpose, but still...I'm tired. And you're always mad at me, like nothing I say is actually enough."

"I'm not mad at you. Why do you say that?"

It crosses my mind for a split second that I have been thinking "this guy's an idiot" a lot lately when I hang up the phone, but I swat the idea away like a fly.

"This is really hard for me," he says apologetically. "But it's like that song. Remember? The Mr. Kilombo one: I want you to love freely, even if it's not with me."

"Don't quote that crap at me."

Tristan gathers up his things from the table. His phone, his watch, which he always takes off when he sits at the table with me, his wallet...

"You're leaving? You're just going to leave me hanging? You're going to be a fucking coward?"

He sucks his teeth again and stares at me.

"No, but as you can see, you've already decided to be pissed at me for something I wasn't even going to do. A perfect example of what I was trying to say."

"That's so stupid."

"Miranda, I want to end this relationship and you have to respect me, because you don't know how much willpower it's taken for me to make this decision. Please, respect the fact that I feel it's the best for both of us. Yes, I'm putting myself first over a relationship that has kept me up so many more nights than it should have. Let me want to be healthy. And responsible. Because I love you, Miranda, and I don't want us to hate each other. I deserve the things that I dream of. And now, if you'll allow me, I'm going."

He stands up and, without looking at me, distributes his things among the pockets of his suit that makes him feel so disguised. I think about his strong legs wrapping around mine in bed. I think about the short hair on his chest, rough against my cheek...I think, but all my thoughts are so jumbled it's impossible to see any idea clearly beyond not believing anything that just happened.

"If it's okay with you, I'll come get my things from your house tomorrow morning, while you're at the magazine."

"It's not my house," I whisper.

"What?"

"Don't say 'my house.' It's our house."

Tristan stifles a sigh before he responds.

"No, Miri, not anymore. Now it's just your house."

I keep waiting for a kiss goodbye, mostly because I'm an idiot and I haven't absorbed any of the conversation. He dumped me. Tristan just broke up with me. He broke almost five years of a relationship and the thing that pisses me off the most is that he didn't give me a kiss goodbye when he left. And while I watch him disappear into the crowd, I wonder what the fuck just happened, who I am, who that guy is, what I'm going to do and how I'm going to get up tomorrow morning knowing that he doesn't want to live with me anymore. Or even kiss me goodbye.

I can't believe it.

There's no way that just happened.

I don't know how much time passed from when he left to when I throw a five euro bill on the table and get up, not caring whether it's enough money to pay for our two drinks or not.

The wind whirls through the streets picking up papers dropped on corners, cigarette butts and dog hair as it goes. I hate the cafes on Fuencarral Street because they're all sad chains with fluorescent overhead lights, but we met up in one of them; it was the closest place between both our offices. I appreciate that it didn't happen in one of my favorite cafes, because I never would have been able to go back. Or at home. Imagine not being able to go back to your own house. Though I don't think I can go back anywhere. I think I'm dying.

I walk along hugging myself and go right past the metro stop. I stumble on. My intuition carries me home. To my home. A home that doesn't belong to anyone else anymore. And what will I do with his stuff tonight? With his fastidious side of the wardrobe. With the sheets, that still smell like him. With the book he's reading that he left on his bedside table. It's not possible. This has to be a tantrum. Like that other time, right?

I haven't even made it a kilometer when I feel the first raindrop. By the time I get to my door, I'm drenched. My teeth are chattering, but I'd be lying if I said I feel cold. What I feel is a ball of heat in the middle of my chest that radiates an intangible but real pain from my head to my toes. It's a ghost pain that I don't know whether to describe as squeezing, stinging, burning or stabbing. It's a pain that suffocates, that shrouds my chest, that digs claws into my scalp like it's going to flay me. A monumental migraine that crouches in wait by my temples, like a wild animal. I'm a hiker lost on a mountain full of hungry and rabid bears.

I can't even cry. Crying would help me...but I can't.

~~~~~

I peel off my clothes in the bathroom and leave them in a heap on the white tile floor. I never liked these tiles because they show every piece of hair I shed. But he loves them. Loved them, I should say. The juxtaposition of the tiny white tiles with the black faucets and the iron finish on the showerhead was one of the things he liked most about my apartment. And the light. It's such a bright apartment... exactly the opposite of how I feel. Right now I'm darker than Sauron. I'm the Dark Ages. I'm darker than the inside of an asshole.

I crawl into bed just as I am. In my underwear. I pull the duvet over me and slide over to his pillow with my heart in my mouth. I sniff it. His cologne...When I met Tristan his scent gave me mixed feelings. It seemed too much to me…I don't know. It was overwhelming. I thought it was the typical cologne that dudes who like themselves too much would pick. Stupid, preconceived images from working where I work, I guess. It seemed to me like the cologne a guy who just wanted to brag about his conquests would wear. Someone who wasn't special. Someone with no style, but with money in his pocket. How wrong I was about that first impression…He was always the complete opposite.

Over time, among other things, that intense, dense smell with a touch of the exotic, that trace of bergamot and vanilla excited me, calmed me, made me feel at home and ready to leave my life behind to run away with him…All at once. Fucking Tristan.

It's not possible. He'll be back. It can't be. I'm going to die without him. Fine, nobody dies from love, but I'm going to succumb to this pain in my chest. A pounding and horribly hot, throbbing headache settles in above my eyebrows.

What am I going to do without him?

What's going to happen to all the things we were going to be? We're not "us" anymore, have we died? How can something that was never born die?

The phone and internet bill are in his name. I'm going to have to do paperwork. For fuck's sake.

How am I going to tell my father? He adores him.

And Ivan? Ivan will say something tremendously practical like, "there's a reason for everything," or "just say fuck it and dance, darling." And I'll feel miserable because my best friend won't understand that I'm going to die. Because this has to be what it feels like when you're dying, I'm not fucking around.

Has he told his family? Definitely his sister…and that pig would have celebrated. His sister and I never got along and she definitely will have poisoned his head, telling him that I'm too independent for him. That I'm too strong. That I'll never want to have kids and he'll be miserable with a life he didn't choose.

God. The pain. I open my eyes and a light that shouldn't be there blinds me. Great. I probably have a brain tumor. Or aliens have chosen this moment to take me to their planet. I close them again while the sensible voice in my brain reminds me that it's just a migraine. A fucking terrible migraine. The mother of all migraines. Everything is spinning.

Tomorrow morning I have to go to a cover shoot. And they'll see me with my face like a newborn rat. Isn't tomorrow the quarterly advertising meeting? I have no fucks left to give about the phrase "our sponsors" being used for the 372nd time to justify decisions about our content that I'm sure we would never otherwise agree to. It all seems a little surreal to me. Is this my life? Are these the "important" things? I can't get my head around having to get up tomorrow with this version of reality dragging me down.

Tomorrow Tristan will come get his stuff.

No. I need to talk to him. There are so many things I haven't told him. There are so many things I didn't know how put into words. Not today or for the past few months.

What if I call in sick?

Yes. I'll wait for him here. And I'll tell him how much I love him. He didn't give me the chance to say it. I'll explain to him that he can't leave me. That you don't abandon the person you love. Who is the love of your life, like I am for him. I'll remind him of all our plans. Like starting to eat less meat, buying more plants, or saving up to go to Japan. I'll promise to complain less, to cook more, to not be a slave to the magazine, to think about us. Yes.

Yes.

Tomorrow I'll tell him everything. And he'll see that I'm right. And he'll stay.

With a little luck this headache will have disappeared by then.

Damn you, Adele. I finally understand all those sad songs.

ABOUT THE AUTHOR

Elísabet Benavent is a graduate of audiovisual communication at the Universidad Cardenal Herrera CEU in Valencia, and she has a master's degree in communication and art from the Universidad Complutense de Madrid. She worked in the communication department of a multinational company until she became a full-time writer. She is an international bestselling author of twenty novels, and she lives in Valencia, Spain.

Website: betacoqueta.com
Instagram: @betacoqueta